DARK STAR

Paul D. Alexander

First Edition: December 2010

Dark Star

Cover Art by Joshua Medling

ISBN-13: 978-1463745776 (paperback)

For information: www.pauldalexanderbooks.com

EPIGRAPH

If the semi-diameter of a sphere of the same density as the Sun were to exceed that of the Sun in the proportion of 500 to 1, a body falling from an infinite height towards it would have acquired at its surface greater velocity than that of light, and consequently supposing light to be attracted by the same force in proportion to its vis inertiae (inertial mass), with other bodies, all light emitted from such a body would be made to return towards it by its own proper gravity.

-John Michell
November 1783

Michell, a geologist, speculated: When the escape velocity, at the surface of a star, is equal to or greater than light-speed, the star's gravity will trap the generated light. Some proportion of any double-star system should contain at least one dark star.

Within the tenants of Newtonian Mechanics, a dark star's own gravity traps any light emitted from its surface and renders the star dark.

The Star's gravitational pull devours its own light.

PROLOGUE

"DEAR GOD," down on his knees, James David *Deacon* Jones prayed in a loud, clear voice to the eerie, black Missouri sky. "Please forgive me my sins and for the life I have led. Lord, if you cannot absolve me, please take from me this wretched existence." Inside his jacket pocket, he clinched the cold pistol, his instrument of salvation. His cries for help were loud, but his voice made not a sound. No one was there to hear. *Perhaps,* he thought, *not even God.* Deacon, at nearly thirty years old, was a tortured, suicidal, self-ruined man.

The promise he made to Doc Edwards, only hours before, reverberated in his mind; all thoughts of self-sacrifice were overshadowed by honor. *If I can't keep my word to Doc, I'm truly worthless; this is a coward's way out.* He relaxed his grip on the pistol, clasped his hands tightly together, and prayed as though his life depended upon it.

He had not always been this way, but his life had changed. Circumstances altered; the past caught up with him. His destiny became his reality. It was time for Deacon to pay for his sins.

James David Jones dropped out of High School in April of his senior year. He could easily have finished. However, rebellion was sweeter than the ceremony.

The same month, his father the Reverend attempted to summon him to his study; James David flatly refused. The Reverend searched for James David and found him on the street. A cruel and un-Christian verbal tirade ensued. James David had not expected it to go easy. *After all,* he later thought; *if it were going to be easy, it wouldn't have happened.* He was surprised to learn from his father's rant that he was two-months old before they named him. Against her husband's wishes, his mother insisted on naming him for the Reverend's brother. The news was a distressing confirmation of the fact he was an unwanted addition to the Reverend's life.

This night, down on his knees, alone in the dark, struggling with thoughts of suicide Deacon remembered that day in the street, and suddenly understood why he had spent his nearly thirty years trying to make his life an exact opposite of his reluctant father.

This night he found himself at the vortex of a frenzied death-spiral that surreptitiously began months before. Oddly enough, the genesis of his demise was not the Reverend; it was innocuous junk mail. Unsolicited religious propaganda which was delivered by the postman with alarming frequency. Because of the excessive quantity, Deacon speculated that every right-wing religious faction, on the planet, had his name.

He should not have opened it, but he did. The graphic images leaped from every page and burned a hole in his mind. The pamphlets contained watercolors of Jesus and his disciples fishing and ministering, serpents, crosses and vibrant interpretations of Bible stories like those, which his father, the Reverend, verbally and physically beat into him throughout his childhood. The words and pastel-laced depictions awakened memories of an existence he despised. A life he thought he had left far behind, long ago, forever.

Next, the dreams came; they rapidly mutated into unspeakable nightmares. Eventually, overcome by insufferable desperation, Deacon crawled inside a bottle of Jack Daniels; the booze became his best friend. Prostrate inside his dank, self-imposed distillation of an existence, he subsisted for nearly a year before the true, physical horror began.

The first night of the flesh-based maelstrom occurred behind a bar on the St. Louis riverfront. It was early evening, and Deacon was long since inebriated. The Bartender mentioned that a gorgeous, brown-haired woman was asking about him. Horny and drunk, he unsuccessfully searched every corner of the converted factory building. After last-call, he staggered outside. While fumbling to put the key in his motorcycle ignition, a compelling voice urgently called to him. *Check behind the building. She's waiting. If you **want*** *her, look behind the bar.* Although it came from inside his head, the insistent chatter was not Deacon's voice.

In the pitch-black alley, he stumbled over of an eviscerated corpse, and fell face down in a pile of rancid garbage. An acrid stench, of drying blood and putrid food, overpowered him. He turned his stomach, repeatedly, until he lay unconscious in a shallow pool of his own vomit.

Rapidly, following that unforgettable night, he saw his father's prophecy begin to come true. He plummeted, tumbling, cascading over his own frailties into a personal apocalypse.

"You're a whore!" Estrella del Rio screamed at the reflection of Star in the mirror. Against her own will, she shifted her wrath from the striking blonde image with perfect make-up, to a newly printed photograph taped to the glass. A handsome young man, in a leather jacket, leaned innocently against a motorcycle.

She shouted at the man in the photo. "You made her a whore; you made me this!" Her hysterical rants grew louder with every word. "You, and your fucking family, made us what we are!" She gasped trying to refill her lungs. Her knees buckled; she sank to the black marble floor.

At almost twenty-nine years old, for the first time in her adult life, Estrella cried authentic tears. "Help me," her ruptured voice echoed against the cold, expansive walls of the bathroom. "Help me find my revenge." She pleaded with the lone woman in the looking glass.

The polished gold fixtures, in the otherwise empty room, remained silent.

Bridget Luna was Star's idea. Estrella resisted at first, but Star argued that a third was necessary. *We need the help,* she insisted. In the end, she had her way; Star always got her way.

The child, Estrella, was fourteen years old, alone and desperate. She sensed Star's presence, and discovered an ally in grief. Together, they lay on Estrella's mother's bed, their legs spread beneath the crushing weight of the man who took their flower. Estrella might have died that night if Star had not come. Instead, they lay there together protecting each other against the stench of the john having his way. The paunch of his belly, pressed hard against their stomach, repulsed them. A morsel of dark chocolate, melting beneath their tongue, comforted them. Together they survived.

Beginning that night, Star took control. She made it clear, first to Estrella and later to Bridget that she was in charge. Regardless of whose turn it was to *lead*, meaning whomever Star chose to represent the physical presence of the three, Star reigned supreme. *Estrella, if it weren't for me...* Star continually reminded her. *If it weren't for me, we would still be sleeping in the bitch's closet.*

Gradually, as the years passed, the childlike Estrella, who merely wanted to feel loved, came to appreciate Bridget, a professional woman who preferred a feminine touch. Star, in immeasurable contrast to the other two, became a whore because she was enamored with the power it gave her over people.

Estrella wanted to confide in Bridget, but Star heard her thoughts and said *no.* There was no such thing as privacy in their world. Star knew everything, and bent Estrella and Bridget to her will. They were three, yet one. Star influenced every thought and every action. Only she decided who should *lead,* when and why.

In the outside world, each of the three had her own friends, clients, and acquaintances. Very few of those people ever learned the truth. The three were obsessively protective of their separate identities. Star insisted they could only appear one at a time as only one person. No one, *outside,* was to know that hiding inside the one physical being were two others, watching, listening, and waiting.

When the equally chubby, middle-aged couple from Jehovah's Witnesses came to her door, Star took it as a sign. They gave her the idea for the inundation of religious mailings. It was simple enough to execute; she merely sent a note to each religious organization using *his* name and address.

Star began the execution phase of her grand plan. After years of waiting, she contrived their first meeting. Her prediction proved to be correct; Deacon believed her to be perfect. With her guidance, he experienced heart-stopping love at first sight. All of his life, he had known something was missing. Without warning, out of nowhere, she appeared. She made sure he knew, from the first touch of her lips, she would fulfill his destiny.

It was always part of her scheme to tell him about *Star* when the time was right, when she was ready, and when everything aligned in her favor.

Deacon kept no record of their time together or the extraordinary, unrelated events, which swirled about them. Not surprisingly, she was camera-shy. *Lots of people don't like to have their picture taken,* he reasoned. He gave a second thought to nothing that transpired. However, in the end so much occurred, he had no choice. He had to put it all in order. He forced himself to remember. Much later, he was able to conjure it all back up; he began to remember things he never knew.

When James David Jones first met Estrella del Rio, after eighteen years of fanatical, bible-based oppression, nine years of joy, and one year of nightmares, he sensed the potency of their consolidated magic, their tangible connection. From their first moment together, he knew she was what he needed. She was exactly for whom he had been searching.

Unquestionably, she was his cure.

ONE

O<small>N THE DAY</small> that James David turned two years old, already a skilled toddler for thirteen months, Reverend John Jones sat solemnly at the kitchen table, and observed his dark-haired son's activities. Only two guests attended the birthday party: a little boy, whose mother was the church secretary, and a little girl, whose father was the choir director. James David's chocolate birthday cake, made painstakingly from scratch by Mrs. Jones in the course of an entire afternoon, sat waiting on the table while the children played on the floor. Their parents sat at the table with the Reverend.

When the little boy guest reached over to play with James David's new toy truck, James David grabbed it away, and let out a scream. Shocked, the boy scooted himself back and stared with wide, frightened eyes.

The Reverend felt his blood boil at his son's unruliness, but he believed that birthday parties were a mother's work. In addition, he wanted to maintain his stature, especially in front of the two members of his staff.

Mrs. Jones, glancing nervously at her husband, tried to coax James David to play. She pushed back her sandy-colored hair, with the backs of her hands, and announced in her whispery voice. "Let's cut the cake, shall we?" After herding the children to the table, she lit the candles on the cake and put James David in his chair. "Now, James David, blow. Make a wish and blow out the candles." She moved the cake closer to him.

He stiffened his arms and held himself back, away from the pastry.

Her face turned red with embarrassment; she coaxed him again, softly. "Please, darling, it's tradition. Mommy will help you. Be a big boy and blow out your candles."

The Reverend felt his own face redden, but not from embarrassment. As the candles burned down, he waited silently with fury as his son resisted his mother's promptings. Just before the tiny fires reached the rich chocolate icing, James David leaned forward stiffly, and blew out the two candles.

Candles extinguished, Grace Jones let out a sigh of relief. "Wonderful, darling, now let's cut the cake together and serve our guests." Her shy voice was nervous and tentative. Her son was unpredictable; she could only imagine how this might end. She placed the cake knife in James David's right hand, wrapping her fingers around his, and gently tried to guide him through the first cut.

She winced as she felt him resist. Even though she had expected the worst, Grace was startled when, without warning, he screamed, "no." The scene at the table exploded in chaos; the other children began to cry. Their parents corralled them and raced for safety, away from the table and the out-of-control child with a knife.

James David stretched his upper body, as far as he could reach, across the table. He freed his hand and the knife from his mother, issued another ear shattering "no," and hurled the utensil across the room, splattering cake on the wall. As the creamy icing oozed and slid down the faded blue wall, it gave the appearance of a house bleeding chocolate.

Well before the cake knife came to a complete stop on the yellowing tile floor, any self-control that the Reverend Jones had maintained was gone. With one highly exaggerated, uncoordinated movement, he ensnared his son with his arm around the child's waist.

He plucked the baby from the chair and carried him into the living room. John Jones was incensed. Too angry to utter even a single word, he violently shook the child like an oversized rag doll.

The Reverend could not think clearly. The banal creature, trapped in his arms, seemed surreal. *We have guests in the house,* he thought as his mind began to clear, *and I must compose myself. I am the Pastor.*

Holding James David at arms length, he looked deep into his eyes. "What kind of a child are you?" He whispered as he put the boy on the sofa and released him. It felt like an electric connection severed; he sighed. Reluctantly, he took the boy up again; embarrassed, he returned to the kitchen.

Only Mrs. Jones remained.

In the few minutes that the Reverend and James David were out of the kitchen, the guests hastily scooped up their children, made quick nonsensical excuses, and left through the carport. Grace anxiously cleaned the chocolate from the wall and floor. Without knowing the reason, she left the knife where it lay.

What am I going to do? She thought worried most about the Reverend's reaction. The child had always been a point of contention. Grace dreaded the day when James David would commit one infraction over the limit. Many rebellions and tantrums occurred of which the Reverend knew nothing, nor would he ever.

When father and son reentered the room, they looked like two aliens with absolutely nothing in common, like water and oil. With all of her being, Grace feared they would never mix. "Reverend, please let him go," she implored, "he's just a child."

He cleared his throat, "Woman, baby or adolescent, birthday or not, he must learn right from wrong." His stern tone was devoid of emotion. "It's our job to teach him. If we ignore his actions, they will only get worse. You remember, as well as me, what happened with David. We have a reason to never forget."

Grace was surprised. Her husband had uttered his brother's name for the first time in more than two years. *Will he ever forgive me and accept this child?* she wondered. A question she often asked herself.

"I will raise this child in the path of Jesus. I'm going to teach him right from wrong; it starts now, today. *'Do not withhold discipline from a child; if you beat him with a rod, he will not die.'"*

Grace recognized the scripture from Proverbs.

He continued reciting the passage; his voice took on a certain cadence as though the timing of the delivery was as important as the words themselves. *"'If you beat him with the rod you will save his life from Sheol.'"* He pushed past her, and carried the rigid child to where the cake knife lay on the cold floor.

The Reverend knelt down. "James David, pick up the knife," he said without inflection. "Pick it up now."

The child did not budge. Grace gasped, fervently hoping her son would do what his father asked.

The Reverend took control of the boy's clinched fist, pried his fingers open one at a time, and positioned the unwilling hand on the plastic handle. James David remained frozen.

Using both hands, the father wrapped tiny fingers around the utensil, and squeezed the child's hand until it closed around the knife. He carried the boy to the kitchen counter, held him above the sink, and dropped the knife.

He placed James David in his mother's arms, and wordlessly, went straight to his study. There he stayed until the house slept.

Grace heard her husband into the night, through the thin walls, murmuring repeatedly to himself with a chant-like rhythm. She did not need to hear every word to know what he was saying.

"Even though I walk through the valley of the shadow of death, I fear no evil; for thou art with me; thy rod and thy staff, they comfort me… Even though I walk through the valley of the…"

Grace found her seven-year-old son playing alone in the backyard. Gazing through the kitchen window of the dilapidated house, she nervously wrung her hands. *When I touch the door, he will know his father sent me,* she told herself. *He will know he's in trouble again. Why must I always be the one to deliver bad news?*

With her face cradled in her palms, she muffled her sobs. Any sound made in the kitchen telegraphed through paper-thin walls to the Reverend's study. *How many times can I do this before my own son will come to hate me?* Grace willed her tears to stop. She wished their family could be different, that father and son could get along.

Mesmerized by the innocent child, she stalled, suffering an eternity of moments. *Everyone says he is such a handsome boy. If they only knew how much he looks like his father, they would understand. He's going to be such a heartbreaker.* She admired his big brown eyes, long eyelashes, and thick hair. She sighed. *He would make a beautiful girl.* The idea made her shiver with regret.

Should I have been a stronger disciplinarian when he started Kindergarten? She questioned herself. *I could have done a better job of helping him to learn to play with other children. If I had taught him to socialize, he would have no reason to rebel. If I had just stood between my boy and the Reverend, I could have been strict and still treated him fairly. It's so difficult for a minister's son; everyone expects him to be perfect. If I had not allowed his father to demand so much of him, make him into something he's not, things could be better.* Grace let out a deep breath; she could delay her assignment no longer.

When the rusty hinges of the wooden screen-door cried out, James David lifted his eyes from his toy. His face filled with dread. He knew her look; he knew why she had come. *I wonder what I did this time.*

"Your father would like to speak with you." He had heard the same submissive tones a thousand times. She spoke in the same manner to the Reverend. She nervously wrung her hands never looking at his face.

Without uttering a word, James walked past his mother. He knew his father was in his sanctuary, waiting. He reluctantly entered and took his place, at attention, in front of the old oak desk. He knew his father's expectations as he knew every object in the room. The study had once been a bedroom exactly like his. The closet was directly behind him; there was a small television hidden inside. He heard the news commentator's scripted speech sift through the walls every night at six-o'clock.

What did I do this time? He wondered again.

With his head down, the Reverend worked silently at his desk. Handwritten pages, along with two open Bibles, covered the desktop,

He's watching me. James's mind raced. *He enjoys making me wait. He loves this shit, making me suffer...* He was careful not to waver. *If I move, it'll set him off...* James held his arms at his sides, hands wide open, and palms pressed against thighs. A fist would provoke his father.

He stared straight ahead. *I wonder where the old man got all these Bibles. Why would anyone collect Bibles? Hell, I don't wanna read one.* The timeworn books, drenched in natural light, which poured in through curtain-less windows, perched on homemade shelves. The room was the same as all the other studies, in all the parsonages, in all the towns.

Many times, James had overheard his parents talking about the moves. His father often blamed him. However, he had also heard his mother say, sometimes the congregation, or the Bishop, requested they move. *Me, thrown out of school might have caused some of the moves,* he admitted. *There'll come a day when I can really do whatever I want; there won't be any fuckin' Bibles in my house. There won't be a study, rug rats, or rules. Shit, I'll do whatever I want when I...*

"James David," the old man raised his eyes from his work and focused on his young son. "Your mother and I are very disappointed..." It always began the same.

Grace slipped noiselessly into her sleeping son's room. She ran her fingers adoringly through his hair, and gently touched James David's tranquil, innocent face. "David," she whispered, awash in remorse. The boy-child sleeping before her was the embodiment of lost love, her final chance at happiness, a symbol of purloined joy. In him, she saw the mischievous smile of her husband's only brother.

She closed her eyes; from the deepest recesses of her mind, she heard David laugh, a joyful, uninhibited laugh. Grace knew a side of her brother-in-law that no one else knew, not even the Reverend. David was sweet, docile, and hard to anger. He loved his older brother, and continuously tried to convince him that their differences did not matter. His calm voice was clear in her mind as though he was in the room.

Dear brother, please don't be so angry with me. Just because I've chosen a life different from yours, doesn't mean it's wrong.

Your life isn't just different from mine, David, it's unacceptable. How can you possibly think that living like a gypsy, riding that motorcycle, drinking, and running with harlots is anything other than evil?

John, I understand how you might interpret my life as sinful. You give me too much credit for total debauchery. I'm not a minister, but that doesn't mean my life is wrong. I'm living my life; doing what I want. I'm sorry you don't approve. Nevertheless, I love you.

You, who loves the dark side of the world, love me. With every word, the Reverend became angrier. *You have chosen to live as a pagan in total opposition to Jesus' teaching... You come into our home, tell your stories, and distract my wife from her duties to the church and me. You encourage her to comb out her hair and wear curls. You're not satisfied with wasting your own life. You want to take us with you, and I will not allow that.*

David cowered and withdrew. It broke Grace's heart to watch. David had often said that all he really wanted was his brother's blessing.

David, leave this house and never return. Never again, call me brother. To me you are dead. He threw open the front door, and stepped aside.

Without a word, David walked past his older brother and into the street. The Reverend pivoted and slammed the door. With both hands, he grasped his collar. The sound of tearing fabric ripped deep into Grace's heart.

Dead to me, dead to me... he repeated as he walked to his study.

Eight months later, at the age of twenty-two years, David died in an accident. One month after that, James David Jones was born.

Grace gazed, once more, at her still sleeping son. She ran her fingers through his hair. He stirred and licked his lips. "Shh, shh, shh," she whispered, "go back to sleep, my darling, and dream wonderful dreams." She tenderly kissed his cheek, and silently slipped into the hall.

Guadalupe del Rio moved from St. Louis to Los Angeles sometime before her baby girl was six months old.

Star knew two versions of her mother's story. One, the woman had told hundreds of times. It always ended with Guadalupe blaming Star for everything that had gone wrong in her life. The other variation, she heard from Lupe's limited friends. Star was sure there was some truth in the stories. She also knew the sometimes distorted recounting came from too much cocaine, self-loathing, and a desire to be something she was not.

"You're the reason," Lupe would often scream, "I'm a whore! Before you come, I have *mis sueños*, me dreams, I have me man."

It was always the same old song, "*¡Que la canción!*" Star would shout back at her ridiculous bitch of a mother.

Sober or high, Lupe always repeated the essential facts of the story the same, word for word. The tall, thin, powerful man, whom Lupe consistently described, was the love of her life. He was the father of an unborn child, but not a husband when he died on a motorcycle and left Lupe to fend for herself.

Guadalupe was born in the Republic of Mexico, the State of Jalisco, the daughter of *campesinos*, migrant farmers. She was thirteen when they crossed the *Rio Grande* with all their possessions on their backs. They were twenty-seven Mexicans in all, including her parents and siblings.

Before they left Mexico, they spent many nights around the campfire eating *tacos* of rice and beans while listening to Lupe's father retell the numerous stories of *Los Estados Unidos y las calles de oro,* the United States and the, so-called, streets of gold.

There were no streets of gold, and in the end, they all lived in a cramped, drafty apartment in East St. Louis, Illinois. The family slept shoulder-to-shoulder in one shabby room; it was bitterly cold in the winter and blazing hot in the summer.

They nearly starved before Lupe's father found a job, as a barge hand, hauling coal on the Mississippi. Fortunately, for the hungry children at home, there were tasks on the boat that no legal worker was willing to do. He lived and worked on the boat for thirty days, then spent an equal number of days at home. When papa was home, the family ate in restaurants and lived like kings. The *Talavera* bowl, which sat in the center of the kitchen table, brimmed full with rich Mexican chocolate. When he was gone, they made broth from boiled meat scraps and begged in the streets. The *Talavera* bowl sat empty.

Lupe was eighteen when her dream came true. She met her green-eyed American, and they fell in love. She was proud that she was a virgin when he first lay with her. As she felt him fill her, she prayed to her *tocaya*, her namesake the virgin Guadalupe, for the warmth to bring a baby.

"Me seesters told me…" This part of the narrative always angered Star. *If she can't blame me*, Star thought, forced to rehear the saga, *she has to blame her sisters or my grandparents*. "…if I had a baby, it would be American, and me too. A baby would be good, but *hijo de puta*. I got you and lost me man. It's your fault. You didn't make me American; you made me whore."

Lupe never actually told Star that at one time, in the first few months, there was money in her purse. Star learned this from others.

Once, when Estrella was thirteen, she found a bill-of-sale for a car. Lupe had purchased it when Estrella was only seven months old. It was nearly new, and cash was paid. A year after she found the receipt, drawing upon Star's courage, Estrella confronted Lupe, who was high on cocaine. Brandishing the scrap of paper, she demanded to know what it meant.

"Momma, did we have money? Where did you get it; what did you do with it?"

The woman's swollen pupils floated in languid pools of red. "None o' you fuckin' business, I got paid for what I not say."

People laughed at Lupe's accent and her grammar; she blamed Star. Because she had a baby, Lupe could not get a job. They moved often because no one wanted a child around. When the money ran out, Lupe's only option was prostitution; Star was to blame. Everything was Star's fault.

For as long as Estrella could remember, up until the time that she began to earn money, she slept in Lupe's closet. Night after night, she lay in the cloistered, dark space listening to some smelly stranger, grunting and sweating, on top of her mother.

Estrella was her Mexican name, and she hated it. Guadalupe was her Mexican mother, and she despised her. Somewhere in Missouri, a green-eyed American was rotting in a grave; he was her father. Without even knowing his name, she loathed him. Estrella was the only daughter of a cheap, drunken whore and a dead man.

In a *barrio* of East Los Angeles, Guadalupe enrolled six-year-old Estrella in school.

Estrella loved the time away from her mother. Although shy around the other children, she was a good student and a fast learner. At home, her mother forced her to set aside her situational shyness and learn other lessons like panhandling and grifting. Most importantly, Lupe taught her: "Men are the enemy; they have money in their pockets." Her mother relentlessly repeated, "It's our job to get their money, all of it."

When James David was eight years old, he walked home from school one Friday afternoon right past a house where he had lately seen a young girl playing with her puppy. As he passed the house, he saw the yellow puppy alone in the yard. He did not know why, but he wanted the puppy.

Looking in both directions to make sure no one was watching, James David lifted the latch, pushed open the gate, and softly called, "Here, boy. Here, boy. Com'ere, boy." The dog ran to open arms. James stuffed the puppy into his coat and ran home. He hid his prize in his fort in the backyard.

On Saturday at noon, a knock came at the front door. James peeked out of his bedroom as he heard his father cross through the living room.

At the front entrance, there stood a tall man and the girl who owned the puppy. Tears stained the girl's cheeks.

"Sorry to bother you, Reverend," the man said in a deep voice, "my daughter and I have been canvassing the neighborhood looking for a small, yellow puppy. You haven't seen one runnin' around, have you?"

"James David," the Reverend Jones called.

Moving slowly down the hallway, James David kept his eye on the girl. He stood back a little ways from his father and waited.

"James David," his father asked in a typically severe tone, "this little girl has lost her yellow puppy. Have you seen it?"

"No, father, I haven't seen any dogs." A cold shiver ran up James's spine. He leaned against the doorframe, stared at the girl's shoes, and supported his overly warm face against the back of his hand. The smell of the dog, still on his skin, was strong.

"James David Jones," the Reverend's voice grew increasingly harsher with every word. His face reddened, "Tell me the truth. Where is this girl's dog? Tell me what you know, or God help me, I'll beat you within an inch of your life. For the love of all that's precious, boy, speak!"

James lifted his eyes warily and looked at the man and the girl standing uncomfortably on the steps. The girl was sobbing; he saw a look of horror on her father's face.

"He's out back," James whispered. The Reverend did not hesitate. James felt his vice-like grip on his bicep. He grimaced as the pain shot through his muscles. The scene around him began to swim as he felt himself being half carried, suspended by only his right arm, half dragged toward the back door. The man and the girl followed at a safe distance.

"Show us," the Reverend ordered. He released his grip on James David's arm. His hand felt hot; his heart pounded in his fingertips. A desire to strike the boy flooded over him. The Reverend glanced at the two strangers, standing on his back steps, and he struggled not to embarrass himself anymore than his son already had.

James David retrieved the puppy from its box inside his fort, and handed it to his father.

Reverend Jones forced himself to take the puppy, and immediately returned it to its owner's arms.

He turned to the man. "Sir," he could feel his voice quiver, "I am very sorry for any inconvenience my son has caused you. I assure you he will be dealt with; this will not happen again." The Reverend felt his composure rapidly slipping away.

"James David," he clenched his fists as he spoke, "you owe these people an apology and a commitment of penance." He looked hard into his son's face. The boy stood unmoving, his eyes trancelike. The Reverend saw no sign of emotion in the grim countenance. "James David, atone for your sins; tell these people you're sorry. Now, James David, right now. I command you!"

Finally, James David began to speak, but his were not the words of an eight-year-old. "You say that God's creatures are not chattel," he calmly began.

A familiar discomfort swept over the Reverend. He had felt this way many times before when he read of the crucifixion of the Christ.

James David continued; his voice seemed devoid of feeling. "You teach us that we are a brotherhood, equal and sharing, in the eyes of God. I have as much right to that dog as anyone."

The Reverend was dumbstruck. *This is not right,* he thought. *This boy cannot use my teachings and my example against me.* Desperate to save face, he searched his mind for a scripture with which to respond.

"Very well, young man," the words came slowly at first, "remember King Solomon. He faced a similar situation with two mothers fighting over the same child: *And the King said, 'Divide the living child in two, and give half to the one, and half to the other.'* Is that your wish, James? Shall we cut this innocent dog in two?" The Reverend glared at his son, ignoring the neighbors. The daughter hung from her father's arm sobbing uncontrollably.

"Enough, I've seen and heard enough," the other man yelled. He stuffed the puppy under one arm, took his daughter's hand, and rushed away.

Reverend Jones left his son alone in the yard, and hastily retreated to his study.

Within the hour, he dispatched Mrs. Jones with a summons for her son. He left James David to stand at attention, for more than an hour, while he tried to unravel the lines of meaningless words in the Bible on his desk. Seething, he studied the pages, careful not to look at the boy.

Finally, overcome with rage, he abruptly stood. The reluctant wheels of the old desk chair squealed in protest against the wooden floor. The chair slammed into the wall. The Reverend removed his belt. He searched James David's face and found no remorse. The boy's big brown eyes were empty.

He lashed the boy, repeatedly, until his heart ached more than his arm. "Now," the Reverend's words were grim and flat, "James David, you will remain here, and repeat this scripture one hundred times." He took an open Bible from the desk and handed it to the child.

James David wept as he read the words. "*And the King said, 'Divide the living child in two…*"

The new parsonage was a little bigger, however more isolated than ever before. James had to ride the bus to school. The moves never mattered to him. Friends were easy to make when he wanted. He lived in his own world with very private thoughts and dreams. Nothing outside that world made any difference. It was all just monotonous details. An unwelcome existence, he was perpetually lonely without being alone.

Reverend John Jones repeatedly forced the story of his son's second birthday upon him. James believed it was a milestone; the day he became a rebel. He never understood why he resented his father so deeply. His mother had seemed different when he was very young. He mostly felt sorry for her now. Sometimes he thought of them both, himself and his mother, as victims.

Occasionally, he dreamed of running away and taking her with him. Then the wrath of his father would again fall upon him, and his mother never intervened. He hated that the Reverend used her as an implement, always sending her to bring him to that awful place. *My father's chamber of horror,* he called it. James came to see his parents as a discordant pair, the master and his disciple.

Inside his private world, his dream world, James lived a very separate life. There, his house, the yard, and his room were always the same, warm and welcoming. There, his father was not a minister, and his mother spoke her own mind. In his imaginary existence, James had friends, many friends. There, they liked his jokes and valued his opinion. There, he was a part of a group, an important part of something very special, a society, his community, a place where he belonged. There, he had no desire to rebel. There, suspension from school was not a possibility, and best of all there were no summons or waiting for punishment.

Estrella at ten was tall for her age, gangly, and a clever, gifted pickpocket. Her inquisitive brown eyes were full of life and hope. Only her olive skin hinted at her heritage. She learned everything with ease. At school, the boys admired her from a distance and the girls envied her. No one befriended her.

Every afternoon Lupe supervised her daughter's homework, which had nothing to do with books or school. They were lessons of the street, lessons of survival in an indifferent world. In all that she touched, she excelled. Her marks never knew she was there. She routinely lifted wallets, cleaned them out, and put them back unnoticed.

When she was twelve, her favorite panhandle was telling old men she was lost; they gave her cab fare and food money. When she pretended to be blind, she doubled the take.

The money went straight to Guadalupe's purse. Lupe counted the scores individually regardless of their dollar value. For each one Estrella received her reward, a tiny bar of rich, Mexican dark chocolate. Trapped beneath her tongue, the candy slowly melted and the natural effects oozed through her body. Often, when the pilfered money first touched her hand, she could taste the phantom cacao.

Two

THE REVEREND carried his 5'11" frame perpetually erect and rigid, like a duty-bound Beefeater. His long sinewy arms were discretely muscular. His rapidly graying, sandy-brown hair continuously diminished, leaving behind an ever-growing, waxen scalp. Outdoors, he wore a black fedora, a protection for his pale skin. Parishioners cowered when he entered a room as though they feared him. James David definitely feared him; he believed were he to openly resist or rebel, the last thing on the elder's mind would be any consideration of personal pain, for either party.

James read book after book, in secret, and loved them all: fiction, non-fiction, biographies, even textbooks. He found Shakespeare, history, science, and mathematics to be especially captivating. Had the Joneses known, they would have been overjoyed, which was exactly the reason James read late at night when his parents slept. He perfected a facade of disinterest, and worked hard to seem remedial to his teachers. Everything in James's world was a secret, including what he knew.

At twelve years old, his hormones attacked his judgment. He began to openly rebel against his mother.

"James David, do you have any homework today?" Grace asked one day right after school.

"No," he answered dully.

"I don't understand this," she began more assertive than normal. "I talk to the other mothers of children in your grade. They tell me there's homework almost every day."

"They're liars," he rebutted. "They're just dirty stinkin' liars."

"James David, don't talk like that. You mustn't call other people liars." She forced a commanding tone. "You have certain responsibilities, and you will have throughout your life. You must do your homework."

He stood up directly in front of her. His brown eyes bulged and his face reddened. Already taller than she, he looked down upon her with contempt. On a smaller scale, he shared his father's physique; his olive skin matched no one. James David clenched his fists tightly, his knuckles whitened. He began to speak in a dry, cruel monotone. "Yeah, well let me tell you somethin'. I'm an American, I'm twelve years old, and I have rights." His words sent his mother straight to her room where she wept for hours.

The next day, for Grace, was like the inquisition. The persistent Reverend spent nearly two hours evoking a thorough explanation for her swollen eyes.

The summons came immediately after school, delivered in a scratchy, broken, almost apologetic, tearful voice. "Your father would like to see you."

The Reverend was working at his desk. The light from a tattered table lamp cast an eerie shadow across the darkening room. James entered and took his place at attention.

More than three excruciating hours passed. The Reverend closed his Bible. He carelessly tossed aside his wire-framed spectacles and rubbed his eyes. "James David, you are right. You are an American, caused by an accident of birth and not by my choice. You *are* twelve years old. For us all, the passage of time is a natural phenomenon. You do have rights. Now, young man, I am going to tell you exactly what those rights are.

"You have the right to remain silent. Children should be seen and not heard. You have the right to do exactly as I say. You have the right to live in this house for as long as you follow my rules. You have the right to address your mother and me with absolute respect. You have the right to go to school every day and do the best work possible. You have the right to attend church every Sunday.

"If you choose to give up, take advantage, or ignore any of these rights, I will hold you accountable. Moreover, may God help me; you will wish you had never been a miserable wretch born to this earth. Do you understand me?"

The boy stood as still as a stone. He stared straight ahead with unflinching eyes.

"James David, do you understand me?" The Reverend asked again, openly agitated.

"Yes," James David whispered.

"I can't hear you."

"Yes, sir, I understand," he said in a still quiet voice.

"Before you sleep tonight, you will memorize Proverbs 29:18. *'Where there is no prophecy the people cast off restraint, but blessed is he who keeps the law.'*

"In the morning, first thing, you are to come here and recite this passage to me, flawlessly. Do you understand?"

James David nodded.

"Do you understand?"

"Yes, sir," he answered in a clear, determined voice.

"Very well, you will apologize to your mother, and you will do your homework. After your recitation, I do not wish to hear of this again. You may go."

Grace accepted James David's apology, although, she knew nothing would change. She knew many things she could never tell the Reverend.

On the day they brought the yet unnamed baby, James David, home from the hospital, Grace agreed with her husband. "One child is enough. Let's do our best with what we have," she said.

"It is God's will." Reverend Jones answered. "It was sin that brought us to this moment; consequences must now be paid for what was done."

She lovingly cradled the tiny baby in her arms; the smell of newborn and hospital was strong. "I know we must pay for what has happened," she conceded.

As he drove, the Reverend glanced at her with remorseful eyes then with contempt at the baby. "The two of you led us here. You were complicit, and for all I know, you encouraged him to act."

Tears filled her faded blue eyes. "He needed me; you cast him out, and he needed family."

"He may have needed a sister-in-law, but not an *intimate friend* as you once called it." Clearly agitated, he increased the car's speed. The next hour dragged by in silence.

That same night Grace knelt by her bed for a very long time, praying and crying. "Lord, dear God, why must thou forsake me? Why hast thou decided to strip my womb and make me barren? Please, forgive me my sins. I know the book of Matthew, and in that, I have violated your seventh commandment. For what I have done, I am truly sorry. Please, help me teach my child well that he might come to know the true nature and spirit of his father."

Much had changed in the Reverend since Grace first met him. When he was young, he was happy and playful. He made no secret of his love for life and God. It was circumstance, family, and disappointment that changed him, gradually at first, then more rapidly as the years passed. Once, when he was in his mid-forties, he confided in Grace that he felt his opportunity to achieve his goals lessening with each passing year. He said it in a moment of melancholy, quite unlike his normal demeanor. "I once hoped to save the world," he said with remorse. "I intended to begin with my little brother; I have failed in every aspect of my life."

Months before Grace first met David; she heard all the stories. The Reverend saw his brother as young and foolish. At the same time, he possessed exceptional intelligence and huge potential. When he spoke of David, he was animated and excited.

"Darling, wait till you meet David," he laughed. "I'll have to be careful or he'll steal you away. He looks like a cigarette model in a magazine. With his boyish charm, I'm sure he breaks hearts every day. He's tall and thin with big, wondrous, green eyes and a charming smile."

"It sounds like you're describing yourself, John." She said lovingly.

"If I can get him started down the right path," he continued as though he had not heard her, "his capabilities are unlimited. I've never known anyone so intelligent and gifted, although I loathe his friends. He tends to make bad choices; he's a terrible judge of character. Nevertheless, he is my brother and I love him. I'm going to do everything I can to help him achieve success and make a contribution to the world. Once you and I are married, we will all be one happy family. Our life together, all of our lives, are going to be so good."

On Thanksgiving Day, the year before she married John, Grace finally met David.

The sun arose to find its reflection glittering like precious stones embedded in a heavy blanket of frost. The frozen dew succumbed to the warming, yellow rays, and vanished before the extraordinary rumble of the motorcycle filled the quiet subdivision.

John Jones's expression turned into a broad toothy grin when he heard the sound. He took his fiancée by the hand, and nearly dragged her to the front door.

A magical sensation swept through Grace when David crossed the lawn. *He does look like John,* she thought. She felt an instantaneous and absolute link to him. Everything good the Reverend had said about his brother was true. David was charismatic; he made the right jokes, cast appropriate glances, and honored meaningful silences, all with perfect timing, yet his presence disquieted Grace.

The Thanksgiving meal went quite well save a few pointed, caustic, mostly ignored remarks, which the Reverend made regarding David's goals.

After lunch, Grace cleared away the dishes and began to wash them.

David casually sauntered into the kitchen. "Can I help?" He immersed his hands in the soapy water before she could answer.

They worked side by side in nervous silence. Once, accidentally, he touched her hand; she gasped for breath.

On Valentine's Day, of the following year, the thirty-eight year old Reverend John Jones made twenty-six year old Grace his bride. David, then eighteen, was his brother's best man.

At the small reception, David asked Grace to dance.

She was timorous in his arms. Startled and flustered, she pushed back and looked anxiously into his eyes. "I have to go," were her only words as she slipped away. In the corner of her eye, she saw her husband watching.

In the following four years, the brothers seldom shared a civil word.

"David, I have nothing more to say to you." The Reverend told him; his voice was cruel. "You're wasting your life; we both know it."

In spite of the Reverend's attitude, David worked hard to build a relationship with him.

When the Reverend was away, David sought out the warm counsel of his sister-in-law. Enthralled by his brilliance and the depth of his capacity to experience emotion, she encouraged him to follow his heart. Their intense conversations became long and intimate; they became best friends. Grace was more open with David than she had been with anyone in her life, including her husband. They trusted each other completely, and shared their deepest secrets.

David visited John and Grace often, frequently *dropping by* even when he knew the Reverend would not be home. David and Grace were always very careful.

David had a girlfriend. Yet, he never took her, or any of his motorcycle friends, to his brother's house. The Reverend made it clear that he was sure they were all *scum*. In the final year of David's life, his twenty-second, the Reverend spoke not a word to, or about, his brother.

David Jones rolled through the fatal intersection on his motorcycle a late, cool Missouri Saturday night. A night that for most people was no different from a thousand other nights.

The police said David did not see the drunk driver careening through the red light with his headlights off. David's prized 1954 Harley-Davidson was a pile of mangled steel, bent beyond recognition. Only the motorcycle's fiftieth anniversary solid bronze medallion was unscratched. David was *Dead on Arrival*.

John Jones did not want to be a father. Actually, as he remembered it, he never really wanted the responsibilities of a husband. Still, a loyal and obedient wife was necessary for a successful ministry, and Grace was easy to look at, a good cook with a tolerant heart. All John really wanted was to be the Reverend Mr. Jones. He resented his parents because their second son was born when they should have been planning their retirement. They said it was *God's Will.* He called it *ineptitude.*

When David was just a brother, an innocent little brother, John adored him. They played together during John's infrequent visits to the home of their parents. He liked to tuck the child in to sleep and read aloud his favorite passages from the Bible.

The elder Joneses went on to a better place, and carelessly left their eldest son to be a father to his brother. That not being bad enough, his brother could have been Chinese for all their dissimilarity in belief. The only things they had in common were their parents, and a shockingly similar appearance. They could have been mistaken for twins had it not been for their glaring chasm of years.

The summer when John first met Grace, the July before they were married, the two brothers buried their mother alongside their father.

Because of the death of their parents, his brother became his son. Outwardly, in the beginning, he praised his younger sibling. He spoke often of opportunity and responsibility. He even tried to convince himself that he could make a difference. However, alone with his thoughts, the Reverend believed, that at eighteen years old, the mold was set; David was already what he was to become. *The course of the ship is laid in, and I, unlike the wind and waves, can have no bearing on the destination. My brother is too old for me to change.*

Occasionally, Reverend Jones regretted his critical treatment of David. Although in the end, there was no time to make up for his actions. His final, malicious words were nearly a year old when David died.

Reverend John Jones stood by the open grave, alone, for a very long time after the mourners left. The coarse gravediggers sat on their heels, far off, waiting, watching, and talking. Occasionally, the wind carried a word or phrase across the granite garden. "He must be the boy's father." The Reverend heard one of them say.

"I would not have made a good father." The Reverend said to the pine coffin. "I was never even a good brother." At forty-two years old, he gazed forlornly at the grave of his only brother, his baby brother; the pain ripped him apart. He was mad and bitter, a failure in the eyes of God.

"I am a wretched sinner," he said to God, "I beg for your divine forgiveness." He knew when he heard his own words, that his opportunity to atone on a mortal level was forever lost. "God, I pray my brother walks with you. Please, tell him I am woefully sorry, and I love him." At length, his will escaped, the old man shuffled away. His steps guided only by instinct.

Eight months later a child was born, a boy, a baby whose semblance, for the perpetually grieving Reverend, was too much like his dead brother. He struggled to look upon the child's face.

The infant lived the first sixty-long days of his life referred to only as *the baby*. Haunted by remorse, the Reverend finally acquiesced; he agreed to a mendacious name, James David Jones.

The night when he unenthusiastically agreed to the name, the Reverend sat alone in his study, buried in unpleasant thoughts until midnight. From the depths of his mind, a cacophony of voices reminded him of his failures. Amid the turmoil of guilt, he heard the final pleading words of a compassionate David. Through it all, he found not a modicum of peace, only swelling resentment.

Another child to raise, he thought. *It is my burden, my penance from God for my sins, for my failure with David. Could it be God wants me to have another chance to lead a disciple down the road of the righteous? This child will be mine from the beginning. I will not repeat my parents' errors with this one. I will make up for the life my brother threw away.*

The Reverend raised James David in the only manner he knew, like a man. James David was a baby saddled with the responsibilities of an adult, an innocent child dragged into a world of unachievable expectations. The rearing was much more than a single mission; it was an arcane crusade.

Open rebellion billowed up when James David was twelve. The Reverend, convinced of some emotional or mental deficiency, ordered an IQ test followed by a Rorschach test and a battery of other psychological exams.

His IQ score exceeded 180; the psychologist told the Joneses he had never encountered a child with more of a contradictory personality. After that, the Reverend concentrated his energy on containment, avoidance, and survival. Everything he tried produced negative results, the antithesis of what he had hoped.

Estrella was fourteen when her mother first introduced her as *Star*. Guadalupe changed the child's name on the same day she sold the blossom off her baby's flower to a portly, beak-nosed businessman for two, greasy hundred-dollar bills and an equally repulsive fifty. She dressed her gangly Star in a short, tight-fitting, plaid Catholic-school uniform skirt, a white cotton blouse, white ankle socks, and black size-seven pumps. The shoes, one size too large, scraped her heels as she walked. Lupe bought the whole outfit for two dollars in the Goodwill Store.

From the doorway to her own room, Lupe watched it all unfold. She stood, callously by, listening as Estrella cried out with pain. Minutes after his violent thrusts began, the scruffy man found culmination; his fleshy form melted from the release, and his whole weight covered the child.

She felt his paunchy stomach pressed hard against her navel. Her long brown hair filled her mouth; chewed ends scratched her throat.

He grunted with the effort as he lifted himself off; a putrid, sweaty blast from his armpits assailed her nostrils. Instinctively, she closed her legs and tucked her knees to her chest.

The obese caricature dressed without a word. His thick silhouette darkened the door. He paused as he turned to leave and glanced back at the trembling child. "Thanks," he said gruffly and disappeared.

Together for the first time, Star and Estrella felt hot tears fill their ears. It was Star's idea to bite hard on the, prematurely dispensed, partially melted chocolate trapped beneath their tongue. The dominant, stimulating cacao flooded their mouth; with it came relief.

Star quickly became the princess of the streets. The other hookers were cruel because they were jealous. She was what the johns always wanted, *the schoolgirl*.

In her first year, she earned substantially more than her mother had in the previous five. Star's per-interlude *donation* equaled more than three times what the other ladies-of-joy in the *barrio* could command, and Star managed twice the number of customers.

She rested one week each month. Unlike the *others,* she stayed in her room with the shades pulled and the door locked. Lupe confiscated most of Star's money and parsimoniously replaced it with dark chocolate. The small amount of money, portioned to Star, she spent carefully, and hid most of it in a secret compartment in her mattress.

Lupe's years on the street took their toll. She became increasingly more volatile with each passing year. Raising a child and turning cheap tricks meant there was never any money for the extras. However, with Star as her benefactor, Lupe explored life's pleasures; she discovered the sublime effects of cocaine.

THREE

T HE NIGHT before Star's sixteenth birthday, Lupe turned her last trick. After that, she spent her time alone in her room sucking her daughter's money up her swollen nose.

Star taught herself the art of maximizing her per trick income. She quoted one price on the street; when they were alone, usually in the back seat of a car, with her hands in their pants, she raised the price. She liked to tease and touch, sensuously, until they spent themselves too soon; often she never even lifted her skirt.

At sixteen, James's hormones and intellect raged; he was out of balance, and out of control. Nothing was ever right, fair, or what he wanted. His mother endeavored to comfort him. He would have none of it. He seldom spoke to her, and he skillfully avoided the Reverend.

Saturday dawned like any Saturday, like any other day. The moon took cover behind the earth, and a swelling, yellow sun took its place. In the Jones's home, there had been no conflict, no argument, or poorly received orders for compliance of any kind. It was just another Saturday.

Except, James David felt different. He awoke with his heart pounding. *I feel trapped in this house—in this life*, he thought. *I have to get out; I need to be free.* He was bewildered, confused, distressed, and he knew not what to do. He knew only that he had to get out, to be free, and to get away from his parents, away from everything. *Tomorrow is Sunday; they'll make me go to church.* He told himself. *That'll be one trip to the sanctuary over my limit.*

Escaping was easy. Both of his parents were out, his mother at the grocery and the Reverend visiting at the hospital. James threw a few essential articles of clothing, a crude homemade weapon, and some canned fruit into the army surplus duffel, which he kept stashed under his bed.

The rickety screen door, with rotting mesh, slammed behind him. Three separate bounces of the door resonated loudly against peeling paint. With the last bang of wood on wood, James felt free.

He slipped cautiously down side streets; with each step, he made his plan. "Serious times and serious circumstances require serious actions," he said aloud to the empty sidewalk, certain that it was a quote from someone of extreme importance. "I bet President Kennedy said the same thing during the Cuban missile crisis," he guessed. He had skipped school the day they discussed it in history class.

The Saturday arcade was perfect; all the wrong people were there. A small group of kids, of whom he knew something about most everyone, loitered near the miniature golf course smoking and laughing.

"Well, lookie at what we have here." said Mike, a twenty-one year old, high-school dropout with a spotty, week-old attempt at a beard. James had seen Mike around; he had a reputation for hanging out with younger kids. "It's the young Reverend Master Jones," he announced with a dramatic flair.

James stared at him in silence.

Mike laughed and blew smoke through his nostrils like a puffing dragon. He tilted his head and followed with a series of miniature, perfect rings of smoke. The other boys jealously eyed every wispy, translucent circle in awe.

Mike's young wife, Tina, hung on his arm and looked admiringly at her husband. Her tight tank top accentuated tiny breasts and nipples. A miniskirt barely hid her panties. One long, feathered earring dangled provocatively from her left ear. James David had seen her before. She was five years older, and he liked that she looked more like a stripper than a toddler's mother.

Upon hearing Mike's words, the others laughed, nervous, forced laughs. The chortle died down, silence hung in the air for less than a minute, and everyone turned to James.

He smiled, then chuckled, "yeah, right, Master Mike, you're just afraid I'm gonna blow my magic flute and steal your disciples."

Mike paused, cocked his head, and frowned almost indiscernibly. Appearing befuddled, he snickered.

James smiled, pleased with his own cleverness. *I'm sure,* he thought, *Mike doesn't know I just mixed a religious reference with a fairy tale and insulted him.*

Mike's manly giggle abruptly stopped. A look of bewilderment crossed his face. James squirmed. It seemed as though Mike had understood after all. Mike's features relaxed. A smile crept across his face. He started to laugh anew. This time it was a deep, robust guffaw.

A titter bounced through the others. They seemed cautious at first, but in a matter of seconds, it became a whole-hearted, gut-busting howl.

Tim was fifteen and a year behind James in school. They had a few classes together, including gym, and knew each other pretty well. He appeared to be the youngest member of the clique. James was sure Tim held the dubious honor of worst reputation. "My old man," Tim had once proudly told James, "dropped a dime on me, and I done time in reform school."

"So, what's your story, Jimmy boy?" Tim wrested control of the conversation. "What's with the bag?" He leaned precariously against a wobbly, white picket fence, which surrounded the miniature golf course. "Takin' care of your mommy's laundry?" He spouted.

Tim was small for his age, barely more than five feet tall. His long, stringy, dirty-blonde hair was oily and uncombed. His once-white tee shirt with wide yellowish stains at the armpits, hung loosely over greasy jeans. Rolled up in his left sleeve was a pack of Camels. His right sleeve, rolled to match, exposed unremarkable biceps. A mangled toothpick dangled from his mouth and counted out his words like a bandleader's baton.

James's whole life had been nothing less than formal. His parents always called him James David, and his current state-of-mind was to non-conform with regard to anything set forth by his parents. However, *Jimmy* sounded repulsive and childish, not acceptable.

With the strength of belligerence welling up inside, James began to speak forcefully. "Let's get a few things straight, up-front." He addressed the group, but he looked mostly at Tim. "No, this is not my old lady's laundry or her anything else, and my name is not, I repeat, not Jimmy. You all may call me JD."

"All right, JD, now we're talkin'." Mike seemed to admire the way he had stood his ground against obvious odds.

James felt a degree of respect from the group. With a single declaration, he had gone from outsider to member.

Mike continued. "So, what's your story? We're all dyin' to know what's in the bag?"

"Okay. Here's the deal. I'm sick of bein' tagged Reverend Jones's son. I've had it up to here," he touched his nose, "of bein' told what to do by people who don't understand me, who don't understand us." He reached out and encompassed his audience with a sweeping motion.

They all nodded and grunted in agreement.

"So, I've done it; I've left home. I'm washin' my hands of the whole damn deal. I don't need parents. I don't need school. Those teachers don't have anything for me, and they don't care anything about any of us. All they care about is quittin' time and payday. I especially don't need the stinkin' church. This bag is full of everything I need; as of today, I'm on my own."

"Welcome to the club!" Tim shouted exuberantly. "So, what's next JD? You got a place to sleep?" Tim's experience was obvious. "Any cash in that green bag of yours?"

"Well, no, I've got a couple bucks. Hadn't thought much about needin' a place to sleep. Left home in a kind of a hurry. What do ya think, Tim, what do you usually do?"

"Back in the day, I made some of the same mistakes, but I've learnt to plan my disappearing acts in advance. I usually steal money from my old man's wallet, a little at a time, so he doesn't miss it. I always try to crash at someone's house. Hell, plenty a times, I've spent a week or better at a friend's house, and their parents didn't even know I was there. Once, I slept with my girlfriend every night for a month, ate in their kitchen, even smoked her Dad's pipe, and never got caught. Shit, if we hadn't had a fight, I'd probably still be livin' there."

"Okay, so what do I do now?" JD asked again. "What do I need?"

"You'll need cash for food, smokes, incidentals, and a place to sleep. It's too cold this time of year to sleep outside without gear. You need a place to sleep tonight. I can sleep another night at home, no problem. That'll give us time to work out a plan. You know, the Reverend's gonna come lookin' for ya, right? You've either gotta avoid gettin' caught or have a plan for if ya do."

Tim's words made what had been a spur of the moment action seem like a long-term commitment. It all made JD more than a little nervous, but he had already set the wheels in motion. His parents, by now, had undoubtedly discovered he was missing. He knew it would not matter if he changed his mind and went home today or in a month; the consequences would be the same.

"For tonight, at least, you can crash on the floor at our place," Mike offered. Tina, still hanging on his arm, nodded her assent.

"Okay, that's great, now we're workin'." Tim said excitedly. "What about cash?"

"I'm pretty sure my old man keeps some money hidden in the desk in his study." JD answered.

"Perfect." Tim was obviously pleased. "You've got a key, right? Alls we hav-ta-do is sneak back in there and lift the dough. It'll be a cinch—like tak'n candy from a baby."

"I forgot my key." James shyly admitted.

"No prob', I've made that mistake; we'll just break in. Don't worry, your old man's a preacher; he ain't gonna call the cops. You're his only fuckin' kid. He won't want his flock to find out that there's trouble on the home front." Everyone laughed.

"Here's what we'll do. If it's okay with Mike and Tina, let's move this gig to their place. You've gotta get off the streets and lay low. You hide out there for tonight. I'll go home and rip off my old man, son-of-a-bitch 'ill be drunk before dark. Tomorrow we'll meet up, get the cash, and maybe a few other things, then head for the woods."

"I have a sleeping bag and some camping gear," JD remembered.

"All right, cool. I've got a sleepin' bag and a tent. Hell, we can live off the land. It'll be a fuckin' adventure. We can work our way, doin' odd jobs, up to Canada. They'll never fuckin' find us."

Tim's face darkened; he took on the expression of a concerned mentor. He rolled the cream-colored, soft-pack out of his sleeve, tapped it three times on the back of his wrist, and lit up. He offered the pack around, everyone accepted. Smoke curled up from Tim's cigarette, which clung to his lips next to his toothpick.

He began to speak in serious, contemplative tones. "We're gonna have ta time this thing just right. We've gotta figure out how ta get in and out quick and without bein' seen. Besides, we've gotta lot gear ta carry. It'll have to look innocent, like a couple a Boy Scouts goin' on a campin' trip." He grinned, exposing tobacco stained teeth between pursed lips. "A Boy Scout, now that's a fuckin' hoot."

"I can drive you." Tina's offer caught JD by surprise. "The two of you can hide in the back seat of my car. I'll drive you to the Joneses' and wait, and then I'll take you to the woods. Tomorrow's Sunday. JD, won't they be in church?"

"Yeah, sure, my old man leaves before daylight every Sunday, and my mom is always gone by nine."

"Mike has day shift at the station tomorrow. I can take him to work, and by the time church starts, we'll be all set."

Mike nodded his consent. He seemed pleased.

Mike and Tina's impromptu party rocked until midnight. JD drank liquor, cheap bourbon and coke, for the first time. Tina mixed his drinks. The first couple were mostly coke. After that, she made them much stronger.

By ten o'clock, the party ended. Underage guests made their excuses, and left JD alone with Mike and Tina. Mike took a final swallow and staggered off to bed. Through clouded eyes, JD watched as Tina carried extra blankets from a closet and made a pallet on the floor. Every time he closed his eyes, the room spun wildly around. Eventually, he found a reluctant, fitful sleep.

Sometime around three o'clock Sunday morning, JD awoke. He tossed and turned on the hard living room floor. Mike's whiskey-filled exhalations sawed through the thin walls of the shabby apartment. JD caught a whiff of the familiar perfume only seconds before he heard the floor creak beneath whispered footfalls. The provocative scent flooded his senses. Tina lifted the blanket and slipped in beside him.

She pressed her taut, warm body hard against his, and put her hand between his legs; JD gasped. She covered his mouth with her free hand, blew a *shh* in his ear, and followed it with a sloppy wet, exploring tongue.

On the grimy floor of the Spartan living room, JD's innocence urgently and quietly vaulted into the warm, inviting, luxurious folds of adultery.

Grace was first to realize that something was wrong. Late Saturday morning, she returned from shopping.

She called for James David, but he did not answer. *Out with friends,* she hoped. She unloaded her groceries and unconsciously put them away.

When James David missed lunch, she began to worry in earnest; by dinnertime, when the Reverend returned home, she was frantic.

"Don't worry, Mother," he said, although he never called her mother. "I'm sure he's with his friends; they've just lost track of time. It gets dark so late these long, spring days."

"We should look for him." She paced the floor. "He has never done this before."

"It won't be necessary. I'm sure James David will be home shortly." His tone was more demanding than comforting. "Now, calm yourself."

The Reverend spent the evening alone at his desk. He seemed only to stare at a blank sheet of paper, which was supposed to have been Sunday's sermon. Grace situated a chair just outside the open door to his study, and passed a sleepless night staring blankly at a wall.

At a little after three o'clock in the morning, she experienced an acute attack of anxiety, and sat desperately gasping for air for more than a minute. The inexplicable, succinct, yet indistinct, outside force that overpowered her, further convinced her that something devastating had happened. She feared for her son's safety. This occurrence marked the third time that day during which she felt a profound change in the tangible connection she shared with James David.

"Nothing can be done until after church," the Revered insisted. "If anyone should ask, we'll simply say James David is under the weather." He reinforced his point with a partial quote from the Bible. "As Paul wrote in his first letter to Timothy: '... *for if a man does not know how to manage his own household, how can he care for God's church?*'"

The windowpane shattered easily with one short swing of the tire tool, which Tim borrowed from Tina's trunk. He wielded it like a professional. Shards of glittering crystal sprinkled JD's bedspread; thousands more slid across the worn hardwood floor, and wedged in every crevice. Tim snapped the latch, lifted the broken casement, and crawled through the opening. He let JD in through the back door.

Tina circled the block.

Tim wanted to ransack the Joneses' bedroom and loot for anything of value. Total violation of his parent's privacy was more guilt than JD could manage. He refused, and insisted they stay together. "Tim, you're the expert, I need you to open my father's desk."

The study door was easy; JD found the spare key in its usual spot. The desk was an entirely different matter. Only one key existed, and the Reverend kept it in his pocket at all times. JD, assured that Tim was an expert, expected him to produce a paper clip or some special tool, press his ear against the drawer, and the lock would click open.

Instead, to JD's chagrin, Tim deftly wedged the tire tool under the lip of the drawer and jerked; the wood splintered in agony as the drawer snapped open. The damage done; fear echoed through JD, but it was too late. All he wanted now was to find some money and escape.

The drawer brimmed full with papers. On top, yellowed and faded, two roughly torn halves of a black and white photograph lay; in it, the Reverend was standing behind a massive grin and in front of a motorcycle. He wore a white tee shirt, and it looked as though there was a pack of cigarettes rolled up in one sleeve.

Beneath the picture, he found a faded-yellow 9" x 12" envelope. JD flexed the sheath of papers. Something about the size of a travel alarm, and very heavy, slid back and forth inside. Printed on the sealed flap, in the Reverend's irregular hand, was only one line: *PERSONAL AND CONFIDENTIAL, OPEN ONLY IN THE CASE OF MY DEATH.* JD had never before seen inside the drawer. Standing there with the envelope in his hand, he felt like an interloper in his own home. He released a heavily burdened sigh of relief; on top of the remaining contents, two neatly folded twenty-dollar bills peeked out of a letter-size envelope.

"Let's get out of here," he urged, already halfway across the room.

"What about the other stuff," Tim asked as he followed, "the campin' gear?"

"Forget it; I wanna get outta here before we get caught!"

Late in the afternoon, Tina picked Mike up from work. JD and Tim hid in the back seat. They gave Mike a report of the day's events, and everyone agreed that it would be best to wait until Monday morning to head for the woods. Tim made another trip to his father's house, and JD spent a second night with Mike and Tina.

The *wild thing,* as Tina called it, was enticing and delicious, and JD was reluctant to leave.

Three nights in the woods were something less than the adventure Tim had described. Their food was always raw or burned. The hard, cold ground was unforgiving. A persistent rock under JD's side of the tent left his back sore and bent every morning as he hobbled around the camp.

Tina's prearranged, clandestine visits were the only good thing in JD's long, lonely days in the woods. Her forbidden society was unforgettable, and he spent every minute, after she drove out of sight, waiting for her to reappear. Intoxicated by her lingering smell, he was recalcitrant to wash away the magic.

Five days seemed like forever, five days of guilt, five days of remorse, and five days of Tim, pushed JD to his limit. "I've had it." JD began as he threw another broken branch on the sputtering campfire. "I'm gonna turn myself in and just deal. We're never gonna have the money we need to make it to Canada. Even if we did get there, then what do we do?" He did not pause for an answer. "Their winters are really rough. We'd probably just starve to death, or freeze, or both. Tim, I gotta go home; you can do whatever the hell you want."

Tim nodded in approval.

Monday morning a concerned parent called Grace. She had overheard her daughter say that James David had run away from home, and was camping with another boy.

With potential camping locations as his focus, the Reverend followed one ambiguous lead after another, and searched the back roads all day Tuesday. Finally, on Wednesday morning, he topped a remote hill, and caught sight of the two boys walking.

Tim's submission was a signal; it was time for JD to take control of the situation. "It's a long walk back to town," he said abruptly. "We're gonna have ta leave some a this shit."

Tim scooped up his personal backpack, and started toward the road.

They left the woods and walked, side by side, down the middle of the deserted gravel road; the going was easy. They had made less than a mile when they saw dust boiling up, like a rooster tail, behind the old car speeding their way. JD gulped hard; a cold chill flashed down his spine. His heart pounded and his vision blurred. "It's my father," he whispered.

"Oh shit," were Tim's only words.

The Reverend stood stoically next to the open car door. JD dared not look at his father. He knew, all too well, the old man's resolute face. As he drove, the Reverend spoke only to Tim. "Where do you live, young man?"

The Reverend sat uncomfortably behind his old desk. The big file drawer hung crookedly from the frame; splintered wood fanned out from its face like a porcupine. He ran his palm affectionately around the jagged edge. A splinter lodged in his finger; he jerked his hand away. With his palm close to the stark light, he studied the tiny black lance embedded just below the skin. A drop of blood oozed from the pinpoint entrance to the wound. With his other hand, he gripped the spot and squeezed with all his might. Pain shot up his arm. He looked again at the damaged drawer, and then turned his attention back to the desk itself. *This was my father's desk*, he thought with regret.

Using all of his strength, he pulled the drawer free. With a few minor adjustments to the slides, the drawer slid in and out with only a few rough places. He took out the large, faded-yellow envelope, and touched the muted-blue words. It was sixteen years since he had written them, and on the same day, he had sealed the vessel. He anxiously checked the seal; the envelope was unopened. Forty dollars were missing from the drawer. A bent and grieving widow had given him the two twenties for his kind words over an open grave. *The money does not matter,* he told himself. *The envelope is intact.*

He held the two torn halves of the photograph under the lamp, and touched the smiling face of his brother. With self-reproach, he taped the photo together, unsealed the envelope, and without looking at the contents, slid it inside. The envelope lay on his desk for two days before he resealed it and locked it away.

Grace had never seen her husband in such an obscure mood.

In a severe tone, he barked the order. "Bring me scissors and a razor; then tell your son I want to see him." He stood between his old desk and the open door on a piece of clear polyethylene, which covered the floor.

The unsteady tenor of his cold voice and the rustling plastic beneath his feet sent a chill down Grace's spine.

With each passing hour, JD became more nervous. *This is just like the son-of-a-bitch,* he thought, *he knows it's always worse when he makes me wait.*

JD waited in his room, alone. The summons finally arrived on Friday afternoon with a reluctant, familiar knock at his door.

Mrs. Jones's swollen eyes and red nose appeared in the three-inch opening between the door and its frame. "Your father would like to see you, James David." She said in her whispery voice.

This is my fault, JD thought as he looked into his mother's mournful, blue eyes.

The anomalous film rattled under JD's cautious steps when he entered the room. He knew not to speak; warily, he closed the door and stood at attention just inside. He held every muscle in his body stiff; nervous tension made it difficult to breath. He locked his arms straight down, directed his eyes to the floor, and waited.

JD loved his thick brown hair; he kept it neatly cut, washed it every day, and combed it often. The women in the church frequently cooed when he came around. "Grace," they would gush to his mother as they ran their fingers through his hair, "do you know what a handsome son you have?"

At sixteen years old, JD was already nearly six feet tall; he was embarrassed, and a little flattered, when his mother's friends surrounded him and stood on their toes fondling his hair.

The Reverend sat behind his desk. He appeared to be deep in thought. Eventually, he began to speak. "James David, you are a disappointment to me. I have made great sacrifices for you, and you thank me with rebellion, humiliation, and deceit." His words were paced and deliberate. "I have asked myself a thousand times where I went wrong." He became more animated; at length, he stood. "What should I have done differently?" He supported himself with his arms, his palms flat on the desktop. "No matter how often I ask these questions, I have no answers. We have given you every opportunity: a good home, a family, the church, and creature comforts that are unknown to many in the world. In spite of everything, you persist in hurting us. What you have done is reprehensible, unforgettable, and almost unforgivable.

"As if all that you have done is not malicious enough, you have stolen from me. You took money that was not yours—forty-dollars, forty hard-earned dollars, paid to me by a widow for ministering to her in her time of loss. You will repay the money, and you will never steal from anyone again, ever.

"I have studied scripture and prayed for divine guidance. It should not be necessary for me to learn to cope with you. You are the child; you should live in my shadow. The Bible is very clear on discipline. It is the perfect and only life guide. In its pages, I found the answer. You will accept that answer, your punishment, in silence and with remorse." The

Reverend's face glowed red; he pounded desk with his fist. "You will learn from this, and you will follow the path of the righteous from this day forth."

JD trembled.

"In the book of Jeremiah, Chapter 7, verses 28 and 29, it is written: *And you shall say to them, 'This is the nation that did not obey the voice of the Lord, their God, and did not accept discipline; truth has perished; it is cut off from their lips. Cut off your hair and cast it away; raise a lamentation on the bare heights, for the Lord has rejected and forsaken the generation of his wrath.'*

"James David, accept this punishment in the spirit of love. Repent your sins, and do not repeat them," he pounded his fist again. "No good can come to you if you do not change. You, my son, are on a path that can only end in a fiery hell."

From a drawer, the Reverend produced the scissors and razor. As he came around the desk, James David flinched; every muscle in his body tensed. He understood what was to be next. He had heard the scripture, and now he saw the tools. Only fear kept him still.

For JD, the sound of hair falling on plastic was deafening. Each snip from the scissors felt like a knife slicing his heart. The fragrance of coconuts and spring sadly became less distinct as the locks slid down his neck. The Reverend finished with the scissors, and took up the razor. With purpose, he pulled the blade in a distinct and repeated pattern across JD's scalp. Twice he nipped an ear. The pain was minor, yet it unnerved JD. He mustered all of his remaining strength, and continued standing.

JD saw many things change that week.

On Sunday morning, he asked his mother for permission to skip Sunday school. Her answer was monotone; she looked at the floor as she spoke. "I guess it will be all right this time."

JD, confused by the quizzical look on her face, thought. *Does she feel sorry for me or guilty for her part in this?* He ran one hand across his bare head, and felt the stubble of new growth. *Either way, she'll have to deal with him for lettin' me out of Sunday school.*

She called back as she left the house. "Do not miss church."

JD arrived as the final peal of the huge brass bells resonated against red brick and stained glass. He slipped through a side door and up the back stairs into the deserted choir loft. The choir no longer used the loft; instead, they occupied folding chairs behind the pulpit and in front of a large, arched-top, stained glass window. The morning sun drenched the sanctuary in deep and varied shades of light.

I am here, he thought as he glared at the Reverend, already behind the pulpit. *Look at me. I want you to know I'm here.*

JD sat numbly through the service. He listened, but did not hear. It was as though the Reverend's voice had lost its authority. His presence seemed diminished. JD felt it more than he heard it. The preacher's words no longer rang out; they lacked passion and conviction. Most profoundly of all was the way he read the scriptures. For the first time in his life, James David Jones was not afraid.

Am I free of him, of his control, he wondered, *or am I just no longer able to feel?*

The hair came back; the feelings never did..

Four

THE BOY they called James David Jones, was summoned to the Reverend's study at least once per week. His physical being always went, always took its punishment, and never complained.

Mrs. Jones rarely spoke to her son. When she did, she seemed nervous. After a time, JD began to notice she was no longer perfectly dressed. Loosely wrapped braids of graying hair lay in inconsistent rows and formed a lopsided bun. Long, rebellious wisps protruded at various angles and hung haphazardly from the back of her head.

I wonder if she feels like I do, he thought. From time to time, he tried to catch her glance. Her once bright blue eyes never looked directly upon him. *This is my fault.*

A long time in coming, his senior year of high school arrived. *Passed by the grace of God,* he thought, *or by the mercy of the teachers,* he concluded.

Secretly, he was pleased with the transformation he managed under the Reverend's nose. He grew hair long enough to partially hide his ears and parted it down the center. At 6' tall, he towered above most of the students. *A thug*, he thought as he admired himself in the mirror.

To everyone, except his parents and the teachers, he was JD. He spent all of his free time with Mike and Tina, mostly with Tina. Their little boy called him *Unca JD*; he liked that.

The second day of April of the following spring, he celebrated his eighteenth birthday. From a shelf in the supermarket, he selected a small chocolate cake and a box of birthday candles. In the alley behind the store, hidden from the street by a smelly dumpster, he hurled the pastry against a concrete block wall. The icing slid down the dirty white building. From the crawling goo, thin wisps of smoke curled up from two extinguished candles. JD smiled, turned, and strode away in silence.

Three weeks later, one month before graduation, JD left school for good. Instantly, the rumors began to circulate and evolve. *Maybe he dropped out because someone provoked him. I heard he did it because it makes him seem cool.* The complicated exaggerations all came back to him. The truth was simple; *The Reverend wanted me to graduate.*

Her eighteenth birthday marked four years since she had been born again, not as a Christian, born again as Star. Kept in the shadows, the innocent Estrella had no practical purpose, no reason to be *out. I need a change,* Star told herself, *my life is boring; I need a fucking change.*

"Make me blonde, a natural blonde," she told the young hairdresser as she relaxed in the chair, "like Marilyn Monroe. It's my birthday and I've earned it." She said in perfect English without the slightest trace of an accent.

Her Spanish, and her Spanish accent, were equally good. When Lupe was away or passed out, she practiced for hours in front of a dirty mirror, watching her lips and her tongue as she enunciated the words in English, then Spanish. She emulated the accents she heard on television from well-spoken commentators in New York and Mexico City. She read every book she could find, in both languages, and filled a stack of notebooks with vocabulary words.

The pale redhead skillfully blew Star's hair dry, and combed every strand until she was perfectly coiffed. The tall, newly blonde, self-proclaimed debutante slowly lifted herself from the chair, leaned over the counter, and admired the change. The new Star looked out from the mirrored wall. "Perfect," she said conceitedly to the image, "I am perfect."

Outside on the busy sidewalk, she turned her face to the warm, spring, west-coast sun, closed her eyes, and smiled thinking of the two other major changes, which were soon to come.

The first few days, after JD left school, were exciting. Kids came up to him in the street and asked to shake his hand. He was a legend. When he was alone and afraid, he turned to Tina. She comforted him. She was his island of refuge until one day Mike came home unexpectedly, and the tide of reality washed away the island. Mike and Tina divorced; Tina told JD it was over.

"But—but, I love you." He pleaded with her to change her mind.

"I'm sorry, JD, I thought you understood. What we had was sport sex. It was forbidden and exciting, but I have a little boy to consider. We need a man to take care of us. I'm sorry."

Eleven years after James David Jones left high school and his home, he was unable to remember his final conversation with his father. He could not recall the last thing his mother had said to him. Haunted by the look of shock on her face, branded on his consciousness were the three parting words he wrote on the note to his mother: *I am leaving.*

JD burned too many bridges; all lay in ruin. He mostly walked the day he wrote the note. He managed to catch a few short rides on the state highways, which wound through the hills and led him to the edge of the Ozarks. The last car dropped him at the top of an eastbound on-ramp. He walked wearily down the incline; the sign on the shoulder of I-44 read *St. Louis 70 miles.* "May as well be a thousand," he said dejectedly.

Cars and trucks raced past seemingly indifferent to his outstretched thumb. It was nearly an hour before the old brown car braked hard and swerved to a stop. "Where ya headed, son?" The driver shouted above the howl of passing trucks.

JD tossed his duffel on the back seat, and slipped nimbly into the front. "St. Louis, sir," he said with intentional respect. "I'm very grateful for the ride."

"That's where I'm goin'. Looks like I can take you all the way." The man smiled. Deep wrinkles drew long lines across his thin leathery face. Bushy gray hair protruded from the band of the worn brown fedora casually cocked on the back on his head. "We'll be there in no time; traffic ain't bad t'day."

"That's great. I really do appreciate the lift. Been standin' there nearly an hour; nobody even slowed down."

"Yeah, I figured as much. I stopped 'cause I thought you might be a soldier headed home from the Fort. I really appreciate what all you boys do, especially after all that shit in the Gulf."

"I'm just goin' to visit some friends." JD lied. "I just got outta high school, haven't thought much about the military."

"That's fine. You seem like a nice young man. I'm glad to help anyway. I'm goin' to visit my mother. She just turned ninety, and she ain't doin' too good. Don't wanna miss out on what little time she's got left. Old gal gave up a lot for me. I owe her."

JD squirmed uncomfortably.

"What's your story?" The man asked. He glanced over and caught JD's twitching eye.

Hell, JD thought. *He seems nice enough; what do I have to lose.* In less than an hour, he told the quiet stranger his life's story.

"Good luck," the man said as he stopped in front of the youth hostel. "I've heard this place is nice."

JD felt the frown crawl across his face. *I wonder what it costs.* He fingered the fourteen one-dollar bills, and rattled a few coins, in his jeans pocket.

The stranger looked, knowingly, into JD's big brown eyes and smiled. "Maybe this'll help." He said as he passed over a tattered twenty-dollar bill.

"Sir, I can't take your money." JD protested weakly.

"Sure you can. I just hope someday you'll go see your old mom. When you do, think of me."

The twenty dollars lasted four days. Every one of those he looked for work. The answer was always the same, "Sorry, we only hire graduates."

Star del Rio took pride in the well-written newspaper articles. Both buried on the sixth page, the two articles appeared on two separate days. *This is cool,* she thought. She touched the words on the page and felt connected.

The same reporter wrote both stories. However, he mentioned no connection between the two, which pleased Star. In the first story, he reported that the police had found a known prostitute who had died of a blow to the head. They had yet to determine if it was a homicide. There was strong evidence found at the scene, which was consistent with heavy cocaine use. Star spread the paper out on the breakfast table, and admired the brief three paragraphs.

On the following day, she found the second story. A neighbor had discovered the body of a well-known pimp, also killed by a blow to the head. Star read aloud the first line of the second paragraph. *"The suspected murder weapon was found at the scene."*

She paused gloating. *"The police recovered a large obsidian ball, a common volcanic by-product typically found in Mexican handcraft markets."* Next, she thought as she closed the paper and took a delicate sip of hot espresso from a demitasse cup.

Nearly a year before, on her eighteenth birthday when she walked out of the salon with newly blonde hair, the plan first came to her. The same afternoon she purchased a *chic* spaghetti-strapped summer dress and heels. She kept them wrapped in plastic in the back of her closet. At least once each week, she took them out, put them on, and admired herself in a full-length mirror. In her mind's eye, she saw *Star* making small talk at a cocktail party or getting seductively into the back of a black limousine. She imagined the intoxicating leather interior, and a bubbling glass of champagne freshly poured by a generous man.

The day before she left the *barrio*, she dropped all of her old wardrobe in a dumpster. That night was a full moon, and the *barrio* was crazy. The next morning she dressed in the crisp summer dress, carefully applied her make-up, and walked casually down the street without a care in the world. Her oversized shoulder bag, stuffed with banded stacks of one hundred-dollar bills and a bag of Mexican chocolate, was a comforting burden.

For JD, everything changed the day his money ran out. It was as if the motorcycle shop appeared out of nowhere. One minute he was walking, dejectedly, down the street, the next he was peering through the plate glass showroom window. A voice told him to push open the door and go in. *What do you have to lose?* The voice asked. JD swallowed hard, touched the last lonely coins in his pocket, took a deep breath, and entered *D-K Choppers.*

"Woman," Reverend John Jones harshly began again, "how can you just sit there day after day? You seldom eat, I never see you sleep, and you have not uttered a word. Is your silence supposed to teach me a lesson? Do you want me to suffer even more than I already am? How can you blame me? The boy was always a rebel. I—we did the best that we could with him. Sometimes it just turns out this way. You know good kids from bad homes, and bad kids from good ones. Was I not always a good father? Have I not provided a good home? I tried to set a good example. Why would he do this to me?"

His words varied only slightly from one day to the next. The general context and meaning of the minister's litany of justifications and excuses, describing how and why he was not the reason James David had run away, were always the same.

The second day of James David's absence, Grace had moved silently around the house systematically closing the curtains and methodically pinning them shut. Not a single ray of natural light breeched her self-imposed prison.

That job finished, she had taken residence in her favorite chair next to the sealed living room window. There she sat, day and night, in total silence for four weeks. The tiny scraps of food, which she forced down, were to ensure that she had the strength to suffer.

The Reverend came and went. Every time he opened the door to the outside, spring came crashing in. The intermittent drone of lawnmowers, the sweet smell of freshly cut grass, and bright invigorating sunlight, a cacophony of the season, all rushed into the dark room. Grace sat unmoving, indifferent to everything except her self-recriminations.

She blamed the Reverend, but not as much as she blamed herself. *It was me,* she reasoned, *who did my husband's bidding.* She had fetched her son when ordered to do so, knowing the demand meant a terrible punishment. On every occasion, she had stood in the next room listening, suffering, but never intervening. It would have been so easy to intercede, to invite the wrath of the Reverend upon herself, but she did not. She could not.

This is your fault! Her mind screamed at her. The sound of her own voice was deafening. *I should not have been so timid. I could have stood up for myself, put my fears aside, and defended my son. If I had, he would still be here, and we would be happy.*

During those weeks of silence, another thought occurred to her many times. *We could have just left; I could have taken James and gone anywhere, anywhere, but here. We could have gotten out of this awful house.*

She imagined a life free of tirades fueled and sanctioned by select passages from the Bible. She wondered how she might have found the inner strength to tell her son the secret, the truth about his birth. She believed, in her moments of self-deprecation, that it would have been better. *After all,* she reasoned, *wasn't keeping the secret a lie.*

She believed things would have been different if she had it to do over again, starting with the day they brought the tiny dark-haired baby home from the hospital. *I shouldn't have spent so much time apologizing for my actions and my feelings. I'm human, too. I have desires. I make mistakes. If I repent and God forgives me, shouldn't the Reverend also forgive me?*

Reverend Jones repeated his words, only this time, much more loudly. "Why would he do this to me?"

Grace snapped back to consciousness. Towering over her slumped figure, he stood in front of her chair. For the first time, in a very long while, she looked directly into her husband's eyes. Incensed with the Reverend for his self-pity, disgusted with herself for long years of ambivalence, and angry with God for his lack of guidance, she was suddenly furious. He had never once answered her prayers.

"Why would he do this to you?" Her outburst carried an amazing strength of passion. "Would you listen to yourself? How can you think that you, that we, are absolved of all guilt in this? All those times you punished that child in your sacred study, I stood by allowing it to happen. We were preparing him for the day when he would turn his back on us. Every time he asked a question about his Uncle David and we answered with a lie, we pushed him further away.

"Of course, we justified what we did by telling each other it was for his own good. We should have told him the truth about everything as soon as he was old enough to understand. If we had done that, and if we had really been good parents, it would not have mattered. He would have forgiven us; he would have forgiven me." She let out a heavy sigh laden with twenty-eight stark days of emotion. "He would still be here today."

The Reverend stepped back. "How can you say that to me?" He looked upon her in awe; the raw truth and simplistic reality of her words mesmerized him. What she said held much closer to the true intent of the Bible than his calculated interpretation. Intellectually, he knew that she was right and he was wrong, but a lifetime of pride prevented him from saying so.

"I was always there for him, for both of you. What I did, I did to protect you both. I could have refused to take him into this house. I could have allowed them to label him a bastard. Instead, I defended him against the evil of the world. I gave him everything that any child could hope for, including my name. All I ever expected in return was a little respect."

In his heart, he knew he should have told her he loved her, but he never had. He had never told her, or anyone else, he was sorry. He had never admitted he was wrong. When the truth about anything became too personal, or got too close, he had always run away.

"I have forgiven you for what you did, for what you felt," he said. "I have struggled every day since to forget all of that. Burned in my mind, on the night he was born, is the look on your face when you begged me to accept him and to raise him as my own. In spite of everything that happened, I did as you asked."

"That's not true. You never forgave me, just like you never forgave your brother. He went to his grave with that knowledge. You say you gave my son everything, but did you ever love him? Did you ever show him even a little affection? Don't you think one of the things that help a child love a father is the father's demonstration of his love?"

"Woman, I am not his father!" He said adamantly, but with a weak voice.

"You promised we would never speak of this," she sobbed. "We agreed. You gave me your word. We both know, and we knew then, we agreed that parenthood is a state of mind. You could have been a father to him if you had wanted, if you had really tried. Had you done that, he would have loved you back. The truth would not have mattered to him. All he ever wanted from us was love, and we never gave it to him." She spoke without breathing; the strength of her words began to wane. "You promised to protect me, I promised to protect your precious ministry, and we promised each other that we would protect James David, no matter what. We let him down, Reverend Jones. We failed."

"Perhaps you let him down, but I never did." He disagreed with insincere conviction. "*Spare the rod and spoil the child*. I demonstrated my love to him through discipline. The problem was always with him. He has an evil essence; it is a terrible, black thing that is impossible to clean. Mark my word; he will end up in a six by eight cell, exiled from the world. As far as I'm concerned, he has set the course for his own destiny. To me, he is dead. I have no son. I have no brother. I have nothing."

"Then, sir, neither do you have a wife. I have no choice but to stay with you; I have built my life around yours. I have washed your clothes, cooked your meals, run your errands, and done my duty in the church. We have been a package. There is not a single congregation, to whom we have ministered, which would have believed for a moment that they were not getting their money's worth. They expect me to teach Sunday school, organize church socials, and sing in the choir. Your career has become my shared responsibility. Because I have spent every waking hour supporting you, I am now ill prepared to make my own way in the world. My only chance of survival is with you."

She lifted her emaciated frame from the chair; her unguided hands trembled as they brushed the wrinkles from her cotton dress. "This time it is me telling you. We shall live in the same house, and I will continue to carry out my church duties. To the outside world, everything will seem normal, but we will not sleep in the same room. I will no longer cook your food or wash your clothes. To me, when we are alone, you are dead, and so you shall remain until God decides to judge us both for our sins."

Grace kept her word. The only occasions during which she spoke to her husband were in the presence of others. The manner in which she carried out the facade was unquestionably perfect. Anyone would have thought the Reverend and Grace were the happiest of married couples. She keyed off her husband's conversations at exactly the right moments, and finished his sentences with finesse. She spoke fondly of him when the occasion presented itself, and was a model church member. At home, however, she slept alone, she ate alone, and she lived in a world where only she and memories of her son and his father existed.

Edward Williams's mother was dismayed when she found her young son, in the middle of his bedroom floor, with his brand new robot completely disassembled, parts scattered everywhere. "Edward, what are you doing?" She asked hysterically. "That toy is brand new."

"I'm makin' it work better, Mommy." He answered without taking his eyes from his task. "You'll see, I'm gonna make it faster."

Mr. Williams arrived and laid a comforting hand on his wife's shoulder. Edward looked up when he heard the deep familiar voice. "He looks like a surgeon, hon. Maybe we should call him Doc."

Doc Williams stood in the center of the cramped showroom floor, surrounded by a chrome sea of custom motorcycles, pleased with what he had accomplished. *It's been a long time coming,* he thought.

A customer entered wearing his *cut*. Doc admired the colors sewn on the back of the leather jacket. The three-inch-wide white upper rocker, trimmed in crimson-red, looked like a fat horizontal parenthesis open on the bottom, and served as background for *Sons of Darkness,* the club name Doc and six other *originals* chose for themselves seven years before. This member was one of nearly fifty who proudly wore the colors; all were Docs' friends and customers.

Parenthetically, between the upper and lower rockers, the Grim Reaper's stark-white skeletal profile lurked in the shadow of his own black hood; a single, empty eye-socket glared. He held his sickle, ominously, in front of his macabre visage; the business end curved backward, suspended threateningly above the dirty shroud.

Doc touched the buttons of his own *cut*, a black-leather vest. He closed his eyes and saw identical colors with *Doc* embroidered in the center of the lower rocker as were all the members' *road* names.

"Doc." Dawg, the parts man called out.

Startled, Doc snapped back to reality. "Yeah, Dawg."

"Somebody on the phone fer ya, boss."

Doc lifted the black plastic receiver from the heavily scratched, stainless-steel counter. The caller asked when the repairs on his custom bike would be finished. "You can pick her up this afternoon." He answered, pleased to fulfill a promise made the week before. "We're finishin' her up right now; she'll be better than new." He smiled sheepishly, thinking of his mother and the robot.

The showroom door inched open and a cool spring breeze rushed in. A frightened young face appeared followed by a lanky frame. The nervous young man loitered for a time, then timidly approached, stopped at a safe distance, and waited.

Doc studied the boy as he moved about the showroom. The caller thanked Doc for the news and hung up. Fascinated, Doc, with the receiver still clamped to his ear, continued to monitor the young stranger who studied each of the motorcycles. He seemed awestruck by the machines. Finally, Doc noisily dropped the receiver back in its cradle.

The young man immediately approached. "Sir, I am JD Jones, and I am looking for work." He said clearly, without breathing; he extended his right hand.

Doc took JD's hand and looked curiously at the boy's jittery eyes. In them, he saw a determined soul. Resolve telegraphed through his strong grip. An aura of something special surrounded the boy. "How do you do, JD, I'm Edward Williams; people around here just call me Doc," he smiled, "and if your willing to work, I believe we can find something for you to do."

JD Jones, bike washer, he thought with pride. *I'm gonna be the best damn bike washer they've ever seen.*

He washed every motorcycle with the precision of a surgeon; the hours flew by. Doc stopped by his work area every day, and seemed genuinely interested in what JD had to say. Doc, who looked young for a thirty-year-old father of two, at six feet tall, stood shoulder to shoulder with his young protégé.

Edward first noticed Katherine when they were both high school freshmen. They sat across from each other in English class. She was a popular cheerleader, and the star of the volleyball team. Her father was a well-to-do business professor; Doc's was a second-generation janitor. Doc was all but invisible to Katherine.

At the end of their junior year, she was elected senior class president. Thanks to Doc and the campaign, he waged in her favor.

It was an unseasonably warm, Tuesday evening in late October of their senior year when they bumped into each other after cheerleading practice.

"Hi, Katherine, how ya' doin'?" Doc tried to sound cavalier. He had long since memorized her telephone number and never had the nerve to call her.

"Hi," she answered shyly. "Thanks for your help with my campaign last year. If I can ever return the favor..."

"When you put it like that, there is one thing." He paused; it was too late to turn back. "The dance—one dance, Friday?"

"I'm sorry, what?"

"You don't owe me anything, but if you really want to do something, save me one dance on Friday night." He explained.

Perhaps it was the music, the finality of senior year, or the fact that he refused to give up; for whatever reason, they fell in love.

From behind the morning paper, Katherine's father peered over half-lens reading glasses. "Is his father not the janitor," he pressed.

"Father, you know he is. How many times have I heard you say, what a nice family they are? Just the other day, you were saying what a fine and diligent man old Mr. Williams was before he retired, and how his son had done an excellent job filling his shoes. I think you even mentioned that the world would be a better place if more people had the work ethic of the Williams's men."

He answered without lifting his eyes. "You, my child, will not become the wife of a third-generation janitor."

After three nights of listening to her husband prattle on about the new kid, Katherine *Kat* Williams was intrigued and wanted to meet JD Jones. "Okay, okay," she said. "I'll stop in tomorrow. I want to see for myself what's so special about this guy. He must be somethin'. We've had summer help before, and you never said a word."

"I'm telling you, Katherine, there is something special about this boy. He's only eighteen, but he doesn't treat this job like summer work. He goes after washin' those bikes like he was killin' snakes. He's meticulous about everything he does; I've never even used this word before, but I think he's charismatic. Tomorrow then, tomorrow you'll see for yourself."

Shit, she thought, *Doc was right.* After fifteen minutes of conversation with JD, Kat was convinced he was special.

"Where do you live, JD?" Kat got right to the point.

"In the youth hostel," he answered shyly, his eyes locked on the floor.

"Is it comfortable; do you have your own room?"

"It's okay, but no, ma'am, all the boys bunk in the same room."

"Well, we'll have to see about that." Kat said sternly like a mother to a child. She pivoted and went straight to the office.

It was late Sunday afternoon when Kat, Doc, and JD finished cleaning out the storeroom in the back of the motorcycle service area. Most of the clutter was junk and went straight to the dumpster. The bathroom, next to the storeroom, was fitted with an old fiberglass shower enclosure. It was also full of junk, but it worked and the water was hot. The area rug had been a gift from Kat's mother. It fit perfectly, and covered the concrete floor from wall to wall.

Doc brought a rusty, steel-frame single-bed from the basement at home, and Kat made it with well-worn sheets and a blanket. Down on her knees, she smoothed out the last wrinkle of the red, white, and blue bedspread. Doc had used it as a college freshman living in the dorm. She looked up at her husband and the young man. *Three days ago, he was a stranger,* she thought, *now he is our ward.* She admired their equally strong faces. *In another life, they could have been brothers.*

"Kat, why are you smiling?" Doc asked. "You look like the cat that ate the canary."

"Nothin' really, I just think the room is nice," she answered, reticent to say what she really thought. "I think JD will be very comfortable here, that's all.".

FIVE

I CAN'T BELIEVE *I've been here three years,* JD thought as he brushed his teeth in front of the dingy mirror in the small, familiar bathroom. *It seems like yesterday that I started work and moved in.* He wiggled into tight jeans, and pulled on black boots. *Maybe I need new jeans.* He checked the pant leg, which was just a little too high on the side of his boot. He had grown his final inch, and matched it with an extra inch of hair.

It was Saturday and he had asked for the day off; Doc agreed without question. JD had long since graduated from bike washer. He started with simple tune-ups and worked his way up to mechanic. He studied the factory and aftermarket service and parts manuals until he knew them all by heart. *If I'm going to be a mechanic,* he thought, *I'm going to be the best.*

He combed his hair, and took one last look in the mirror. The face seemed wiser than what he remembered. Behind the veneer, still lived the boy, the preacher's son. *Am I really twenty-one? My life didn't even begin until I came here.* The face in the mirror smiled. *I guess I grew up right here.*

He opened the back door to the showroom, and walked right into the middle of a cheer. The membership of the *Sons of Darkness* formed a semi-circle, and began to chant. "For he's a jolly good fellow…" Someone put a beer in his hand. JD was swept into their midst.

The bike shop was officially open. However, no one worked. The drone of bikes arriving and leaving was constant. Beer coolers occupied every corner of the showroom. In the center of the room was a sound system, and a makeshift dance floor.

"Doc, this is a real party." The somewhat-drunk JD hugged his friend. "Thanks, this is really great, you're amazing."

In mid-afternoon, Doc stopped the music. JD was in the middle of a slow dance with someone else's girlfriend. "Mr. Jones," Doc began with an official and prophetic tone, "We are here today to celebrate a very important event, the anniversary of your birth. Not just any anniversary, this is the day whereupon the laws of the state of Missouri acknowledge your transition to adulthood. You, sir, have achieved an age whereon you may now legally, and without forethought, buy your own fucking booze!"

The crowd roared.

"Therefore, as the appointed representative of this distinguished group of derelicts, which we call the *Sons of Darkness*, it is with great pleasure that I bestow upon you the honor of full member." Doc reached out with open arms, palms up, "Gentlemen, the cut."

The crowd rippled from the back as they passed it forward. An officer of the club stepped from the ranks, and handed Doc a folded black-leather jacket. He shook it out by the shoulders, and held it up for all to see. The club colors emblazoned the back. Between the rockers, the Grim Reaper waited. Embroidered on the lower rocker was a single word, *Deacon*.

"Mr. Jones, by the power vested in me, I hereby confirm upon you full membership in the *Sons*. I'm sure somewhere in the Bible there's a passage that would make my point. However, only you would know where it is, and that is my point. Because of your prolific use of scripture with which you always make your point, you have divined your own road name. From this day forward, you shall be known as *Deacon*. Please accept this *cut* as a token of our friendship and esteem. Wear our colors proudly."

Deacon touched the black leather, smooth and durable; he fought back tears. M*y armor,* he thought. With Doc's help, he slipped into his new jacket. For the first time in his life, James Deacon Jones was an important part of something. *I'm finally a Son,* he proudly told himself.

The tufted red-leather seat of the custom chopper, resting on its kickstand in front of a plate glass window at the edge of the dance floor, gave Deacon a clear view of the room. The cold Budweiser washed easily past his tongue. He joyfully breathed in the oily-clean smell of the motorcycle shop, the laughter of his friends, and most of all, the brotherhood.

The *Sons* were not one per-centers; they were not outlaw bikers. Deacon noticed a lawyer across the room. *A friend,* he thought. *It doesn't matter what you do during the week,* he patted his knee with the palm of his free hand. *If you're a Son, on Saturday we're all the same. Today,* he smiled modestly, *today, I'm not only a member, I'm Deacon.*

It was almost dark when Doc stopped the party again. He quieted the room; with anticipation, everyone focused on Doc. He whistled a long, low, beckoning call. A path between the dance floor and the door to the service area magically opened. Two members emerged and threaded their cargo carefully through the throng. One guided and the other pushed a large wooden crate, which rode upon a four-wheel dolly.

"A member of an MC has to have a scoot." Doc said as he smiled broadly and touched the oily box, which brimmed full of miscellaneous motorcycle parts. An old Harley-Davidson hard-tail frame, chipped and scarred, protruded from the center of the crate.

"This is mine," Deacon's voice cracked with emotion, "this is for me?" He ran his fingers through the greasy parts. "They're beautiful."

"Yeah, a beautiful, greasy mountain of work," Doc added. "But I'll help ya. Hell, we'll all help you."

The crowd closed around Deacon and his prize. Beneath the crush, he laid his face on the jumble of cold steel and chrome. Warm tears dripped through the pile.

Occasional grease fueled fireballs, belched from the massive outdoor grill, and illuminated the clear night sky. The mouth-watering aroma of barbeque wafted into the showroom and the mob streamed outside.

"Come on, Deac, you have to eat somethin'." Doc coaxed Deacon outside.

Someone shoved a lawn chair against the backs of his knees, and someone else put a plate of ribs in one hand and a glass of Jack Daniels in the other. The crowd, interacting like a single multifaceted organism, whirled around him. One by one, the members came around, shook his hand, called him Deacon, and ceremoniously patted his colors.

"Deac, you don't have a tatt, do ya?" Doc's question came late in the evening; only the hardcore crowd remained.

"Nope, ain't got no fuckin' tatt!" Deacon's drunken speech was, for a moment, clear. "Ya think I need one?"

"It only seems right, my friend, it only seems right."

Led by Ink, a founding member of the *Sons,* the sluggish, serpentine motorcycle processional stretched through the back streets and alleys.

Doc rode second in line. With one hand, he supported a limp Deacon on the back of his bike. They made the last turn and topped a small hill. He killed his engine, coasted the remaining two hundred feet, and stopped in front of Ink's tattoo parlor.

Slumped in the artist's chair, Deacon rolled his head around in a drunken stupor and mumbled something incomprehensible.

"Deacon, Deacon, can you hear me?" Doc caught him by the shoulders and shook. "I need you to talk to me. Listen, Ink's been at this a long time; everybody knows he's the best skin artist around. He's gonna give you whatever you want." He shook him again, only more soundly. "Deac, you're gonna have ta tell him what ya want. He's an artist, not a mind reader."

Through the fog that shrouded his mind, a random thought emerged. It came out of an old part of his brain, the part that was his first life, which had ended when he was eighteen years old. *What will my father say? What will he do to me when he finds out?*

He shook his head as if to expel the memory. "Right here, put it right here." With the index finger of his right hand, he touched his left arm just below the scar left by his smallpox vaccination. "Let's do somethin' my old man would appreciate." He said with a drunken, sinister laugh.

The mental image of the tattoo was crystal-clear as though he had planned it his entire life. Deacon heard his own voice talking to him through the fog. *This must be how divine guidance that the Reverend always talked about works. Hell, maybe this is divine guidance.*

Deacon began to speak lucidly and without hesitation. Perfectly formed words came in a chanting rhythm like a parishioner reciting the Lord's Prayer. With careful precision, as though reading from a script, he described the symbol of his life. "I want a cross, a three-dimensional cross. Not of wood, make it ancient ebony with deep golden trim as though it came from the time of Moses in Egypt. It should be elegant, too ostentatious for Christ, like the possession of a man who wouldn't own a cross or possess the humility its ownership would require."

Deacon became increasingly more agitated. "Give it depth, feeling, and value—enticing to a lover of priceless trinkets, and wrap it with a serpent, a wicked, sin-filled snake."

Ink sketched frantically with colored pencils on a large pad.

Deacon abruptly stopped and looked into the faces of his friends. In their inebriated eyes, he recognized confusion and fear. No one moved. They seemed to be waiting.

Deacon heard his father's voice. He closed his eyes and saw the Reverend Jones pound the pulpit and shout at the congregation. He heard the message as clearly as if the man was in the room. Deacon began to repeat, verbatim, what he heard: "Remember, Brothers, the Song of Moses in the old testament, Deuteronomy, Chapter thirty-two, verses thirty-two and thirty-three:

For their vine comes from the vine
of Sodom,
and from the fields of Gomor'rah;
their grapes are grapes of poison,
their clusters are bitter;
their wine is the poison of serpents,
and the cruel venom of asps."

Deacon returned his attention to the sketch on paper, and resumed his description as though he had never stopped. "A viper with the fury of hell reflected in its burning eyes. Wrap its boneless skin and cold flesh around the entire width of the cross."

Occasionally, Ink held up the incomplete image for Deacon to see. Continually, he erased and redrew the shapes to match the verbal tapestry.

"Its head must tower above the symbol, drawn back and ready to strike; menacing fangs will drip with the evil venom of Satan." Deacon paused; thinking, remembering, knowing, and then he continued. "Paint the dagger of a rich man or pagan king, an anlace. I want the knife to impale the cross through the snake. It will bleed a rich crimson blood from the wound, not the snake, the cross, the lifeblood of goodness and truth. When you've finished, the cross will weep with the blood of the faithful."

The muffled buzz from the tool barely penetrated Deacon's drunken stupor. He jerked at the first prick of the needle.

Ink quickly lifted the tool from his skin. "Easy, Deacon, you're gonna cause me to make a mess of this. You have to sit still, relax." He ordered.

Deacon was aware of the strong, antiseptic smell mixed with ink and sweat, which hung in the thick air. Bikers crowded the chair to watch the work unfold. The pain of the needle was excruciating at first. As he became accustomed to the alcohol numbed stinging, his mind drifted away.

"Oh, shit!" Ink's panicked voice penetrated Deacon's thin veil of unconsciousness.

"What, what's a matter?" Deacon blinked. Ink's face was close to his arm; Deacon could feel his friend's hot, rapid breath.

"Shit, man, you're bleedin'. It's the booze. It's a fuckin' blood thinner."

"What's that mean to me?"

"It means the ink might not stay, and it makes the work harder for me."

"It'll stick, just finish." Deacon ordered; he looked up at the schoolhouse style clock on the wall. It was 3:50 A.M. *Wow,* he thought, then closed his eyes and drifted away.

Daybreak devoured the remnants of darkness; the tool buzzed for the last time, and the artist leaned back to admire his handiwork.

"Your best ever." Doc said with amazement. He held a mirror so Deacon could see the full image imprisoned in his arm. Deacon grinned. *From God's lips to my arm,* he thought.

Late Sunday afternoon, consciousness found Deacon; he looked around the unfamiliar bedroom. *Where am I?*

A naked, apple-face woman lay sleeping by his side. She opened one eye and yawned. "Afternoon, sleepy-head, I thought you'd never sleep it off."

"How'd we get here?" He asked nervously. "Did we…"

"The guys dropped us; this is my place, and you bet we did, more than once." She pecked his cheek. "I volunteered for this gig, and man, am I glad I did. Happy Birthday to me," she laughed.

Deacon closed his eyes against the light; his head throbbed, even his eyelids ached.

When the protective bandage of gauze and ointment came off his arm, no one laughed. The frightening image was exactly what Deacon had described. No one was able to look long at the carefully stained skin. The most anyone, including Deacon, could manage was a sideways glance.

Occasionally, as the weeks passed, people who had heard about the tattoo would ask to see. At times, in a bar with a little urging and a few beers, Deacon would roll up his sleeve for effect.

Ink was the first to admit that he did not know how he had produced the horror from only Deacon's description. Once, about a week after he created it, Ink asked to see it again. He examined the image closely. "It's like the snake is alive," he marveled, sounding angry. "And the cross, it looks like it's dyin'. He gingerly touched the image, and jerked his hand away as though he had been shocked, then vomited in the bathroom.

Two nondescript envelopes were securely zippered away in a side pocket of her snakeskin purse. Each contained thirty one-hundred-dollar bills. It was early Saturday afternoon, and Star had already turned two tricks. *Shit*, she remembered, *it's my birthday; I deserve to celebrate.* She patted the side of her purse thinking about the money inside. *I'll do two more, and then make it a club night,* she promised herself. *Hell, maybe I'll even drive out and spit on my bitch-of-a-mother's grave.*

By midnight, Star was sick of the pawing, desperate men vying to buy her a drink. She looked disgustedly at their faces. *Like I'm gonna fuck any of you for free,* she thought.

In the club's momentarily empty bathroom the pale, skinny woman applied red lipstick with the skill of an artist.

"Hi, I'm Star." Without waiting for the woman to respond, she dragged her painted nails, sensuously, down the brunette's emaciated right arm. She admired the girl's reflection in the spotless mirror, and leaned in until they were cheek to cheek. Star's come-hither brown eyes sparkled.

The girl shuddered at Star's touch, and answered in a faint voice. "Hi."

Inside the locked stall, Star put both hands on the girl's shoulders, and forced her to her knees. She pulled her own skirt up, slid her panties to one side, clutched the girl's hair, and pressed hard. "That's it, baby, get it all!" She purred.

With one hand, from a plastic bag in her purse, Star retrieved a miniature chocolate and deftly removed the individual wrapping. The room was warm and the chocolate was sticky soft. She slid the candy under her tongue and examined her hand in the light. Dark traces of gooey chocolate melted and clung to her fingers. Only the top of the girl's head showed from between Star's thighs. *Perfect,* she thought as she wiped the chocolate in the girl's hair. *This cunt doesn't know she's mining gold for free*, she smiled, remembering the twelve thousand, newly earned, dollars hidden in her purse.

Every eye traced every sensuous step as Star returned from the ladies' room. She surveyed the faces, assigning a numerical score to each. She checked the plastic bag in her purse; it was empty. *Assholes,* she thought. "Barkeep, call me a cab." She ordered.

The bedside clock showed midnight; she pulled the covers up and closed her eyes. *Gotta get some rest,* she thought.

An excruciating pain shot through her naked left bicep. "What the hell!" She exclaimed to the empty room. She checked the clock. "Shit, I've barely slept an hour. This sucks. She closed her eyes again; the effects of the alcohol were nearly gone. She cleared her mind and tried to sleep.

She heard the electric-mechanical buzz clearly, as though it was in the room. The phantom pain of a non-existent needle on her sensitive skin seemed real. A profoundly frightening image flashed across her mind like a shooting star. *I understand,* she told herself with clarity of vision. *I know what I must do.*

By ten o'clock Sunday morning, Star had begun to put her plan in motion. Star del Rio took the first step toward that which she knew at her core was the fulfillment of her true destiny.

Grace Jones skillfully traced the distinct lines of her tightly braided hair. Her fingers followed each painstakingly wrapped cord confirming the bun on the back of her head was perfect. *I don't need a mirror to remind me.* She thought, remembering the last time she had seen her reflection. From behind tightly closed eyes, she saw her own sad image of a woman barely past fifty, prematurely gray, ever deepening wrinkles, and worst of all, faded blue eyes. *I don't need a piece of glass to remind me of what I've done.* She pried open her eyes and hurried out of the dusty house.

During the first few years, after James David left, Grace looked for him every day. Some days she stood in the doorway of the house watching the street, hoping he would walk in to view. Her resources were very limited, but she called the police every week. It was the same with all the public agencies. "Sorry, ma'am, your son was eighteen; he left of his own free will. If he doesn't want to be found, chances are, he won't be."

"I cannot accept that." Her adamant response was always the same. "I will not accept that—I will find my son. With or without your help, I will find him."

She fervently wished to see again his shy, handsome face. She wished, but she never prayed. For Grace, God had failed. She had asked for His help, repeatedly, but it never came; God never answered. She knew that the messages from God, which the Reverend interpreted for her, came from the Reverend. "These are your words; you do not speak for God!"

During those same years, the Reverend experienced his own contempt-laced memories of James David. *If he had followed my instructions, he would have stayed on the path of righteousness*, he reminded himself. *I did all I could.* With each passing year, John Jones went full circle through every possible emotional stage: regret, anger, remorse, then began again with all consuming regret.

Mrs. Jones was right, he admitted to himself. *Without her, the congregation will feel slighted; I need her and she needs me. Without me, she can't survive, and without her, I cannot minister. I am tired of the transfers; I am tired of this life.* He cringed with the knowledge of his own reality.

SIX

FOR THE FIRST TIME, Deacon Jones was truly happy. His life was as he had always dreamed. The members of the *Sons* treated him with respect, and Doc was the older brother he never had. They talked about everything, drunk or sober. Eventually, Deacon told him every sordid detail of his first eighteen years.

For nearly a year, following Deacon's twenty-first birthday, they worked almost every night on his motorcycle. The scattered parts from the big wooden crate began to take shape.

Deacon threw his leg across the tan-leather solo saddle, and rested his right hand on the throttle; the reach and drop were perfect. He lowered his head, and with one eye, aligned the center of the tachometer with the centerline of the front tire. Extended forks, raked thirty degrees, made the nineteen-inch, hand-laced wheel seem far away. He smiled a dreamy smile. "Doc, this is so damn cool."

Doc sat, low to the floor, on a mechanic's stool drinking beer from a long-necked bottle. "Yep, exactly what you said you wanted." Doc answered, obviously pleased with the work. "This wasn't a project; it was a fuckin' mission!"

"Yeah, but it's worth every minute, every dollar." Deacon proudly proclaimed.

"Last thing we gotta do is get her painted," Doc noted. "You got somethin' in mind?"

"Absolutely, I wanna make her dark blue with gold accents. The paint's gonna be the icin' on the cake."

"What about decals or airbrushin', some kinda art?"

"I've been thinkin' about that, but you won't like it," Deacon said nervously.

"Great, what the fuck ya thinkin'?"

"I wanna ask Ink to airbrush the tattoo on the tank."

Doc gave a kick and shot backward across the floor. "No fuckin' way!" The stool's casters carried his weight smoothly. He rolled to a stop ten feet from Deacon and the bike. "Ink won't do it. He already told me. He can't stand to look at the fuckin' thing."

"Well," Deacon persisted, "I'll just get him to paint the snake and the dagger. He'll do that. Without the cross it's no big deal."

"Yeah, maybe, I doubt it."

"Widowmaker's gotta have a look. I'll convince Ink, you'll see."

"What's Widowmaker?"

"It's her name." Deacon beamed, white teeth flashed, and brown eyes sparkled. He smoothly flipped his long hair away from his face. "A cool bike's gotta have an awesome name. She's Widowmaker 'cause she's gonna be a badass motherfucker. Let's have a few more of those beers and celebrate." He slid effortlessly off his creation, and crossed the room to the dented refrigerator.

Doc, with a highly practiced hand, painstakingly painted the tank and fenders a deep translucent blue over a gold undercoat.

Ink protested with every stroke. When he finished, the snake pierced by the dagger or anlace, as Deacon had first called it, was a perfect partial-reproduction of the menacing tattoo.

"Listen to me now, Brothas and Sistas," he climbed upon a wooden box in the middle of the showroom floor next to Widowmaker. The club members drew close. "Raise yo hands and say AMEN if you hear me."

Beer bottles lifted in a mock salute. "AMEN," the crowd called out in unison.

"AMEN," Deacon returned, emulating a zealous preacher calling his flock. "Widowmaker is ready for the street."

"AMEN!"

Deacon rented an apartment, bought furniture, household goods, and even a car for the Missouri winters. *I'm a fuckin' cager.* He told himself when he slid behind the wheel for the first time. *Hell, I'm like a real person.*

Every head turned as Star strutted down Rodeo Drive. Precise, deliberate clicks from spiked heels gave audible rhythm to her movements. She tossed her long blonde hair back nonchalantly. *See how they look at us.* She told Bridget and Estrella with pride. *Look at those faces; they're all dying with envy.* A white-leather miniskirt accented unbelievably long, tanned, and toned legs.

Bridget Luna rented an elegant, furnished apartment, and filled the closets with beautiful dresses.

Italian marble, in the exquisite bathroom, was cold beneath her bare feet. She admired her reflection in the slick black floor. She laughed aloud. "I—have arrived." Her words echoed against the imported stone wall.

The massive, far-away, king-size bed beckoned. She charged the width of the sitting and bedroom combined; nine long steps were required to reach the four-poster. Her last became a leap, then a twist. She landed on her back and slid, with a bounce, across the silk comforter. "This is the fucking life!"

Star never spoke of her real business, or her true private life, to anyone. The apartment was her sanctuary; there she continued her self-education and planned preparations. The spare bedroom, with its door always closed, was a grim addition to the finely appointed apartment. Its only furnishings were an old wooden table, a four-drawer metal file cabinet, and an exercise machine. She covered the only window with thick black paper. On one wall, she hung a large blackboard. The opposite wall supported an equally sized cork bulletin board. The remaining surface she covered with mirrors, which bordered the always locked door.

The new chalk screeched as it marked the green surface. Star cringed. A miniature puff of white dust rolled out in front of the soft eraser as she removed her first attempt. The board did not resist the softened edge of the chalk, and she silently printed: *To Do.* Beneath the heading, she began, thoughtfully, to make her list.

She wrote and rewrote the items until she was sure they were chronological and comprehensive. The first three were:

1) Improve me

2) Respectable image

3) Find the family

Down around item twenty was *get high school and college degrees*. That part was easy; Benny's reputation for forgery was impeccable, and he even framed the certificates. As she accomplished each item on the list, Star drew a diagonal line through the corresponding number.

Respectable image meant a profession through which Star could meet people, wealthy people, and the LA real estate market was burgeoning. The school for real estate brokers was too easy, and practically overnight, Star was respectable.

Star was self-aware; she knew that it would be fruitless to try to judge her essence and true character. Her mother's lessons had long since wiped all emotion from her countenance. Life, Star's life, supported by Estrella and Bridget, had become a series of premeditated, carefully orchestrated events designed to achieve one end. Every time she entered her *war room* and read the list, thoughts of revenge and the settling of scores overwhelmed her. Her focus was on three far-away people, whom she blamed for stealing her happiness.

She had never actually met, or even seen them. In spite of this, she had put it all together from the bits and pieces pried from her mother. Time and cocaine had gradually unsealed the tomb of her mother's bought and paid silence.

When I do face them, she promised herself, *I will make everything right. I'll settle the score just as I did with my own bitch of a mother.*

"Good afternoon, Doctor, I'm Bridget Luna." Star firmly shook his hand, and then settled comfortably in a muted-yellow leather chair in front of the plastic surgeon's massive glass desk.

"How can I possibly make you more beautiful, Miss Luna?" He smiled. His face filled with a familiar look of wanting.

"Doctor, please, you're too kind." She contracted the muscles in her face and forced a blush. "I would like for you to make my nose a little smaller, more petite, enlarge my breasts, and explain to me the ramifications of liposuction."

"I will be happy to help you, Miss, with whatever you want. However, I am truly surprised that a woman as stunning as you feels the need to make such changes."

"Doctor, oh, Doctor sounds so formal." She leaned in, provocatively, exposing her tanned breasts. "After all, you are going to see me naked and unconscious. May I call you, Robert; it is, Robert, isn't it?" Star looked past him to his vanity wall, papered with diplomas. "Well, yes. Yes, it is, but my friends call me, Bob."

"If you don't mind, I prefer Robert. It sounds so elegant, so—so sophisticated."

Es muy importante siempre ser coqueta. She heard her mother's voice repeating the words. *It is always important to be a flirt.*

"By all means, call me Robert, and may I call you, Bridget? It's such a lovely name; it fits you perfectly. Your mother must have great compassion."

"Thank you. Please do, and yes, my mother was a very compassionate woman." She willed a face of sadness, and with both hands pulled her hair back behind her ears.

"I'm sorry, you're so young; I just assumed your mother was still living."

"Don't be sorry." Star began to cry, softly. "My mother was a wonderful, loving woman, but she lost a three-year battle with lymphatic cancer just thirteen months ago, and I miss her so."

Doctor Robert, painstakingly, triple checked every instrument and every measurement. Star reveled in the attention, and after surgery, awoke to three-dozen red roses.

In her bedroom, she made sure that he believed he was *making love* to her. *Two more easy procedures,* she thought as she stared at the ornate crystal chandelier, which hung above the bed. *Two more visits to this room, and we will be even.* She caused her mind to drift away.

The doctor, firmly entrenched between her sculptured legs, continued to hammer her pelvis in short desperate thrusts; his moans grew to a wail.

Star, relieved, slid the chocolate from beneath her tongue and bit it in two, matched his sound, and added to it in her own sensuous, guttural rasp. "Oh yeah, baby, that's it, doll. Give it to me. Give Bridget what she wants."

In less than two weeks, the final two procedures were complete, and the corresponding payments delivered. The last of which, she decided to make special by allowing him to finish in her mouth.

Breathless, Doctor Robert reluctantly withdrew his rapidly softening penis from her collagen-enhanced lips. Bright-red lipstick drew uneven streaks on white skin. He sighed. "In two days, we can remove your bandages and give you one last check. Sweetie, you're finished." He lovingly nestled between new breasts. "You have everything you wanted."

"Thank you, doll, you're right." She smiled with a predictive countenance. "I got exactly what I wanted."

"Oh, Robert," large teardrops gathered in thick mascara, then streaked down tense cheeks, and disappeared into the hospital sheet, "it's the guilt. I just can't live with the guilt. I keep thinking about your wife and children crying. I know in my heart my mother would never approve."

"But, Bridget, darling, I love you. I'll get a divorce; I'll do anything. I just want to be with you."

"I love you, too, Robert. That's the problem. I love you too much to allow you to give up your family. Even if we were together, I could never forget that I destroyed your marriage. No, my dear, sweet, Robert, it can never be, but I will always love you."

Even before the discoloration in her skin completely faded away, she had forgotten his first name. Star drew a line through the number one on her list with a flourish.

The only other person who ever saw the inside of the *war room* was the telephone man. Star stood mute in the doorway, and watched him work. After he left, she plugged in a small black phone with a built-in answering device. She hummed and counted until she was convinced; the low, tonal quality of her voice was its most seductive. She pressed her lips against the tiny microphone. "Hi, this is Star. Your message means everything to me. Tell me a story, and I'll make it worth your while."

Next to the phone, she placed a small, brown permanently bound ledger. She breathed in the primal aroma of freshly tanned leather. A single leather strap, wrapped around a solid-brass button, held the book securely closed. Diagonally across the cover, as though she was adjusting a work of art, she positioned a deep-burgundy fountain pen.

Among Star, Bridget, and Estrella, they called it *the circle of the sun.* All who fell in this group were Bridget's responsibility. Their interest was Real Estate; Bridget called herself *their agent.* The light of that circle fell in a great arc and encompassed lunches and dinners, tennis games, and cocktail parties. She quickly and adeptly became a member of their elite group. From that circle, under Star's expert tutelage, Bridget meticulously extracted people who, by nature of their personalities, financial status, and minimal indicators, showed themselves to have an additional interest in a very different place, in the *shadow of the moon*, within the overpowering influence of Star's gravity.

At first, when Star talked to herself (that is to say, in conversation with Bridget and Estrella) she thought of them as her johns. Later, when face to face with her own reflection, she decided to call them *night people*. Eventually, she waxed poetic and discovered she liked much better to simply call them *moon people*.

Her goal was to amass a great deal of money, a fortune, in a very short time. To achieve this, she would not limit herself to one market. Lavender ink flowed across pages of the brown book as it filled with masculine and feminine names. Star, totally disengaged, was not in the least contrite about the depth of her service; ecstasy, self-realization, and fulfillment, came from the power to control the *moon people*.

Daily, in a private ritual, she methodically bound the stacks of one hundred dollar bills. They accumulated in such abundance that they became difficult to store. By the time she turned twenty-five, her key fob held safe deposit box keys from more than a dozen banks. Her freezer was chocked full of packages, which, with amusement, she labeled as frozen vegetables in every variety of green imaginable.

Each of the sleazy detectives, whom she hired year-after-year, was happy to accept Western Union wire transfers from the mysterious woman in exchange for the information they sent. Not one ever questioned her strange requests. As ordered, they traveled from one small Midwestern town to the next investigating and taking pictures of an old minister and his wife. Later, in stark contrast, they investigated a young man who worked in a motorcycle shop and rode with a club called the *Sons of Darkness.*

The battered-wood table slowly began to disappear beneath a mountain of notebooks labeled by year, each filled with a chronological sequence of events discovered in the Missouri investigation. Star marked the pages, which contained what she considered *substantial events* with colored tabs. In the center of the table, usually open to one specific page or another, was a large Bible, which she had purchased at a used bookstore.

To her it was not a religious guide, or even a symbol; it was merely a reference book. Its big pages, broad margins, and large print facilitated highlighting and handwritten notes. There was a family tree, drawn by the publisher, on the cover page. Along each of the printed branches were handwritten names of long-dead family members of some unimportant family. Star laughed aloud when she first found the diagram. In crimson ink, she drew a large circle and bisected it with a single diagonal line.

On the blackboard, she neatly printed a list of scriptures, which she had learned about from the detectives' reports; she copied them verbatim from the Bible. Tacked to the corkboard were organized rows and columns of 4" x 6" photographs, stolen at a distance by one zoom lens or another. Star financed every scrap of information and every photograph with money earned from a lascivious man between her legs, or her between the legs of a salacious woman.

"What's bothering you, Edward?" Kat laid her fork on her now empty plate, and dropped her hands to her lap. You've barely touched your dinner, and we haven't really spoken for more than a week. You should be the happiest man alive. I looked at the P&L today; we just finished our best quarter ever. Business is good, like we always dreamed. Even my father has finally admitted, in private of course, that you were a good catch. At one point in the conversation, I think he almost said he was wrong. So what is it? Tell me, please."

"It's nothin'—just stupid stuff—nothing worth discussing."

"I don't mind hearing about unimportant things, but you've been moping around here for more than a week; it has to be something."

"I don't want to talk about it, really. It has nothing to do with you; I'm afraid if I say it out loud, it'll sound more stupid than even I think it is."

"Try me. Come on, Edward, we have a deal, no secrets. Remember?"

"You're right as always, Katherine. I'm sorry. What happened is—well the thing is—okay—here it is—I think I'm jealous of Deacon." He blurted it out.

"What, what on earth are you talking about? You two are best friends. I've heard you say hundreds of times, he's the best thing that ever happened to the bike shop. The customers love him; you love him."

"Exactly my point, people hardly ever ask for me anymore. It's Deacon this and Deacon that. I feel like our success is due to him. I'm just there as a witness and an occasional sounding board."

"But, hon, isn't that the point? You're the boss, the founder. If you had not recognized his potential, if you had not taken him in off the street and taught him most of what he knows, he would be nothing. His success is your success because it's you who masterminded the grand scheme, the concept, the plan, the initiative are all yours."

"All right, so what's left for me? Do I retire and let him take over?"

"No, of course not, you use that handsome brain of yours to figure out the next step. You decide how to best use that which is at your disposal, and make the store grow even faster. We can have more free time, for you and me, to do the things we've always talked about."

"Have something particular in mind? Changes in the business, I mean."

"Not really, all I'm suggesting is that you give yourself credit for what has happened, and propel us to the next level."

"The obvious next level is to expand." He said, thinking aloud. "We can expect only so much from each of our customers. To grow, we need more customers."

"Okay, Edward, so how do we do that, how do we grow? What must we do?"

"Offer something new and different, market ourselves; maybe change our image. I guess our best marketing tool is Deacon. The customers treat him like the voice of their desires. He seems to know what they are thinking even before they do. To expand our business, will mean a lot more work. Kat, how can I ask Deacon to work harder?"

"Don't ask him, let him ask you. Why can't we make him a partner? Give him a stake in the expansion. He'll be so excited; he'll work harder than ever. The business will grow and our share will increase geometrically."

"You see, Katherine, it isn't me running this business; it's you and Deacon. I'm just watching."

"Oh, don't be silly. I'm just verbalizing what you're already thinking."

"I came home worried about losing control of my business, and now we're talking about giving up part of it."

"We won't give up anything. We'll grow due to the neural dynamics of vested interest."

"Katherine, you're starting to sound like your father."

Deacon Jones was twenty-five when Doc offered him a partnership. It changed all their lives.

SEVEN

REVEREND JOHN JONES pounded the massive oak pulpit, and shouted his Easter message at the congregation. "Jesus died slowly on the cross that Friday. He hung between two criminals who, unlike our Savior, died quickly." His voice elevated. "Around three o'clock in the afternoon, Jesus drew his last breath, and knowingly moved from the physical life to our Father's promised, eternal life. At the same time, the massive curtain, which hung in the temple and concealed the Rabbis' inner sanctum, tore from ceiling to floor and fell. The sacred chamber was revealed, and the Rabbis' deepest secret uncovered..." The Reverend paused; he took a burdened breath. *It's Easter,* he reminded himself. *Friday was his birthday; he's twenty-six now.* The congregation squirmed in anticipation of the rest of the story. He took his time and scanned the room. Spring dresses, in every color of the rainbow, spotted the wall-to-wall pews.

The main door to the sanctuary creaked open; sunlight flooded in, blocked only by a tall featureless form. The Reverend strained to know the face. Intense light blinded him. The room hung in anticipation. He took another deep breath, and struggled to finish. "In that moment, the secret was known to all; the sacred and holy arc of the covenant was missing," he shouted. Once more, he attempted to identify the man. The door closed and the face became clear. *The head usher, not my son,* he was disappointed, *not James David.* He gasped. Pain struck his chest. He crumpled to the floor. His side went numb, and his world went black.

A sea of curious faces rippled and parted; the EMTs ran, with the gurney, through the church.

Grace held tightly to a stainless steel bar on the inside wall of the swaying ambulance. The Reverend labored to breathe; the clear plastic mask fogged, and the respirator clicked in an uneven tempo.

"Is it a stroke?" She asked the young EMT.

He took his eyes from his patient, "Yes, ma'am."

"Will he survive?" Her voice cracked.

"We're doing everything possible, ma'am; we'll be at the hospital in a minute. The doctors will take good care of your husband."

The doctor pressed his stethoscope against the Reverend's chest and held his wrist. Grace watched nervously through the glass wall of the ICU.

"Mrs. Jones?" The doctor asked as he left the small room.

"Yes, I'm Grace Jones."

"I'm Doctor Conrad," he said thoughtfully. "We have stabilized your husband, and now we need to wait."

"Thank you," she said simply.

"We'll need to keep him here for several days. It's too early to know the extent of the damage."

Alone in the hallway, Grace waited with only her thoughts. *I have lived eight years in silence without my son,* she told herself angrily, *now this. Why, God, why me, have I not paid the price for my sins? I have lived all this time with only a shell of a husband. Am I to now to become his nurse?* A single tear rolled down her cheek. Instinctively, she wiped it away. Her skin was cold. Wrinkles, which bordered her mouth, felt deep. Grace believed herself old.

After a few days in the hospital, Reverend Jones came home. The doctor said the Reverend should walk again. His slurred speech would slowly improve. His eyesight was the problem; it was permanently impaired.

At twenty-eight, Deacon believed his life was perfect. He thought of his past only on holidays. He occasionally wondered where his parents were and what they were doing. He thought that if they had died, he would never know. It was about this time when the demons began to visit. There had been a recent deluge of religious propaganda in the mail; the colorful images caused Deacon to think much about his father and the Bible.

Deacon was naked in a street of ancient cobblestone. Clothed people, strangers, surrounded him. The crowd began to scream, then to run away. The ground shook; *an earthquake,* he thought. From nowhere, enormous black bulls, with massive horns, charged dangerously close. He pivoted and ran as fast as he could. With every footfall, arrows of slicing pain shot up his legs. An acrid smell of blood flooded his senses. He looked down; bright red covered his feet.

The street was empty except for Deacon and the monstrous bulls, whose demonic eyes glowed hell-red; deadly, white horns sparkled in unnatural light. Solid brick buildings, with no windows or doors, closely lined both sides of the street. Deacon ran harder. He twisted his head and glanced back; mucus erupted from snorting nostrils, and sprayed Deacon with hot spatter.

From the center of the street, a towering, ominous cross, blocking any passage, appeared to grow. A greenish viper was laced upon the ebony and gold cross. Angrily, it writhed and thrashed upon the dagger that impaled it, striking the air repeatedly with fangs that dripped yellow venom. The poisonous excretions splashed on rough cobblestones; droplets sizzled as they burned acid holes through the stones. Odors of death, filth, and phosphorous blasted Deacon and burned his nostrils.

The satanic reptile turned its attention to a fully exposed Deacon. Its eyes were vacuous, red holes, dimensionless evil. It tensed, and drew back its head as though to strike. Deacon cast a fleeting look over his shoulder; the bulls were almost upon him. He dropped to his knees and covered his face with crossed arms. "God, forgive me my sins!" He screamed, preparing for certain death.

The impact with the bedroom floor awakened Deacon. Wadded, sweat-soaked sheets bound him. He curled into the fetal position and cried.

Star del Rio sat alone on the edge of the massive, empty bed. She dragged red painted toes meaningfully across luxurious carpet, drawing asymmetrical shapes against the soft white background. She closed her eyes, canting her head all the way back. Her upper spine popped softly. An uninvited thought broke through her daze. *You've been a whore half your life.* The thought was indifferent, factual. *You chose this life. This is your destiny and your penance.*

She closed her eyes and invited sleep. Shadows in the room were a distraction. The clock ticked in slow motion. *They have only come twice before,* she told herself unconvincingly. *They were just an aberration. They mean nothing. What do I care? All I need is sleep, just dreamless sleep.* She rolled to the center of the bed, repositioned the covers, and stared wistfully at the ceiling.

This is only happening, she thought as she scrubbed her face in the blistering hot shower for the third time, *because I've been reading that stupid Bible. How can people, so-called Christians, study that violence and those stories of evil, vengeance, and curses, and call it the Word of God? Isn't God supposed to be benevolent and forgiving? If I believed in something, or someone, greater than myself, I would at least pick something that was always good.*

No wonder Christians are tormented and confused. Their life guide is contradictory and tragic.

If it gives me nightmares, what does it do to the people who live by it; who believe in it? An archaic book is not going to get the best of me. It's a reference book; nothing else, a fucking tool, with which I intend to achieve an end that will bring me satisfaction and revenge."

"What do you want from me?" Star screamed at the shadow on the foggy surface of the glass shower door. Reflexively, she pulled back and slammed her fist into the textured glass. A thousand crooked lines fanned out from bleeding knuckles. The fractured panel hung motionless, as if holding its breath, then crashed to the marble floor.

In spite of Star's resolve, the nightmare came every night.

The entryway seemed common enough, but the compulsion to take the knob irresistible. A multitude of discordant voices filled the place like an unearthly choir. Perhaps they were the dead voices of the unknown family inscribed in the secondhand Bible, names she had unemotionally defaced with a few strokes of her red pen. The voices demanded that she enter the cave-like room. Numbed by a cacophony of sights and sounds, Star only sensed other beings.

As the recurrence of the nightmare amplified, it became increasingly more threatening. Eventually, the other entities present were unmistakably clear. What she had suspected, but feared and denied from the beginning, was true. The man, the woman, and the boy child were faceless, yet Star knew exactly who they were.

The boy seemed frightened and disoriented; the old ones were confused. All were oblivious to her.

She watched the boy cross the room and enter a semblance of a second room. The old ones followed. She trailed them, or she was part of them. It was unclear. Sometimes Star thought she was seeing the events through the boy's eyes. They moved unceasingly from room to room. Each was similar to the last, only smaller, and more rancid. Walls and floors were all roughly hewn abrasive stones. The final room, if that was what it was, was blistering hot.

Star touched the wall. It seared her flesh. She screamed, but could not hear the sound. There was no other way out. She looked back. The entrance had somehow grown shut. She saw the final instant of closure, like a high-speed healing of human flesh; yet, the wall was stone.

The others disappeared, and she grieved their loss. They had not acknowledged her presence; still their absence broke her heart. The ambient temperature increased. The masonry changed from glowing red, to a straw-colored hue, and finally, to white hot. She realized, for the first time, that she wore no clothing. The blistering stone walls of the room blurred, and transformed into something like a honeycomb of human cells.

Trapped inside the semi-consciousness of a man, extraordinarily empowered, she was able to arouse him. At will, she could affect the nerves that directed his libido; he tossed and turned. Her image was real to him. She could feel it, but his identity was a mystery. She discovered his erogenous zone, and hovered there; culmination raced to him. She commanded his desire to lessen. She was his succubus, and he was her marionette. The power was rich and fulfilling. With one slight gesture, she brought him to orgasm.

As quickly as it had begun, Star crashed out of the stranger's consciousness. She awoke, alone in the Queen Anne room, tangled in wet sheets. For the first time in her life, she was truly afraid. Star's personal demon had come. She found it, or it found her, and she saw its face. She knew it too well; the face was her own.

Star arose, fatigued, as if she just returned from a long journey. She stumbled down the hall to her *war room*. With disgust, she examined the pictures of her enemies. Sickened, she drew a finger across the chalkboard, making a line through the lists of scriptures. She spoke to the words, written in her own hand, and to captured images on photographic paper. "You are all my enemies!" she screamed. "Your time will come. It is coming. Each day I become more ready. You can't frighten me with cheap parlor tricks, and childish intrusions into my dreams. I am not a demon. You are the evil ones. You sneaked away in the darkness, and took with you my chance at happiness. Soon, I will take back that which is rightfully mine, that which has always been mine. You will all pay; you will pay for what you have done."

One week after Deacon's first nightmare, it came again. The second time was more vivid. The frequency of its visits increased during the following month until it came almost every night. Driven to total despair, he climbed inside a bottle and hid from the demons. Jack Daniels quickly became Deacon

Jones's best friend. His work suffered. Doc begged him to get help. His friends staged an intervention, but he was too drunk to care.

The plan crept slowly, surreptitiously, into the Reverend's mind. It evolved by installments over a number of years. As the plan took shape, it became a driving compulsion. It germinated in the soil of his cerebral garden. Lying dormant at first, then through the cold winter of realization, it found its true beginning. He would compensate for all of the low points of his meager and miserable life. Fiercely, he cried out, "and it is good." In the court of God, and humankind, he would have his moment of retribution, which would lead to contentment, even if he had to create it himself.

The nightmares convinced Star that it was time for the next phase; she thirsted for vengeance.

O'Connell, probably an alias, was an ex-IRS accountant laundering money for the mob. With his help, Star transferred nearly all of her assets to offshore banks. He assured her that it was fully accessible, and completely untraceable.

Reverend Jones was secretly pleased when he realized that he was improving much faster than the doctor's prognosis. He was able to speak, walk, and even see with almost no impairment. However, in the presence of Mrs. Jones, he continued to play the part of an invalid.

He returned to the church. He sat through the majority of each service, standing only to deliver the sermon. His personal stock, with the congregation, rose as word of his devotion, in the face of adversity, spread. He stood in good stead with his wife and the church. *Somewhat helpless* worked to his advantage. Behind the guise of an invalid, he could implement his plan in secret.

Locating James will be the hard part, he thought. The Reverend had saved a little cash every payday for many years. He would need it to pay a private investigator. In the back of a magazine, he found his first bit of good luck. For one hundred dollars, the advertiser could find anyone, anywhere, guaranteed. Two weeks later, he had a phone number and an address. James David was close by, living in Kirkwood, a suburb of St. Louis. The next challenge was to get there without Mrs. Jones knowing. When she did leave him alone, she took their only car.

In the lobby of the nursing home, he found a two-day-old weekly paper from a small-town thirty miles away. Locked in a stall of the men's room, he anxiously flipped to the classifieds.

Bridget Luna was excited with the cocktail party invitation, which arrived with her name elegantly inscribed on the expensive, cream-colored linen envelope. Star, displeased by the distraction, said it was impossible. She was obsessed with the complete erasure of Bridget Luna's existence, their escape from California, and the *circle of the sun.*

Bridget, who did not agree with her own erasure, argued that her absence would cause too many questions. Star saw the logic in her words and agreed. *Enjoy yourself, this is the last time,* she said coldly.

We are leaving here in four weeks, and we'll all be ready, no matter what.

"*Who cares,*" Bridget, with her hands on her hips, said indignantly to Star, whose image looked back at her from the mirror in the deserted hotel restroom. *"I know you make more money, and you found Estrella before me, but that doesn't mean I'm less important. This party is a perfect example. Some self-important woman has invited me here because she thinks my presence will make her more popular."*

The conversation was unusual because Bridget, Star, and Estrella did not usually speak aloud to one another. Tensions ran high among the three. The stress of the move, the intensity of Star's plan, and her obsessive control of their life was all taking its toll. Estrella cowered nervously *inside,* listening to the too-public argument.

"*Stupid sluts,*" Star laughed at Bridget, *"Both of you, what our hostess doesn't know, and what you seem to have conveniently forgotten, is they all want this body; not for the houses you sell, but for the pleasure I bring. Hell, how ironic, the woman who desperately wanted us to come, and is so excited to see us, has no idea how excited her husband gets when he's inside me. I wonder what she would say if she knew, her loyal mate gives me three thousand every week for an hour in my bed.*

"*You're going to this party. Just don't think for a minute that you're the lead. You can watch, but I'll do the talking. We'll do this my way. I'll show you how to take advantage of your marks."* Star chuckled and finished painting Bridget's deep-red lips.

Talk around the hotel pool was a mixture of gossip and business, laced with hidden meanings and double entendres. Out of habit, Star sized up the starlet who only a few months before had received a best supporting actress nomination.

The tall, finely chiseled thespian seemed distracted as she made small talk with Bridget. Star recognized the look in her eyes. They were secretly screaming; *take me, lick me, drive me crazy, I want you.* Star correctly interpreted the signals, and sent her answer in the same, nonverbal, code. She was effective. The young woman squirmed. A welcome feeling of power and control swept through Star. *See, I told you,* she whispered to Bridget. Like a starving vampire, Star moved in for the kill.

"Do you know all of these people?" Star casually asked with a sweeping glance at the *A-list* gathering.

"Hardly anyone, at least not personally," the woman answered in a discrete voice. "I was only invited because of my nomination." She paused. "Do you—do you know them all?"

"Yes, I know everyone here." Star let Bridget answer while she admired the girl's alabaster complexion. "I know them well enough to say you're probably right about why you were invited. There's really no such thing as friendship here."

The actress seemed to hang on every word. The hook was set; the starlet was Star's prize to reel in at her leisure. She could do whatever she wished, and when *the mark* went beyond all previous comprehension of ecstasy, at exactly the right moment, Star would offhandedly mention some exorbitant sum. The *naïve* woman would gladly open her purse and produce the money. She would think of it as a gift, something special for her lover. She would never say she had slept with a prostitute, or that she had paid for anything, especially not sex.

"Why don't we get out of he…" Before Star could finish, she caught a glimpse of a tall African-American man in a shiny black linen suit threading his way through the guests. From across the pool, she saw the look of anger and contempt in his eyes. Fear swept over her. Garvin Brown was a pimp from East LA. He was the younger brother of Star's ex-pimp who the police found with his head smashed in almost ten years before, the day after they found Lupe, and the same day Star disappeared.

"Sorry," Star gasped, "I don't feel well; I have to go!" Before the young woman could answer, Star disappeared through the shrubs.

She slapped a one-hundred-dollar bill in the valet's hand and ordered him to run for her car. "I'll wait around the corner." She pointed to the place.

If he found me here, she reasoned, *he could know where I live.* She threw a few personal items, including her ledgers and journals, into the dark-green Jaguar and abandoned the rest.

One day later at a used car lot in a small town in Arizona, she traded the Jag for an older-model red Chevy Camaro. The Jag was worth ten Chevys, but she traded even. The salesman, also the owner and a part-time barber, pulled his mouth up in a big toothless grin as Star sped away.

The back roads felt safe; it took nearly three days more to get to St. Louis. Star envisioned her deserted *war room,* and drew a mental chalk line through a corresponding number on her *To Do* list.

EIGHT

THE NEWSPAPER AD described the van as *perfect condition, 100,000 miles, priced to sell,* and the color as *black.* It sounded ideal, exactly what the Reverend wanted, something innocuous. High-mileage meant a low price, and he did not intend to drive it far. He concealed the torn ad in his wallet, and buried the paper in the trashcan.

"It's a cherry Ford van," the man on the telephone convincingly told the Reverend. "But I can't drive thirty miles to show it to you. If you don't buy it, I'll be out the trip." He complained.

"It's exactly what I am looking for," the Reverend argued, "there's just no way I can get there to look at it. Come to my home this Thursday morning, precisely at ten, and if it's everything you say, we'll have a deal. I give you my word."

"I don't know, mister. I've already been burned a couple a times by agreeing to meet someone who didn't show."

"But, I'm asking you to come to my home. I promise you; I'll be waiting."

"I just can't do it, not thirty-miles, sorry, mister."

"Wait a minute. Don't hang up!" The Reverend was desperate to make a deal. "Tell you what, today is Monday, I'll put a fifty-dollar bill in the mail today. You'll have it by Wednesday. You drive over here on Thursday. If I don't show, you keep the fifty for your trouble. Otherwise, you put the money against the price. Okay?"

"Make it a hundred bucks and you've got yourself a deal." The man bargained.

"Okay, a hundred bucks, but be here Thursday at ten; don't be late." The Reverend sternly cautioned the man.

Reverend Jones sat nervously at the well-worn kitchen table. Across from him, Mrs. Jones, apparently deep in thought, quietly sipped coffee from a big china mug. Guardedly, the Reverend glanced at the wall clock. The minute hand shuddered reluctantly, and then snapped to dead center on the twelve. It was exactly nine o'clock Thursday morning.

"Grace," he began, "I think I'm out of my medicine, and it's time for a dose. Can you check?"

She glanced up from the steaming cup, shook her head, and left the kitchen without a word. Minutes later, she returned. "Reverend," her tone was slightly agitated, "why didn't you tell me sooner that you were out?"

"I don't know how I missed it. I'm sorry." He tried to sound remorseful. Earlier, he had secretly emptied the remaining few tablets into a plastic bag, locked them in his desk, and left the empty pill bottle on the bathroom vanity.

"All right," the disdain gone from her voice, "I'll go to the pharmacy as soon as I finish my coffee." She sat back down.

He glanced again at the clock; it was fifteen minutes past nine. "You know, I'm supposed to take my medicine every twelve hours," he hinted. Mrs. Jones continued to sip her coffee. "Don't you think you should go now?"

"I'm going, I'm going. You aren't going to die if you pop one of those pills at one minute past eleven, you know!"

"I know, but I worry less when I take my medicine on time. I want to get better."

Mrs. Jones, moving at a relaxed pace, thoughtfully chose a dress and shoes. He agonized as she searched for her purse. Finally, at precisely 9:53 A.M., the door snapped shut behind her. The Reverend exhaled a deep sigh of relief, and sat down in his chair to wait.

He gasped when the door sprang open; she was back. "What—what happened?" he asked with incredulity. "Aren't you going?"

"Of course, I'm going; I forgot my car keys, that's all. What's the matter with you? You look like you've seen a ghost."

"Nothing—nothing, I'm fine; just anxious for my medicine."

"Too bad you've never worried about the well-being of others as much as you now worry about yourself," she said, peeved, as she scooped up her keys and slammed the screen door behind her.

"You have no idea," he began with pride of conviction to the closed door, "what you are saying, or to whom you are speaking, woman. I'll show you soon enough. I'll show everyone the real strength of the Reverend John Jones."

Less than a mile from her own driveway, Grace met the black van and the woman in the car that followed. They caught her attention because the car tailgated the van so closely that it looked like they were connected.

She returned with the prescription at eleven o'clock. The van, parked in the driveway of the vacant lot next door, beside a wooden skeleton of charred remains, was a surprise. No one had parked there since the house burned to the ground.

"Where'd the van come from?" Grace asked as she handed over the small white pharmaceutical sack.

"Is it a van?" He asked trying to sound surprised.

"Yes, a black van." "A man came to the door and told me that he had car trouble, and had rolled in over there. He asked me if I thought he could leave it until he could come back with help. I told him, I didn't think it would make any difference to anyone."

"Where's the man now?"

"He asked to use the phone, called someone, and got picked him up within just a few minutes. Why all the questions, do you think I was wrong to tell him it was okay to park there?"

"No, I don't suppose it matters. I just don't want it to turn into a junkyard."

"I'm sure we have nothing to worry about." He said feeling his way along the wall to the kitchen for a glass of water.

The Reverend began with short excursions through the countryside. He always wore dark glasses and a wide-brimmed black fedora pulled down to his ears. The trips were nerve-wracking because the brevity of Mrs. Jones's errands limited him.

When the Reverend suggested that Grace volunteer at the hospital, she was relieved. For a long time, beginning shortly after his stroke, she felt trapped. He had always discouraged her from any kind of volunteer work, saying her place was in the home. His unexpected change in attitude was a startling, but welcome, revelation. She immediately made the call; the hospital scheduled her for work the next day.

Everything is perfect; he thought when she told him the news. *At last, I'm free to make it all happen.* He was careful not to let her see him smile.

Deacon Jones was barely twenty-nine years old when he stumbled into the alley and tripped over the two halves of a black man's body. He lay in a pile of garbage, convulsing. Just before he passed out, overcome with terror, he had a vision. The image so vivid, he was sure it was real.

His father, the Reverend, towered over him; he had not aged. In his arms was a small yellow dog. His booming voice was unchanged; he spoke with authority and absolute conviction. *Very well, young man, remember King Solomon…*

A dense black shroud enveloped Deacon's mind; its weight overpowered him, and his knowing disappeared.

Deacon awoke to a throbbing headache, bewildered and queasy. *Where am I?* A narrow shaft of sunlight found its way through mauve curtains and bisected the half-light. Two floral-papered walls contrasted two bone white walls. The door was ajar, open just a few inches. Deacon, struggling to recollect what had happened, squirmed in search of a position that would bring relief to relentless, full-body pain.

A woman entered. Her short blonde-streaked hair and lithe frame were a welcome sight; Deacon breathed a sigh of relief. "Kat, I'm so glad to see you. How did I get here?"

"Take it easy, James." She sat on the edge of the bed and helped him settle back. "You've had quite a time. You need to rest."

"Katherine, how did I get here?" He asked again. "Where have I been?" "Perhaps you know more than I do, James. Edward said he found you passed out in an alley on The Landing. He brought you here, and we put you to bed. But, James, there must be a lot more to it than that. When Edward brought you home, he was shaking. I have never seen him so terrified. All he would tell me was that it was ghastly. He wouldn't say what. Did you see what Edward saw, James, do you remember what happened? Were you involved in something?"

Her rapid-fire questions were too complicated for Deacon's whiskey-muddled mind. "How long have I been here?" He feared the answer.

"Since about daylight, morning before last. You've been fitfully unconscious and puked until I thought you would dehydrate. It wasn't until early this morning that you settled down and seemed to rest."

"My bike, where's Widow…"

She cut him off. "Don't worry about your motorcycle. Some of the guys took it to the shop."

"Thanks, thanks for everything, but I've gotta get outta here. I've gotta get to work. Where're my clothes?" He tried to sit up, but his stomach growled loudly and cramped. He dropped his bedraggled mop on the pillow.

"You're not going anywhere, mister, except maybe to take a bath." She pressed her finger against her nose. "You've really done it this time. Just lay right here and get well. Then, you, Edward, and I are going to sit down and have a long talk. We love you, James; you're our partner and a member of our family. We want to help you, and based on what I've seen, you need a lot of help. Now, rest and I'll bring you some soup."

After their first dance, during the fall of their high school senior year, Edward and Katherine parted only once when Edward went off to attend a state university, one hundred miles away. It was a miserable, lonely year for them both. The following spring, Edward dropped out of college, and they were married.

The first several years were difficult. Katherine's father cut her off, and Edward worked evenings, driving a forklift in a warehouse. He earned extra money by repairing motorcycles for his friends during the day. Katherine attended beauty school, and after graduation, she rented a chair in a popular shop.

Soon, Doc was spending at least eight hours each day on his side job. He rented a small garage for eighty-five dollars per month; *D-K Choppers* became a real business.

Two children were born in the ensuing years. Kat gave up her job to raise their family. Her formal childhood spilled over, and she endeavored to keep their personal and their biker life completely separate. She only called her husband by his nickname when they were away from home.

Business improved. Doc left the warehouse and bought an old building in Kirkwood, Missouri, and remodeled it. He worked seven long days per week; it was a frugal, but comfortable and rewarding life.

It was a day more before Deacon could dress himself and sit upright. Katherine was convinced he was suffering from a combination of alcohol poisoning, withdrawal, and shock. He refused to go to the doctor. "I've never had a broken bone or gotten more than a shot, and I'm not about to let some doc poke around on me now. I'm not sick. I'm just a little hung over."

In the living room, Katherine served coffee from a hand inlaid wooden tray; classical music decorated the silence. "A lot has been going on around here for the last several months, maybe even for the last year." She began. "I feel there is much I don't know, and I, well—what I do know, I don't understand. Whatever it is, James David, it has to stop.

"James, I—we have no intention of letting you ruin your life. Mostly because we care about you, but in all fairness, you must realize that what happens to you also affects us. First, because you're part of our extended family, we experience your pain; we worry about you. Second, you are our business partner. As bookkeeper, I can honestly say we did not offer you a partnership only because of how we felt. You're smart, perceptive, and people really respond to you. You bring a lot to *D-K-D Choppers.*

"However, for the last year, we've all been treading water. It's as if we're back to owning our jobs again. James, this has to change.

"Now, let's get the whole thing out on the table. Edward, why don't you begin by telling us what happened the night you brought James home."

"Katherine, it's repugnant, I don't think…"

She cut him off. "I don't care how disagreeable it is; let's get it out in the open. I want to know."

"Okay, but, just remember, I warned you."

He, reluctantly, began. "I knew that Deacon, excuse me, James, was at the bar and out of control. Some of the guys called me before I left the shop; it was probably close to eight o'clock. They said he was already ballistic. By the time I got down there, it was nearly nine, and I couldn't find him. So, I left and made a couple of other stops, still no luck.

"I rode around, checking bars, and finally went back to The Landing. It was around closing time. He wasn't there, but someone said they thought they had seen him outside trying to start his bike.

"The alley was so dark I couldn't see anything at first; so, I was feelin' my way around, and I nearly tripped over a man layin' face down. I apologized for kickin' him. By then, my eyes were beginning to adjust to the dark, and I saw him clearly. Guts and blood were everywhere; I puked on the spot.

"It was unbelievable. I had to press against the wall to get around him without stepping in his blood.

I was so sick, I thought I was gonna pass out. I was in the process of getting out of there when I found James lying in his own puke. I threw him over my shoulder, took the long way around, and came out of the alley three blocks away. I hid him there, and flagged a taxi.

"The cops called me the next day. Someone had told them I was at the bar. I told them I didn't see anything. They said there was a murder in the alley, someone from out of town. They did mention it looked like a professional job, not even his wallet was missing."

The color was gone from Katherine's face. "James, it's your turn. Tell us what you remember."

"I had hardly slept the night before, and I started drinkin' that morning. I must have eaten at some point, but I don't really remember.

"I hit a bunch of bars and finally ended up in that one. I don't know what time it was, but it was dark. The bartender told me that a woman had been askin' about me. I thought it was probably some of the guys playin' a practical joke, but I looked for her anyway.

"When I couldn't find her anywhere in the bar, I went outside. I must have been pretty hammered, 'cause the next thing I know I'm standin' in a pool of blood between two halves of a man. That's all I remember."

"James, are you sure you didn't see anyone else, or anything unusual, and you never found the woman?"

"I've been in that bar plenty of times, and there was nothin' special about that night. But, you know, now that I say it, there was somethin'. The parkin' lot was full of all of the typical rides, you know: Beemers, SUV's, some bikes, and a few West-County

Mommy-Wagons. What stuck out was an old black van sittin' on the edge of the lot, like a sore thumb. It was a Ford van like we used to joke about. You know—no windows only a little convex porthole in the back too small for an adult, and too high for a kid, like an out of place teat.

"Oh, and I had something like a dream, or a vision, but it seemed real. I saw my father; it was like something from my childhood, a thing I haven't thought about in years."

"Maybe, there's some connection," She pushed. "Why don't you tell us the story?"

"It happened when I was something like eight years old. I saw this girl playin' with her puppy every day when I walked home from school. I guess I was jealous because my father wouldn't let me have a pet. So, I stole it, and hid it in our back yard. When the Reverend found out, he went on one of his rampages and quoted scripture, the one about King Solomon going to cut the baby in half. He actually threatened to cut that little dog in half. I'm sure the whole thing was designed to make me feel guilty, and it worked.

"Anyway, I don't know; there was something about the dead body that made me think my father was there. I imagined that somehow he was still tryin', after all these years, to make me feel guilty for stealin' that dog."

They listened to the story, but said nothing. Then Katherine, her voice trembling, began to speak. "What else has happened, James?" The questions came in torrents. "Why do you drink so much? Why can't you sleep? We're best friends; yet, you never talk to me anymore. What's going on? Please, let us help."

James shook his head and buried his face in his hands. "It's a nightmare!"

"We know," she agreed.

"No, I mean I'm having one, the same one, over and over." His muffled voice escaped through his fingers. "At first, it only came occasionally, but now, it comes so often I'm afraid to sleep."

"What kind of nightmare?" Katherine asked. "What do you think is causing it?"

"It's—my—tattoo." His voice weakened as he blinked back tears. "The snake in my tattoo is trying to kill me. My father was right; God is punishing me for my blasphemous life."

"It's okay, sweetie." Katherine slid over and gently touched his shoulder. "Let's look at this thing logically. If it's your tattoo, let's tape over it so you don't have to look at it. I'll call the doctor and see what our options are for having it removed. I hear they work wonders with this new laser removal process, and we're going to keep you away from the booze. At the rate you're going, if you don't stop, you're going to kill yourself.

"The murder can't have any relevance." Edward injected. "It's just a coincidence. As far as the woman who was looking for you, who knows, maybe you imagined whole thing. You saw your father, and he wasn't there."

"Let's put all of this behind us." Katherine insisted. "You stay here and rest for a few more days. We're going to get you healthy, happy, and back into the world." Katherine smiled. "You need something to look forward to, like, maybe, a woman in your life?"

"No, no, I don't think so," James protested. "You know how bad my luck is with women. They all think I'm really exciting at first, but that wears off pretty quick."

"You've got it backwards, James." Katherine was adamant. "Let me tell you how I see it. Just remember, this is from a woman's point of view. I think you're afraid to get close to any woman. You, my dear, have a fear of intimacy. I've known several of your girlfriends. Some were serious, but every time they got close to you—you became indifferent. In the end each one just went away, usually with a broken heart."

Deacon settled deeper into the creamy-white overstuffed sofa. Protected in his best friends' bastion, he closed his eyes. *Maybe they're right*, he thought hopefully, *just maybe I can get my life under control. Wouldn't that be something?*

"I'm going to throw up again." On rubbery legs, Deacon ran for the bathroom. An hour later, he crawled back to bed.

Cold sweats and convulsions racked his body, day and night, until he thought he was losing his mind. Katherine served him soups and crackers, and forced him to eat. After five days, of convulsing in the dark, Deacon began to feel like himself.

"Katherine, I have to get back to work." He pleaded as he leaned against the doorframe.

"Not so fast, mister," Katherine replied, "we agreed you would stay here a week. I will not settle for a minute less. Besides, last night I had a nightmare of my own. In it, I imagined how your house must look. No argument, just give me the key. Tomorrow morning, first thing, I'm going over there to clean it up."

"How could you live like that?" She asked when she returned.

He looked at her sheepishly.

"By the way, I noticed something odd. What's the deal with the pewter picture frame on your bedside table?"

"What's wrong with it?" He asked.

"It's empty; there's no picture."

"There never was a picture. It's my family portrait. I keep it to remind me how good my life is, that my happiness is up to me."

"I see." She shook her head,

Deacon avoided his tattoo, and any thought of it. He gathered up the mountain of religious brochures and booklets, which had come in the mail, and put them in the trash. He returned to work, ate dinner with Kat and Doc every night, and drank not a drop.

Three weeks passed; Deacon felt more like himself than he had in a year.

NINE

FOR THE TENTH TIME in as many minutes, Star anxiously checked the rearview mirror of the Camaro. *I'm worrying about nothing.* She tried to convince herself. *There's no way he'll follow me from California.* The roadside sign announced, *Welcome to Missouri.* She breathed a heavy sigh of relief as though the invisible boundary between Oklahoma and Missouri would protect her. The final few hours on the road were easy; traffic was light, the red two-door Chevrolet ran well, and she rolled into downtown St. Louis in mid-afternoon. She chose the first hotel that looked like Four Stars.

For the first several days, she was very cautious. The drab downtown apartment was easy to find, and easier to rent. She signed the lease, Estrella del Rio, and paid the landlord in cash, eight months in advance. He did not ask to see her identification. *Exactly enough time,* she calculated.

She required only ten minutes and fifteen one-hundred dollar bills at the secondhand store to buy enough furniture to fill the apartment. She spoke in Spanish to the two Mexicans who loitered outside the store; for twenty dollars each, they readily agreed to deliver the furniture.

Shit, Star thought as she awoke her first morning in the depressing confines of the furniture-choked bedroom. *I'll kill myself if I have to sleep here every night. I may as well be sleeping in Lupe's fucking closet.* The caustic memory of her mother tasted like sour milk. *I may need this place, but that doesn't mean I have to sleep here for a month while I get everything ready.* She arose, resolved, rolled her head about her shoulders in tight limbering circles, and headed for the bathroom.

"Do you want me to wait, miss?" The cab driver with perpendicular elephantine ears asked politely as he pulled into the lot of *Plaza Motors* on the west side of the city.

Star leaned into the window and intentionally displayed her cleavage. "No, that won't be necessary." She smiled and handed him the fare plus a twenty-dollar tip.

The dark-blue Mercedes sedan, just inside the showroom, gleamed in the morning light. "It's a ninety-seven." The well-trained salesman said as he approached her, smiling broadly.

"What?" She asked without lifting her eyes.

"It's an early production ninety-seven. It's next year's model." He explained.

Star drank in the man's closely shaven face; she recognized the familiar wanton look. *Hmm,* she thought, *I like his tan, electric-beach; this might actually be fun.*

It took twenty minutes for the small army of salesmen to move the other cars, open the massive plate-glass doors, and drive the blue car outside. It took only twenty more in the alley, with her skirt shoved up around her waist, for Star to negotiate the lease down payment to a number that pleased her.

"I'm sorry, miss, we only sell apartments." The man's tone was apologetic. "Here at the *Chase*, we cater to a very special class of people; we don't have anything to rent."

"Are you absolutely sure?" Star asked in her most solicitous voice, with a drippy-sweet southern accent. "I'd just love to own an apartment here, but I don't know how long I'll stay. My daddy, he sent me up here from Dallas to oversee a new acquisition, and I just don't know how long it'll take."

"What business is your father in?" The man was intrigued. He glanced past her to the sparkling Mercedes.

"Why, just oil, but he is buyin' somethin' of a more of a sportin' nature if you get my meanin'," she said hinting.

"You don't mean the Cardinals, our baseball team?" He probed.

"Oh, now, sugah, I'm not supposed to tell; you're goin' to get me in trouble with my daddy." She rolled and batted her eyes.

"Maybe I can help you, miss. We do have one apartment. It's furnished. The grand old lady that lived there died recently, and her family asked me to see what we can do to help defray the ongoing costs while they decide if they want to sell. I can call them, and ask if you like," he offered.

He seemed surprised when she produced bundles of cash and paid eight months in advance. Star counted the stacks as she placed them on his desk. "Is it a problem?" She asked, fidgeting with her hemline and crossing her legs. The wet heat of the car salesman lingered deep between her thighs.

"Oh, no, no problem at all," he answered quickly. "It's just that no one pays cash anymore."

She smiled. He was well dressed, but older and balding; his rotund belly hid his belt. *Not worth a discount,* she told herself repulsed by his physical characteristics. *Maybe, Lupe would have done this guy, but not Star.* The uninvited memory of her mother disgusted her. She shook her head, trying to throw the mental image aside.

"This is perfect," Star shouted exuberantly, standing on the broad hardwood sill of the massive casement window in the opulent Penthouse. "This is more like it." *Forest Park*, from the twenty-seventh floor, was a mansion-lined garden of the gods. Verdant trees cradled the yellow afternoon sun as it took its final breath. "Shakespeare understood," she whispered, remembering the hours she had spent as a child hiding from reality among his words. *...the fire that severs day from night.* This life is mine, my destiny. When I am finished, this will again be my life. Only in a place like this can I be myself."

Volunteer May flowers spotted the countryside. Inside and outside *D-K-D Choppers,* motorcycles were everywhere. The machines of summer sparkled, ready for the season.

"Business is good my friend." Doc slapped Deacon's back. "I almost forgot. Kat called. She said with all the excitement last month, we missed your birthday. So tonight, we're goin' out to dinner. She wants Italian; we're goin' down to *The Hill*. She said to tell you to dress nice, and pick us up at six, sharp."

"Shit, Doc, I don't want to drive my fuckin' car in this weather." Deacon protested. "It's bad enough bein' a cager when there's snow on the ground."

"Deac, haven't you learned your lesson? Don't fuck with Kat. Besides, there's somethin' goin' on. She even made reservations. We've been married for twenty years, and I can tell she's up to somethin'."

Kat checked her watch, and glanced again at the door. She repositioned the napkin on her lap. Their table, which Katherine had apparently requested, was semi-secluded in a small alcove near the back of the cavernous dining room.

Deacon watched her continuously fidget, but he remembered Doc's warning and said nothing. Her nervousness was contagious; Doc squirmed. Deacon looked around, searching for the reason for her behavior. Perched on the few unoccupied tables, thick black napkins elegantly folded in the shapes of miniature Bishops' Hats accented starched white tablecloths. The wait staff, also dressed in black and white, skillfully glided through the labyrinth of crowded tables.

Kat took a tentative sip from the stemmed water glass, and nervously cleared her throat. "James, I've met someone."

Deacon chuckled, "Kat is this something we should be talking about in front of Doc?" He looked quizzically, first at Kat, then Doc. They both turned their eyes away.

"Oh, goofy, you know better. You know what I mean. I've found someone for you, a woman."

"Well, that's a relief. At least you're not tryin' to fix me up with men. But now that I mention it, I'm not so sure that the last girl wasn't a man."

"Stop it. Ellen wasn't so bad. She had some very endearing qualities."

"I'm sorry, Kat, you're right. I thought it very romantic that she and I shave our beards with the same brand of razor."

Kat thrashed him with an icy-quieting look, and then continued, undaunted. "This woman is different. In fact, I'm absolutely convinced she's perfect for you. It was mystical, actually, the first time I met her. I instantly knew she was the one. She's the new waitress down at *Krispy Kreme*. I meet some of my friends there for coffee twice a week. Even her name is cute. It's Estrella, and you pronounce it just like that. It's spelled with two L's. She told me that together they make a J sound. It's Es-TRE-ja," Kat carefully sounded out the Spanish name. "She's outgoing, and I'll answer your first question before you ask. She's beautiful!"

"Well, I guess that about covers everything." Doc commented dryly. "When are they gettin' married?"

Kat ignored her husband's comments. "She told me she doesn't have any plans this weekend; so, I took the liberty of arranging this dinner for the four of us. Now, boys, please no arguments. Mother knows best."

Deacon looked over at Doc and shook his head.

When the tall blonde entered, she captured Deacon's attention, along with everyone else in the restaurant. The room seemed to grow quiet as she threaded her way through the closely set tables. *She*, Deacon thought, *cuts through the conversational din as neatly as Moses must have parted the Red Sea.*

At five feet ten inches in black four-inch closed-toe pumps, she towered over the sitting patrons. Her tight, black skirt stopped six inches below her knees. A side-split, which was at least eighteen inches in length, broke with each delicate step revealing a muscular tanned leg. A large golden buckle on a wide patent leather belt, loosely counted each step. Long shapely arms protruded from a short sleeve sculpted white sweater, which outlined statuesque breasts. Natural-blonde locks spilled over semi-bare shoulders. Big, blue, intelligent eyes sparkled, jeweled accents to a refined nose, high cheekbones, and full red lips.

Without hesitation, she walked to their table. By the time she arrived Kat was already on her feet. They hugged. Deacon's heart pounded. A magnetic field swept through him; dizzied by emotion, his breathing stopped.

"You must be Deacon," she said in a raspy, sultry voice.

Their connection steamed over Deacon like a freight train. He attempted to stand, but his knees were rubber. It was much more than animal attraction.

It was a supernatural bond. Deacon had always hoped that magic existed; in that moment he was sure it did.

After an embarrassing silence, he found his voice. "Yes, yes, I am, and you must be Estrella." He strived to pronounce her name correctly. "I am very happy to meet you." The train left the station; there was no getting off. It did not matter. Escape was the last thing on Deacon's mind.

Before that Saturday night in May of his twenty-ninth year, Deacon Jones did not believe in love at first sight, or the absolute connection between two people, which can transcend time and space. In the span of a breath, one he had not expected to take, he felt as though he had always known Estrella. Everything she said made perfect sense.

By the time dessert arrived, Deacon was convinced she was the woman with whom he would spend the rest of his life. *I want to take this slow*, he told himself. *I'm sure of the outcome, but this is the time when memories are made.*

Deacon gingerly kissed her cheek, a cautious, good night kiss. They stood, toe-to-toe, in front of the battered door of her apartment. Kat and Doc waited in the car with the engine idling. His lips touched her skin; electricity ignited his whole being. *It's going to be even better than I imagined.* He thought.

"May I call you tomorrow?" He hoped his question was rhetorical.

"You, my dear, may call me always. Deacon, I believe I know what you're feeling. I just want to say, I feel the same."

He kissed her again, sweetly, on the other cheek. He backed away, reluctantly, holding her hands until they could reach no further.

Estrella remained in the open doorway; she waved as the car pulled away.

Deacon held her in his frozen gaze for longer than he could see. He faced forward, oblivious to his mute friends. A few blocks from their home, Kat twisted in her seat, and looked knowingly into his eyes. He smiled. "Kat, you were right."

After the taillights disappeared, Star backed into her drab apartment. She kicked off her heels, laughed aloud, and admired her flawless image in the hallway mirror. "Perfect."

Estrella and Deacon were inseparable. They were only apart during the workday. The first week was gradual and sensuous. Deacon's courtship pleased Star very much. It was Shakespearean, like Bridget's hero, exactly what she had planned and expected. He bought fresh flowers every day; every meal, in or out, was eaten by the light of flickering candles.

The first time their lips touched, she felt him tremble. *That's It, doll*, she thought conceitedly. *You're all mine.*

A week to the moment had passed since they met, Deacon collapsed on the tan fabric sofa in Estrella's tiny living room. It had been a joyous day in the blistering sun with the wind in their faces. Widowmaker did not miss a beat. They returned exhilarated from the ride, still tingling with the phantom vibration of the machine.

When Estrella returned from freshening up, it was as though an angel entered the room. Her thick blonde hair, piled atop her head, looked like a natural crown held in place by a golden bow. Gold rope earrings reached her shoulders. She wore only a white diaphanous silk blouse with long sleeves and tails. Backlit, by a light in the bedroom, the silk appeared to glow. Scooped sides framed a white satin garter. White silk stockings disappeared into red-soled white pumps.

With seductive steps, she glided across the room, and stretched out her hand. Long perfect pink nails beckoned. He took her hand; it felt as though he levitated to his feet. Her silk veil fluttered, and resettled on erect nipples.

Without a word, she thrust him lovingly back, straddled him, and formed her body to his. Her delicate scent was intoxicating. She loosed her hold, leaned back, and captured his eyes with hers. Penetrating blue orbs floated in an ocean of passion. With her palms on his cheeks, she drew him into a long, sensuous kiss.

Deacon labored to breath; every muscle tensed. He looked up, searching for firmer emotional footing. He closed his eyes. His mind went blank. Her delicious lips parted. Her tongue explored.

She responded to the stirring in his jeans. Her movements centered on the bulge. He tried to concentrate, to control overwhelming desire. Elusive yellow light, from legions of burning waxen strings, danced on white walls, and illuminated luscious skin.

Deacon struggled to slow the natural ascension to ecstasy. His bodily need grew, geometrically, beyond mental control. He ached to be one with the love of his life. He grasped the silk with both hands. Her firm grip covered his; she took control and slid the fabric down.

"Let's wait." She whispered urgently. "I want you, doll, but I want to wait." She kissed him, and resumed a slow, sensuous gyration.

"Estrella," Deacon gasped, "I want you, now." Her intensity increased. She kissed him again, more deeply than before. It washed over his entire being, like a tsunami. He arched his back and tightened his grip. "Estrella," he whispered hoarsely.

With a single powerful movement, she pushed away and lifted herself off. She spread her muscular legs, placed her hands on her hips, and looked down upon him. Perfect white teeth sparkled. "Oh, doll, you are so good."

"Wow," he sighed.

The complex aroma, of chocolate and macadamia nut Hawaiian coffee combined with bacon, permeated the air and dragged Deacon from a deep sleep. Estrella, wearing only a short cotton bathrobe decorated with tiny pastel flowers, was busily turning bacon.

Deacon quietly slipped up behind her and wrapped muscular arms around barely covered shoulders. Using only his nose, he pushed aside her straight damp hair, and sensuously kissed the back of her neck.

They did not go outside that day.

"How'd you hurt yourself?" She asked as she traced the edges of the large bandage on his upper arm.

"It's a long story," he answered dully.

Deacon stretched out on the sofa; Estrella curled up beside him on the floor. "I have all day," she whispered between wet kisses.

"For you to understand what's under this bandage, I must tell you all the dirty secrets of my life. Are you sure you want to know?"

"Doll, I want to know everything. Trust me. We're going to be together always, no matter what. Your story is just that, your story. It can't—nothing can—change how I feel."

"Okay, but I have to go slow. A lot of this I haven't thought about for a very long time. I should start by telling you about the Reverend."

It took hours for Deacon to tell the story of his life; he cried often. When he spoke of his mother, his voice softened. Not a single memory was funny. He never smiled in the telling of the emotionally draining details.

"But, I don't understand, it sounds like your parents tried to give you a good life. There are a lot of people who would give anything to have two parents, or even one, especially parents that love you."

"If my father loved me, he certainly had a strange way of showing it. I don't know. Maybe it wasn't his fault, but I never felt like I was a part of them. I never really felt like a son."

He saw sadness and understanding in her concerned face. Estrella dropped her watery eyes and turned away. "Show me the tattoo," she whispered.

She gently caressed his painted skin.

"I have already told you. I lost my parents a long time ago," Estrella said as she traced the atrocity on

Deacon's arm. "I don't want you to misunderstand my reaction to your story. It's important that you know, and understand, what it's like for people who have no family. After my mother died, I was alone. I lived with people who didn't want me. At least your parents loved you, even if they didn't know how to show it." She paused, padded off to the kitchen, and returned with glasses of Coke.

"Here," she handed him the glass, "get comfortable. Let me tell you my story. I'll begin at the beginning."

Deacon propped himself up, and took a sip from the glass. "Is this old?" He frowned.

She took his glass and tasted it. "It's just *Coke*, plain old cola from one of the little bottles. I think they're stronger—where was I?

"My mother was a Mexican, and my father was American. He died fighting in Vietnam not long after I was born. The only memories that I have of him are from the wonderful stories my mother used to tell. He was so kind to her. Their life together must have been like a dream, the great American dream.

"Then, he was killed, and with him, they buried a huge part of her happiness. But, you know what, she never showed her sadness to me. She only talked about all the marvelous things from their life together.

"Mother was a vision. She was so beautiful, and delicate beyond description. She spoke perfect English and Spanish. She was the bilingual assistant to the president of a large import-export company.

"She used to tell me that when I was born, I was like a little angel sent to save her. Not a day passed that she didn't remind me of what a precious part of her life I was. She named me Estrella, which is Spanish for Star. She always called me, *mi Estrellita,* which means *my little Star.*

"Our house was really small, but she decorated it with beautiful Mexican things. She said all of our treasures would help me to know, and appreciate, my proud Mexican heritage. My favorite souvenir from Mexico was a big hand-carved obsidian-glass ball created by volcanic eruption. For me it was magic. It was probably about four inches in diameter, but it seemed huge. We kept it on a basket-weave stand in the center of the coffee table in our living room.

"Every afternoon, after school, I would sit on the floor next to that table at eye level with that beautiful black ball. When the sun was low enough, the rays would capture my ball and mystically illuminate an otherwise invisible band of gold. Pure gold, I always thought. It ran completely through the center of the sphere. In those moments when that gold band glowed, I would make one wish, always the same one. I wished that my life would never change, that my mother and I would be happy, and we would be together for the rest of our lives.

"Then, when I was seven..." Estrella's voice trailed off. The color drained from her face, and her eyes welled up with tears. In a broken, halting voice, she continued. "She became ill. I didn't really understand what it meant to have cancer. All I knew was that my mother spent too much time in bed. She stopped going to work. Our Christmas tree was still in the living room when she died. It was May, a few days before my eighth birthday." She sobbed.

Deacon wrapped his arms around her and held her tight.

She sighed deeply. "Almost immediately, they took me to a foster home. I had no other family. They wouldn't let me take any of our things. They didn't even let me pack my own clothes. My foster mother packed for me. I remember that day vividly, as if it was yesterday. They took me away, half-dragging, half-carrying me. I remember begging for my magic black ball.

"I still have nightmares about that day, with my arms outstretched and my fingers helplessly grasping at air. It's always the same. The closer I get, the further away the ball." She rocked back and forth. "Then, it disappears into an open grave, and I'm falling, falling, and bam—I'm awake."

"Oh, Estrellita, it must have been awful. I'm so sorry. You can tell me the rest another day. Let's just be together. I understand why your mother thought you were her little angel because I think you're my angel, too. Sent here to save me from myself; sent here to cure me.

"Before I met you, I was drowning in my own life, at my own hand, and my existence had no value. I was a lost soul, but from the first moment we met, I knew you were special. I knew you would become an important part of my life. I'm so drawn to you, so revived by you; all my problems seem like nothing."

"I know," she said, "I was sent here to change your life by something much greater than either of us."

Sunday morning, shortly before daylight, Deacon fell, arms flailing, soaked in sweat, from Estrella's bed. His impact with the well-worn pine floor made a resounding thud. The serpent had returned.

"Easy, doll, take it easy. It was only a nightmare. You're okay. I'm here. I'm here for you."

She knelt beside him on the floor, and massaged his back. After several minutes, she whispered. "Don't move. I'll be right back."

Deacon leaned against the mattress, trembling, absorbing the therapeutic heat from the steaming stoneware vessel. A slice of lemon floated just beneath the rippling surface of the greenish-clear liquid. "What is it?" He asked weakly as he lifted the cup to his nose.

"It's your cure, doll. Put your faith in me. You said I'm everything you need, and I'm going to prove you right. I'm going to take care of you from now on. Drink your toddy."

He took a cautious sip. The bitter taste of bourbon assaulted his senses with an abstemious alarm. Perplexed, he looked first at the cup, then incredulously back into the innocent face of the woman he adored.

"This is whiskey. I can't drink! I can't handle it! Wait a minute, last night, the *Coke*. No wonder it didn't taste right. It was rum, wasn't it? I can't do this. When I drink, I go out of control. I black out," The cup slipped from his shaking hand.

"Estrella, darling, please, you have to help me not drink. It's only been a few weeks since I went through withdrawal; it was horrible. When I drink, I do things I can't remember. Worst of all, I have the same hideous goddamn nightmare."

Deacon crawled to his feet and steadied himself against the second-hand bureau of drawers. From the mirror, an incredulous stranger examined him. Perspiration dripped from his disheveled hair; his skin was pale.

"Oh, doll, I'm so sorry." Her voice cracked. "I put a little rum in your coke last night, but only to help you sleep. I've known plenty of alcoholics and addicts, and they weren't anything like you. Your only problem is drinking to excess. A little booze won't hurt you. On TV the other day, they were talking about how a little red wine every day is actually good for your heart."

"What about the nightmare?" He asked as he splashed cold water on his face. "I haven't had it since I stopped drinkin'. Then, last night I drink some rum and coke, we uncover the tattoo, and it starts all over again."

"Doll, those things are totally unrelated. It was just a coincidence. Listen to me, alcohol is not your problem. The tattoo is not your problem. Your problem is your parents, your childhood, and your past. It's guilt, or unfinished business, or regret, or longing, or God only knows what else. Whatever it is, and no matter how long it takes, we're going to work through it, together. Don't push me away. I want to help." Tears ran down both cheeks.

Deacon's demeanor lightened; she slipped into his arms. After several minutes, she stepped back and took his hands in hers. "Why don't we talk about your dreams?" She suggested. "I'll tell you what I know about their interpretation."

They dressed and sat together on the sofa. "I told you about my nightmare when I lost my mother's obsidian ball. What I haven't told you is that I used to have a lot of nightmares. They started right after my mother died, and they went on for years. There was one in particular about a man, a big ugly man who was missing part of his face. He had me pinned down on my back, and I was screaming at the top of my lungs, but no one heard me.

"In another one my father was dressed in camouflage fatigues and walking alone through the jungle. Small featureless men, dressed in black, were sneaking up behind him. I cried out, but he couldn't hear me. The men were closing in, and he couldn't see them. I tried to run to him. I could feel myself moving, but I wasn't getting closer. The men started shooting; the bullets ripped through my father. He screamed. The rifle fire was deafening, but I heard nothing. It was deafening silence, if that makes any sense."

"What did you do?" Deacon petted her. "Do you still have nightmares?"

"Those three are just a sample. There were a lot more. Some are just too hideous to discuss.

"A couple of years ago, a friend told me about a book called, *How to Interpret Your Own Dreams*. When I read it, I discovered that anxiety, and the trauma of losing my parents, were most likely the cause of my nightmares. After I identified the nature of my problems, the nightmares became less frequent. Finally, they stopped." She smiled contentedly. "I haven't had one in years. The good news is now I dream, beautiful dreams. Sometimes they're in color, sometimes black and white, but always vivid."

"That sounds incredible, but do you think it can help me, your book? If I understand my nightmare, will it stop?"

"Absolutely!"

"I feel like I have two lives, and it's not good. For the past year, I've had my daytime life where I didn't do my share of the work. I was hung over and miserable. Then, there was my other life. I was drinking in some bar, starting early every afternoon, sometimes at lunch, and eventually I was drinking *Jack* for breakfast.

"My memory of that year is blurred. I was out there doing God-only-knows-what. I can't imagine, and I remember almost nothing. The thing that separated my two lives was my nightmare.

"One of my father's favorite scriptures was, *He that is without sin among you, let him first cast a stone at her.* I'm a sinner; I'm just unsure of the extent."

"Deacon, together we can overcome anything. You'll see. Very soon everything will be perfect, absolutely perfect." She pulled him close and kissed him.

Deacon put his faith, absolute childlike faith, in Estrella. She became his guiding light. Every day was hers to direct, hers to fashion. The nightmares continued. She was always there, always comforting.

When he pleaded with her to make love with him, her answer was always the same. "Oh, doll, to give myself to you, to any man, is such a big step. I need to wait. I want to be absolutely sure."

"But, I am committed," he protested. "We are committed, aren't we?".

TEN

THE LATE AFTERNOON JULY SUN beat down. Widowmaker roared. Deacon searched his mind for the right words. The throaty bark of the V-Twin engine echoed against the houses, which lined the street. People on the sidewalk turned to watch him pass. He leaned back in the saddle; he felt good. *They must think me quite a sight.* He thought noting their curious faces.

He stroked the blue over gold gas tank. "Good girl. Estrella will never take your place. She only adds to our family." He affectionately reassured the inanimate object.

A smile crawled across Deacon's countenance as he made the last turn at the intersection. The red Camaro was in his driveway. *Good, she's already here.* A rich smell of simmering spaghetti met him at the door. Estrella followed with open arms, her face gleamed. "Welcome home, doll." She kissed him deeply.

Deacon felt the familiar sensation in his jeans. Waiting for consummation was taking its toll. *Maybe tonight will be the night.* He told himself hopefully. *Maybe tonight she will really be ready to make love to me.*

"Come with me, doll." She said in a wanton voice. She caught his shirt collar between two fingers and led him to the sofa. She dropped to her knees, and unbuttoned his pants.

Deacon gasped; his eyes rolled in their sockets. "Oh, baby," was all he could say. Her long blonde hair draped down her chest and disappeared between luscious breasts. "Oh, baby," he said again as her hand closed upon him.

Estrella relaxed her grip and skillfully dragged her fingernails up and down Deacon's penis. "That's it, doll," she whispered, "close your eyes, and let me take your worries away."

In the blackness of his own consciousness, he felt each individual fingernail. Corresponding tremors racked his being. "Oh, baby, let me make love to you!" He begged desperately. "I want to be inside of you. We've waited long enough. I love you. Please, make love with me."

"In time, doll, it will all come in due time." She said plainly with no interruption in her strokes. "I want it to be special, to be forever. Be patient, doll, you will get what you deserve. If you love me, you will wait." She pressed him with the familiar admonition. "I won't let you suffer. We can do plenty. Don't I always take care of you?" She asked.

Her hands stopped. He opened his eyes and looked into her insistent face. "Yes, you always take care of me." He whispered. "I don't mean to pressure you. I just want you so badly."

"I'll give you the next best thing." She resumed the delicate strokes.

Deacon watched through clouded eyes. Long slender fingers encircled him; her mouth opened. He gasped. Warmth, from deep inside her mouth encompassed him. He shivered violently, and felt her swallow hard.

"Isn't that better?" she asked. "You only want what you can't have."

"Guess what?" He asked chasing a mouthful of spaghetti with a sip of red wine.

"What?"

"One of the Sons, Blade, has cancelled his trip to Sturgis." He said repeating the words he had so thoughtfully rehearsed. "You must know him. I saw you talkin' to him last Saturday at the party."

"No," she answered flatly. "I don't know him. Anyway, what does this Blade's trip plan, have to do with you?"

"Not just with me, with us," he said excitedly. "He has a motel reservation for Sturgis. The big rally in South Dakota I was telling you about. Anyway, someone put sugar in the gas tank of his bike. He's so pissed he isn't goin'."

"Okay, so—" She put both palms flat on the table, and gave Deacon an impatient look.

"I bought his reservation!" He almost shouted. "I want to take you to Sturgis. It'll be our first ride. I want you to understand how special it is to sit in the wind, and Sturgis is incredible. There will likely be a half-million bikers there. Gettin' a reservation is a big deal. You have to make them, and pay a deposit, at least a year in advance. We'll leave in two weeks. Please, baby, let's go. Let's get away from here—just you and me, out on the road."

"I don't know, doll." She answered with a reluctant tone. "What about my job? I've never ridden with you for more than a couple of hours." Her protests lacked conviction. "I don't know if I'm ready for a road trip. Besides, your bike's a chopper, a hard-tail you say. In case you haven't noticed, so am I," she touched her firm buttocks. In my book, two hard-tails might make a sore-tail, and that'd be mine. Anyway, there's no room to pack anything."

"I've got it all figured out. I've already called your boss; she agreed to give you the week off. Last month we took a Harley Low Rider in on trade. It has saddlebags and a sissy bar. You'll love it. I promise. You'll be comfortable."

Estrella scooted her chair back. She cupped Deacon's face in her palms. "If this is what you want, doll, I'll go."

"You're gonna love it!" He exploded with joy. "Too bad for Blade though, he needs a complete overhaul. It's gonna be expensive. Why would anybody put sugar in a guy's gas tank?"

The corners of her mouth lifted. She kissed him. "Yeah, why would anyone do that?"

Estrella pressed her lips against his ear. "Deacon, my butt is killing me, and I have to pee." She peered over his shoulder, only 100 miles registered on the Harley's trip odometer. She had counted the miles all day, and knew he wouldn't even begin to look for gas until they had ridden at least 130 miles.

"Okay," he shouted back, his voice carried away by the wind. "We'll find a room in Sioux Falls."

Dim light crept in beneath heavy curtains. The rusty air conditioner in the rented room growled as it labored against the Sunday morning August heat.

Estrella peered out through the condensation-fogged window. "Shit!" She said loudly.

Deacon's eyes snapped open. "What, what's wrong?"

"It's raining." She answered disgustedly. "It's fucking raining. Do we have to ride in this shit?"

Deacon crawled off the hard bed and crossed the room. He used the curtain to wipe away the moisture. Rain, from a dreary sky, pelted the glass. Bikers, fully clad in rain gear, were streaming out of the parking lot. "We don't have a lot of choice." He said apologetically. "It's either ride in the rain, or sit here all day hoping it'll clear. Let's go to the Harley store, buy some rain suits, and make the best of it. We only have another four hundred miles or so. If you sit close to me, I'll block most of the rain. It won't be so bad."

Westbound Interstate 90 was crowded, mostly with motorcycles. Deacon stayed in the right lane, and held his speed at a steady 60 miles per hour. A strong, left-quartering crosswind whipped across the asphalt; he compensated with backpressure on the right handlebar of the Harley, and leaned into the wind. Passing tractor-trailer rigs showered them with a wall of water as they passed.

The right shoulder of the roadway, beneath every overpass, served as temporary shelter. Every one was crowded with bikers sharing their storm stories, watching the western sky, and trying to dry out.

After eleven miserable hours on the rain soaked, red asphalt of South Dakota, they rolled down the last exit into Sturgis. Deacon found the motel, near the bottom of the ramp, on the outskirts of town. Leather clad bikers and road-grimy bikes streamed everywhere like army ants. The high decibel din of the engines was relentless. Giant tents, a multi-colored patchwork of vinyl and canvas, lined the streets and spotted the surrounding hills.

Deacon coaxed the metal key into the lock of the motel room door, then dragged the rain soaked T-Bag inside. Estrella, her arms piled high with dripping road gear, followed. Even with the door securely closed, the constant, muffled beat of the engines throbbed. The road weary travelers collapsed on the bed.

Monday morning they awoke to the persistent hammering of rain against the window. "Man, am I glad we're not out on the road today." Deacon said. He rolled over and drew invisible circles on Estrella's bare arm. "One hard day in the rain will do me for a while."

Estrella stirred. With both hands, she carefully massaged her still-closed eyes. Her fingers followed a distinct path around her eyelids like a doctor performing a procedure.

With her eyes barely open, she slipped off the bed and into the bathroom. "I thought you said this was going to be fun?" She called back. "A road trip, you said, with beautiful scenery. The Black Hills were black all right, so black you couldn't fuckin' see them. The only thing I saw all day was rain dripping off your fuckin' hair, which was in my face."

"I know, sweetie, I'm sorry. I guess it's just a bad weather pattern. Listen to it, it's pouring. Let's not let this ruin our vacation." Deacon crawled out of bed and pulled on his jeans. "I've been here before when it rained, and it doesn't affect the party. Come on. Let's get breakfast. You'll see."

It rained every day, but the convivial mob ebbed and surged in sync with the downpours. Sturgis, South Dakota, a normally non-descript cow town, was drowning in leather.

The television weatherman forecast clearing skies across the state on Thursday. Deacon and Estrella agreed that would be the day to head for home.

"I want to see her again," Deacon enthusiastically remarked, "I want to watch Sam Morgan ride her Indian in the Motordrome one more time. Today's our last chance."

"Don't you think twice is enough?" Estrella asked shaking her head. "What's the appeal of watching some broad ride an antique in a barrel?"

"I can't explain it. It's just an amazing thing, that's all. People call her the queen of the *Wall of Death.* Please, just go with me. You have to see. When they ride the *Wall,* they defy the laws of physics and nature. I'm worried it's a dying sport."

"I can see why," she said sarcastically.

"Oh, come on, sweetie, it won't kill you. It's a twenty-minute show. You've already shopped every vendor's booth, and we've tasted every ethnic food imaginable. I really want to go once more, but with you this time."

In the bottom of the giant, machine-cluttered wooden barrel, the lanky blonde effortlessly side-cranked the 500-pound 1936 Indian Scout. It popped, and started, on the first kick. Blue smoke belched out of the exhaust and swirled up to the sparse audience.

Perched on a narrow platform atop the exoskeletal structure, they were separated from the rider by a solitary braided-steel cable. *The Reverend took me once.* Deacon remembered as he drank in every detail of the scene below. *It must have been at the state fair in Sedalia.* He chuckled. *If he was trying to scare me, his plan backfired.*

Samantha Morgan threw her leg over the sixty-year-old Indian, and in one seamless motion began to circle and climb the vertical walls. She held her arms high above her head. Curly blonde hair, accented by a thin braid on each side of her face, whipped in the wind. At 60 miles per hour, the red, white, and blue machine screamed. It carried its fearless rider within inches of the safety cable, and 10 meters above the machine-strewn floor.

Deacon shouted excitedly into Estrella's ear. "My father brought me once to see this show!" His words nearly lost against the high-pitched whine of the engine. "It was incredible!"

"He probably meant to throw you in!" She shouted back. A look of loathing distorted her face. "Let's go to *Jack's* and get a drink."

Every waking hour of the rally, *One Eyed Jacks* brimmed with rowdy bikers. Wednesday noon, with the mob driven inside by the rain, the bar was packed.

"Let's drink beer," Estrella insisted. "Come on, Deac, you promised me a good time."

By four o'clock, after eight bottles of beer, Deacon had enough of the hard wooden barstool. He pressed his lips against Estrella's ear. "Baby, let's go." His voice diluted by blasting music and the shouting mass.

"Just one more," she shouted back, "let's try one of those naval shots." She put her hands on his biceps and held him at arm's length. Her erect nipples pushed against the silk tank top.

He drank her in with his eyes. "Damn." He held up a twenty-dollar bill, folded lengthwise, for the bartender to see.

The crowd hooted and howled. Estrella climbed confidently from barstool to bar top. A tantalizing Amazon balanced on high-heeled boots. She opened her arms to her audience. With a rubber band, she secured her hair in a tight yellow ponytail, and lay flat on her back.

On tiptoes, the bartender wildly waved her arms; her panties peeked out from beneath her miniskirt. The mob howled. Deftly, with the tequila bottle held high above Estrella, she filled her naval. Whipped cream blasted from a can and surrounded the tiny pool. She positioned a cherry at the peek of the unstable white mound. The crowd roared. "Drink it, drink it…" they shouted in unison.

Deacon pressed tight against the bar. Using the wooden rail as a step, he lifted himself up and buried his face in Estrella's belly. He sucked up most of the tequila and a modicum of whipped cream. He raised his head and swallowed hard. Whipped cream dripped from his face.

The crowd clapped and chanted, "Cherry, cherry..."

Deacon leaned back into her stomach and caught the stem between his teeth on the first try.

Estrella propped herself on her elbows. In one fluid movement, using only her teeth, she snatched the fruit from his mouth and swallowed it whole. The horde erupted.

Deacon sat alone on a barstool. Through a drunken haze, he checked his watch. The hands showed straight up eight o'clock. He scanned the expansive bar searching for Estrella. Surrounded by the clamoring crowd, two brunette bartenders, dressed as prostitutes-in-prison, frantically poured drinks.

He shook his head as though it would clear his vision, and tried to focus, still no Estrella. On his third visual pass around the room, he found her twenty feet away lying on the bar top.

A tall, square-jawed woman with closely cropped copper hair, bent over Estrella. A long stemmed maraschino cherry hung from the woman's mouth. Whipped cream dripped from her cheeks to Estrella's face. She released the cherry, and it disappeared into Estrella's eager mouth, followed by a long, soulful kiss.

Deacon blinked in amazement. The woman pulled Estrella to a sitting position; then lifted her from the bar. They kissed again. The woman put something in Estrella's hand, and said goodbye with a languorous French kiss.

Estrella squeezed in beside Deacon and snaked her arm through his. "You doin' okay, doll?" she shouted. "Let's have another round." She dropped a crumpled hundred-dollar bill on the bar.

A little after midnight, Estrella led Deacon toward the exit. "Let's go, doll." She said in a seductive voice. "I have a surprise for you."

Deacon started down the wooden stairs. A tall man forced his way through the crowd and up the stairs, nearly knocking Deacon off his feet. Deacon caught himself and glanced up at the man. Stringy coal-black hair surrounded an acne pocked face. Deacon did a double take. Short white horns protruded from greasy hair.

The giant stared down. "What are ya lookin' at, bud?" The menacing voice boomed. His eyes took Deacon by surprise. He shook his head, and looked again. Swollen black pupils floated in a pool of solid red.

Deacon caught up with Estrella, threading her way through the haphazardly flowing throng. He squeezed her elbow. "Did you see that big guy? Back there on the steps. Did you see his eyes? He looks like Satan."

"Yeah, I saw him," she answered unimpressed. "It takes all kinds. He's wearin' theatrical contacts. People use them all the time to change their eye color."

Artificially cooled air blasted from the noisy box under the window. Peeling his tee shirt off with one hand, Estrella led Deacon across the room. She turned him around and pushed him to the bed. She struggled with his boots; then effortlessly removed his jeans and boxers. She caressed his hairy legs and smiled. "Tonight is your night, lover."

She slipped out of her jeans, straddled his waist, and stripped off her tank top. Moisture from curly rain-soaked blonde hair dripped on bare shoulders. Traces of whipped cream spotted the inside of her naval. She hunched over, and devoured his mouth. "This is what you've been waiting for, doll."

"Ohh, baby," Deacon moaned. Through enamored eyes, he saw the love of his life towering over him. Dark nipples engorged, her face began to change. She skillfully guided him to the place of his desire. "Oh, my, God," he cried out as ecstasy washed over him, "oh, my, God."

Her hand was heavy on his throat. He gasped for breath. Her grip tightened. Above her head, her free hand snapped from side to side like a cowboy on a runaway horse. She sucked her cheeks into her now gaunt face. Wild blue eyes glared. She screamed. "This is it, doll, now it's my turn… Bitch, you're done. It's my turn to *lead*!"

Every nerve in Deacon's body pulsed in synaptic disarray. He stiffened and passed out. Deep red, then black, and finally consciousness came. He opened his eyes. She had not moved. "What," he said weakly, "what did you say?"

She draped her limp body over his. With her lips pressed against his ear, she whispered. Her delicate, raspy voice was more sensuous than ever before. "Don't worry about it, doll. Now I'm here. Finally we are one." Her breath was chocolaty sweet.

She nimbly stood; still straddling him, she hopped backward, and landed gracefully with both feet flat on the floor. She backed toward the bathroom, and paused in the open doorway. Harsh incandescent light painted a reddish, phosphorescent outline of her naked torso. In a strangely different, commanding tone she said, "From now on you can call me, Star."

She backed into the brightly lit room and closed the door in front of her.

ELEVEN

HER HANDS on her hips, Star stood in the middle of the cluttered apartment. "Give it all away, to charity, or whoever will take it!" She said emphatically. "I don't give a shit what we do with it. I don't fucking need it. I only want my clothes."

Deacon opened the closet, shook his head, and stepped back. "Whoa," he said, obviously amazed. "I knew you had nice things, but I really had no idea. This is unbelievable. We'll have to make two trips."

"A girl likes to look pretty," she answered unimpressed.

"All this must have cost a fortune."

"What else have I had to spend my money on? When I was living in California, I moved often. I always found roommates with furniture, and I spent my money on clothes. This was the first time I bought any furniture." She canvassed the room with a sweeping hand motion. "I got it all at a secondhand store."

"Why did you come back? I have never really understood. I thought you loved Los Angeles, the climate, the excitement, and the movie stars."

"I did, I do, but I felt ungrounded. The Midwest is my real home. This is the place where I lived with my mother." *Sad face, make a sad face*, she thought. "I thought that if I moved back, some of the old feelings, the happiness, would return to me. It sure worked out better than I expected. Thanks to Kat and providence, I found you. We found each other."

"You're glad you came back?" Deacon sounded anxious. "You're really happy here? It's only been a week since our first time. You're not going to leave me, are you?"

"Never," she smiled and nonchalantly touched his two-day stubble. "Everything is much better than I'd hoped, than I'd planned."

"Close your eyes and relax." Star spoke softly in an unwavering monotone. "Imagine yourself alone in a room. It's white, all white—the ceiling, the walls, the floor, everything. You are standing on a luxurious carpet. It isn't too warm or too cold. It's perfect, comfortable, and safe. The light is dim, but you can see clearly. It's candlelight, but you see no candles. Are you there? Don't open your eyes. If you are, simply say yes."

"Yes." Deacon answered obediently. Slumped on the sofa, his chin rested on his chest.

"The room is large. At the end opposite you, is an entryway, but there's no door. Leave this room, and enter the next. It's much like the first one, comfortable and safe, only smaller. Look, your parents are here, the Reverend and Grace; they're smiling, happy to see you. Look into their eyes. They're telling you that they love you with their eyes. Can you see them? Do you feel them?"

"Yes," he whispered.

"Your parents want to take your hands, one on each side. Put your hands in theirs and walk with them. Walk through the next entryway; don't be afraid. This room is a dull red. The stone floor is hot, scorching hot. It is burning the soles of your shoes. Relax. Your parents are strong. They'll protect you. Feel their strength. If you see this, say yes."

"Yes."

"This room has no exit. Look behind you. The place where you entered is gone. It has become a solid wall. It's hotter now. Look, the other wall, there's a cross. It's your cross, Deacon, the cross on your arm. Look at the serpent and into its evil eyes. Now," Star commanded urgently, "now run. Run to it and rip the snake from the cross. Tear it down, and destroy it before it destroys you!"

Deacon experienced exactly what she described. In his semi-dream state, he saw the cross and the serpent. The heat was suffocating. He felt trapped. Something was wrong. He was alone. The monstrous serpent thrashed and hissed. Deadly venom dripped from its fangs. Deacon screamed, and ran back to where the entrance had been. There was nothing there; it was a solid wall. He heard his father's faint voice in the distance. *He that is without sin among you… He that is without sin… He that is without… He…*

Deacon's nightmare world went black; he lost consciousness.

The acrid blast, from the smelling salts that Star pressed against his nostrils, jerked him back to consciousness. His sweat soaked shirt clung to his chest; his jeans reeked of urine.

"It's okay, doll, I'm here." She said in a low, soothing voice. "You're okay, you're safe. You did well. We're making progress. Relax and go to sleep. We're done. Tomorrow we'll go there again, and you'll win, once and for all. I'm sure of it, absolutely sure."

Deacon fell fitfully to sleep; the serpent came, bigger, angrier, and more violent than ever before.

Near the bed, Star casually rocked and watched her doll toss and turn. She smiled contentedly, and dragged a wooden match slowly across the rocker's arm.

The black market *Cohiba* glowed fiery red in the dark room.

"I remember the day he first walked through that door." Doc Williams said pensively. He gestured toward the locked plate-glass entrance. "It seems like yesterday."

Doc and Kat were alone in the middle of the showroom floor comfortably reclining against custom motorcycles. They sat a few feet apart. Their legs dovetailed, not touching. He brandished a half-full bottle of longneck Budweiser. It was his sixth. Kat was one behind.

"He was just a kid, a scared, wet-nosed kid. He must've looked at everything in here ten times before he finally got up enough nerve to ask me for a job."

"I remember that day, too. Only I remember that you were a little short on compassion." She giggled drunkenly as she lifted her tee shirt and freed her breasts. "You and your long thoughtful pauses, you almost had Deacon in tears before you gave him a job. At least you made up for it later. I was proud of you the way you took him under your wing."

"Kat, this is serious, put the twins away. We need to talk about Deacon. I'm really worried. Maybe what's happenin' to him is my fault." Doc said somberly. "It was my idea to make him a member of the *Sons*. I introduced him to this life. I could have turned him away, sent him back to his folks. Instead, I helped him make it without them. Hell, I'm the one that suggested he get the fucking tattoo. Now look at him. He drinks too much, he blacks out, and God only knows what else. Shit, even I have nightmares about the butchered pimp in the alley."

"Pimp, how do you know he was a pimp?"

"Didn't I tell you? When the cops questioned me about what I saw, they told me the guy had just arrived, a few days before, from California. There was a warrant for his arrest in LA. The charge was pandering."

"I'll be damned," Kat's eyes were beginning to dull from the beer. Her shirt slipped partially down. One naked breast remained. "You can't blame yourself, Doc. You've done so many good things for Deacon. You gave him a chance. He wouldn't have gotten that any place else. If you had turned him away, no telling what might have happened. He would probably never have gone home.

"As for that hellacious tattoo, I was there. When he described what he wanted, it was as if he was possessed. It didn't even sound like Deacon talkin'. I'm haunted by the memory of the look in his eyes, and the way he talked. After all these years, I remember it like it just happened."

"The last ten years have been great. He and I have hardly ever argued, and the business has done better than I had ever hoped. I just wish I knew what went wrong. What caused the nightmares and the drinkin', and what do we have to do to get it stopped, to get Deacon back?"

"Hon', at least he has Star. The first time I saw her I knew she was perfect for him. Have you seen how he dotes over her? If he can be saved, she's the one that can do it."

Doc's reaction was strong and immediate. "Yeah, whatever—shit, what's up with her, anyway?"

Kat's eyes flashed, surprised. "What, what are you talking about?"

"Her name, that's what. All these months, all I've heard is Estrella this and Estrella that. Nothing would do, but I had to learn how to pronounce her name. Now, all of a sudden, we're supposed to call her Star. I'd like to know what happened to fucking Estrella. I don't know what went down in Sturgis, but since he got back, Deac's been actin' goofier 'n shit."

Kat's drunken slur became a stern, clear admonition. "Edward, let's not forget you have your nickname, or road name, or whatever you want to call it."

"Okay, I see your point. I'm just tryin' to put it all in perspective, that's all, and I'm havin' a hard time rememberin' to call her Star and Deacon keeps correctin' me."

"You'll get used to it." She switched back to sweet. "Star is good for Deacon, and right now, more than ever before, he needs someone. Doc, he needs happiness in his life."

"I don't know, Kat. It just doesn't seem right. She's too perfect. If she's so good for him, why doesn't she stop him from drinkin'? Instead, she's drinkin' with him."

"You don't understand. You men are all alike. He'd been drinkin' for a long time before they met. If she tells him he has to stop, it'll drive him away and make everything worse." Kat hiccupped. She covered her mouth. "She and I have talked about this. She told me that she always makes his drinks, and puts in as little *Jack* as possible. She's keepin' him occupied, so he won't feel sorry for himself and obsess over the nightmare."

"What do you know about her, really?" he asked.

"She's had a hard life, lotta tough breaks. Her father died in Nam when she was a baby. Her mother died of cancer when she was, umm, like seven or eight, I think. She bounced from one foster home to another. Nobody wanted to adopt her. She was already too old. Everyone wanted a baby.

"Right after high school, she took off for the West Coast with her boyfriend. She was sure they were in love. She got a job waitin' tables, and he hung out lookin' for movie stars. She finally got tired of supportin' him and threw him out. She stayed, took acting lessons, went to auditions, and kept waitressing. It never worked out, so she decided to come home to St. Louis."

"But why, baby? If her parents are both dead, and she has no family, why come back here? What'd she hope to find?"

"I don't know. I'm sure I don't understand. I still have my parents, and I can't even imagine my life without them. I've thought about that, when they die, I mean. My memories of my childhood are stirred by special places. You know, by certain little things. Maybe that's why Star came back. Maybe she's looking for places that she went as a little girl with her mother. She's probably lookin' for stuff that reminds her of a happy time in her life. Doc, I think she's lookin' for somethin' better, just like we're all lookin'."

"I guess so. I hope you're right."

"I am. 'Sides, Deacon isn't a snot-nosed kid washin' bikes anymore. They'll work this out. You'll see. Now, come here you big hunk, and give me a little of that special medicine that only my doctor can prescribe."

"Deacon, Deacon, you all right?" Doc touched the motionless figure slumped over the desk in their office. His skin was too warm. He breathed irregularly. Doc shook him.

Deacon awakened roughly, flailing his arms and yelling incoherently. Where his eyes should have been, bloodshot slits glowed red like dying embers in a hardwood fire. Sour alcohol, mixed with sweat, emanated from every pore. He smelled like an empty whiskey keg in the men's locker room.

"What? Yeah—yeah—I'm, I'm okay." Deacon answered sluggishly. "I must've dozed off."

"You look like hell, man. You won't make it 'til lunch. Why don't you just go home?"

"No, I don't want… I don't need to go home. I have work to do. Don't worry 'bout me."

"Listen, you smell like shit. Why don't you at least go in the back and get cleaned up? Hey, I've got an idea, get yourself squared away, and let's go out for a burger?"

"Doc, I'd love to, but I'm pickin' Star up for lunch today."

"What's with you two? Sometimes I think you're joined at the hip."

"I can't explain it, but for me, it's like she's a part of me, the best part. I think about her all the time. She drives me crazy. I've never known anyone like her."

"That's great. I'm happy for you, you know that. Everybody needs somebody. Deac, I know this is none of my business, but I thought you were gonna stop drinkin'. What's up with that?"

"Doc, you worry too much. I don't have a drinkin' problem. I'm fine."

"What about the blackouts and the nightmares? Have you looked in the mirror lately? You sure seemed to have a problem when you spent five days at my house dryin' out. Even you thought so."

"That's unrelated. I don't have a drinkin' problem, and I'm gettin' rid of the nightmares. The blackouts are history, and I don't drink heavy anymore. I drink when I want to. Star's helpin' me. Everything's great."

"If you say so." Doc, shaking his head, walked slowly back to the showroom.

"Kat, I'm just not sure about this." Doc said as they walked toward the lawyer's office.

"Doc, we've been over this a hundred times." Kat answered without breaking stride. Hand in hand they crossed the busy street. "It's just a precaution. If there's nothing wrong with Deacon, then as soon as this is over, we can put it all back. Okay?"

"I guess. It just feels wrong, that's all."

"Edward, you should have had an exit strategy from the beginning. I wish you would have come to me years ago." The balding middle-aged lawyer said. He sat, stoically, on the other side of the massive desk.

"It was a different time." Kat added in defense of her husband. "It all just happened. One day we were a sole proprietorship, and the next we formed a partnership. It was no big deal."

The lawyer explained that under their current partnership agreement if anything happened to either of them, Doc or Deacon, the matter would go into probate. He seemed condescending as he described how the courts would handle the case. He suggested that they restructure the agreement. "We can make it so if one of the partners should die, or otherwise be unable to contribute, due to permanent disability, imprisonment, or institutionalization that partner's share would revert, in its entirety, to the remaining partner with appropriate compensation."

Doc shook his head. "It sounds so sinister."

Kat nudged his knee, and gave him a familiar, disapproving glance.

"Okay." Doc reluctantly agreed.

Deacon was in a drunken stupor when he signed.

"Ooh, doll, come on let's party!" Star slid her wet tongue into Deacon's ear. A mimosa-dampened charge shot through his body. "Careful, baby," he caught the fragile stemmed glass just before it crashed on the granite counter. A splash of orange cocktail slopped across the dollop of peanut butter, which formed a rough mound on white bread.

"Come on, doll." She implored. "It's Saturday, let's have some fun!"

He pushed the nearly empty flute away and turned to face her. Her palpable allure was irresistible. Their arms intertwined as they sank to the cool tile floor. She urgently spread her legs. Her black pleated miniskirt bunched around her waist. "C'mon, doll, c'mon, Deac, give it to me. Give it to me hard. Show me the wild thing. Make me pant."

"I don't have protection," he mumbled.

"Don't worry. I'm on the pill. We don't need those fucking condoms anymore. Now shut up and give it to me." Her voice fell to a hoarse whisper. "There— there—that's it—that's the spot. Don't stop—don't stop. Yes—yes—yes."

"Let's go dancin'." She pulled him to his feet. "We can ride Widowmaker. Let's live a little, and do up the town." She hurried out of the room.

"Hey, what's goin' on?" He stumbled after her. "Don't run off, wait for me." The bathroom door slammed in his face.

"Star, let me in." He knocked on the locked door. "C'mon, baby, I gotta wash my face."

"Hold your horses." She found the zip-lock plastic bag hidden beneath a towel in the back of the linen closet. "Can't a girl get any privacy around here?" Wearing plastic gloves, she removed her diaphragm, sealed it in the bag, and stashed it in her purse.

Knee-high black leather boots protected Star's legs from the heat of Widowmaker's throbbing engine as they rode the quiet back streets.

They stopped at three different clubs. Star danced at every one. Between songs, she made sure Deacon had plenty to drink.

By the third bar, Deacon's head was spinning. Alone in a bathroom stall, he supported himself over the toilet. The white porcelain blurred and he passed out. Subconsciously, he heard Star whispering in his ear. *Fight the serpent...resist your father...defy the cross.* His world spun. The voice continued. *Discipline...the rod and the child...the valley...the shadow...death...death...death... Bring me his head...his head on a platter...for me... his head on a platter...*

I'm dead, he thought; *this is hell.* The absence of reality was all too real. *What time is it?* He thought he heard himself say.

Where am I? The same feminine voice asked. *Eight o'clock,* the voice answered. *Day or night? What day and where?*

The scriptures droned on; Deacon was lost somewhere inside his own mind.

A cruel ray of afternoon sun crept through the tightly closed lid of Deacon's eye and bore into his brain. Consciousness came like an exploding bomb. He flailed wildly. Every muscle ached. *Is it Sunday?* He thought remembering bits and pieces of Saturday night. *Where is Star?* He called her name; the house was dead quiet.

Deacon half-crawled, half-walked to the kitchen. He made coffee, took one sip, and poured the rest in the sink. His stomach ached with hunger, but his eyes abhorred food.

He made his way to the front door, and looked out on the deserted street. The *Sunday Post-Dispatch* lay in its usual spot on the front porch. He hobbled back to the kitchen and collapsed on a chair. He rolled the string off the paper. The thick roll uncoiled, and the massive headline assaulted him.

SECOND MUTILATION SEVERS CITY'S NERVE

Deacon's mind reeled. "Oh, my, God," he said. "Has the whole world gone crazy? Am I going mad?"

He forced himself to swallow two aspirin, and sat down to read.

Soulard, for the second time in as many months, a ruthless mutilation has shocked the city.

Early Sunday morning, following a 911 call, police found a woman, in her early twenties dead in her apartment, allegedly murdered sometime late Saturday night. The name and address of the victim, along with the details of the crime, are withheld pending further investigation.

Deacon's throat constricted, and his heart began to pound. He couldn't remember exactly where he had been, or how he had gotten home. Twenty hours were lost; his only memories were fragmented snapshots, fleeting and inconsistent.

He finished the article. *However, in an independent Post-Dispatch investigation, we have learned from a source close to the police that the victim was a twenty-three year old white female who lived alone in a Soulard apartment. Sources allege that the cause of death was severe mutilation, reportedly decapitation.*

"Oh, Jesus, my nightmare," he said to the empty room. "The voice said something about bring the head, or give me his head, like somethin' my father would say."

From the bottom of his closet, he dragged a scarred green metal trunk into the bedroom. From the garage, he retrieved a large standard-blade screwdriver and a ball-peen hammer. Two light blows and the worn chrome latch willingly popped open. Near the bottom of the trunk, he found his small black student Bible.

Inside the cover handwritten in blue ink was his name, the date, and *Promotion Day*. On the opposite page in adult script was a note:

Do your best to present yourself to God as one approved, a workman who has no need to be ashamed...II Timothy 2:15, Prayerfully, Reverend Jones

"Shit, my father couldn't even sign my Bible." He said to the tattered book. "His secretary wrote the same thing for all the kids. The son-of-a-bitch was impersonal in everything he did."

It took only a few minutes of anxious skimming to find the book of Mark, Chapter 6. The message leaped from the page, and burned his eyes with the weight and fire of the words.

23And he vowed to her, 'Whatever you ask me, I will give you, even half of my kingdom.'

25And she came in immediately with haste to the king, and asked, saying, 'I want you to give me at once the head of John the Baptist on a platter.'

27...He went and beheaded him in the prison,

28and brought his head on a platter, and gave it to the girl...

Deacon dropped the book, rushed to the bathroom, and dry heaved until his throat was raw and sore.

At the kitchen table, after a long antiseptic gargle, with one hand resting on his Bible, he looked again at the newspaper. *Sources say the police are investigating all leads. It is rumored this may be the work of a serial killer. Experts say we can probably expect more murders that are similar.*

Early Sunday morning the Chief of Police, in his first brief press conference, announced that he has assigned the major case squad to the investigation. The Federal Bureau of Investigation is aware of the case.

"You've been up," Star commented when she returned home late that afternoon. She leaned over the bed to kiss him.

Deacon caught her by the neck and pulled her into his arms.

"What's all this about?" Star petted his hairy chest. "Are you all right?"

"I feel a lot better, but, sweetie, I'm frightened. Where have you been?"

"What do you mean? You drank a little too much, that's all. Everything's fine. Don't worry. You were sleeping soundly, and I was bored. I went to the zoo."

"It's not just about the drinkin. It's about the not remembering, or the remembering. I'm not even sure which."

"What don't you remember?" She seemed surprised.

"Almost nothing after our second stop, the only thing I remember is like a nightmare. There was a voice, almost like yours, repeating one of my father's scriptures. Star, were you talking to me?"

"Of course, I was talkin' to you, but not about the Bible for crissake. I told you I was going for the car. When I returned, I talked to you while I helped you into the car. By the way, what happened to your shirt? When I came back, it was gone."

"You left me?"

"I told you I had to. I couldn't get you home on the bike. So, I got a ride back here and drove back in the car to pick you up."

"You left me passed out in a bar?"

"No, the bar was closing. I left you outside around the side of the building behind some cars. No one could see you. I knew you'd be safe. When I returned, you were still layin' in the same spot, next to your bike, but your shirt was missing."

"How long were you gone?"

"I had a little trouble getting a ride. Something more than an hour, I guess."

"Wow!" He shook his head, and then laced her fingers with his. "This is all so strange, but here's the worst thing. There was another murder, a mutilation, in Soulard. It's already in the paper. It couldn't have been too far from where we were."

"So, doll, what does a murder have to do with you, with us?" She had a perplexed look on her face.

"Remember, I told you about what happened back in March. There was a guy killed in an alley, and I was there. What are the odds of me being in the vicinity when the two most violent crimes in years are committed?"

"Deacon, you're making too much of this. It's no coincidence. This is the city. Crime happens every day. Forget it."

"Maybe you're right."

"Sorry, I missed work yesterday." Deacon told Doc early Sunday evening. I'll be in tomorrow. I think I just had a little touch of the flu this weekend." He dropped the receiver back in its cradle, folded up in the fetal position, and fell, fitfully, to sleep.

Doc hung up, pushed his chair back from the desk in his home office, and stared at the ceiling. It was unusual for a whole weekend to have passed without seeing Deacon. On Saturday morning when he called, Star told him that Deacon had gone to the store.

Several times Monday, Doc tried to drag Deacon into a conversation. He resisted.

Deacon slipped into the service area and began an engine overhaul, something he had not done for a long time. *Surely, sane people don't hear voices,* he pondered. *Okay, Saturday, what happened?* He began to make a mental list: *Drank mimosas in the morning, tipsy not drunk, made love on the kitchen floor, and first time without condom. After that, it's bits and pieces. I got sick, a kaleidoscope of people, music, dancing, blackness, and the voice in my head.* He stopped. *I have to write this all down.*

A crazy person wouldn't do that, he argued. *A crazy person wouldn't keep notes, would he? Crazy people babble and wave their arms, they don't make sense, and they don't make lists.* He felt better. He was going to write it all down and organize his thoughts, just like a sane person.

He walked to *Spencer's Grill.* The classic furnishings were a flashback to the fifties with stainless steel and well-worn wood. It was a comfortable place. He slid into the same booth in the back where Doc had first proposed their partnership.

Deacon's stomach growled. It was early afternoon, and he had not eaten. He ordered a milkshake, half-chocolate, half-vanilla. From his shirt pocket, he took a small red spiral-bound notebook. Over the years, he had kept a precise record of every deal he had ever made, every sale, every trade, every motorcycle, and every customer.

He flipped to the first unmarked ruled page and printed, *KNOWN FACTS,* at the top. Beneath the title, he made a list of everything that had happened during the past year. It was painful, especially at first, but with ink spilling from the black pen, he painted a prosaic image of his recent life.

There were blank spots in the sequence of events. Those were the blackouts. For the first one, the first time that he was sure it had happened, he wrote, *BLACKED OUT*, in capital letters. Next to the words, he drew a straight horizontal line across the page, a symbol for lost memory. After he established the key, for subsequent entries he used only the line.

The final entries were the chain of events beginning on the previous weekend. The remaining traces of ice cream, in the bottom of the glass, were a thick warm liquid by the time he finished. He leaned back against the high flat back of the booth, closed his eyes, and stretched.

Details, or the lack of certain details, bothered him. *How about when I was passed out?* He gave himself a mental quiz. *Star said I was alone. She said I was in the same place when she returned. Did I stay there? Was I capable of moving? Either way, what happened to my shirt?*

TWELVE

STAR SAT ALONE in the living room. Glowing flames from half-burned candles flickered; tiny reflections danced on the glass of empty wine goblets.

"I'm sorry, I'm late," Deacon said as he hurried into the room. The smell of overcooked dinner hung in the air.

She crossed the room with open arms. Her short white dress accentuated every curve. "Doll, I've been worried sick about you. Where have you been? I called the shop. Doc said you left hours ago."

"I'm sorry; I didn't mean to worry you. I just needed a little time alone. I needed to think."

"It's okay, doll, you don't need to explain yourself to me. Whatever you do is fine. I was just worried, that's all. Now, come with me. I've prepared a wonderful surprise. I just hope it's not all dried out."

The chicken breasts baked in white wine were crispy, but the presentation was perfect. She filled two goblets with chilled white wine.

"Sweetie, I don't think I should drink."

"Ah, doll, I've told you. Your problem and drinking are completely unrelated. Besides, it's only wine, a German Spatlese. It doesn't even taste like liquor. How can we eat an elegant chicken dinner without a little glass of wine?"

They spoke of unimportant things. Finally, Deacon steered the conversation to his unanswered questions. "I mentioned that I was thinking earlier," he began.

"Yes," she answered. "I didn't ask any questions because I don't want to pry."

"I have questions," he continued. "There are many things that don't make any sense."

"Like what, exactly?"

"For starters, Saturday, tell me again where was I when I passed out. How did I get outside?"

"We hit a total of three clubs, right? I didn't think you had had that much to drink, but I went to dance and you disappeared. Some guy came out of the bathroom and told me you were sick. I found you passed out on the floor of a stall. The guy offered to help, and we carried you outside because it was closing time."

"I don't remember the third bar, but okay, then what?"

"Well, you had vomited all over your shirt, and no one wanted to give us a ride. I decided to leave you and go for our car. I bummed a ride. I drove back, picked you up, and brought you home."

"And I was there alone, passed out, for more than an hour?"

"Yeah, I guess, something like that. I wasn't wearin' a watch, so I don't know exactly. What difference does it make? You've passed out before. What's the big deal?"

"My shirt is the big deal. How could I have lost it? If you didn't take it off, who did?"

"There must be a logical explanation. Maybe a bum stole it, or someone tried to help you and took it off so you wouldn't smell so bad. In fact, that's what I should have done in the first place. I just didn't think of it."

"Maybe you're right. I guess I'm making too much out of nothin'. Forget it."

Star smiled sweetly. "Now if we're done, I'll clear the table. Oh, by the way, I can't find my favorite scarf, the dark-green silk one. Will you be a dear and see if I left it in your saddlebags?"

The first leather bag he opened was empty except for a tool kit. Deacon unhooked the nickel buckle of the other and lifted the latigo flap. His heart raced and his hands trembled. Wadded up inside the leather bag, he found the missing shirt. The stale, putrid stench of dried blood and vomit reminded him of Garvin Brown.

"Deac, did you find my scarf?" She asked when he returned, trance-like, from the garage. "Deacon, Deacon." Star called his name.

He disappeared into the master bath and closed the door without answering. He staggered to the toilet and sat down on the lid. With his face in his hands and his elbows on his knees, he rocked back and forth, softly moaning.

"I did it—I did it—I did it." he confessed repeatedly, his voice ripe with self-immolation. "Why can't I remember? What am I going to do? If I have a split personality, surely I can push that other person, that evil part, out of my life and make myself whole again. It must be possible. Surely, I can be saved. My father said there is forgiveness and restoration of the soul."

For the first time in more years than he could remember, maybe even for the first time in his life, Deacon, with a sincere heart, got down on his knees and prayed. "God, if you can hear me, if you know me, remember me. Please, please help me. Show me the truth or help me find it. I need to know. I have to know what I have done. Father, help me."

He splashed water on his face and dragged himself to the kitchen.

"Doll, didn't you hear me? Did you find my scarf?"

"What? Oh, your scarf, no, it wasn't out there."

"Deacon, you look like you've seen a ghost."

"I'm fine. Sorry, I was just in a hurry to get to the bathroom."

The bedside clock showed three o'clock in the morning. Deacon slipped silently out of bed careful not to wake his soul mate. He tiptoed through the dark rooms to the garage. The rancid smell assaulted his olfactory senses as he stuffed the shirt in a plastic trash bag, and tied it tightly. He put that bag in another, and another until the odor was indiscernible.

It was ten blocks to the neighborhood restaurant on the corner. Sticking to the shadows, the walk took less than ten minutes. Without a second thought, he dug down through the garbage in the dumpster as far as he could reach, and buried the bag beneath the stench of rotting food.

Deacon washed his hands and arms with cold water from a spigot in his yard, crept back into the house, and slipped back into bed.

Deacon began nervously, "Doc, can we talk?" They were alone in the showroom.

"Sure, what's up?"

"Not here, I mean we need to have a real conversation in private."

"Okay, Deac. Give me a minute; I'll tell Dawg to mind the store."

In *Lone Elk Park*, on the far western edge of the city, they found a picnic table in a vacant clearing. Two elk grazed at the edge of the trees. A six-inch carpet of dry leaves blanketed the ground.

Deacon was nearly an hour into the story before he got to the bloody shirt. "If I do have a multiple personality disorder, is it possible that my other personality committed those murders?"

"Deacon, we aren't certain of anything. You're just speculating and imagining the worst."

"Don't you think it is all a little too fortuitous? How can I be innocent? Twice now, I was near a murder. My nightmares and fragments of memories match, and now, the fucking bloody shirt. Hell, what am I supposed to think?"

"Calm down. Yelling at me isn't going to solve anything."

"You're right. I'm sorry. I'm just really on edge. I can't sleep, Doc, I'm scared!"

"I know you are; so am I, but we're going to work through this thing together. We'll find the answers."

"Then what, what will we do? What if I'm—I'm a killer?"

"We'll cross that bridge when we come to it. In this morning's paper, the police are saying that maybe it's not a serial killer. The first victim wasn't sexually assaulted. The young woman last weekend, Cynthia something, was raped and decapitated. Her apartment is in Soulard. Do you know anyone down there?"

"I don't think so. Does it matter? What about my bloody shirt, it wasn't my blood. I didn't have a scratch on me."

"Man, Deac, your imagination is really workin' overtime. Listen, I'll tell you what. You know John Candella, right? He's a member of the *Sons*; everybody calls him Shield. He's tall with red hair, and his wife's a bleached blonde with great teats."

"Sure I know him, so what?"

"He's a cop."

"What, Shield a cop? No way."

"Yup, he's a major case detective downtown."

"What do you want me to do, turn myself in and beg for mercy?"

"No, course not, what I'm thinkin' is that I ask John, just as a buddy interested in knowing what's goin' down, to share some of the details of the two cases."

"Why would he do that? He'd risk his job. He won't take the chance just to satisfy a brother's curiosity."

"Maybe not, but he's been tryin' to convince me to sell my bike for a couple a years now. If I offer him a once-in-a-life-time deal, he'll be so happy. He'll do anything."

"Doc, I can't let you do that. Your Harley's your life, man. She took years to build. It'd be like me givin' up Widowmaker; it's just too much. I can't let you do that for me."

"You've missed the point, Deac, that machine isn't my life, you are, you and my family. You're my brother. You've always been there for me. This is something that I can't, not do."

Doc caught John Candella off guard when he offered him the deal. "I don't like this, Doc. If I get you copies of those reports and somebody finds out, I'll get fired for sure, maybe even busted."

"Okay, John, I just figured you, of all people, would understand how exciting it is to be able to get somethin' you aren't supposed to have," Doc insinuated.

"All right, all right, I give. I'll help you, but you read the reports, destroy them, and don't tell a soul, okay?"

"Deal."

"No, you have to swear."

"Okay, I swear. Now, when can I have them?"

"Tomorrow afternoon. When can I have my bike?"

Looking up from the report, Doc shook his head. "Deacon, look at this. It's worse than I imagined."

It was nearly midnight, and the two men were alone, locked inside their bike shop. A single tarnished banker's lamp illuminated the windowless service area. An incandescent bulb caused the thick green shade to glow. Clinical white light spilled onto the gray metal desk lighting a single oblong area.

Doc's index finger flushed white from unconscious pressure on the paper. He marked his place on the poorly copied report, and read aloud. *"Victim's head, positioned upright on a large plate, was found in the kitchen. Eyes were open and small amount of dried blood formed a pool around severed neck."*

"Oh, my God, Doc, that's unbelievable! Jesus, what if I did that?"

"Come on, Deacon, help me. Let's get through this. Make notes in your little book. Let's get all the details. I promised Shield I'd destroy the report, but he didn't say anything about takin' notes."

"Should we copy it word for word? It'd be easier if we just make a photocopy."

"Yeah, I know, but I gave my word, and there's no difference between this copy and one off our machine. All we need is the pertinent stuff," Doc turned his attention to the page. "Look, they call it rape slash homicide. The woman's name was Cynthia A. Thomas. Are you sure that name doesn't ring a bell?"

"No, like I said, I don't think I've ever heard the name." Deacon pointed to an entry on the form. "She was born April nineteenth, 1972. Poor girl turned twenty-four this year."

"This says the time of death is estimated at somewhere between one and two in the morning, Sunday. Where did you say you were?"

"According to Star, I was passed out behind a bar on *The Landing.*"

"She lived on the corner of Sidney and Salena. Probably less than fifteen minutes from *The Landing,* especially at that hour of the morning. Deacon, even though you were close enough, surely you didn't ride over there. You were passed out, right?"

"Do you think that if what I consider to be my normal-self is unconscious, that another personality could be conscious?"

"You're talkin' about somethin' that's out of my league. If it doesn't have spark plugs and valves, I don't know much about it."

"What else does the report say?"

"They found a straight razor at the scene."

"Wow, imagine what a mess that must have been." Deacon cast his eyes down as if trying to remember. "There was blood on my shirt, but what about my jeans? Cutting off someone's head would have made an incredible bloody mess, right?"

"Yeah, I don't know anything about crime scenes, but I saw Brown in the alley and I've never seen so much blood. A rapist would have to have his pants off, or at least down. The killer must have had blood all over him."

"Great, now I'm a killer and a rapist." Deacon slumped over in the ragged shop chair.

"That's not what I meant, Deacon. I was just thinkin' out loud. I'm trying to help you prove that you didn't do it, not that you did."

Doc read the rest of the report aloud. "*Reporting officer arrived at 1956 Sidney Street, Apartment C, at zero three hundred hours in response to an anonymous report of a homicide. Caller thought to be female, overly excited, spoke broken English with a very heavy accent, possibly Spanish.*"

"R/O found the apartment door closed, but unlocked, with no sign of forced entry. All windows were locked and unbroken. Female victim's torso was completely naked; hands and feet tied to the four corners of the bed. Total bleed out occurred in the upper one-third of the bed. Sheet and mattress uniformly severed directly below neck laceration, indicating head was removed while the victim was prostrate on the bed. Victim's head was found in the kitchen... Okay, Deacon, we've already read this part. Let's work on the list of facts." Doc ground his fists against his eyelids. "We're missin' something."

"Maybe we can get something more, like a copy of the autopsy." Deacon suggested in a tired voice. He looked at his watch. It was three o'clock in the morning.

"There you go, that's a great idea." Doc sounded excited. "If we can get the medical examiner's report, it should have blood type and all sorts of shit, maybe even somethin' about the assailant. Do rapists use condoms?"

"You're asking me? How will we get our hands on the ME's report, and what can we do in the meantime? Doc, I'm too nervous to sit around. What—what if there's another murder?"

"I understand. I don't want to wait around either, but it'll probably take a couple of days for John to copy another report. I just hope he's still grateful. By the way, Deac, what's your blood type?"

"I don't know. I've never had a test, least ways, not one that I remember." He sighed, "Just another example of what a worthless piece of shit I am. I've never even donated blood."

"Continually beatin' yourself up, over every fuckin' thing, isn't gonna help. First thing tomorrow, why don't you go to one of those independent labs? I know one. My kids' dermatologist sent them. If your blood type isn't a match, that alone will disqualify you as a suspect. Now, go home and get some rest. You look like shit."

"Thanks a lot."

"You know what I mean. This shit is takin' its toll on you. One other thing, we're friends, right? I mean best friends."

"Of course, we are, Doc, you know that. Why?"

"Good, 'cause I don't want you to take this the wrong way."

"Take what the wrong way?"

"Deacon, I don't think you should drink anymore. I know you and Star are convinced you're not an alcoholic, and I'm no expert. So, I'm not saying that you are. But as your friend, as your best friend, I'm just tellin' ya that from where I stand nearly every time you drink somethin' gets fucked up."

Deacon's forlorn gaze was riveted to the ceiling. He answered in a deliberate whisper. "I know. I know you're right. I don't think I'm a drunk, but I can't take that chance. I'm not going to drink anymore. Just please, please stick with me; help me. I have to know. I have to find the truth. When I do, I promise you I'm going to do something about it."

"Do something?" Deacon's choice of words and the way in which he said them set off a subconscious alarm in Doc's mind.

"I don't know exactly, but if it's me—if I'm the one, somehow, I have to stop it. Somehow, I will have to stop me."

"Hi, doll. I'm glad you're home." Star met Deacon at the door. "I've missed you. You're all right, aren't you?"

"I'm okay. Doc and I were catchin' up on some work. I'm sorry it's so late, I should've called."

"It's okay. All that matters is you're safe. I'm just a little over sensitive. The crazy stuff that's been happening must be rubbing off. Come sit with me." She led him, by the hand, to his favorite chair. "Let me make you a drink, and something to eat."

Deacon squeezed her hand. "Star, we need to talk."

"Sure, doll, what's on your mind?" She knelt at his feet. Her big blue eyes glistened with compassion.

"First, I want you to know—I want to remind you, that you mean everything to me."

"Oh, my God, this sounds like a *Dear Star* conversation." Tears welled up, and she squeezed his hands.

"Oh, sweetie, Star, Estrellita, never, don't even think that for a moment. This is about being together, not apart. This is about loving you, about our future, our happiness, and our life. There's just so much happening to me that I'm confused.

"On one hand, I have you. Without question, you're the best thing that's ever happened to me. I assure you, I am prepared to do anything necessary to protect that, to protect us. On the other hand, as you already mentioned, there's plenty of weird stuff going on. Ordinarily, I'd just say that's life; it's not my problem, and continue doing whatever I was doing. However, I can't do that this time because it's all too close. Mostly, I'm scared to death by my nightmares, and especially the blackouts.

"Star, I have to find out what's happening to me and why. I have to confront my demons. Then, we can be truly happy. We can be together forever."

"Deacon, we are going to be together forever." She said emphatically, wrapping her arms around his legs. "You feel our connection, don't you? Nothing, or no one, can ever come between us. What's happening is just part of a crazy world, a civilization off balance. It's been this way since the beginning of time. Today, in some way, outside forces are affecting us, but it's all in the odds. It doesn't have to mean that it has anything to do with us, with you."

"I wish I were as convinced as you. It just doesn't feel right." He shook his head. "It's all too personal. Maybe if I were alone, it wouldn't matter so much, but I'm not. I have you to consider. For the first time in my life, I truly love someone, and she loves me. I've waited too long for you. Our life is too perfect. I refuse to put us, to put you, at risk."

"Deacon, that's so sweet, you're so sweet, but I don't understand. What does this have to do with me? How can I be at risk?"

"I need to explain. There may be a serial killer out there, and he seems to be moving in our circle. What if you're his next target? Then, there's me, what if I'm sick? What if I am losing my mind?"

"You're not losing your mind, and nothing can change our love," she argued.

"I'm not talking about changing it. I know that's not possible. I have for you, what I'm sure, is unconditional love. I will do anything for you. Star, I would die for you. Just imagine, if we die for the person we love, we might save that person's life, but the survivor will suffer to endure the loss. Which is worse, dying or surviving the death of the love of your life?"

"Deacon, I'm lost. You're talkin' crazy. Nothing's going to happen. No one's going to die."

"I know this must sound bizarre, and maybe it is. Regardless of the outcome, at least I've told you. Now, I need your help."

"I'll do anything you ask. You know that."

"Sweetie, I know we've agreed that I don't have a problem, but I don't want to take any chances." He said unflinchingly. "I want to stop drinkin', cold turkey, not a drop, and I want you to help me."

She answered without hesitation. "Whatever you say, doll, not a drop, not ever. You can count on me." She climbed onto his lap, wrapped her long arms around his neck, and squeezed. With moist lips nestled against his ear, she whispered. "You can count on me. Doll, you're so tense."

She slid down, disappeared into the kitchen, and called back. "I'm going to make you a steaming cup of chamomile tea. My momma used to say there's nothing better for what ails you than chamomile."

Deacon settled into the over-stuffed recliner, and closed his eyes. His mind drifted. What seemed like a single, luxurious moment later, the glass teapot whistled.

"Be careful, don't burn yourself," She whispered in an ethereal voice.

He gingerly sipped the strong, bitter elixir. *Even tastes like medicine,* he thought.

"Drink, lover, drink it all. Relax. I'm here; you're safe." She coaxed him until he had drained every dram.

Deacon evaporated into a troubled sleep, to a place void of warmth and comfort, the demons' sanctuary.

He swam alone in a murky brown river. Instinct kept his head above water. In the middle, a great distance from either bank of a very wide channel, he tried to touch bottom, but found nothing. He tried to relax, and concentrated on slowing his breathing.

In the distance, a long bridge, supported by massive moss-covered gray stone arched-top legs, stretched across the water. The current broke against the supports, and emanated out like two great Vs until they gradually diminished. The elevated roadway loomed large as the current swept a powerless Deacon down the ever-widening channel.

It sounded like a surfacing submarine in an old World War II movie. Startled, Deacon looked back over his left shoulder. The huge open mouth broke the dark surface. Fear tore through his body; he felt the dark tongue-filled cavity surround him. He screamed into the sky lit by a black sun.

He thrashed, and fought for his life, breaking free of the giant hippo's bite. Instead of plunging into dark water, he fell through the air. A hard, flat surface stopped his fall.

A beguiling voice spoke to him. "It's okay, doll, I'm here. It was just a nightmare. It's all right.

C'mon, let's get you unwrapped. How in the world did you get so tangled up in the sheets? Maybe you don't have to drink to have nightmares after all. Try to get some sleep. We'll talk tomorrow."

Deacon awoke long before daylight; his head throbbed. *What is it that haunts me?* He pondered. *What have I done to bring this upon myself? I haven't touched a drop for two days, and still I feel like I've been on a forty-eight hour drunk.*

Star yawned, and made a waking noise. "Are you okay, doll?" She stroked his muscular chest. "Did you sleep okay?" She asked anxiously in her husky morning voice. "I was out like a light after we got you back into bed." She rolled onto her side, propped herself up on her elbow, and held her face three inches from his. "Deacon, are you okay?" She repeated louder than before.

He did not flinch. "I'm okay." He answered faintly. "I have a killer headache, that's all."

"Relax. I'll get you a glass of water and some aspirin. Did you hit your head when you fell out of bed?"

"I don't know what happened. I don't have any lumps, but I feel like I really tied one on."

"I hate to say I told you so again, but all you drank was a cup of chamomile tea, and you had a nightmare. See, everyone has nightmares."

"Maybe you're right. Either way I know for sure that drinkin' doesn't help, so why take the chance. Besides, I've already dried out once, and I don't want to go through that again."

"Okay, Deacon," she tossed the curt words at him, "it's your life."

He dozed off. He awoke to find Star sitting next to him. She gently wiped the back of his neck with a cool moist cloth. "I thought you were mad at me?" He asked peeking from under the black sheet.

"I'm sorry." She continued mopping his neck. "I just get stuff in my head, and sometimes I'm not very understanding. Forgive me?"

"Darling, there's nothing to forgive." He drew her close. "I adore you."

She placed two aspirin between his lips. "Take these. You want to tell me about your nightmare. Talking might make you feel better."

"Do you want to get your dream book? Maybe we can figure out what it means."

It took a while, but he described to her, to the best of his memory, the river, the bridge, and his escape from the mouth of the hippo.

"I think you have to balance the book's interpretation with general definitions of events." Star sat, her legs crossed under her, in the middle of the bed. She flipped through the pages of the book. "The bridge probably represents a transition between two periods in your life. Maybe it means things are changing for the better?"

"If I'm getting better, how come it's so damn scary?" He asked glumly.

"The unknown is always scary."

"What else?" He touched the book as if to hurry the process. "What about getting eaten?"

"I'm afraid that doesn't sound quite so encouraging. It could be, symbolically, the hippo is assimilating your strength. It's possibly a manifestation of the jaws of death or the extinction of consciousness."

"Great, none of that sounds good." Deacon said apprehensively. "Extinction of consciousness and awareness is what I fight against every day."

"Deacon, are you really sure you want to know all of this? They're just one person's idea; maybe, it doesn't apply to you."

"Yes, I want to know. I have to know. Tell me all of it, no matter how difficult."

"The way I read it, the only possible meaning of a black sun is the death of active intelligence, and the river probably represents the twists and turns of fortune. The fact that your river was wide shows that you have a great destiny, whatever that means. You know what seems odd. The ancient stones, arched supports, and big muddy water, it's as if you're describing the Ead's Bridge. You know, down by Laclede's Landing."

"This is all so complicated. I feel like I need some professional help."

"Doll, I can help you. I'm all you need. Together, we can get through this. Trust me. I'm here, Deacon. I'm with you. I'm part of you. I promise."

Deacon dragged himself from the bed, showered, and drove to the lab for a blood test.

THIRTEEN

"WELL?" Doc asked as Deacon entered the office.

"Well—what?" Deacon's mind was elsewhere.

"What did they tell you at the lab? What's your blood type?"

"I don't know yet. The place was a mad house. I asked one of the nurses if they're always so busy. She said their business has quadrupled since Magic Johnson announced that he has AIDS."

"I don't give a shit about Magic Johnson. When are we gonna know your blood type? Shield said he'd stop by this afternoon with the Medical Examiner's report."

"They said it would be two days because of the backlog."

"Shit that means we have to wait until Friday."

"Actually, no, the HIV scare got me to thinking. I asked them to do a whole battery of tests, including HIV and drugs. I don't know anything about all this shit. But, I thought maybe all the booze has caused some kind of a chemical imbalance, or somethin'. I'm just grasping at straws and hopin' for answers. Maybe, with your help, I'll bump into one. Or, with my luck, someone will cram the answer down my throat. Either way, at least I'll know the truth."

"Deacon, you're off on a tangent." Doc sounded impatient. "When are we going to have the lab report?"

"Monday afternoon."

"Shit, at least we have a date."

The autopsy report, from the murder of Cynthia Ann Thomas, arrived that afternoon. Locked in their office, Doc read it aloud.

"Victim was a twenty-four year old blonde Caucasian female; her clothing was found scattered around her bedroom. She was completely nude.

"Articles of clothing, found closest to the bed, were a black pleated mini-skirt, thigh-high opaque stockings, black high heels, and a white silk blouse. Detectives noted they found no undergarments in the room. No traces of blood or other foreign objects found on clothing.

"Body was free of lacerations or bruises with the exception of extreme, inverted, Y shaped bruises on wrists and ankles. Victim's legs and arms were bound to four bedposts with silk scarves. Single, surgically precise, laceration to the throat was consistent with scalpel or straight razor. Larynx severed between Hyoid and Cricoids cartilages.

"Victim blood type, O negative. Stomach contents and toxicology results show high, oral consumption of champagne. Victim's pubic area was combed;

twelve dark brown pubic hairs were found, which were inconsistent with victim's hair. Foreign strands tested as male, blood type AB negative, consistent with sperm residue found inside vagina. Note: Also present were female secretions, blood type AB negative, which were inconsistent with the victim.

At the end of the report, the Medical Examiner rendered his opinion based upon the medical evidence.

"It is my opinion that Cynthia Ann Thomas, a twenty-four year old female, was entertaining a male lover. The presence of what was close to a liter of champagne in the victim's system would indicate that the man was probably not a first time caller.

"The victim's clothing had been worn, but contained no foreign particles, except those consistent with objects found inside the apartment. It is unlikely that the victim had been outside the apartment in that clothing. The lack of evidence of a struggle and the absence of under garments would indicate that the victim was expecting her lover, had willingly allowed, or had removed her own clothing, and helped in the tying of her restraints.

"The victim participated in sexual intercourse. At some point, the victim struggled in her bonds, which caused bruises on her ankles and wrists. The assailant then cut her throat. The cause of death was loss of blood caused by the complete severing of the larynx.

"The presence of fluids from a second female, mixed with the assailant's semen and the victim's secretions, indicate that the assailant had intercourse,

with a second woman, sometime within the preceding eight hours.

"The victim's head was found on a platter as though it was put on display. Absence of male fingerprints indicates premeditation. The manner was homicide.

Doc and Deacon, both pale as ghosts, looked away from the report and each other.

Ten minutes passed in silence. "Now what do we do?" Deacon was the first to speak.

Doc answered in a matter of fact tone. "It's horrific, I know, but we have to keep our cool and focus on the details. The killer is AB negative. That's an extremely rare blood type. No doubt, on Monday, we're going to find out that you're type O, or something equally innocuous, and that'll be that."

"I hope you're right, Doc. I pray you're right."

Star stretched, diagonally across the bed, and pressed her warm feet against his bare side. With a single, powerful thrust, she scooted him to the edge of the mattress. "Deacon…Deacon, your goddamn alarm…get up and turn it off."

Deacon awoke, startled. His thoughts clouded with an irrepressible sensation of impending doom. He rolled over, hit the alarm, curled up, and exhausted a heavy sigh. *Blood test results day*, a feeble voice inside his head, whispered. He had not told Star about the test. Too much was at stake. He could not risk losing her.

The variations in her personality were enigmatic and often a strain. When she was alert, everything was always perfect. She was caring, devoted, sensitive, and sweet. When she drank too much or was not fully awake, she could be caustic, abrupt, and even cruel. The caustic, cruel part he feared. However, it was his fear, and his alone, not to share with anyone, ever. Never did a single syllable, of a solitary word pass his lips that might be construed as a negative reflection on the love of his life.

Ten minutes of snooze time passed in the unblinking of an eye. The alarm resumed its irritating wail. A light tap and the clock radio stopped its incessant buzz. He resisted the urge to crawl back into bed.

The steaming shower was invigorating. Aided by fragrant lather from green soap, it washed life back into every pore. *It's a shame,* he thought, relishing the pelting hot water *that not every moment can be like this one. I have to go back out there and face my problems no matter how terrible. I suppose, if there were only good times, they would not seem so great. I only hope this hole is not too deep.* He closed the faucet and wrung the water from his wavy hair. The thick cotton towel felt reassuring as it wicked away every drop of moisture.

Deacon strode anxiously to the kitchen, thinking of cereal. His stomach growled, eating itself. He thought soft food might help. He drank most of a glass of orange juice in one gulp. A sharp, nerve-induced pain struck. He retched in the sink.

"So much for eating," he told the trashcan as he dumped the cereal.

Deacon was the first to arrive in the laboratory parking lot. He showed his ID, paid the bill, and walked back to his car. He sat and stared at the sealed envelope for a long time. His hands trembled. With his switchblade, he slit the fold and reluctantly pulled out the pages. Printed across the top, he verified, *James David Jones* along with his address. Mostly meaningless information filled the sheet. *HIV negative* leaped off the page. His search ended with *blood type*. Deacon gasped.

Exhausted and tightly wound, Doc paced the showroom floor. He had hardly slept all night and had arrived at 4:30 in the morning. It was 11:00 A.M. still no word from Deacon. He checked the time; a minute later, he looked again.

At 11:30 A.M., Doc spotted Deacon's car in the parking lot. Deacon sat motionless behind the wheel. Doc ran to the car, and tried the locked door.

Deacon stared straight ahead with steadfast, lifeless eyes.

Doc tapped on the glass, but Deacon did not move. The car's engine was idling, and the automatic transmission was set in drive. The combination of the parking lot incline and a curb, located about four feet from the white laid-block wall, held the vehicle in place.

Doc pounded the glass with his palms, "Deacon, Deacon," no response. He removed the large folded knife from the case on his belt and banged on the glass.

Deacon jerked and looked wildly about. His was the visage and eyes of a crazy man. Deacon swung his arms; his head rolled unevenly about his shoulders. He bumped the accelerator, and the car leaped over the curb.

Astonished, Doc fell backward. With a low thud, the car came to a stop against the building.

Deacon's erratic movements ceased; a semblance of cognizance returned to bewildered eyes. The car rolled backward, stopping with the front tires resting against the inside of the curb.

Doc tapped on the glass. Deacon unlocked the door, and Doc pulled it open. "Deacon, you all right, what happened?"

Deacon handed him the crumpled paper. Doc scanned the words, *AB negative*. He sat down, hard, on the tarmac. "Oh—my—God, holy shit!" He read the words again. There was no mistake. Deacon's blood type matched that of the sperm, and the pubic hair, taken from the body of Cynthia Thomas. "Shit!"

The pair sat in their office. No words passed between them. Palpable fear and distrust hung in the air. Everything was wrong, even their friendship. Doc considered the possibilities. He struggled to convince himself that Deacon was innocent, but there was so much evidence. The facts were incontrovertible. He stared hard at a single marred spot on the tile floor, unable to lift his eyes, unable to look across the room at the distorted face of his partner.

Deacon fixated on an over-sized calendar in the middle of an otherwise blank wall. His life was over; his arrest was eminent. He hated himself. He would never again be able to look at his reflection or say his own name. He had become his nightmare. His father was right. He had walked willingly into hell, and now he was a part of the evil.

Dawg, the counterman, knocked loudly. "Deac', there's a couple a suits out front. They wanna see ya."

"I'll go," Doc whispered. "You stay here, out of sight. Keep a low profile 'til we sort this shit out." He switched off the lights and slipped quietly out of the office.

Deacon sat alone in the dark, very afraid.

"Gentlemen, good morning, how may I help you?" Doc threaded his way through gleaming motorcycles. He extended his right hand.

The taller lanky man spoke first. "Are you James David Jones?"

"No, I'm Edward Williams, his partner. Can I help you?"

Deacon clamped his ear to the door. Thin ribbons of light invaded the small office and drew uneven lines on shadowy walls. He listened intently but heard only muffled voices. He thought of his trips to his father's study. *The waiting is always worse than the punishment.*

"I'm Detective Jensen; this is Detective McNeil. We're with the St. Louis Major Case Squad. We would like to ask Mr. Jones a few questions."

"I'm sorry. I'm afraid he's out."

"Sir, do you know where we can find him?"

"No, I don't. He took the day off. He told me he had some errands. He said he would be in tomorrow."

Jensen handed Doc a business card, an embossed gold badge marked the corner. "When you see him, tell him to call me at this number. If we don't hear from him, we'll be back in the morning."

"I'll be sure and tell him."

"Was it the cops?" Deacon asked nervously.

Doc sighed, leaning against the closed door. He shivered. "Yeah, two Major Case detectives, I told 'em you weren't here. They're comin' back tomorrow."

"Now, what are we gonna do?" Deacon cradled his face in his hands. "It's over, isn't it, Doc? I'm finished."

"Deacon, I need to ask you a question. Bud to bud and you have to tell me the truth. No matter what it is, or what it means. Promise to tell me the truth."

"Doc, you have been my only family for years. You and Katherine are the best. Until I met Star, I thought you would be the only real family I would ever know. I promise to tell you the truth."

Unblinking, Doc locked on Deacon's gaze. "Did you do it? Did you murder those people?"

Tears streaked Deacon's cheeks. "I don't know. I wish I did, but I can't remember a thing. Doc, I'm losin' my mind. There's just so much evidence against me. I'm terrified that I did do it. I just don't know. Doc, please help me." Deacon dropped sobbing to the floor. "Help me, I'm begging you."

Doc knelt beside his friend. "What do you want me to do, Deacon? You are my brother. I'll do anything to help you, but we can't—I can't, cover up two murders. I taught my children to tell the truth and always obey the law. I told them since they were very small that honesty is the cornerstone of society. Without respect for others and the system, everything would break down. We would descend into chaos. I taught them these things because it is my value system. I cannot contradict those beliefs, not for anyone, not even you."

"I understand. I wouldn't ask you to help me cover anything up. The sane part of me agrees with you and shares your principles. I'm asking you to help me find the truth, once and for all. When I know what it is, then I can do something about it."

"What do you mean, exactly—do something about it, turn yourself in?"

"No, if I'm locked up, I may never know—I may never be able to find the truth. Hell, they could convict me with circumstantial evidence. I'd spend the rest of my life in prison, or in an institution with only the memory of what supposedly happened. That would be unbearable. I couldn't live with the guilt."

"Deacon, what're you tellin' me? Do you think there's an easier way out, like suicide? You can't do that. I can't let you. It's wrong. It's a shortcut to the chaos, a permanent solution to a temporary problem. It's against the laws of God and man."

"Doc, remember all of the conversations we've had about wearing helmets?"

"Of course, I do. But, what does that have to do with this? You're anti-helmet, so what. You sayin' not wearing a helmet is like a death wish?"

"No, I'm referring to something you said."

"What did I say?"

"You told me you believe riding a motorcycle is dangerous, with or without a helmet. You said it's possible to be killed, or permanently injured, either way."

"I remember, but what's that got to do with suicide?"

"You've always said that if anything catastrophic was to happen, you'd rather someone pull the plug than live the rest of your life as a vegetable. For me to live with the memory, with the realization that I'm a monster, is unacceptable. I'd rather be dead. If necessary, I'm prepared to pull my own plug."

"I understand your analogy, but I couldn't stand by and watch or allow you to do it."

"I hope if it comes to that, you're not around. But, now you've gotta make me a promise as my best friend."

"You know I'm willin' to do anything for you just as long as it's not illegal or immoral."

"It's both, but, more importantly, it's humanitarian. If I am guilty, if I completely lose my mind, if my dark side takes over, and the Deacon that you know totally disappears, I want you to do this service for me. Doc, I want you to pull the plug. I want you to end my life."

"Oh, my, God, Deacon, I can't do that. How could I ever live with myself? The answer is no, absolutely not."

"I am not asking you to kill *me* as you know me. Don't you see, it will be the monster I have become? You'll be saving my soul. You will set me free. Perhaps God will forgive me. Maybe I'll end up in a better place. Certainly, he would pardon you. Doc, you're the only person that can help me. You are the only one that I can ask to do this."

"Deacon, do you realize what you're saying? Have you lost all touch with reality?"

"In this moment, I'm completely aware of what I'm saying. I am begging you to do a good thing, a just thing. You won't have to be ashamed. If I'm a killer, an amoral creature, you will be doing society a favor. No one will ever question your morality for having defended yourself from a crazed murderer. As far as living with yourself, you can be happy. You will know that you have shown me the greatest love of all, unconditional love. You will have saved my immortal soul. Please, Doc, if it comes to that, do it for me."

Doc stumbled weakly to a chair and sat down. Ten minutes passed. "I hope it doesn't come to that, but if it does, if we find irrefutable evidence that you're guilty, if you lose your mind and become that thing you describe, I swear—I swear that I will end your suffering. I know you would do the same for me."

The deliberate tick of the clock was the only sound in the room. It was well past dark before either man moved.

Deacon finally broke the silence. "What should we do now?"

"First, we need to know exactly why the cops want to talk to you. If it's just routine, then maybe you should talk to them. However, if you're a suspect, that's a different story. We can't afford to chance you being arrested. You need to be able to move around. We have to conduct our own investigation, and we'll have to do it on the DL."

"I agree. But, how're we gonna find out what the cops are doin'? We can't very well ask them."

"No, but we can ask Shield. I just hope I have one favor left." Doc thumbed through his Rolodex, then dialed the number.

Detective John Candella answered on the second ring, "Candella."

"Shield, it's Doc. How ya doin'?" he casually asked.

"I can't talk to you anymore, Doc."

"What? I'm just callin' to see how the hog's runnin'."

"Bullshit, your partner's in big trouble, and I've already given you too much information. If anyone finds out about the reports, I could be suspended or fired. Doc, I'm not a one per-center. I'm a cop. This job is my life."

"Shield, just tell me what you know. Why do you say Deacon's in trouble?"

"Aw, come on, Doc, you know, as well as I do, what's goin' on. Jensen and McNeil told me they talked to you this afternoon."

"That's right. They came in the shop and asked to see Deacon, but they didn't say what they wanted."

"Doc, I know you're fishin'. So, I'm gonna fill in some blanks for you, then I'm out of it. If anyone asks me about this, I'll deny it all. Here's the deal. Deacon is a suspect in the pimp murder downtown and the Thomas murder in Soulard."

"How's that possible?' Doc asked surprised. "What link could the police have found between Deacon and two unrelated murders?"

Deacon listened pensively to Doc's side of the unsettling conversation. The blood drained from his brain. He touched his cheek; it was cold and clammy. The room began to spin. His elusive consciousness was slipping away.

"They were tipped off by an informant." Candella answered curtly.

"Tipped off, by whom, a rat on your payroll?"

"No, it wasn't a CI. It was an anonymous call," Candella explained, "a woman with a heavy Spanish accent. She had details that were unknown by the press and the public. Deacon is the number one suspect. Doc, they're going to pick him up."

"Shield, what can we do? Deacon couldn't have done this. Someone's got to be framing him. Can you help me get some answers? All I'm askin' is to see a copy of the report from the first murder. Please, John, I'm asking you, friend to friend. It's important, life or death important. You know Deacon, he's a good guy. Give us a chance to clear his name."

"Edward, it's too late. I don't think anyone can help Deacon. If you want my advice, you'll get out of this while you still can. I've heard the evidence. I'm afraid you're mistaken about your friend. I like Deacon as well as the next guy, but you have to admit, he's a little weird. I've seen his tattoo. One more thing, we're finished, no more favors. Don't call me again."

Doc turned toward Deacon, whose pallid face and glassy eyes caused him to look like a bad photograph. "Deacon—James David, can you hear me?" Doc shook him. Deacon displayed no a sign of cognition. "Come on, buddy, snap out of it. I need you with me.

We've got a lot to do. Come on, James, don't leave me now."

Doc noticed a quiver; first in his eyes, then his hands as though a wave rolled through his body from top down. His whole body shuddered. He struggled to his feet, ran to the bathroom, and threw up.

"I'm scared, Doc," Deacon said in a phlegm voice. "I may as well give myself up. They're going to arrest me anyway."

"You can't do that. We need to prove your innocence. I can't do it without you."

"Shield must have told you to get out. You'd better take his advice. I'll take care of this on my own. There's no place for me in this world. I need to write some letters; put some thoughts on paper. Why don't you go on home and get some rest. I'm going to leave some things on the desk. Please take care of them for me."

"What kind of things? What are you planning?"

"Don't worry, just some letters and personal stuff. It will be self-explanatory."

"Deacon, if you're still talkin' about suicide, it's out of the question. We agreed…"

Deacon cut him off. "Doc, you're letting your imagination run away with you. Everything will be fine."

"I can't let this go, Deacon. No matter how you say it, the meaning is the same. You're planning to—to take your own life."

"If I am, would it be such a bad thing? Look around, Doc, what do I have? I haven't spoken to my parents in more than ten years. You, Kat, and Star are my only family, and everything that I do is bad for you. I have systematically hurt everyone in my life. There's nothing left for me. I have no reason to live. People who care about me are suffering. Innocent people are dying. No, my friend, this is for the best. Let me do something right for a change. Let me save all of you. Perhaps, by so doing, God will know I've repented, and he'll forgive me."

"Deacon, I can't—I can't let you hurt yourself. We don't know the whole story. Just give us some time, a couple more days. Let's get the facts, and then decide what to do. If we don't do everything possible, I won't be able to live with myself."

"I don't know how much more of this I can take. I have to end it one way or the other. Doc, I know I sound like a broken record, but our friendship has been the highpoint of my life. I will do what you ask, for as long as I possibly can, until I can't bear another moment. I'm beginning to question if I even know right from wrong. My father said, on more than one occasion, that he doubted if I even have a conscience. Maybe he was right."

"You certainly put a lot of stock in everything your father said. Has it ever occurred to you he was the one with the problem? Hell, maybe the Reverend's crazy."

"He and I may not have gotten along very well, but he's still my father. He was only doing what he thought was right. He tried to raise me to be a good person. *Let he who is without sin cast the first stone,* is one of his favorite quotes. To my recollection, he seldom cast stones at any one. When he did, he punished himself after. Wouldn't you consider his actions an admission of guilt, or a sign of human frailty? Don't you think he knew that he was not perfect?"

"Deacon, listen to you. You're proving my point. Your old man was always pushing, always demanding that you be something even he was incapable of being. He expected you to be perfect, and all the time he knew that it was impossible. No one's perfect. He set you up to fail. Just how sane is that? What loving, caring father drives his child to fail?

"Let's consider another possibility with the evidence in the two murders. Their connection to your father's favorite scriptures is a big part of why you think you could be the killer, right?"

"Well, yeah, what are you saying? Do you think my father has something to do with this? For all I know, my parents may not even be alive."

"My point exactly, you know nothing about them. After ten years, out of nowhere, your father's prophecy begins to come true. People die exactly as the scriptures say. He repeated those same scriptures to you so often that you still use them in everyday conversation."

"Maybe my father was right. My sins have come to haunt me. His prophecy is self-fulfilling. Evil spills from my mouth, and people around me suffer. There are two dead bodies because of me."

"Deacon, I feel like I'm wasting my fucking breath. What if there's someone out there intentionally making your father's prophecy come true? What if you are being framed in such a way, even you believe you're guilty?"

"Who would possibly do such a thing? I don't have any enemies. Besides, how could anyone know enough, or care enough, about me to go to all that trouble? What do they accomplish?"

"That's it, exactly!"

"What, what's it?"

"Deacon, it could be the Reverend John Jones. He knows all that shit, and he sure has a mean streak. My dad never punished me anything like yours did."

"Impossible, my father would never hurt me. He loves me, or at least loved me. He just has a different way of showing it." His voice cracked. "I'm the one—I ran away. I deserted them."

"Is making you stand at attention, awaiting some unknown punishment for hours, loving? What your father did to you is not normal. Today, children call the child abuse hot line. Parents end up in jail for that kind of behavior.

"Maybe the Reverend finally drove himself crazy. Maybe he quoted the Bible so many times he's lost touch with reality. He's described the angels of the Lord so often he believes he is one. Didn't King David send Bathsheba's husband to the front lines to ensure he was killed in battle? Your father could be out there making prophecy, his prophecy, come true. This whole thing is so bizarre. Anything's possible. Try to see this from another perspective. Be honest, your father could be enacting what he thinks is God's will."

"Not possible, Doc, my father wasn't a perfect parent, but he's not insane."

"Why are you so anxious to believe he's innocent; yet you think you're not? Let's not close our eyes to any possibility. When we talk motive and knowledge, I can certainly make a case against the Reverend. He has both."

"I don't even know if he's still alive."

"That's something we have to find out."

"I guess you're right. Besides, I've been thinking about my parents a lot lately. I'd like to know—no, I guess what I mean is I need to know what happened to them. No matter what else happens, I want to ask for their forgiveness for my part in everything that happened."

"All right then, it's settled." Doc said relieved. "Let's rest here for a few hours. We can ride into Illinois before daylight, and find you a safe place to hide while we investigate the murders and the Joneses. Deacon, no matter what we find, we'll see this through together."

"Okay, but I need to get out of here for a little while."

"Deacon, we've settled this, I am not going to let you do something that I'll regret. I'm going to keep an eye on you until I am sure you're not in the mood to do something stupid."

"It's not like that, I give you my word. I just need to get outside. This may be hard for you to understand, but I need to go somewhere quiet, to be alone in God's creation. I need to get down on my knees and pray for salvation. I'll be back soon, I promise. Doc, I have to do this; I have to do this alone."

"Dear God," down on his knees, James David *Deacon* Jones prayed in a loud clear voice to the eerie, black Missouri sky.

FOURTEEN

Doc's BOOMING VOICE shattered the predawn silence. "Well, I'll be damned!" He stood in the office doorway holding a large white envelope.

Deacon rubbed sleep from his eyes. "Where'd you get the envelope?"

"Found it in the showroom. Someone slid it under the door."

"What's in it?"

"A police report, the pimp murder, our friend Shield came through after all."

"What's it say?"

"I don't know; haven't read it yet. Let's get our shit together and get outta here. It'll be daylight soon; we don't want to be seen."

"I need to make a quick stop at my place and pick up some gear."

"Deacon, we can't risk it. The cops might already be there. We'll buy whatever you need."

"Doc, I can't..."

"You can't, what?"

"I can't leave, go into hiding, or whatever it is we're doin' without saying good-bye to Star. I don't want her to worry."

"Deacon, it's too fuckin' risky."

"I know you're tryin' to do what's best for me. I appreciate that, but I have to do this, no matter what the risk. If she were to disappear without telling me, I'd go nuts. I can't do that to her."

"Okay, but ten minutes, and we're out of there."

"I knew you'd understand, ten minutes."

Guided by Doc's concise hand-signals, Deacon carefully backed the loaded motorcycle trailer through the gate. Doc's form, illuminated only by taillights, glowed red in the moonless predawn. Without a word, the two men loosed the straps and unloaded, first Widowmaker, then the Harley-Davidson Low Rider. The ancient door screeched in protest as Deacon slid it open. Lovingly, he rolled Widowmaker inside, and left the Low Rider and a Heritage Softail, which Doc had ridden from the shop, parked behind the trailer.

Inside the massive brick structure, which was once a thriving manufacturing concern, Deacon studied the cobwebbed walls. He remembered the day, three years ago, when he and Doc had agreed to buy the building. It had been the home of one of the first manufacturers in downtown St. Louis. *We can use it for storage for now!* Doc had said adamantly trying to convince Deacon and Kat that the building was a good idea. *Later, we can restore it and have our own museum. We can buy and sell antique motorcycles. It will make an excellent second location for our business.*

Deacon admired the long rows of motorcycle frames and miscellaneous parts. Even the elevated walkways, which surrounded the cavernous room, were stacked high. *Nothing more than a bone yard.* The macabre thought was unwelcome. *Nothing more than a place to store our dead until we're ready to bury them. This building is like all my dreams, obsolete.* He put his weight behind the door, forced it closed, and locked it. The Low Rider willingly responded to his touch. Already outside the gate in the street, Doc sat on the idling Heritage, waiting.

"Baby, it's me." Deacon whispered in Star's ear. Sound asleep, her breathing came in a measured rhythm. He slipped one hand under the covers. Warmth radiated from her nearly naked body. Her luscious, warm skin caused him to tremble. She filled him with need. His physiology began an involuntary cycle of response.

Star squinted. "Doll, where've you been, you all right?" she asked in a sleepy voice. She rolled on her back, pulled him down, and spread her legs. "Give it to me," she whispered.

"I can't—I can't stay. I only have a couple a minutes," he said urgently. "We need to talk."

She sat up and drew the sheet to her breasts. "What's going on, Deacon, what's the matter?"

"Star, the police are lookin' for me. They think I had somethin' to do with the murders. I'm gonna hide out until Doc and I figure out why. I came to say good-bye, and to tell you to be really cautious."

"There's no reason for you to hide. Let's go to the cops. You didn't do anything wrong. For the times you don't have an alibi, I'll say you were with me. Don't leave. Let's face this together."

"I love you for what you are trying to do, but I can't let you get mixed up in this."

"Where will you go? When will I see you? I have to see you. Deacon, I love you more than I dreamed possible. Without you, my life has no meaning. Let me go with you. I can help." She spoke rapidly, pleading. "There must be somethin' I can do. I need to be with you."

"I—I love you, too, but, for now, it's best you stay here. I'm not exactly sure where I'm going. Even if I did, it's better if you don't. I don't want you to lie for me. If the cops come here, tell them the truth. You don't know where I am."

"How long will this take? Can I meet you somewhere?"

"I'll keep in touch. We'll see each other very soon. I promise. I'm lost without you. There's one more thing. I want you to be able to protect yourself. It sounds crazy, but it might mean protecting yourself from me."

"Deacon," Star twisted her face quizzically. "What do you mean? You're scarin' me."

"I don't have time to explain. Just promise me. If I try to hurt you, you'll protect yourself."

"You're talkin' crazy. You could never hurt me."

"I'll tell you the whole story as soon as I can. When I do, you'll understand. Right now, there's no time. Promise me, please?"

"I don't understand, but I promise."

"That's my girl." From a special leather-lined pocket inside his jacket, he pulled a black handgun. "I want you to take this."

She pulled away. "I don't know anything about guns. They frighten me."

Without hesitation, he popped the loaded magazine out of the handle, checked it, and snapped it back in place. "I know you don't like this. Take it for me. Make this one of the things you do because you love me."

"That's unfair; you're using my love against me."

"Not so. I'm using your love to cause you to protect yourself. I'm outta time. Please, just do as I ask." He moved closer and held the pistol in front of her. "This is a forty caliber Glock. It's completely legal, registered to me. It's a powerful semiautomatic weapon. The same gun the state cops carry. The safety is built-in. It's here in the trigger.

"I'll put a round in the chamber. When I pull this slide back," the mechanism made a metallic click, "it's ready to shoot. Don't point it at anyone unless you intend to shoot. When you're ready, just squeeze the trigger; the safety will release as you squeeze. After every shot, it'll reload and cock itself. Be sure you hold it with both hands, like this, and line your target up in the sights. Baby, I'm sorry I have to go. If the time comes, you'll know what to do. You always seem to know."

"I love you more than life it…" The bark of the Harley's engine severed his last word.

Star waved from the open doorway. Dried leaves swirled and danced in the street behind the speeding motorcycles. Two brake lights, a meter apart, flashed once simultaneously; they disappeared around the corner. Fading stars were rapidly melting into the light of day.

Star smiled. She undid her sash. The short robe fell open. With legs spread, she massaged the back of her neck using both hands, and then fondled her breasts with a languorous, circular motion. She stretched her arms around her back, as far as she could reach, closed her eyes, sighed deeply, and traced the imprinted image that lurked beneath her skin.

The resounding blast from a single gunshot echoed though Deacon's house.

The phone rang twice. Only the glowing blue digits from the microwave clock lit the kitchen, 6:27 AM. The fourth ring, *I know the son-of-a-bitch works from home,* she thought. *This early, he must be there.*

The line clicked in the middle of the fifth ring; an answering machine engaged. "Mahoney Investigations…" the tinny man's voice began. "Hello," said the same voice, only groggy and human, cutting into the recording. "Hello," he repeated.

"Mahoney," Star said, "you know I don't like to be kept waiting."

"Ms. Luna," he asked sheepishly, "is that you?"

"Of course, it's me, who else?"

"Yes, Ms. Luna, I'm sorry." His whiskey voice was beginning to clear.

"How can I help you?"

"I need you to go out again today; it has to be today."

"Yes, ma'am, as you wish. Do you want more pictures of the old couple or the biker?"

"It's a little more complicated this time, Mahoney. I need you to go inside the preacher's house." The line was silent. "Mahoney," she said agitated. "Did you hear me?"

"Yes, I heard. That's breaking and entering. You've never asked me to do this before."

"I don't give a shit what you call it. I want it done today. I've paid you plenty. You'll do this, or I'll get someone who will. Besides, all I want is copies of documents. You aren't going to steal anything. I don't want you to leave any evidence that you were there. I'm in a hurry, so I'll even sweeten the fucking pot. I'll pay you four times the usual."

"I'll do as you ask. What am I after?"

"Their house is in California, west on Highway 50, right?"

"Yes, ma'am, they live on the edge of town."

"Do you think they'll be away today?"

"Yes, ma'am, I'm pretty sure. Most days, they visit at a local nursing home."

"Good, inside the house you should find one of the bedrooms set up like an office. There will be a desk with at least one locked drawer, probably a file drawer. Inside you'll find a large yellow envelope. It should be marked personal and confidential, or some such shit. I want a copy of everything it contains. If it's sealed, steam it open. Leave everything exactly as you find it. Now, get movin'. I'll call you at four this afternoon to set up a meeting."

"Yes, ma'am, you can count on me."

"Mahoney," her tone changed.

"Yes," he answered. There was trepidation in his voice.

"This will be your last job."

When the Mississippi River came into view, the October sun was beginning to peek through the treetops on the Illinois side. The paved surface of the expansive *New Chain of Rocks Bridge* was no different from the highway, which led to it.

Three car lengths behind Doc and halfway across the bridge, Deacon turned his attention upstream. A line of a half dozen barges, piled high with coal and pushed by a single tugboat, crawled slowly upstream. Directly above the mountains of mined black mineral, the *Old Chain of Rocks Bridge,* rusting in the morning light, traversed the debris littered river.

The guttural sound of the V-Twin engines echoed against the newer bridge in an even cadence. Each rail post, which bordered the roadway, added its own note to the song. Deacon released his grip on the rams-horn handlebars and momentarily closed his eyes. Sweet fall air, foul water, and caustic diesel fumes sent a convoluted potpourri of neural messages. The first rays of the morning sun sliced through the cold air and warmed his face. His mind drifted for a moment more; his eyes popped open. The reality of his situation came crashing back. *Mixed signals,* he thought, *the story of my life. Fucking mixed signals.*

On the east side of the bridge, safely in Illinois, Doc led the way to a station for gas and breakfast.

"We'll find a small out of the way resort or motel, something, somewhere north of here along the river." Doc said casually between bites. The three symmetrically cut pancakes on his plate were dotted with minute splashes of pure maple syrup.

Across the table, Deacon nervously hacked an identical stack into jagged chunks drowning in a concoction of peanut butter and syrup.

"Deac, how can you eat like that?"

"This may be my last meal."

"Yeah, right, so how come you always eat that way?"

"I dunno," he answered with a full mouth. "Maybe I eat like this when I'm nervous."

"You eat like that when you're nervous, excited, happy, sad, everything. It's a wonder you don't weigh three hundred pounds."

"When I was growing up, I was in trouble a lot. If the Reverend summoned me during dinner, I didn't get to finish my food. I ate fast so I wouldn't lose out."

The young, knobby-kneed waitress picked up the dirty plates. Doc fanned the pages of the police report across the table. Brandishing a blue highlighter, he began scanning and marking the sheets. "Let's see what we have." He highlighted all pertinent information, and added commentary as he went.

Deacon transcribed what they agreed were relevant facts in his pocket notebook.

"Garvin Brown was a thirty-seven year old African-American from East LA," Doc cleared his throat. "Why would a mother name her son Garvin? Can you imagine what a ribbing he must have taken in school?"

Deacon looked up, incredulous, "This from a guy who calls himself, Doc."

"All right, wise guy." Doc brushed off the jab. "It says here that Brown's 'Cadi' was found parked and locked in front of the bar where he was killed. The only clear fingerprints were his. In the opinion of the reporting detective, the victim was alone."

"It doesn't add up. What business did he have in St. Louis, and why was he killed? Doc, do you think we're goin' at this from the wrong angle? We keep tryin' to establish my connection to the murders. Maybe we should be thinkin' about what they have to do with each other."

"Hmm, now you're thinkin'. We need to get some background on both victims and look for a common thread. Plus, we need to find the Reverend and Mrs. Jones. This will take a few days. Don't you think?"

"I guess. One problem, if the cops have put out an APB, there's no way I can ride any bike with D plates registered to us. I'm not even safe in Illinois."

"There would be if the license plate wasn't registered to us. With a helmet and sunglasses, all bikers look alike."

"What do you have in mind?"

Doc dug into his travel pack and pulled out a current Illinois license plate.

Deacon turned it over in his hands. "Where'd you get this?" The ubiquitous numbers were computer selected, and the plate was unblemished.

"You know the wrecked Road King parked in the southeast corner of the shop? It'll take weeks to get the parts. So, I lifted the plate. The irony is that the owner is a Chicago Judge. He won't even come down until his bike's fixed. Obey all the traffic laws, don't do anything unusual, and you can go anywhere you want, no problem"

Deacon traced the edge of the license plate. "Perfect, this is unfucking believable."

Doc continued with the report. "This says that Brown has a record all right, but not for dealin'. He was arrested three times for pandering and once on suspicion of murder."

"Do you think Cynthia Thomas was a prostitute?" Deacon asked surprised at the possibility.

"I don't know, but if she was, that could be a connection." Doc nodded in agreement. "It's an angle we can check by talking to her neighbors. I'll do that, and maybe get a look inside her apartment."

"What else do we know about the pimp? What happened with the murder charge?"

"I'll be. Deacon, you're not going to believe this. They picked him up for the murder of his brother, another pimp. Says here that cause of death was a *subdural hematoma*, and the police thought it was a territory war. You'd have to be pretty damn cold blooded to smash in your brother's head over a few city blocks."

"What happened? How come they let him go?"

"They closed the case for lack of evidence. When he was in custody, Brown told the police that the real killer was a Mexican hooker. He vowed to find her and bring the police *her head on a platter*." Doc tapped the page, "That's an exact quote from his signed statement."

"Doc, remember what the bartender told me the night of Brown's murder? There was a woman with a heavy accent asking about me. Could this be the connection?"

"I don't know how. A woman with an accent might have had some connection to Brown, but that all happened way back in April, almost seven months ago. How could Brown be connected to the Thomas murder and more importantly, with you?"

"Who knows. At least we have a few clues. Can you go back to the bar and ask the bartender if he can remember anything else?"

"No problem. I'll go tonight."

"Doc," Deacon's features softened, his eyes filled with tears, and he lowered his voice. "I can't tell you how much what you're doing means to me. I—I don't know what I'd do without you."

"Forget it, Deac. You'd do the same for me." Doc's voice quivered like a wavering violin note. "Let's get movin'. We have a lot to do."

They secured their helmets to their travel packs. The throaty Evolution engines cranked once, and called out through straight pipes in Harley voices. Sunshine filled a crystal-clear blue sky, and reflected dully off the muddy Mississippi. They wound their way, side by side within the confines of a single lane, north on Illinois Highway 96, the *Great River Road*.

In less than an hour, Doc signaled a right turn. A small sign at the intersection announced: *Riverview Inn,* underscored by an arrow. He slowed and turned into a small paved road, which lead through the trees. The narrow artery snaked into the woods, turned to pea gravel, and became a switchback, which twisted through dense foliage. The engines chugged up the steep incline in first gear. In a clearing, atop the bluff, they found a panoramic view, which included miles of river and thousands of acres of farmland.

Six small red clapboard cabins formed a semicircle on the edge of the wooded precipice. In their center, was a small matching structure, the office and manager's residence. Each cabin, meticulously accented by a colorful array of late season flowers, was identical to the next. A thirty-year-old Oldsmobile Vista Cruiser station wagon sat in front of the office. A Corvette Roadster, its top down, sat in front of the first cabin on the right, number six.

Doc pressed his face against the rusty screen. Inside, in the shadows, a slight feminine figure bent over what appeared to be an antique brass cash register. A yellowed *OPEN* sign hung crookedly in the corner of a dusty window, smeared with a labyrinth of tiny fingerprints.

He swallowed, rolled his head clockwise once around, and opened the door. Two long steps brought him to the front of the register. The door squeaked, and bounced twice against the frame.

The young woman looked up from her work and smiled. Short dirty blonde hair framed a round, innocent face. "May I help you?" she asked. A small boy crawled noisily around the end of the scarred counter pushing a battered fire truck.

While Doc was peering through the screen, Deacon leaned back and threw his long legs across the handlebars. With his head cradled in the T-pack, he closed his eyes against shafts of sunlight that broke through uneven openings in the thinning oak leaves.

"Hi, my friend and I..." Doc motioned toward the motorcycles. *He looks like he doesn't have a care in the world.* The thought distracted Doc for a moment.

How can he be so relaxed while I'm terrified? He sighed audibly and then continued. "...we're out for a couple of weeks of peace and quiet." He towered over the miniscule woman. "We saw your sign. Do you have a vacancy?"

"Sure do. My husband and I bought this place last year. It's our dream, but no one knows we're here. You can have your pick. All the cabins have kitchenettes and two beds. How long would you like to stay?"

"I don't know. We're just livin' day-to-day. How 'bout I pay you for a week in advance, and we'll go from there?"

"That's fine. Cabins one through five are vacant. Do you have a preference? There's a honeymoon couple in six. I haven't seen them in three days. I keep thinking it's going to rain, and he'll have to put his top up. My husband works at the St. Louis airport. I run the resort with little Billy's help. Oh, listen to me carry on. You'd think I don't ever get to talk to anyone." The woman stopped, and then laughed at herself.

"Cabin one will be perfect. That'll give your newlyweds some space. Are there phones in the rooms?"

"No, sorry," she laughed again nervously. "There's a payphone on the back of this building. If you need an emergency number, you can use the office number. I'll come get you if someone calls."

"You're very kind, thanks, how much for the cabin?"

"Fifty a day or three-hundred for a week, how often would you like clean sheets?"

Doc looked at little Billy. He cooed as he made another circle. A wave of compassion swept over him, for the woman, for Deacon, and for Katherine. He wanted to protect everyone, to keep them all safe. Compassion gave way to dread. He felt inadequate; the unknown was untenable.

He refocused on the woman's childlike face. *I wonder why she came here, her husband's idea. Could she possibly have wanted to be alone with a baby on top of a bluff; her only company strangers who never leave their room, and never tell the truth about their lives? Would she have come here if she had known?* "If you clean once every three days, that'll be plenty. We'll be out sightseeing most days. I have friends in St. Louis. I may not even sleep here that much." He laid three, one-hundred-dollar bills on the counter and signed *Al Stephens* at the bottom of the registration card.

The cabin was small, decorated in an antique fishing motif, and meticulously clean. Deacon tossed his bag on the bed next to the window, then went outside, and helped Doc back the bikes up to the building. With a screwdriver and pliers from his saddlebags, he switched the Missouri Dealer plate for the purloined Illinois tag.

"Deacon, it's gettin' late. I need to get back. I'll go straight to *The Landing* and talk to the bartender tonight. Hopefully, I can find out something more about our dead pimp and the mysterious woman."

"Okay, I guess. Doc, when am I going to see or hear from you?"

"Relax, Deac, this won't be so bad. I'll call you in the morning. I don't want to call from home or the shop. Tell you what, I'll take the number of the payphone," he pointed across the parking lot. "Let's agree on a time. I'll call you from a payphone in town. If you have to call me, do it from a phone away from here, give me a number, and hang up.

"Don't use any credit cards or your name for anything. You have plenty of cash?"

"Yeah, I've got a little more than five-hundred."

"That should be plenty. If you run low, I'll bring you more. I know this all sounds very cloak and dagger. We don't know who's doin' what, and I'd rather err on the side of safety."

"You're right, like always, can we talk at eight in the morning? After that, I'll ride into Missouri and look for my parents. I'll start at the central office of the Methodist Church, which probably doesn't open before nine. Even if he's retired, or something has happened to them, the church people should know."

"Doc, one more thing, I've been thinkin'. I'd like Star to know where I am and that I'm okay. I'm sure she's worried."

"Deacon, I don't think we should tell anyone where you are, or what we're doin'. The fewer people that know the better off we'll be. This way no one has to lie to the cops but me. Kat and I can let Star know you're safe. That'll have to be enough."

"Okay," Deacon reluctantly agreed.

"Good, it's settled, until eight. You take care of you." The Harley sparked to life.

With one fluid movement, Deacon leaned over and put a trembling arm on Doc's shoulders.

Doc snapped the transmission into first gear, idled past the lonesome Corvette, and started down the hill.

A moment before he disappeared behind the crest, without looking back, he raised his left hand and made a fist.

Deacon struggled, holding back his tears. He saw Doc raise his arm; he saw the clenched fist. He understood: *Power, united we are strong; together we will prevail.*

FIFTEEN

DEACON LEANED against the red clapboard. The morning sun was beginning to devour the thin frost. He shivered, and checked his watch for the fifth time. The minute hand showed one past eight.

The payphone's rusty ring shattered the silence.

Deacon gingerly answered, "Hello."

"That you?" Doc asked.

"Course it's me. Who'd you expect, Jimmy Hoffa?"

"Very funny, just bein' cautious, no names, okay?"

"Okay. Have you talked to my lady. She all right?"

"She's fine. She called my wife and was told you're safe.

"Excellent, thanks. What about the cops, they lookin' for me?"

"'Fraid so. They've been to my house, your house, and our business. They have a warrant for your arrest."

"Jesus." Deacon supported himself against the building.

Doc waited while the news soaked in. "You, okay?" his tense voice exuded fear.

Another minute passed in silence. "I'm here," Deacon's voice cracked.

"Hang in there. We talked about this. We knew it might happen."

"That was talk; this is real. Something is actually happening to me, something that maybe can't be fixed."

"We'll get it straightened out. This isn't the end of the world. We'll prove to them and to you, that you didn't do anything."

"What are the charges?" Deacon asked.

"Rape and murder. Apparently, they haven't been able to tie you to the pimp. If I'm correctly reading between the lines, they're definitely trying to implicate you for both. We have to get on the stick. The longer you stay in hiding, the more convinced they'll be you're guilty."

"Did you talk to the barkeep last night?"

"Yeah, his story's basically what he's been sayin' all along. From the mug shots they showed him, he thinks he saw the pimp early that evening. The place was packed. He poured the guy a Scotch, neat. The girl made quite an impression. Believe it or not, he actually seemed excited when he was talking about her. He said she was hot except for a ragged scar on her left cheek. Spoke broken English. He barely understood her. She had long dark hair, dark eyes, and was wearin' a micro mini."

"Can he recall what she said?"

"She asked for you by name. Do you have any idea who she is?"

"None, if I have a split personality, I guess it's possible she would know me as that person. I've read that people with alternate personalities actually function like separate people."

"We don't even know if you have other personalities. All we know is you've had some blackouts. I see you almost every day, and you're always you. Let's stick with what we know for sure."

"The description doesn't ring a bell with me. Did he see them together, the woman and Brown?"

"He's sure they were together, at least once, near the front door. Of course, you know the bar. It's a long way across. If it was as crowded as he says, I don't know how he could have seen much. Supposedly, there was a lot of arm waving like an intense argument. Then the crowd surrounded them and blocked his view. He saw her once more, right before closing. She came in and went straight to the bathroom. Somethin' else odd, when she came back, she was wearin' jeans."

"Did he see the pimp after the fight?"

"Nope, that was the last time. He didn't even see him leave."

"What'd he say about me? Did I act normal? He's seen me in there plenty."

"He said you were outta-your-mind drunk. He offered to call you a cab, but you blew him off. When he told you there was a good lookin' woman askin' about you, you made a rude remark and walked away."

"What'd I say?"

"It doesn't matter. You were drunk."

"I want to understand my mental state. Word for word, what did I say?"

"You said something like: 'Cool, maybe I'll just fuck the bitch.'" Deacon's stomach was trying to eat itself; his skin burned. "Doc, why do you bother?" he shouted. "I'm hopeless, not worth savin'. I'm not worth your spit!"

"Calm down. Come on, if off color remarks were a felony, most of the population would be in jail. You can't handle the booze, that's all. Let's get back to business, and no names."

"Sorry, it's just that—sometimes I can't believe the things I've said and done. Maybe I really do need professional help."

"I'm not a judge of anything, buddy, but I believe in you. Because of that, because of who I know you really are, I'm certain you didn't do this. One other thing, do you know anything about a black van?"

"A black Ford van, maybe, why?"

"The bartender told me that every night you were in there, including the night of the murder, he saw an old black van in the lot. He noticed it because it stuck out like a sore thumb. How'd you know it was a Ford?"

"Because, I remember it, I even told Ka... your wife, about it. Hell, I don't know anyone who owns a van."

"I'm sure it's nothin', maybe a vagrant livin' in his van.

"I haven't been to the last vic's apartment yet. I intend to go today. Are you ready to hit the road?"

"I found the address of the church's district office in the phone book, and I'm ready to ride."

A computerized voice broke in: "Deposit seventy-five cents for three minutes."

"I'm outta change," Doc said hurriedly. "I'll call you in the morning, same time, same place."

"Right, 'til then, good luck," the connection dropped. Deacon Jones was suddenly and sadly alone.

The plump secretary was pleasant enough although she seemed impatient. The district office of the Methodist Church was quiet. Deacon was the only visitor. He checked his watch. It was five minutes before twelve and probably her lunchtime. He lied nervously telling her he was Reverend John Jones's nephew from California.

She lumbered over to a metal file cabinet. Within a minute, she returned with a thick, tattered file. She opened the folder, looked up, and smiled. "Isn't this a coincidence," she said politely. "You just came from California, and your uncle lives in California, Missouri."

"Yeah, a coincidence," Deacon breathed a sigh of relief. He heard Tina's voice the day she broke up with him. *Don't ask a question you can't stand the answer to.* With a fearful voice, he timidly asked. "What about my aunt, my Aunt Grace?"

The woman answered without looking up. "This lists them both at the address." She tore a page from her note pad, surreptitiously glanced at her watch, and quickly copied the address.

Deacon left the office with the neatly folded paper and mixed emotions.

State Highway 50 wound through the Missouri countryside. Vibrant fall foliage created a colorful collage in bright red, orange, and yellow against a vivid blue sky. After two hours on the road, Deacon easily found the aging white clapboard parsonage. He stashed the Low Rider, just off the county road, a quarter of a mile away. Two hundred meters from the weathered house, he hid behind a sprawling oak tree. A lone, faded green Chevrolet Impala sat in the driveway. The last time he had seen the car, it was nearly new.

The house was still. While he waited, Deacon methodically studied every detail of the property. Beyond the house, he glimpsed an out-of-place shape. He pushed his sunglasses down his nose and strained to see. A burning pain shot through his body. The rough bark of the tree scraped his back as he sank to the ground. He rubbed his eyes and looked again. He was not mistaken. It was a black Ford van.

Sixty minutes passed; still no movement in the house. The first eighteen years of Deacon's life wormed their way through his memory. He tried desperately to seize upon the good times, but failed. For every good recollection, there was something bad attached, trumpeted by a visit to his father's study. He battled to imagine his father smiling or laughing. Instead, he saw him towering overhead, arms crossed, glaring.

The front door opened. Deacon was shocked back to awareness from the distasteful regurgitation. He held his breath. Two relics appeared on the porch.

The old man, hunched over, limped stiffly. A black, threadbare suit hung loosely over his emaciated frame. A short, narrow tie lay haphazardly against a wrinkled white shirt. The jacket of his Sunday best pulled open as he walked. He wore baggy pants, braced by clip-on suspenders, plus a belt. A rumpled, familiar, black fedora perched in stark contrast upon long, thin wisps of snow-white hair.

"Jesus." Deacon whispered.

Mrs. Jones kept stride one-step behind her husband. Her brown, belted shirtwaist dress buttoned snugly around her neck. A vinyl purse swung from her right arm. Bluish-white, meticulously braided hair wound tightly in a familiar bun. Deep wrinkles marred her face.

Deacon Jones found his parents wearing strangers' faces, a couple who had never known happiness. They called him James David, referred to each other in formal terms, and spoke of themselves in third person.

Out of character, Mrs. Jones walked to the driver's door. The Reverend traced the passenger side of the car with his hands until he reached the door.

"I'll be damned. The old man is blind." A gust of wind swallowed Deacon's words. The sprawling oak's sparse leaves rustled. Unexpectedly, he wanted to be at his father's side. A powerful urge tempted him to rush over, take the old man's hand, and help, again to be a part of their life, to be their son, and to seek their comfort.

He lifted himself from the dry grass and started toward the car. An apathetic force stopped him in his tracts. Pride, shame, or maybe even fear, whatever it was, it paralyzed him.

Yellow *POLICE LINE DO NOT CROSS* tape
stretched in an X across the apartment's doorway.
Doc wormed into lightweight, leather riding gloves.
He glanced down the empty hall, slit the door seal,
and tried the knob. The door was unlocked. *Someone
was a little careless* he chuckled as he entered.

Cynthia Ann Thomas was a secretary at the nearby
brewery. A well-worn sofa and mismatched chair
greeted Doc as he entered the dingy living room. A
small round table, surrounded by battered wooden
chairs sat in the edge of the combination kitchen and
dining area.

A kitchen counter protruded a short distance into
the room, a separation between cooking and eating.
On the counter top, Doc found something he had only
seen in movies. Masking tape formed a crude circle
on the Formica surface.

A repugnant must permeated the rooms. Family
photographs, in quality frames, dotted predominately-
bare walls. Doc turned a hand-rubbed walnut frame in
his hands. "A gift from Mom and Dad, no doubt," he
said to the older couple in the photo.

A mirrored dresser constructed of a plastic-coated
laminate was the most prominent piece of furniture in
the bleak bedroom. The front corner of the top surface
nearest the doorway was broken and missing.

Tape, in the uneven shape of a body, marked the
bare mattress much like the taped circle on the
kitchen counter. A dark bloodstain splayed out, well
beyond the adhesive boundary, in a macabre shape.

The dresser consisted of two stacks of four
drawers each, which Doc systematically searched.
The top left contained socks and stockings. Next

down was underwear. Most of the shabby bikini panties were cotton. Beneath the panties, Doc found a ribbon-tied bundle of greeting cards. The contents of two more drawers down on the left and the top three on the right were nondescript.

Carefully organized with rows of silk undergarments, the last drawer on the bottom right was different from the rest. In the corner, were four large red scarves neatly bundled and identically tied with a single knot near one end and a four-inch diameter self-loop in the other. Doc held a scarf at arm's length. The sturdy silk cord spanned thirty-six inches. He surveyed the fabric. Beyond his reflection in the wide mirror, four bedposts stood four-feet above the soiled mattress. He slipped one of the loops over a turned finial; it fit perfectly. "I'll be damned," he whispered. "Our secretary did like kinky sex."

Near the back of the drawer, and completely out of context, he found a plastic bag of individually wrapped chocolates. He lifted the bag; what was beneath captivated his attention. Doc had seen dildos before, but nothing so big, or lifelike. It was thick, flesh-color, and approximately eighteen inches long with the head of a penis on each end. The soft, flexible latex material was like real skin. *I'm glad I'm wearin' gloves.* He hastily dropped the toy in the drawer.

His hand brushed a mostly hidden velvet box. Inside was a yellow-gold tennis bracelet set with dozens of brilliant cut diamonds. Tucked in the lid was a neatly folded card with an elegant inscription inside: *Precious kitten, I hope you will cherish these stones as much as I cherish your love. Their brilliance are overshadowed only by your own. All my love, B.*

Doc listened at the door until he was sure there was no one in the hallway. He slipped out and walked casually down the hall. He stopped at the next apartment and knocked.

A single feminine eye peered through the narrow opening between the door and its jamb. "Can I help you?" The security chain stretched tight. She appeared frightened.

"Hi, I hope so. My name is Al Stephens," he made up the story as he went. "I work over at the brewery with Cindy Thomas."

"Then, you know she's dead," the young woman replied flatly, and began to close the door.

"Wait, please, I need your help."

She stopped. "Sorry, I can't help you. I hardly knew Cindy."

"The thing is I feel like a heel askin'. I loaned her my CD collection. Now, I don't know how to get 'em back."

"Call the cops." The woman said curtly.

"I'm afraid I'll never get them back if the cops get involved. I just thought, maybe, you might know some of her family or friends, someone who could help me without a big fuss. I'm a forklift driver in the warehouse. Those CDs were a big investment," Doc said dramatically. "I thought when I loaned them to her, it'd be a way to get to know her. I wanted to ask her out. She was so pretty."

"I hate to break the news to you, friend, but I don't think she had family around here. Least ways I ain't seen nobody who looked like a mom or dad go through her door. As far as her goin' out with ya, I'm afraid you aren't a very good judge of people."

"I don't understand."

"I ain't sayin' anything about what kind of a person she was. I'm tryin' to tell ya she played for the other team."

"What?"

"She was a dike, you know, a lesbian."

"Wow, I had no idea," Doc did not have to act surprised. "Did she have a girlfriend? Did you know any of the people who visited her? Someone might have a key and be able to help me."

The tension in the chain relaxed. "My neighbor must have been quite the lover." The eye in the crack sparkled at the sound of its own voice. "She moved in 'bout a year ago; there's been a steady stream of gals in and out of there ever since."

"There was no one special? Someone you would have seen often?"

"Now that you mention it, there was. I've seen the same blonde every couple of days for the past, I'm not sure, maybe six or eight weeks."

"Did you ever speak to her or hear Cindy call her by name?"

"Did I ever!" Her voice raised a decibel, the half-face twisted into a frown, and the eye squinted. "I saw 'em kissin' in the hall. The blonde, a real looker by the way, called Cindy, 'Cat.'"

"What did Cindy call the woman?"

"Bridget, I'm pretty sure."

"What'd Bridget drive?"

"That's easy. She nearly backed into me once. Her car, now that was the odd thing," she added in an uncertain tone.

"Odd like how?"

"I don't know much about cars, but that gal was drivin' a brand new Benz, dark blue. Why would a good lookin' broad with that kind of money be hangin' with a secretary? I guess it takes all kinds."

"Besides good lookin', what did she look like? Can you describe her?"

"Yeah, sure, I bumped into her a couple of times out front before I knew she was seein' Cindy. She was a lot taller'n me, probably close to 5'7". Her blonde hair hung down past her shoulders. She had big blue eyes, a tan I would kill for, and great boobs, prob'ly Ds."

Doc held his breath. Stunned by the familiar description, he stared at the eye.

"Mister, that all you need?" the woman asked impatiently.

"Her voice, what kind of voice did she have?"

"Very distinct, raspy, really sexy. No wonder Cindy was…"

Doc spun around, and started down the stairs.

"You want me to give that woman your number if she happens to come back?" the eye called after him.

"No thanks," Doc called over his shoulder without looking, "I'll be back."

Unhurriedly, Grace Jones drove toward town.

Deacon gave her a safe head start, and then followed. He cast a final glance toward the house as he passed. *The study's probably in the front corner.*

He thought as he opened the throttle to escape the memory.

The sign on the building read *CALIFORNIA CARE, Personalized Care for the Aged*. The Joneses took nearly five minutes to cross the tarmac and enter through the front door.

A few blocks down on a side street, Deacon hid the Harley between two cars. He strolled to the corner, and then followed the main street to the front of the red brick structure. He paused, shifted his weight nervously, and strained to see through the plate-glass windows. Reflective glare from the mid-afternoon sun blocked his view.

It was impossible to cross the lawn discretely, and the sidewalk did not pass directly in front of the windows. The only option was to enter blindly and hope that the Joneses were not standing inside the door. Nonchalantly, he entered the foyer and pretended to read flyers posted on a bulletin board.

A small opaque glass panel made a metal on metal sound as it slid open. A pear-shaped face appeared. "May I help you?" The nurse asked with an indifferent tone.

Deacon froze. "Hi, I'm waitin' for my sister," he answered apprehensively. "We would like to see your facility. I can't imagine what's happened. She's already late and that's very unlike her."

"Do you have an appointment?"

"I don't know, not unless my sister made one. Do we need an appointment? All we want is a general tour."

"We always try to schedule our visitors so we don't disrupt the residents."

"Gosh, I'm sorry. We can come back." Deacon grasped for an excuse to stay in the lobby for a few more minutes. "Do you mind if I wait here 'til she arrives?"

"Tell you what. We aren't too busy today. If your sister gets here in the next fifteen minutes, even if she didn't make an appointment, I'll be happy to show you around."

"That's very kind, thanks. Can I wait right here?"

"Wait in the atrium if you like. There's a sitting area close to the door. You'll be more comfortable."

"Great, thanks." Deacon tried to act pleased. *I hope I'm not walking into somethin'*, he thought. His stomach gnawed. The door buzzed.

Silk plants, sprinkled amid various arrangements of sofas and chairs, lined the walls of the common area. Residents sat in smalls groups on furniture and in wheelchairs scattered throughout the room. Carelessly strewn about, walkers and canes looked like modern welded sculptures.

On the far side of the spacious, well-lit room, a glass wall separated the atrium from an open-air patio surrounded by the building. French doors, propped open, welcomed a pleasant fall breeze to breathe life into an otherwise clinical atmosphere.

"You a biker?" the masculine voice cracked with age like the twang of a tired fiddle string.

Deacon scanned the equally wrinkled faces, a dozen, separate experiences, a lifetime of history for each. *To know what they know,* he thought, *would be to know it all.* He paused trying to see past each visage to the individual who lie beneath. Shakespeare's words, which had secretly fascinated

Deacon as a child, applied to the ancient faces: *"A book where men may read strange matters."*

As though shoved, a wheelchair darted from the wall. The occupant's face was brown and weathered like dry pigskin. Intelligent blue eyes shone like bright marbles against a washed out tapestry.

"I said, you a biker?" An arthritic hand pointed at the Harley-Davidson patch sewn on Deacon's jacket.

"Yes. Yes, sir, I suppose that's what some people would call me." Deacon said respectfully. "I love to ride my motorcycle. I hope you don't consider that a bad thing." It occurred to him that a little light conversation with a resident might serve well as cover. He glanced nervously around. His parents were nowhere in sight.

"Hell, no," the old man answered loudly. "I don't think it's a bad thing."

Several residents looked up.

"Shi-it, in my day, I was one hell-raisin' son-of-a-bitch."

Deacon, caught off guard by the language, was empathetic for the misshapen form. *Wonder how long it's been since he raised any hell.* "Did you ride a bike?" Deacon asked while simultaneously catching a glimpse of the Joneses strolling across the courtyard with another couple. The two women walked arm-in-arm talking.

The old man seemed unaware of Deacon's refocused attention. He continued in his loud, cracking voice. "Hell, I di'nt jus' ride a motasickle, I rode Hawleys all ma life." Hit and miss teeth distorted his crude speech. "Some a da boys rode Injuns. I was most awways a Hawley man. My first sickle was a Injun, a farty-five Scout. It was damn dawg. So, I sood it, and bought me a Hawley sevnty-foor. Now, tha' bastird 'ould strectly hawl ass."

"I bet," Deacon tried to sound interested. The movements of his parents captivated his attention. He thought it odd that they both talked with great animation to their same sex conversant, but never to each other or the other person of the opposite gender. The two men, completely immersed in an intense discussion, communicated with sensational gestures.

The women appeared much more gentile. Occasionally, one would squeeze the other's arm in such a way that convinced Deacon they were close friends. *Funny*, he thought, *I can't remember a time when my parents even had friends, especially not good friends.*

Deacon followed the old biker's colorful recounting closely enough to make an occasional one or two-word comment. From where he sat, he was able to observe the courtyard unnoticed.

Without warning, the foursome turned toward the building entrance. He had only enough time to lower his eyes. They walked through the doorway and passed him. Neither his mother nor his father even glanced in his direction. They were so close he could hear their concurrent conversations. His mother and the other woman were talking about plants and soil. His father's booming voice sliced through the room, and dragged Deacon back in time, twelve years. He delivered the diatribe in his practiced march like the measured tick of a metronome.

"But, Reverend," the other man asked in a timid voice, "how can you speak with such conviction about the feelings of God? I have never seen it so written." His formation and choice of words convinced Deacon that this man was, or had been, a minister.

The Reverend continued unruffled. "God has spoken to me. My words are His, perfect and divine. They are His flawless recollection. Brother, what I am saying to you is *the Word of God.*"

Some things never change, Deacon thought disappointed. The Reverend Jones was still the same pompous, pious man. A sad, mental breeze swept over Deacon.

"Sir, excuse me." The nurse, who had been behind the glass, interrupted the old biker.

Ignoring her attempt, he continued his recollections. "Once, we took over a little town in South Dakota for a two day binge. Next year we went back and it turned into a hell of a party'. I hear tell it's still goin' on toda…"

The nurse did not let him finish his sentence. In a loud voice, she addressed Deacon. "Do you think your sister's comin'? My shift is over, and I really need to get goin'. I've gotta pick up my baby girl from the sitter."

"I can't imagine where my sister is. We'll call and make an appointment for another day."

"That'll be fine. We'll look forward to your call." The woman sounded sincere.

Deacon noticed her left hand. A white line where a ring had recently been marked her finger. "Thanks very much for your consideration." He glanced furtively around. His parents, along with their companions, had disappeared down the hall.

The Low Rider's left foot peg scraped the pavement as Deacon leaned through a tight turn. He breathed a sigh of relief. The rapidly falling sun lit the road ahead in convoluted shades of orange and yellow. He leaned back, his right hand rested lightly on the throttle, listening to the V-twin engine as its song echoed across the empty highway. He thought of the story of the prodigal son and wished someone would butcher a fatted calf for him.

He passed a payphone. Star's face popped into his mind. He pushed on into falling darkness. Doc's warning continuously cycled through his mind. *Don't make contact with anyone.* He had agreed. He argued with himself. After all, it was Star. *I owe it to her,* he reasoned. *She would never do anything to hurt me.*

The payphone called to him; over the howling wind, it screamed his name. He slowed to a rolling U-turn. Doc's persistent tone echoed in his head. He reversed the turn and continued eastbound.

The third payphone, which also knew his name, was irresistible. "What the hell," he shouted to the sky. "There's no danger in a five-minute call to the love of my life!" He braked hard and made a tight sweeping one hundred and eighty degree turn in the middle of the two-lane tarmac.

A busy signal answered. Deacon depressed the switch-hook and dialed again, still busy. He glared at the shiny black and chrome instrument. *This isn't right,* he thought. *I promised Doc I wouldn't do this. The busy signal is a sign; I should leave this alone.*

He spun on his heel and headed toward his bike. Twenty seconds later, he was rolling smoothly out of the parking lot away from the device. Instinctively, with a series of fluid motions that required some action from nearly every appendage, he stopped. Simultaneously, he killed the engine, extended the kickstand, turned off the ignition, and gyrated off the leather seat.

"Sweetie, it's me," he began before she could answer, "you all right?"

"Geez, doll, I'm so happy to hear from you. I've been worried sick. The question is, are you all right?"

"I'm fine. Just missing you too much, that's all."

"Deac, where are you, what've you been doin'?"

"Right now, I'm somewhere in God-only-knows-where po-dunk Missouri. Star, I saw my parents today."

A prolonged silence followed. "Really, did you talk to them?"

"No, I just watched from a distance, pretty close actually. If they saw me, which I doubt, they didn't recognize me."

"I suppose that's good. Did you want to talk to them?"

"I don't know. I'm just not sure. At one point, I thought I did. I heard them. My father was talkin' just like—I mean in the same self-righteous way that he always did. I just couldn't. I don't want to talk about them. What's happenin' there, any news?"

"If you mean have the police been here lookin' for you, I'm afraid so, several times."

"What'd you tell them?"

"I told them you just disappeared without telling me anything. They said they were lookin' for you in connection with a homicide, nothin' more."

"I wish I knew what they know. Our inside source has dried up."

"What do you mean?"

"I shouldn't say more. Doc thinks it's better if you don't know the details. We don't want to compromise you."

"Anything that applies to me should be my decision." She responded sharply. "If I have to lie to the police, it's no big deal. They aren't going to torture me. Doll, tell me," she demanded.

"I can't. Really, I shouldn't. I told Doc I wouldn't."

"At least tell me where you're stayin'."

"I can't, it's for your own good."

"Doll, please…" she cooed.

SIXTEEN

THE BRIDGE across the Mississippi was lit bright as day with artificial light too yellow to be the sun. The rumble of Deacon Jones's finely tuncd Harley-Davidson echoed against the faded green steel structure as he headed east. At the traffic light he turned left, north on the *Great River Road*. Emotionally and physically exhausted, every nerve in his body was on a sort of numb alert.

The nearly deserted highway felt uncertain. An ethereal black ribbon stretched into the night. Occasionally, distant headlights cast ghostly shadows upon the littered surface of the muddy river. Matte finish galvanized guardrail bordered the black tarmac. Deacon slowed to twenty-five miles per hour. In one practiced motion, he loosed his chinstrap and removed his helmet. Cool night air wove its fingers through thick brown hair.

This ride, this night, was different; Deacon ground his teeth. The further north he rode, the tighter the knot in his stomach became. The clear, moonless sky held its bright stars close. One broke free and shot across the sky. In a millisecond, the earth's atmosphere devoured it. A vacuous fear gnawed at his soul. *Why is this happening to me? Dear God, what have I done?* He questioned the Deity who is night and all things, both of this world and beyond. For the thousandth time, he mentally worked his way backward through the years trying to remember every detail. He began during that period of his life before he left his parents. He remembered similar experiences full of trepidation, of impending doom. He had felt like this, exactly like this every time, just before the Reverend summoned him to his study.

His angst increased with each passing mile. The bright headlight illuminated the familiar metal sign, *Riverview Resort, 4 miles*. Still nothing felt right. A nagging voice in the back of his mind began to shout. *You're riding into something!*

Deacon relaxed his grip on the throttle. *Why no cars?* he wondered, feeling like the last man on earth. *How long had it been since he met oncoming traffic?* He tried to remember. He checked the rearview mirror again, and still there were no lights. He glanced to his left. Even the river was devoid of traffic. The strange night, the aloneness, and the sense of impending doom were untenable.

A mile from the turnoff Deacon recognized the terrain and instinctively coasted onto the shoulder. He shifted into neutral, killed the engine, and rolled to the wide bottom of the deep ditch. Totally hidden from the road, he left the machine, and walked the last mile. When the trench became too shallow, he climbed northeast into the forest. The rocky terrain was steep. With short, labored breathing, Deacon quietly worked his way up the incline. At the base of a low, sheer bluff, he stopped. Artificial lights glowed from atop the stone precipice.

"My cabin," he whispered breathlessly. "If there's nothin' up there, I'm gonna feel pretty stupid. Better safe than sorry, the exercise will do me good," he reasoned.

The desolate resort was deadly quiet. Still, nothing seemed out of the ordinary. Only Deacon's uncanny premonition held him back. He peered over a boulder to the top of the bluff. He had a clear view of the cabins and the parking area. The Corvette was gone; there were no cars in sight. One yellow light glowed next to each cabin door, except for one, Deacon's cabin. Three bluish-purple bug zappers buzzed and occasionally popped. Deacon felt relative compassion for the tiny unsuspecting insects. He wondered if he was crazy. *Do sane people care about insects?*

He carefully studied the outline of the buildings. He probably would not have seen the first man had he not scratched his head at exactly the same moment that Deacon's eyes traced the vertical line of that particular cabin. Deacon froze; his heart fought against the wall of his chest. The man dropped his hand and vanished.

One at a time, he found six men. *Police detectives*, he thought.

On the cold, gray-black river bluff in the dark, pre-winter woods, time had no cadence. *How long 'til daylight?* He wondered not risking the movement necessary to remove the chained pocket watch from his jeans. He worried that the polished stainless steel, or phosphorescent clock hands, might reflect a bit of light. Apprehensions hammered his brain like a blacksmith trying to destroy his own work.

Deacon's arms and legs ached; frigid air penetrated to the bone. He wiggled his toes. His feet were numb. He wished for the men to leave. There was no movement around the cabins. It was clear they were awaiting their prey. Deacon was equally sure he was the prey.

How did they find this place? His mind badgered him. *There's no way they followed Doc. He hasn't been back. We've used payphones. Maybe they tapped my phone.*

Darkness overstayed its welcome in the too long night. Indecision became the enemy. If he remained, the first light of day would reveal him. In the dark, he easily blended into his surroundings. Daylight would steal his advantage. To slip away unnoticed, it had to be soon.

Deacon made a mental list of each man's position and calculated every one against his field of view. He noted the devotion with which each individual had manned his post. The odds appeared in his favor. The men lay hidden from anyone who came up the narrow, winding driveway. On that thoroughfare, they concentrated their watch. He reasoned that the two men who were completely out of his sight were of almost no threat. The others would only see him if they diverted their attention from the entrance. They were obviously growing weary becoming easier to study. Their animation increased in proportion to the mounting hours.

I arrived unnoticed, he concluded. *My way in will also be my best way out.* He took a deep breath, made one last visual sweep, and began a meticulous—measured retreat. Deacon took one cautious step; a sharp pain shot up his leg. He checked the four men. No one had moved. He took another step.

When the last suit disappeared from view, he increased his pace. Sunrise began to splash through the trees. It was still more than two hundred yards to the base of the hill, plus a mile to his bike. He covered his face and launched headlong through the heavy under-brush, ignoring the stinging branches that whipped his brittle skin.

It was impossible to push the six hundred pound machine through the spongy, frost-laden grass up the steep embankment to the road. Deacon was reticent to start the loud engine; there was no choice. He threw his right leg over the motorcycle, crushing an empty beer can under foot. Deacon cringed at the loud crunch. He gulped, and hit the start button. At barely more than an idle, man and machine climbed diagonally out of the ditch.

Good, no traffic, he congratulated himself. A quick U-turn and he rolled out south toward St. Louis. The stubborn engine warmed slowly, throbbing and trembling at low speed. Deacon guardedly twisted the throttle. The exhaust barked proportionately. He continuously clicked through every gear until his speed was a steady thirty-five miles per hour in fifth gear. The illuminated analog tachometer showed only seventeen hundred RPM. The emanating rhythm seemed unbearably loud.

The first two miles took less than four minutes, two hundred odd seconds, which seemed like an eternity. With five miles in his rearview mirror, Deacon breathed a deep sigh of relief. He opened the throttle until the speedometer, whose internal light source diminished by the light of day, showed ninety. He looked warily back. No one was following.

The phone rang seven times before Doc awakened. "You all right?" he asked as he rubbed the sleep from his eyes.

"I'm fine. I had a close call. Did I wake you? Sorry for calling so early, I didn't want you to ring the payphone at the cabins. Everything is crashing down around me."

"The time doesn't matter, but we should be careful. We talked about an alternate payphone in the city. Go there; I'll call you in an hour. D, keep the faith." Without waiting for a reply, Doc hung up and quickly dressed in jeans, a tee shirt, and a plain leather jacket. *No colors today*, he thought.

Deacon answered the payphone before the first ring finished.

"You okay?" Doc anxiously asked for the second time in as many calls. "Yeah, I'm all right, but the cops found me. They found the resort."

"How do you know, are you sure?"

"Yeah, I'm sure. When I went back there last night, they were waitin'."

"How'd you get away? There's nothin' on the scanner."

"I don't know. It was weird. I just had a feelin'. It kept eatin' at me. The closer I got, the stronger it was. I hid my bike and climbed up to the cabins through the woods. They were hidin' and waitin', six plainclothes. I was careful. They never saw me."

"Sounds like that intuition of yours is finally payin' off. We need to meet. You sure you weren't followed?"

"Positive, no cars were behind me or in front. They say the good tails stay in front. Is somethin' wrong? Do you have bad news?"

"Nothin's wrong, well, nothin' more than that which is inherently wrong with all of this. Let's just meet. I'll tell you everything then, okay?"

"Shit, Doc, don't do this to me. You know I hate it. My father always made me wait for my punishment. He knew the waiting was worse than the punishment itself."

"Sorry, I don't mean to be punitive. God knows you've been through enough. It's just somethin' I'd rather say in person."

"That does it! I can't stand it. Spit it out. What happened?"

"There's no easy way to say this. There's been another murder."

Deacon propped himself against the phone.

"You still there," Doc asked. "Did you hear what I said?"

"I'm here," Deacon answered with a shaky voice. "But look, there are murders in the city all the time, probably every day." He said hopefully. "This doesn't mean it has anything to do with me, or the first two for that matter. Does it?"

"You're right. There are crimes in the city every day. Probably a lot more than we hear about, but they don't all seem to follow a particular pattern."

"What pattern? Are you sayin'—you talkin' decapitation?"

"No, this one had biblical significance." Doc paused. "It was another woman."

"How do you know it was from scripture?"

"D, let's finish this in person. Please, can we meet somewhere?" Doc sounded anxious.

"Sure, we'll meet, but you know I'm not hangin' up or movin' from this spot 'til you tell me the whole fuckin' story."

"Okay, whatever, fine, fuck! It was a stripper from *PT's*. A cop checkin' the parkin' lot for drugs found her." Doc began to speak rapidly. "She'd been raped, shaved bald, and beaten."

"No fuckin' way! Where was her hair?" Deacon asked without a pause.

"Hell, what the fuck, I don't know. I guess it was still in the fucking car. Who cares? We're lookin' for a psychopath. He took it with him, or it was all over the car. There's no tellin'."

"Doc, why'd you say it has something to do with the Bible? No offense, but you're not exactly a Bible scholar."

"I just think it sounds like the shit your old man made you memorize when he shaved your head." Doc paused, several seconds passed. "Deacon, what did the Reverend do with your hair?"

Deacon ignored the question. "We've gotta find out what happened to her hair. It makes a big fuckin' difference. Meet me in an hour." Deacon heard his own voice change. It was cold and matter-of-fact. "Can you make some calls, and see what else you can find out?"

"I'll try; I've got a friend at the *Post*. I'll see if she can help. Where do ya wanna meet?"

"Remember the place south on the river, the place where I used to go to think?"

"Yeah, I know where it is. I'll be there in an hour."

An hour and fifteen minutes later, Doc found the deserted rock quarry. To the east, loaded barges were creeping up the Mississippi. He pushed his Harley through a gap between the fence and the end of the locked gate.

Deacon, stretched out on top of his motorcycle, had his eyes tightly closed against the bright fall sun.

Why in the hell is Deacon ridin' Widowmaker? Doc wondered. *Does he wanna get caught? This is too fuckin' risky.* He rode closer, and was relieved to see that Deacon had switched license plates. Widowmaker wore the borrowed Illinois plate. Doc recalled the first time he had seen Deacon lay on top of his motorcycle. *He's a biker's biker, born to the wind.*

Deacon cradled himself, comfortably, in the concave leather seat. His buttocks rested on the base of the gas tank. His legs, crossed at the ankles, extended across the handlebars. The lick-and-stick buddy-seat supported his neck.

Doc rolled to a stop and killed his engine.

Deacon lifted his right leg, bent his knee to ninety degrees, and rolled to the left. He landed gracefully on the firm, powdery surface of the quarry floor. *"¿Que pasa?"* He nonchalantly asked.

Standing, Doc balanced his upright machine between his legs. Anger welled up, and his face flushed. "Deacon, what in the hell is the matter with you? Do you wanna get caught?"

Deacon opened his mouth to speak; his face flushed crimson. "What, what have I done now, Doc?" He asked sadly.

The look on his face and the sound of his voice softened Doc. "It's your bike, man. Why are you ridin' Widowmaker? The cops are bound to have a description. Hell, everybody knows your bike."

"Shit, Doc, I'm sorry. Don't be upset with me." He gulped down a breath. "It's just—it's just that—" he stammered. "I felt so alone. I needed something familiar. I know it sounds stupid; ridin' Widowmaker comforts me."

"I overreacted. I'm sorry." Doc said with compassion. "I'm just worried about you gettin' caught before we get this whole fuckin' mess figured out. If you have to turn yourself in, I want it to be on your terms."

"You're right." Deacon visually traced the sheer white quarry wall three-hundred-feet to its uppermost edge. "It feels like any minute could be my last. My life is over; I'm just waitin' for the end. If I have to go, I don't want to go alone."

Doc followed Deacon's line of sight. A switchback construction road connected the quarry floor to the top of the pit. Deacon had once mentioned that when it was his time, if he could choose his own terms, he wanted to cash out in a ball of fire. A fall from the top of the quarry to bottom, man and machine, would definitely create a fireball.

"Deacon, you've gotta put that kind of shit outta your mind. We're gonna solve this."

Deacon dismounted and stood toe-to-toe with Doc. "I wanna believe that, but it's more likely you've got more bad news." His words were certain; his tone was weak. "What else do you know? It's gettin' worse, isn't it."

"I wish I could tell you somethin' different, but I'm afraid you're right. It looks bad." Doc laid his hand on Deacon's back. After a minute, he stepped back, removed his sunglasses, and looked deep into Deacon's blood-shot eyes.

Deacon squinted against the glare of the sun. "Did you talk to your friend at the *Post*?"

"Yeah, she was workin' on this story. That's why I'm late."

"What'd she say?"

"She had a few answers, the who and why are things nobody knows."

"What about the hair, did they find it?"

"Not a single strand was found in the car. She was thirty-four, a single mom with a teenage son. Her stage name was Houston. Her real name was Tina somethin'. She lived somewhere out in the Ozarks— maybe your old stompin' grounds."

"Tina, thirty-four," Deacon repeated pensively.

"When I heard about the hair, it reminded me of how your father punished you by shaving your head. Didn't you tell me that your old man left your hair on a piece of plastic that he had spread on the floor?"

"Yes. Later he put my hair in the trash. The scripture he made me memorize says the hair was cast away." Deacon staggered backward and steadied himself on his motorcycle.

"What else did your reporter friend tell you?" He asked winded. "When'd it happen?"

Doc helplessly watched his friend struggle with regurgitated emotions. "Sometime after midnight, night before last, she was completely naked in the back seat of her car. Deac, I have to ask. It happened during the only night you slept at the resort." Doc posed the question timidly. "Did you leave there at any time?"

"No, I stayed in my cabin all night. You know, Doc, I haven't slept well for a long time. With my history, who knows? We shouldn't base anything on what I remember."

"True, but we have to start with what you know." Doc tried to sound convincing. "If you think you were there all night, that's good enough for me. Anyway, the victim was a popular dancer. She left the club at midnight. Reportedly, as far as her customers go, there was nothin' really out of the ordinary. The bouncer told Janice, my reporter friend, there were plenty of women and men there, some couples, mostly single guys. The manager said it was typical, a busy night.

"A minute ago you seemed interested in her name and age. Does that mean something to you?"

"I dunno, probably not. It's just that a long time ago, I lost my virginity to an older married girl, Tina. We had a thing and she broke it off. She broke my heart. I haven't seen her in eleven years. The age sounds right, and she had a little boy. I'm sure it's just a coincidence. What else do you know?"

"She was raped. They found traces of semen and vaginal bruising." Doc paused. "The most bizarre thing is that the killer wrote on her head in red lipstick."

"What kind of writing?"

"I know what he wrote, but who knows what it means. It was just a letter and a series of numbers like a prison ID number or somethin'. Maybe he's an escaped con taunting the cops. That might explain why he shaved her. You know, some guy gets deloused and shaved in the joint, and when he gets out, that's all he can think about. It's far fetched, I know. So is writing on a dead woman's head.

"The cause of death, at least in the preliminary investigation, was from blunt force trauma. The cops are speculating that he used a club or a baseball bat, something like that."

"Or a rod," Deacon murmured.

"What?"

"You know, a rod, like in the Bible, *spare the rod and spoil the child.* My father used to say that to my mother and me all the time. What letter and numbers exactly?"

Doc pulled a roughly torn scrap of paper from his pocket. Crudely scratched on the yellow paper in blue ink were six characters:

J72829

"Well, I'll be damned," Deacon began. "I'll be damned. I'll be damned." He paused. "It's not someone's ID number. You were right the first time, it's scripture."

"How can you tell? Aren't all of the books of the Bible named after some disciple or somethin'?"

"For the most part, yes, and I know this one. I know it by heart. You hit the nail on the head when you associated the shaving with my father. He made me memorize that scripture, word-for-word. It's Jeremiah 7, verses 28 and 29, J72829." Deacon stopped, closed his eyes, and tilted his head to the bright sun; it canvassed his face. He appeared to be mentally searching for something. Doc noticed rapid movements beneath his eyelids as in the Rapid Eye Movement stage of paradoxical sleep.

Deacon began to speak in an unwavering monotone like the rote speech of a ten year old. *"And you shall say to them, 'This is the nation that did not obey the voice of the Lord their God, and did not accept discipline; truth has perished; it is cut off from their lips. Cut off your hair and cast it away; raise a lamentation on the bare heights, for the Lord has rejected and forsaken the generation of his wrath.'*

"Doc, this is too weird, it can't all be coincidental. The only two people who could possibly do this are my father or me. I saw *him* yesterday. He's not capable of doing anything, other than forcing his opinion on everyone around him. In fact, I think he's nearly blind. That leaves only me. It can only be me."

"Wait a minute, bro. You're not giving up that easy. I won't let you. True, it's all pretty fucking strange, but other people believe the same as your father. You said yourself there were always many people around the church. What'd you move, five or six times while you were growing up? Even if there were only a hundred-fifty or so people in each church, that's close to a thousand total. Some of them had to know about your relationship with your old man. It's hard to hide that kind of dysfunction. Your mother is one. She knew everything, and what about the guy and his kid with the puppy? Your father threatened to cut it in half, didn't he? Hell, Deac, maybe that girl grew up, became a psycho, and decided to ruin your life because you stole her fucking dog."

"You're really graspin' at straws. For goodness sake, Doc, my mother," Deacon said exasperated. "She wouldn't even step on a cockroach. And, the little girl with the dog, shit, I never even knew her name. I doubt that she knew mine. I think we moved right after it happened."

"Look, I know the easy thing to do here is just give up. For you to say, okay, I'm guilty take me away; I can't let you do that. I believe in you, just as you believe in your mother. You couldn't harm a fly. I don't know who is doing this or why. *That* we have to find out, I won't give up until we do. Now, let's get back on track. There's a lot of information which still makes no sense."

"I'm beginning to wonder if it will ever make any sense. There's just so much to process, and only two of us. You haven't even told me anything about Cynthia Thomas. What did you find?"

Doc flinched at the reminder. "Gettin' in the apartment was easy. Cops left the door unlocked. I had a good look around; even talked with a neighbor."

"Good, so share," Deacon demanded impatiently.

Doc told him about everything he had found. He succinctly described the talkative eye in the doorway.

It made Deacon laugh. They discussed every point and what it could mean. He wanted to tell Deacon more about Bridget. He wanted to describe her. *Deacon deserves to know all of this,* he told himself as they discussed the details. *He should know about her voice.* Doc chastised himself for his reluctance to tell all that he knew. He looked past Deacon at the switchback road and the three-hundred foot drop, and he did not tell his friend everything.

"Doc, I feel like the last fucking man on earth. I'm exhausted; I've hardly slept, and the only news I get is bad. I don't know how much longer I can continue to do this. I want out. I need out.

"Before you got here, I was staring at the walls of this man-made pit. I considered riding to the top." Deacon pointed at the rim of the quarry, and lowered his voice to a whisper. "I wondered how fast I could ride before we cleared the brink. I imagined the whole thing. I saw exactly how far we flew before starting the trip straight down."

"I knew that," Doc said compassionately. "What stopped you, James David?"

"You know what. At first, it seemed like the best idea possible. It would put me, and everyone around me, especially you, out of our misery. I got on Widowmaker and started her. We sat here idling. I thought about all the nights and weekends you and I spent building her. In those days, it was you and this machine that saved my life." He paused, and touched the fangs of the airbrushed snake. "In that moment, because I couldn't bear to sacrifice her life along with mine, I couldn't do it. Sounds insane, doesn't it? I'm alive because I couldn't kill my bike."

"It doesn't sound crazy to me. It does illustrate my point. How could someone who can't even smash a machine possibly hurt another human being? James David, we're friends; we'll get through this misery by working together, by solving the mystery, not by you sacrificing yourself. Listen, I've gotta tell you. Every time you mention hurtin' yourself, you scare me. Please, for me, for my piece of mind, promise me you won't do anything like that— promise me."

"I don't know if I can. It's because—it's just that sometimes," tears filled Deacon's bloodshot eyes, "sometimes, I feel so desperate. I don't know what else to do. Suicide feels like my only way out."

"Don't you see, Deac, there are plenty of people who care about you. We all want to help you work through your problems. At least, promise me next time you feel desperate, you'll talk to me first. Talk to me, and tell me what's on your mind. Okay?"

"Yeah, okay, I guess so."

"Not good enough. I want to hear you say the words. Promise me and make me believe you. Do it for me. Do it for our friendship."

"All right, I promise. I won't do anything until we've talked."

Doc breathed a sigh of relief. "Good. Thanks. That means a lot to me." Now, tell me about your folks."

Deacon told Doc, in perfect detail, how he found the Joneses, and everything he had heard and seen. Reluctantly, he confessed that he had been unable to resist calling Star.

"That has to be how the cops found the resort." Doc shook his head disapprovingly. "Your home phone must be tapped. I haven't told anyone anything, not even Kat. The cops must've been listening unless you have another idea?"

"No, you were right. I shouldn't have called. Damn it, what if I've implicated Star just by talkin' to her. I should've listened to you." Deacon paused and smiled sheepishly. "I've already put her in jeopardy. It would be best just to keep her with me. As long as the cops don't know where I am, they won't find her either. Besides, I need as much emotional support as I can get."

"Are you sure you're not lettin' your little head do the talkin' for your big head? I don't want you to take this the wrong way. I'm only trying to look at it from every possible angle. Maybe there's somethin' else to consider."

"Doc, quit beatin' around the bush. What are you gettin' at?"

"Just that we've only known Star since May, and the trouble started about the same time she showed up."

"That's bullshit! I didn't need a lot of time." Deacon was irritated. "I know her; I feel her. I'm connected to her. Don't you believe in love at first sight?"

"I do believe in love at first sight, and there's probably nothing to this…"

Deacon cut him off. "That's right, there's nothin'. Star has had nothin' to do with anything. Besides, the first murder happened a month before we met. Don't forget, it was Kat who introduced us. Shit, Doc, even Kat says we're the perfect couple."

"I'm sorry, Deac, I don't want to argue. If you want her with you, then so be it. Just be open to everything. That's all I ask. Don't completely trust anyone."

"What about you?" Deacon shoved Doc's logic in his face. "Are you sayin' I shouldn't trust you either?"

"Certainly, you have a point. Be assured, I'm on your side. However, I think you should be wary of everyone, including me."

"Will you find Star for me and tell her to be ready? I'll pick her up this afternoon."

"I'll tell her. Where are you headed? We should keep in touch."

"South, some place secluded. I'll know it when I see it. I need to get some rest. That it then?"

"Not quite. There's one more thing."

"More bad news?"

"I don't know if I'd call it bad, more like odd. I reread your blood test results this morning, and I found something unusual. They found a chemical trace in your blood. A drug called Sodium Amytal. I've heard something about it before, but for the life of me, I can't remember where. I've been rackin' my brain trying to remember, but so far no luck. You haven't been takin' drugs, have you?"

"No, other than the booze, I haven't taken anything. I have enough trouble with the liquor. I've never even heard of Sodium Amytal. Who can we ask?"

"I don't have any close friends who are doctors, and we need to be careful. I don't want to give us away. If this thing is rare, my asking questions in the wrong place could cause unwanted attention. Let me see what I can find."

Four o'clock that afternoon, Deacon found Star waiting in a busy parking lot. It had been more than thirty hours since he slept. Exhausted, he rode the back roads, struggling, with every mile, to stay awake. He had only two things on his mind, keep Star safe and a quiet place to lie down.

SEVENTEEN

THE MOTEL appeared out of nowhere fifty miles southwest of St. Louis on a county road, a nondescript blue line on the map. Ancient oak trees nearly hid the weathered building. The parking area, accented by weeds growing from every crack, was behind the structure. Deacon cut the engine. They silently coasted to a stop a safe distance from the office.

Star smiled. Pleased with herself, she signed the register, *Bridget Luna. Bridget's still upset and doesn't want to come out,* Star thought. *I'll use her name anyway.*

Without uttering a word, Deacon, fully clothed, fell fast asleep on the bed.

After twenty tortured hours, he awoke, bombarded by a desperate need to cleanse his soul. He told Star every detail of what had happened over the last few days. He opened his pocket notebook and read his meticulous notes aloud.

When he finally finished, she took charge. "Let's make storyboards," she commanded.

"What?"

"Storyboards," she repeated agitated. "A schematic of what has happened. Something we can visualize and discuss."

"I know what they are. How are we going to do it here?"

She moved gracefully around the small room, spoke dramatically, and punctuated her words graphically with delicate head and hand movements. "Let's find some cardboard, tape it to the walls, and lay out everything in chronological order with a magic marker."

Doc was obviously wrong, he thought impressed with her willingness to make sense of his dilemma.

Even her printing is elegant. From the edge of the bed, Deacon admired his love as she neatly printed a list of events and facts on the fetid cardboard, which smelled like the dumpster where he found it. *She's incredible.* He was fascinated by her every movement. The fat colorfast marker looked out of place in her delicate hand. Thick black lines soaked into the brown paper as she drew them, and swelled like a snake swallowing its prey.

April - Black man cut in half behind bar - The Landing

  A. Known pimp - Garvin Brown

  B. No connection to D

  C. D drunk - no memory

D. Unknown woman - long dark hair - large facial scar - ugly

Star stepped back and admired her work. "Okay, that's what we know about the first murder."

"I didn't say she was ugly."

"What?" Star asked surprised.

"The bartender said she was pretty, but she had an ugly scar."

"It's the same fucking thing. An ugly scar makes a girl ugly." Star snapped. "Now let's move on."

"There was some other stuff about the pimp, remember?" Deacon added.

"Look, Deacon, I know there's a certain amount of information that I haven't written down. It isn't all pertinent." Star said impatiently. "If we're going to solve anything, we're going to have to focus on facts, verified facts. You know a lot of that info is just so much useless background dribble. We can cover our walls, clutter our minds, and not help this process at all. Or, we can just fucking move on."

"I suppose you're right." Deacon responded apologetically. "It's just that, well—it's just that, when we first discovered a lot of those facts, Doc thought, and I agreed, they might lead to somethin'. That's all." He was tired and discouraged. He did not want to alienate his lover.

"Doc's not here, is he? It's you and me doin' the work. At the end of the day, it's just you and me." She shot back. "Besides, I told you a couple a days ago. You need to evaluate your friendship. I know some things that'll shock you."

"What kind of things?" Deacon was riveted. "What're you talkin' about?"

"Nothin', never mind." Star feigned despair for her slip. "Let's get back to work."

"You know this kind of shit drives me crazy. Never give me a hint about somethin' and not finish."

"I wasn't hinting. It was nothing. I assure you."

"I'd like to be the judge of that. If you love me, you'll tell me." He implored.

"Since you put it that way, first, I want to go on the record. When you use my love as a way of getting what you want, it's emotional blackmail—period. Anyway, two days ago, I was dusting the house. I wasn't intentionally looking at your papers, but there was a document on top of your desk and it jumped out at me. It's your partnership agreement with Doc and Kat."

"That, it's no big deal. We had it drawn up years ago."

"Exactly my point, only the agreement I read was written and signed one month ago."

"That's not possible. I haven't signed anything."

"It's definitely your signature, and it was on your desk. Here's the real kicker. It stipulates that if either you or Doc are institutionalized, imprisoned, or die, the business immediately reverts to the other partner. Seems to me, the likelihood of Doc ending up in prison, committed, or killed is slim. If that isn't motive enough for him to frame you, I don't know what is."

"There has to be some logical explanation." Deacon argued. "Doc wouldn't do anything to hurt me."

"People always say money can ruin families and friendships. It looks like he wants your half of the business."

"Doc'll clear this up. Until then, I don't even want to think about it."

"Fine, I won't mention it again; I won't say I told you so, but you'll see. If you're looking for someone with motive," she said the words slowly, dramatically, and one at a time, "he's—your—man. What better incentive than cold—hard—cash?"

Deacon stretched out on the hard bed and closed his eyes. Disassociated thoughts whirled through the darkness of his mind. All of the tenants of fairness and clarity, in which he believed, were crumbling around him. He doubted himself. Doc doubted Star and his parents. Star doubted Doc. There were too many unanswered questions. His world was cloistered and suffocating.

Uncomfortably, he slept. The nightmare came with all the familiar faces, the serpent, the cross, and a resounding cry of absolute hopelessness.

Deacon awoke to Star's sensuous, reassuring voice as she kneaded his taut muscles. "It's okay, doll, I'm here. I'll take care of you. I'll make sure we put an end to this." She gently pressed the arches of her warm feet against his soles.

Throughout the night, he slept for short periods and awoke often. Daybreak was a welcome sight. He took a hot soaking shower and endeavored to collect his thoughts. *Too many details left out of the outline. They have to be resolved.*

Star sat on the edge of the bed. She counted each stroke as she lovingly pulled the big comb through the thick blonde strands.

Tentatively, Deacon began. "I know you want only the best for me."

She answered automatically. "Of course I do. I always have."

"There are a few things about the Brown murder I think we should talk about." He said testing the water.

"Look, doll, I'm sorry about last night. We were both exhausted, and I got a little cross. We can talk about anything you want. Just one thing, let's not write anything down until we agree that it has a definite connection. Okay?"

"Deal. Star, do you know how wonderful you are? Have I told you today how much I adore you?"

"No, silly, you haven't. If you want to tell me, now is good."

"I adore you." He sat next to her, wrapped her in his arms, and nuzzled her neck. "I love you. I'm crazy about you."

She twisted, ever so slightly, just enough to move her hair from his touch and pushed him away. "What's on your mind?"

"A couple a things, the pimp, Brown, was charged in Los Angeles with his brother's murder, and…"

She cut him off. "That has no connection to this murder. Besides, you said yourself he was released; the charge was dropped."

"What about what the bartender? He saw Brown arguing with the scar-faced woman. That might relate to the investigation of his brother's murder. Brown told them the real murderer was a hooker. It could be more than a coincidence.

"Then, there's the black van," he continued. "The bartender told Doc he saw it at the edge of the parking lot on several occasions. I saw it there, too. There was one just like it in the vacant lot, next to my parent's house."

"The van thing is a little strange." She commented as she wrote, *black van*, on the cardboard. "I'll give you that."

She systematically dismissed the rest of his concerns. "The bartender also said the place was packed. We can't be sure of what he really saw across a crowded room. Maybe Brown was talking to the woman, maybe not. It could be he was hitting on her or even tryin' to recruit her. After all, he was a pimp. If they were arguing, it could have been about anything. It's all circumstantial, and hearsay is not a viable connection.

"Let's be pragmatic. Imagine a pimp saying that a hooker in East LA killed his brother. Can you fathom just how many hookers and pimps there are in LA, especially on the East Side? They kill each other all the time.

"You were in the bar at the same time. I'll give you that, but that's all. The second and third murders were both young females. Nothing about them resembles what happened in the first murder. I only put it on the board because you were there. It marks the beginning of a series of events."

"You're probably right," he reluctantly conceded. "Let's move on."

Star poised the marker in front of the cardboard. "Okay, what was the second vic's name, Candy Thompson?"

"Her name was Cynthia Ann Thomas."

"Yeah, right; she lived at 1956 Sidney."

"How'd you know that?" Deacon asked surprised.

Star rolled her eyes. "I read it in your notebook," she answered hesitantly.

"I didn't write it in my notebook."

"You must have told me," she insisted.

"I don't remember talking about the address. Only that it was in Soulard."

Star stepped back, pivoted, and glared at Deacon. "Listen, enough already, quit pickin' at the little shit!" She exploded. "You can barely remember who you are. Maybe the booze has pickled your brain. How can you remember something so specific, and say that I can't. I think not."

Deacon hung his head. "Maybe you're right. I'm in no condition to question anyone, especially not you. Sorry."

"All right, never mind. Let's just keep goin'. I'm getting tired of tryin' to help you and fighting over every fucking detail. I'm not the one who got us into this fucking mess. If you want me to stick it out, just back the fuck off."

"I won't do it again." Deacon whimpered. "I won't question you any more. Sweetie, I need your help."

Star looked down upon her forlorn doll, her beaten puppy. Success opened the floodgates; dopamine surged to her brain. Giddy, she discretely took a small dark chocolate from the side pocket of her purse.

With her back to Deacon, she unwrapped the morsel and slipped it under her tongue. Ecstasy stimulated by dual stimuli washed over her. She bit her lip and trembled. The silent orgasm captured her breath.

They continued making their list. Deacon read the facts from his notebook. They discussed each one. Star wrote, or didn't write, the particular clue on the makeshift boards.

"She was a twenty-four year old secretary working at the brewery." Deacon said spelling her name, "*C y n t h i a   A n n   T h o m a s.*"

Star wrote the girl's initials in bold letters across the top of a large blank piece of dirty cardboard, **_C–A–T_**, and ceremoniously drew a line beneath. "Is that right?" she asked waiting for Deacon's reaction. There was none. Below the line, she started an outline with age and place of employment.

"Doc said he found some really kinky stuff in a drawer in her bedroom." Deacon consulted his notebook. "You know, like sex toys, provocative lingerie, and something he described as a 'double-dicked dildo,' whatever that is."

"Sex toys may be interesting to you and Doc, but I truly doubt that they have anything to do with the poor woman's murder. In fact, I think you are a couple of shits. The very idea of gettin' your rocks off by going through someone's private things, and then laughing about them is sick. I'm disappointed in you, Deacon. I thought you were different."

"We weren't laughing," he said defensively. "Well, maybe a little, but we didn't mean anything by it. How else are we supposed to deal with this horrendous shit?"

"You can start by sticking to the facts related to the poor girl's murder, and by having a little respect for the dead. She was only twenty-four goddamn years old. She will never know the joy of marriage or find the love of her life. Experiences that people like Doc take for granted."

"As far as the joy of marriage goes, I doubt it."

"You can't know that. She was a very pretty girl. Her picture was on the news."

"I didn't say she wasn't good lookin'. I said she would probably never get married. Her neighbor told Doc that Cynthia was a lesbian and had a lover. Doc even found a diamond tennis bracelet with a love note from B. The woman next door said the lover's name was Bridget."

Star turned her back to hide the look of shock and surprise on her face. "Show me," she said as she regained her composure. She reached for the notebook.

"It's not in here. We were outside talkin', and I didn't write it down."

"I need to pee." She said and abruptly left the room.

Hunched over the stained porcelain sink, she splashed cool water on her face. An imperfect countenance looked back from the mirror. Bridget sadly caressed her long blonde hair. Star angrily twisted the strands in her fingers. *Get it together; go away.* Star told Bridget. *You're in mourning. Remember, you didn't want to be out. You're sad. I get that, but I'm on mission. Either help me or stay out of my fucking way. There's no time for this shit.*

"You okay? I thought I heard you talking." Deacon said his gaze transfixed on the wall.

She ignored the question and picked up the marker. "Now, let's see," she spoke with practiced nonchalance, "her head was found on a plate in the kitchen. Right?"

"Right, but, Star, don't you want to note that she was a lesbian? We even know her lover's first name. It could turn out to mean something or if we can find this Bridget maybe she can help."

"Think about what you're sayin', Deacon. The killer raped the woman. They found sperm in her vagina." Star added the two facts to the outline as she spoke. "Even if she was gay, which by the way is hearsay, her female lover could not have been the murderer. Those details have no relevance here. The murderer is a man. The facts are incontrovertible, now, what else?" Star ended her tirade as abruptly as she had begun.

"The police found a straight razor at the scene."

Star added *razor* to the outline. "See, a straight razor is a man thing." She said noting that the victim was found bound to the bedposts, and there was no sign of forced entry.

"Murder reported to 911, anonymously." Deacon read verbatim from his notebook, *"female caller with Hispanic accent."*

"Fucking racial profiling, I doubt that the ethnicity of the caller has anything to do with the murder." Star said indignantly. "Your information is great, but let's limit the storyboards to relevant facts. Is that all we know about this one?" She asked as she went down the list and made a check mark by each item.

Deacon breathed in a deep sigh and slowly let it out. "Yeah, I guess so." He said glumly.

"What's that supposed to mean? Is there something else you haven't told me?"

He answered guardedly. "There's nothing else on my list."

"Deacon, who are you tryin' to kid. I know you. I feel you. When you suffer, so do I. When you succeed, I feel the joy. There' something you're not telling me. It may not be on your list, but it's on your mind. You trust me, don't you?" She said dejectedly.

"Of course, I trust you. That has never been a question."

"If you trust me, you'll tell me everything. No secrets, we promised."

"There is something, but it's so horrible. I've been afraid to tell you." His bloodshot eyes filled with tears. "It's because I love you so much I haven't mentioned it. I was afraid if you knew, you would stop—I was scared you wouldn't love me anymore. Star, you are the one absolute certainty in my life. I can't bear to lose you. Telling you isn't worth the risk."

Star wrapped her arms around him, and pulled him close, burying his face between her breasts. "Don't worry, doll. I'll love you for the rest of your life. Some day soon, I will show you the ultimate love, an experience that man has speculated about since the beginning of time."

"What kind of experience?" Her blouse muffled his words.

"A surprise, lover, one for which you must wait. Be patient. I promise. Once we have resolved all of your questions about your current situation, you'll understand. When you have all the answers, then and only then, will I be prepared to give you the greatest gift of all.

"But, let's not get off track." She lifted his face and smothered him with warm wet kisses. "Tell me what you're holding back. No matter what it is, no matter how awful, my feelings will not change."

Reluctantly, he began. "Do you remember the day after Cynthia Thomas was killed when I was sick?"

"Of course, I do. It was just the booze. You've been hung over plenty of times."

"There's something else. When you came back to the bar to pick me up, my shirt was missing, right?"

"Right, I just figured you had puked on yourself, and thrown your shirt in the dumpster. I didn't even bother to look for it."

"I found it that afternoon." He tested each word as though it was the most important declaration of his life. "It was in my saddlebag."

"So?" Star answered insouciantly. "Your shirt was fucked up, and you stuffed it in your saddlebag. Doesn't seem like a big deal to me."

"No, sweetie, you don't understand. My shirt wasn't only covered with vomit. There was vomit and blood, someone else's blood. I didn't have a scratch on me. I think it was soaked with Cynthia Thomas's blood. The evidence points to me. I have done some research on people with multiple personalities. As I understand the illness, it is possible for the individual personas to do things without the others knowing.

Like more than one person sharing one body. If I have that mental illness, this really could be my doing. Without knowing, I've raped and killed at least two women." He sobbed. "Don't you understand? I'm a monster!"

She jerked backward and pressed against the wall. "Deacon, Jesus, this is worse than I thought." She stared intensely into his eyes with a look of incredulity. "Do you really think it's possible? I've heard of multiple personality disorder, although I assumed that the other personas, as you called them, would be aware of everything. Do you really think this could be you?"

"You see. I knew it," he wept profusely. "Even you are repulsed by me. There is no such thing as absolute, unconditional love. This is more than even you can take. There's no place for me on this earth. I'm sick, an aberration."

"Wait a second, wait just one second. I'm shocked for sure, but it doesn't mean I don't love you. Nothing's changed between us. Everything I said is still true. I'm not going to leave you, no matter what. We're in this together to the end.

"Honestly, I am stunned by so much information that implicates you. Still, let's not forget about the possibility of someone else, like Doc, framing you. He certainly has the motive."

"I just don't believe he would do anything to harm me. He's like a brother to me. Actually, he's more than a brother. Brothers are thrown together by accidents of birth. Doc chose me. He chose to be my friend." With the words, flashed a memory of the Reverend and something he had often said. *Boy, if a*

man has to tell you that he's honest, don't trust him.
In that moment, Deacon doubted his ability to trust
anyone, even himself. He looked into the enchanting,
blue eyes of *the love of his life* and wondered if he
could even trust her.

"Wake up and smell the reality, Deacon. We've
established motive; Doc stands to get your half of the
business. That could be worth real money. He always
knows where you are, and what you're doing. He has
a key to your house. He could have easily slipped into
the garage and put the bloody shirt in your
saddlebag."

"All right, let's say you're right—just for the
purpose of discussion. How could he have gotten my
shirt in the first place?" Deacon proffered. *If I knew I
was guilty, this would be easier.*

She answered without thinking. "That's easy. You
were unconscious outside the bar. I went home to get
my car. There was plenty of time for someone, let's
just say it was Doc, to take your shirt, drive to
Soulard, commit the murder, get blood on your shirt,
and return to the bar before me.

"Or, let's say he didn't have time to do all that and
get back to the bar. He just switched to plan B. He
simply slipped into the house sometime early Sunday
morning, and put the shirt in your saddlebag. Either
way, the result is the same. He makes you think
you're the murderer. You end up in prison or an
institution for the criminally insane. Or, even better
for him, you commit suicide and *viola*, the business is
all his."

Star continued adamantly. "If you prefer, you can
just go on thinking that you have a split personality,

and *Mr. Darkside* is the killer. Either way, doll, you're right. Your life is over. Are you ready to give up?" Her screams ripped through the thin walls. "Are you so fucking weak that you're goin' to roll over and let someone else win?"

"Does it really matter? Either way, the life I was living is lost." He rapidly sank into an extreme depression. "If I'm not who I thought, and if my friends aren't my friends, what do I have? Without a future, friends, or family, what is there?"

"Deacon, your friends and family have betrayed you, fucked you. You only have me. We're in this together, and we can't stop now. We have one more murder to sort out; then we'll put an end to this."

"Is it necessary to continually rehash the details? It's like the difference between reading the obituaries and actually going to the funeral. Being there makes it real, too real. These murders are cold stiff corpses to me."

"Deacon, I love you, but you're pushing your luck. I'm sick of listening to you whine. Your problems are overwhelming. I repeat, YOUR problems. Yet, here I am, still tryin' to do the right thing, still tryin' to help. So, cool it. Bite your lip or hit your head on the wall. Do whatever the fuck it takes. I don't give a shit. Pull yourself together, or you won't have to worry about me because I won't fuckin' be here."

"You're right. I've got to get myself together. Hang in here with me a little longer. One way or the other, I'll find a solution. We'll solve this mystery, and I'll settle it once and for all."

Star moved on as though nothing had happened. "Better, much better. Number three, what do we know?"

Deacon opened his red notebook to the final inscribed pages. Details of the final incident were sketchy compared to the previous two. "Her name was Tina." He began as he remembered his first luxurious night on the floor with his Tina. "She was a dancer at PT's. They found her naked in the back seat of her own car."

"Where and what is PT's?" Star asked innocently.

"It's a strip club on the East Side in Illinois."

"You ever go there?"

"Yeah, a few times."

"What's the attraction to those places? Do you go there to get laid or just to get your rocks off?" She asked angrily. "Have you been with any of those women, those whores?"

"Sweetie, it's not like that," he said defensively, "least not in the places I've been."

"You've been to more than one? I can't fuckin' believe it. You've conveniently never mentioned this before. Fuck, you think you know someone."

"Star, you're blowing this completely out of proportion. It's just my friends and me. You know, just a bunch of guys hangin' out. We go there to look, have a few laughs, and drink a few beers. No one ever leaves with a girl. It's against the rules. It's a fantasy; no one gets hurt. You can't even touch the girls. The guys go home to their wives or girlfriends excited, anxious to please them. There are no victims."

She shook her head disapprovingly. "Tell that to the family of the woman who was shaved and beaten to death in the back of her car." She said sharply.

"How'd you know she was shaved?" He asked surprised.

"I dunno. I think you told me yesterday."

"Did I—Don't remember, seems I don't have much of a memory these days." Deacon stared at the lines of ink, bewildered.

"What else do you know?" Star asked.

"J72829 was printed on her head in red lipstick."

"Which means—what?"

"I think it's a reference to Jeremiah Chapter seven, verses twenty-eight and twenty-nine. Scripture I was forced to memorize as a child. It's a reference about people who don't obey the Word of the Lord. It orders them to cut off their hair, and cast it away."

Star added the abbreviated notations to the outline. "Was it?" She asked.

"Was it what?"

"The vic, the stripper, was her hair cast away?"

"Well, yeah, I guess. As far as I know, it was missing."

"Was she raped?"

"Yes," he answered dismayed.

"Doll, why does that upset you?"

"You know the answer."

She persisted. "I want to hear it again in context."

"It bothers me, 'cause it's all stuff I know. It's like somethin' I've lived, and tried to forget. It all points to me. The night it happened, I was alone. PT's is an easy hour's ride from where I slept, or didn't sleep. It frightens me because I might have been there, because I could've done it. You know the worst thing. It's the wondering, the waiting to find out what's real. My heart is trying to beat me to death. I fear I'll die of internal bruising or a brain hemorrhage before I find the truth.

"This is how my father used to punish me. It's why I can't bear to wait for bad news. Waiting was worst of all, waiting and wondering. I was afraid, but no one cared," Deacon sighed. "I was all alone. I imagined my mother rocking and knitting; totally oblivious as I died a slow, agonizing death."

"I understand better now." Star edged away. "It's really scary. For the first time, I have a feel for what you're goin' through. It really is possible that you're the one. Doc has motive, your father has knowledge, but you; I can't believe I'm saying this, you have: motive, knowledge, and opportunity."

For the first time Deacon sensed her distrust. "I need to speak to Doc!" Deacon said urgently as he paced the room. "There's something I have to do. I need his help."

"What? What do you have to do Deacon? Let me help."

"Star, if you love me, if you have ever loved me, trust me. This one last time, don't ask any questions. I need to call Doc."

"It's not safe for you to go out. You can't risk being seen. I'll walk to a phone and call him for you." She grasped his hands and locked on his sullen gaze. "James David, I have never loved you more. Whatever you need, I probably need it more. Soon, I will explain exactly how I feel. Doll, very soon you'll understand, beyond a shadow of a doubt, what you mean to me."

Deacon's mind raced; the words meant little.

EIGHTEEN

THE TELEPHONE at *D-K-D Choppers* rang twice. Dawg, the surly counterman, answered. "Give me Doc," Star said curtly. A synthesized *Born to be Wild* by Steppenwolf played while she waited.

A masculine voice interrupted the song. "Doc," he answered in a businesslike tone.

"Doc, it's Star. Deacon says he needs you. There's something the two of you have to do together."

"Where is he?" Doc asked coldly.

"In a shitty motel fifty miles southwest of the city on highway PP, it's the only hole-in-the-wall on the fucking road."

Doc's voice vibrated with mounting anger. "I know what you're up to, bitch!"

"What," she feigned surprise.

"I've discovered a lot more than you intended." Doc spoke rapidly. "I know all about you. I know about California; I know what you're trying to do to Deacon, *Bridget*, and I'm going to stop you."

Her rage welled. *They will both know everything,* she thought, *on my schedule.*

She held the receiver at arms length and shrieked at the top of her lungs. "You only think you know me; you don't know shit! Just try fucking with me. You're out of your league. My advice is run and hide. You ain't seen nothin' yet." She swung the receiver like a baseball bat; the black plastic exploded.

Deacon heard the high-speed howl of the lone Harley as it devoured the last few miles. He winced as he pulled on his boot, and then limped hurriedly outside.

He shouted above the dying engine. "Man, am I glad to see you. These last two days have been more like months."

"Deacon, you all right?" Doc practically leaped from his motorcycle. "I was scared shitless."

"Of course, I'm all right. Why wouldn't I be?"

"Where's the bitch," Doc demanded. "Where's Star?" He looked past Deacon at the open door.

"Doc, what's gotten in to you? You're talkin' about my Star."

"Give me a chance to explain. Let's go inside. Where is she?" He started toward the doorway. "Is she here?"

Deacon followed. "She's not here. What's goin' on? She came back from calling you thirty minutes ago, said you were on your way, and then went out for soda and…"

Doc cut him off. "Was she upset?" he asked, then abruptly changed the subject. "What's the matter with your leg? You've been limpin' since the quarry." Doc closed the door and locked it. "Looks like it's worse. Did you hurt yourself?"

"I don't know. Who gives a shit? My foot is the least of my problems. To answer your question about Star, at first I thought she seemed upset. So, I asked her and she said no. After that, she was fine. You know what a quick temper she has. I would have known if something was wrong."

"Yeah, tell me about her temper, but I think she can control it whenever she wants."

"Doc, what's up between you and Star? You come in here ranting about where she is and calling her names, and then you change the subject. Besides, the problem isn't my leg. It's my toes. It feels like I stepped on a nail. I must have kicked somethin' the other night runnin' through the woods. Anyway, never mind me. What about Star, what do you know that you're not tellin' me?"

"Deac, it's a long fucking story. You had better sit down. It doesn't have anything to do with me. I figured some stuff out, so I confronted her. This is strictly between you and Star. I'm just not sure why."

Doc paced back and forth unable to find a beginning to what seemed to be a nonsensical story. He read parts of the outline aloud. "You didn't write this," he stated.

"Well, no, Star wrote it. Together we decided which details were important."

"Look at this. Look at how much you've left out. What's missing tells its own story."

"What story?" In one fluid movement, Deacon was off the bed and face-to-face with Doc. "You're makin' me nuts, Doc." What in the hell are you talkin' about? Cut to the fucking chase, and get it over with!"

"Okay, relax. I didn't want to tell you this. You have enough on your mind. I don't think Star is who you think she is. The way I see it, nothing about her is as it appears.

"When I started checkin' leads and comparing the facts, they didn't add up. It wasn't until I dug deeper into the life of Garvin Brown that it began to make sense. There was another warrant for his arrest in California. One they never served. You'll never guess why they wanted him. This one had nothin' to do with his brother's murder. They think he had something to do with the disappearance of a Beverly Hills socialite."

"So, what's that got to do with Star? She's no fucking socialite. She's a waitress."

"Let me finish. It seems this socialite was at a cocktail party. Brown arrived, she ran away, and was never seen again. They've been searchin' for her since April. The real kicker is the woman's name." He pointed to the storyboard, "Bridget Luna."

"I don't get it. Who's Bridget Luna? You're pointin' at nothing."

"Exactly, her name isn't on the list. Bridget was Cynthia Thomas's lover's name. I told you. It's not here; you've left it off. It just so happens Bridget Luna disappeared something like four weeks before Kat first met Star."

"Are you sayin' you think there's some connection between Star and this Bridget Luna?"

"I think Star is Bridget Luna. Isn't Luna Spanish for moon?"

Deacon gasped as if shot. He covered his face with both hands, fell to his knees, and keeled over. He wrenched in agony, moaned, and writhed in slow motion on the threadbare carpet.

Doc knelt at his side and tried to comfort him.

Deacon jerked away. "Leave me alone. You've done enough."

Doc edged reluctantly toward the door. "What can I do? I don't mean to hurt you, but this is what I found; these are the facts. Tell me what you need. This is as hard for me as it is for you."

"Jesus, Doc, you have no fucking idea what I'm going through. This isn't happening to you. It isn't your problem." He half-yelled, half-cried, his voice muffled by cupped palms. "My fucking life is cursed!"

Doc answered in a subdued voice. "I'm sorry."

Outside, alone, Doc touched Widowmaker's custom seat. He kneaded the soft leather. Doc traded for the seat and gave it to Deacon, who slept that night, and every night until they installed the seat, with his prize next to his bed.

Doc shivered. *What will the future bring,* he wondered. *How will this end?*

The midday sun beat down on the neglected parking lot. Doc ventured back into the room. It was time to face the music. It was time to tell Deacon the rest.

Deacon sat on the bed, an elbow on each knee, his face still hidden in his hands. Without looking up, Deacon spoke in a terse whisper. "It still doesn't make any sense to me. How could Star have been Cynthia Thomas's lover? The neighbor said this Bridget drove a blue Mercedes. Star drives a red Camaro. It would be impossible to confuse the two. When would she have had time for this? Besides, take it from me, she's definitely no lesbian."

"You tell me." Doc said leaning against the doorway. "When was the last time you visited her, or called her at work?"

"I never go out there, and I don't call because she's only allowed to use the phone for emergencies. I talked to her boss a couple of weeks before Sturgis. I guess that was the last time."

"Look, the tennis bracelet must've cost a bundle, the kind of money a socialite would have." Doc entered the room. "The note was romantic, signed *love, B.*" Doc opened the curtains and sunlight flooded in. He glanced expectantly outside. "Even the double-penis dildo makes sense. It's the kind of thing lesbians' use. Deac, there's too much evidence to ignore. There's something else; two other discoveries that I didn't want to tell you about."

"Tell me," Deacon said resignedly.

"The neighbor described Cynthia's lover to me. The description matches Star to a T."

"Means nothin', there are plenty of tall hot blondes in St. Louis."

"I thought so, too, until I asked about her voice."

"What'd she say?"

Doc looked deep into Deacon's pain-filled eyes, "Sexy and raspy."

"It's bullshit. There are tons of those around, too."

Doc took a deep breath. "Worth a thousand words they say," he took a folded square from his shirt pocket and handed it to Deacon.

One crease at a time, Deacon unfolded the faxed copy of a society page photo. Arrows pierced every nerve in Deacon's body. The caption read *Bridget Luna*; the face was Star's.

Doc stood helplessly by as Deacon soaked the information from the page. Deacon's hands trembled. His eyes glassed over. He attacked the page in what seemed to be a muscle spasm, crushing it into a tight ball. He convulsed, and fell backward, a limp, sodden mass.

"Deacon, Deacon, you okay?" Doc anxiously shook his friend. Deacon did not respond. His lifeless eyes were open, the pupils dilated. His hand fell open, and the waded paper dropped to the floor. His breath came slow and labored; all color drained from his face. Doc had seen this once before. Deacon was in a stress-induced coma. There was nothing to do but wait.

"Why murder her lover?" Doc wondered aloud. He drew a circle around *Cynthia Ann Thomas* with the black marker. He doodled and drew a headless stick figure. He reviewed the list looking for common denominators. Star's emphasis on *C A T* caught his attention.

Deacon groaned. "Wha' happe'ed?" He asked with difficulty. He sat up and ran searching fingers across the bed.

"On the floor," Doc pointed to the paper. "There."

With stiff mechanical movements, Deacon retrieved the wad, opened it, and stretched out the wrinkles. Hot tears streamed down his cheeks and splashed on the page.

Doc sat next to him on the bed. "Deac, I know how hard this must be, and I'm sorry. I don't think we have a lot of time. We need to figure a coupla' things out; we've gotta get goin'. We don't know where she is or what she's up to." He tapped the cardboard with the marker. "Look, look at this. Do you think the reason for selecting this particular woman could be so simple?"

"I don't understand."

He touched the bold underlined initials. "The first letters of her name, they're an acronym.

"The spelling's different, but the name's the same. Her nickname could be the same as my Katherine's, like a message."

"Doc, it's such a stretch. You're being paranoid. There has to be a logical explanation for the Bridget Luna thing. The two of you are really making me crazy. Star says I can't trust you; you say she's the one. I love you both. Somehow, you both must be wrong."

"It doesn't seem odd to you this is the only victim that Star drew a line under?"

"I don't know."

"What about the photo? You can't say it isn't Star."

"No, but the caption could easily be wrong or someone could have tampered with the picture."

"Deacon, can't you see what she's doing to you? Since she arrived, everything in your life has turned to shit. I don't know why, or how, but it's her."

"If you're right, she won't come back here because she knew you were coming, right?"

"Yep, there's no way in hell she's comin' back. I told her on the phone that I know she's up to somethin'. She won't risk a confrontation with me, not in front of you. She won't be back, and I'm equally sure we haven't heard the last of her. She's gone to a whole lot of trouble to make you look and feel guilty. I'm sure it isn't over."

"Doc, while we're on the subject of trust, there's something I need to ask. It's about our partnership. Star says she saw an agreement that says if anything happens to me, you get the business. She says you're tryin' to get me out of the way, so *D-K-D* will be all yours again."

The color drained from Doc's face. "Deacon, I was afraid; I didn't know what to believe. The circumstantial evidence all points to you. Even though I always said I was sure of your innocence, I had my doubts. I was worried about my family. Kat called the kids and asked them to stay at school. They think we're havin' marital problems. We thought it better they think that, rather than tell them the truth. With all of your talk of a split personality, I honestly didn't know if I could trust you. Kat and I agreed, like it or not, we had to protect ourselves financially as well as physically and emotionally.

"Deac, I hope you can forgive me. Now I know it was unnecessary. You could never hurt anyone. I had my doubts; however, look at it this way. You still have yours. I've proven to you that it's Star, and not you or me. Still, you don't believe me."

"Doc, you could be wrong. The victims were raped. Star couldn't have done that. If she is involved, she's not alone."

"There are a lot of things I can't explain: your dreams, the bloody shirt, and the rapes. However, there are definite connections between Star and the victims. What about her mood swings, and the way she sometimes treats you? The writing is on the wall. You don't see her walking back through that door, do you?" Doc pointed at the heavily marred door.

"True, she isn't back, but I wouldn't call that missing. She's been gone less than two hours. Let's wait a little while and see. The big question remains. If she did this, how is it that the two women were found with AB negative semen?"

"I agree, it doesn't add up. Let's say, for the sake of argument, she killed Garvin Brown. If she killed him in self-defense, why did she cut him in half? No body does that, except in the movies. You'd need a sharp knife and a saw. It matches with the scripture that your father made you memorize after you swiped the puppy."

"You have a point. Let's even say you're right. Why would she do it? It was quite a risk killing someone in such a public place."

"He could have surprised her at the bar. The brunette with the scar and Star could be partners. Somehow, they got him into the alley, killed him, and as an afterthought cut him in half to make it look like you were involved. Whoever is responsible is doin' a great job."

Doc and Deacon sat side-by-side on the bed waiting for Star to return.

For the first several years, after James David ran away, depression gnawed at Grace Jones. When an Easter Sunday stroke left the Reverend incapacitated, she became his primary caregiver. The responsibility repulsed Grace; however, in the end, the responsibility saved her life. Her life became all about him and left her little time for other thoughts. She was alone and lonely in her own home with her husband in the room. After a time the rote, daily routine became nearly unbearable. She felt trapped. Guilt and obligation kept her mouth closed and her hands busy. For Grace it was living without breathing.

When the Reverend suggested that she volunteer at the hospital, she was thrilled. The children filled an emotional chasm in her life. She looked forward to daybreak, and she resented her husband less.

It was a late October day, more than eleven years since James David had walked away. Grace, who was never sick, awoke with an unusual throbbing headache. Because of her devotion to the children, she took two Extra Strength Bufferin and drove to the hospital with her head still pounding.

The first couple of hours were difficult; she struggled to maintain her composure. An RN saw her steady herself against the nurses' station. She pressed the back of her hand against Grace's forehead and ordered her to lie down in an empty room.

A physician's quick examination came with a diagnosed touch of flu and a prescription for rest. A little before two o'clock in the afternoon she convinced herself that she was well enough to drive. She made her way outside, with uncertain steps, and drove home in a daze. For the first time ever, Grace was three hours early.

The black van on the road ahead looked familiar. Oddly, it led Grace on the route home. *A coincidence,* she thought until it turned into the vacant lot next door. *It's the same one.*

The driver's door swung open. A tall straight man immersed in thought, stepped down, and started toward the parsonage. A shocked Reverend and a perplexed Grace came face-to-face in the edge of the lawn.

"Reverend, mercy sakes!" Mrs. Jones stumbled over a landscape of even grass and broken syllables. "What are you do… your eyes, driving? How…" Without warning, she fainted and fell backward in the thick flora.

The Reverend rushed to catch her, and cradled her head an inch before it reached the ground. "Take it easy," he said in a soothing voice. He caressed his wife's cheek. "Lie still."

When Grace regained consciousness, bombarded with a surreal recollection of what she saw, she was lying on her own bed with no memory of how she got there. *I must be sicker than the Doctor said.*

She focused. The Reverend was sitting next to her. His piercing green eyes traced her movements. She was not dreaming. Reverend Jones could see.

"What happened?" She asked angrily. "I don't understand." She strained to lift herself. Her head throbbed.

"Lie still. Don't try to move. I'm sorry I've given you such a shock. Let me explain. There's so much to say. There's much for you and I to do. Our son needs us. You're burning up. Are you sick?"

"I have the flu. Never mind me, what do you know about James David?"

"Grace, first I want you to know…no…no…no, I'm so stupid. I never say anything right. What I mean is I desperately need you to know that I love you!"

Grace hung on his words, shocked by the sudden change. She looked into his eyes to see if what he said was true. They were clear and unmoving. She saw only sincerity.

"I realize now, actually, I have for quite some time, the error of my ways. In the way I've treated you and James David, I have sinned. In so many ways I have sinned against God, my family, and man. I am deeply and truly sorry."

Tears streamed down her cheeks. With a handkerchief from his pocket, he lovingly caught the warm drops. He continued in low sincere tones. "I have already sworn my repentance to God, and asked for His forgiveness. Now, I am begging for yours?"

This man did not even sound like the Reverend, who had not called her Grace since the day they brought baby James David home from the hospital. He did sound like the young John Jones she had married. "John, I love you, too." She said. Her heart forgave him. She sensed a profound change fill the room, which suffused by the afternoon sun slanting through dingy windowpanes, swelled with magical shadows and shards of light. It purified the inhabitants, awash in shades of crimson and yellow, through recrimination and forgiveness.

Two people who had once known each other found again, first themselves then their half. That aloof part of each, which had been the Reverend and Mrs. Jones, became ethereal and left, first the room, then the house, and finally the planet. John Jones and his wife, Grace, became again a couple with only a trace of a memory that they had suffered together at their own hands and at the will of circumstance.

John engulfed Grace in his arms, and repeatedly told her how sorry he was, how much he loved her, and most important of all, how it was not too late.

She echoed his remorse with her words, and thanked God with her thoughts.

"Now, I have much to explain. I'll begin at the beginning." He stretched out on the bed and slid his right arm under her neck.

She rolled toward him. "Take your time darling. I want—I must understand everything. Tell me."

John explained that, after his stroke, what the Doctor had said was true. He had lost most of his eyesight. His prognosis for how quickly and well he would heal was completely wrong. Miraculously, his vision rapidly returned. It was then, that he had perfected a plan, which had haunted him for a long time. When he lay in the hospital, it all seemed hopeless. Later, when his health improved, he took it as a sign from God, a second chance for an old man who had made more bad decisions than good.

"Grace, there were so many times I wanted to talk to you, to tell you how I felt. I wanted to say I was better, but you were so angry. I believed the only way to restore your faith in me was to carry out my plan. I was convinced that when I did, you would see me as I was in the beginning of our life together and forgive me.

"When I first learned where James lives, it was a blessing and a curse. I had long anticipated that day. When it finally came, I was afraid. I was frightened of what I might find. Some time passed. Finally, I gathered myself up. I prayed to God for guidance and strength, and I went.

"Grace, I was so touched by what I saw. Our son has grown up to be a very handsome young man. He's tall, slim, and looks so much like my brother. His hair is dark brown, and he wears it rather long. In the past, I would have never approved, but I no longer care about those things. I only care about him. Grace, he looks so good."

John paused, cried a little, and then continued. "I followed him. Every afternoon he went to one bar or another, and he always stayed well into the evening. I slipped up to the entrance on several occasions. I saw him always the center of attention in a world, which is the exact opposite of ours." He sighed, and relaxed his muscles. The telling seemed to drain his energy.

"John, how did you do this without me knowing? I understand the van and how you could leave while I was working, but at night you were always here."

"You only thought I was here. We go to bed so early, and you have never checked on me. I would wait a half-hour and sneak out; it was easy."

"Does he really look like David? What does he do?" Sadness swept over Grace. Her expression softened. "Is there a woman in his life? I feel like we have missed so much. More than anything, I want to recover something of those lost years. Maybe we can be a family again." She stopped, and released a thick sigh.

"There is something I need to confess. It has weighed heavily on my conscience for a while now. It's difficult." She took a deep breath as though trying to inhale strength. "After James left, my world crumbled. You and I were at odds. You had the stroke, and I began to feel that God did not care. I am ashamed to admit this. I began to question the existence of God. I decided that if He does exist, He is a cruel and unloving God. John, I lost my faith." She gasped, and drew herself in, clinging to her husband.

"I know, dear. I have always known. I saw it in your face. You couldn't see my eyes through the dark glasses, but I saw yours. I knew exactly how you felt. Because—because, Grace, the exact same thing happened to me."

"Really?" she was genuinely surprised. She pulled away a little to see his face. Tears washed down his cheeks. She kissed the wet streams, and tasted a certain salty relief.

"Thanks, for telling me." She said lovingly. "You know there was a time when you would never have admitted that. I shan't remind you of your faults. However, do you know you've never told me you were sorry for anything, not ever? Not until today."

"I don't mind you pointing out my shortcomings. I want to hear you. It feels like a part of my penance." John's words were foreign to Grace. "I have been my own worst enemy far too long. Everything has changed. I have found myself. I have again found God, my son, and best of all, I found YOU!"

"Tell me more about my son," she implored, "describe him to me, every feature."

"More than anything, he looks like his father, my brother, like David."

"I knew it. I knew he would. John, you know we did the right thing. It was important we raise him as if he belonged to both of us. We owed it to David. We owed it to ourselves."

"You're right. I just had so much resentment. What bothered me most was David's lifestyle, and I was jealous of his connection with you. He lived his life his way. Not me, society, or the church were able to compel him to conform. I resented him for that."

"It's true I loved David. It was a special kind of love. I tried to keep my feelings for him from interfering with you and me. I made a commitment to you. I vowed to love, honor, and obey, and I did my best to be true to what I said. Sometimes it was just too hard."

John's expression saddened, he sighed, and then he answered. "It was never the same for me. I never had the kind of connection with him that you did."

"He wanted a relationship with you."

"I know, I couldn't, and now it's too late. This is just one of the burdens I carry. More importantly, I believe that James David truly needs us. I do not wish to repeat past mistakes. We must help him."

"Is he all right?" Her voice quivered. "What has happened?"

"I'm not sure, exactly. I did know where he was and now he's disappeared. One night back in April in an alley behind a bar, someone mutilated a black man. James had nothing to do with the murder, but he was there. After that, his behavior radically changed. Before, he was predictable. After that night, he was erratic. He works in a motorcycle shop. He dresses well, lives in a nice house in Kirkwood, and appears to be some kind of a manager. He knows where we are. He was here. He followed us to the nursing home just a few days ago."

"What," her voice raised, "he was close to us, came to see us, and you didn't tell me?"

"It wasn't so simple. I wasn't ready to tell you about my deception. If I'd known then what I know now, I would have walked up to him, put my arms around him, and told him I love him; but I didn't. You can add that to my lifelong list of mistakes."

"Don't be so hard on yourself. You had your reasons. I'm disappointed, that's all."

"Thanks, for not making this any harder than it already is. Anyway, he just watched us, and then left. It was the last time I saw him."

"What makes you think he's in trouble? Does someone think he had something to do with the murder? Is he in danger?"

"I have no idea. I'm not suggesting anything. I know that it's complicated; it's bad. Recently there were two more murders. Wait—I'll show you." John left the room and returned with the front page of the

St. Louis Post Dispatch. He handed her the paper. "I wish you didn't have to see this."

Grace gasped when she read the headline: "*Jones Sought for Questioning in Three Murders*." There was a color photograph of James David sitting on a motorcycle.

"I hid this from you. I didn't want you to know."

"It says questioning." She touched the image of her precious son. "It doesn't say they think he did it."

"The fact that they printed his picture on the front page says something. The police have done this to get the public's help in finding him. I don't think they'd go to all this trouble if they didn't have strong evidence."

"He couldn't have done it." She said adamantly. "He has a good soul, a sweet soul. Behind the rebellion, he was as gentle and compassionate as his father. He can't have changed that much. He could never hurt anyone."

"I agree, but there's more."

"More, what could be worse than suspicion of murder?"

"Grace, I saw her. She's with him."

She was unsure of his meaning; yet, a cold chill raced down her spine. "You saw her. You saw who?" She asked cautiously. She waited. It felt like an eternity before he spoke.

"The girl, the other child…" John's words weighed heavily upon him. He sank to the bed.

"You can't have seen her." Grace's voice cracked with fear. "It's not possible. She is God-only-knows where. How could you have known it was her. When they left, she was just a baby—a baby."

"It was so strange. You had to be there. The first time I saw her, I sensed something unusual. She seemed familiar, like *déjà vu*. It wasn't in her face. She doesn't look like her mother or her father. After I saw her three or four times, I realized that she walks like her mother and gestures like her father. "The first night I saw her was the night the man was killed. She was a brunette like her mother. After that, she was a blonde. I only knew it was her because of her walk and those striking movements. Grace, I'm convinced it's her."

"How could she have found James David? We did everything possible to make sure this could never happen. We spent our life savings. Do you think they know the truth? How did they meet, by chance?"

"A coincidence would be a stretch. She must know something. By now, she's probably told him. Her mother swore to me if we gave her enough money for the move to California, she would never tell. I never should've trusted her. Why David chose her in the first place is beyond me. I have often thought he did it to irritate me. If that was the case, it worked."

"No, John, he never wanted to hurt you. He talked to me about her. He loved her. In the hospital when he died, she seemed nice. I think she loved him, too. It was just that, after she lost him, she was out there all alone with a baby to feed." Grace closed her eyes and tried to imagine herself as a single mother. "She made bad choices. She didn't manage her life very well, but we've all done that. If I'd been in her place, I probably would have been bitter and felt deserted. In spite of everything that happened between us, I've been fortunate. You were always there. In your own way you accepted James David as your son."

John gently squeezed Grace. "Now, we must decide what we're going to do. How are we going to help our son?"

Grace reveled in his embrace. "Darling, do you have any idea how good it makes me feel when you say *our son*? It feels so real. Maybe we do have a chance as a family. Let's find him; let's help him."

NINETEEN

THE BOLD HEADLINE reached out from behind the scratched Plexiglas door of the newspaper dispenser and ripped Deacon's breath from his lungs. He snagged the heel of his boot in a crack and stumbled into Doc who was just a step ahead.

"Hey!" Doc swung around and caught his arm.

"You look like you've seen a ghost."

With a limp hand, Deacon pointed to the headline.

Doc read the banner aloud:

FOUR SLAIN, BIKER SOUGHT

"Four," Doc's voice trembled, "there's no four." He wiggled two quarters from his jeans and dropped them into the slot.

Deacon whispered, "What does it say?"

"They think you killed another woman."

"Oh, my, God!" Deacon buried his face in his palms. "When, why do they think it's me. Why do they always think it's me?"

"Says here it happened night before last. A hooker was killed in the street, shot in the head with your pistol."

"That's impossible. There's no way they could match my gun to this. It has to be speculation." He choked. "Besides, Star has my Glock." The meaning of his own words reverberated through his mind.

"They searched your house and dug a slug out of the wall." Doc synopsized the information as he read, "Ballistics match. It says she was allegedly shot in cold blood, and no one saw the shooter."

"I've never fired a gun in my house. Star and I were in the motel that night, all night. Neither of us left."

"Deac, you sure?"

"Are you askin' if I'm sure I didn't leave the room, or if Star didn't leave? I still don't believe she's the one," Deacon argued. "With me, shit, who knows. I'm always doin' something I don't remember. Even if I'm not crazy, if one more fucking thing happens, I will be. I swear to Christ, I'm at my limit."

"You gave her the pistol. If you didn't shoot the wall of your house, it has to be Star. After I confronted her on the phone, she took off and never came back. How much more fucking proof do you need? You gonna wait 'til they fry you for something you didn't do, or until you actually see her kill someone before you believe me? The bitch is out to get you. I don't know why, I just know she is."

Frantic, they rode their motorcycles side-by-side. Less than a meter separated their handlebars. Deacon continually replayed recent events in his mind, searching for a reasonable solution, an alternative to the obvious. He wished it were all a bad dream.

Doc leaned smoothly into a deserted gas station. Where gas pumps had once stood, pipes and bolts protruded from the concrete. Only a window-height payphone mounted on a short pole and a dilapidated building remained. His engine coughed its last breath. He lifted the receiver from the switch hook.

The connection crackled. Her voice was faint. "Edward, you okay?" Kat asked tearfully.

Doc watched Deacon limp to the back of the station. *He must have to pee.* He turned his attention back to Kat. "I'm okay. Shouldn't I be? Do you know somethin' I don't?"

"There's been another murder, a shooting."

"We know. We saw it in the *Post*."

"Edward, is it really James David? They say he's the one."

"No, I'm sure he's not. He isn't convinced, but I am. He's always had the opportunity, and he's so confused. He's unsure of what he has, or hasn't done. There's much more to this than what we know, Kat. Somehow she's in the middle of this. You should'a heard how she talked to me this mornin'."

"She who, Star?"

"Star, Bridget, whoever the hell she is," he answered sickened by the thought.

"Who's Bridget? I haven't heard anything from Star." Kat changed the subject. "Guess what, I remembered where we saw the article about Sodium Amytal. It was in *GQ*. I found the magazine. It was in an article about Michael Jackson's court case. They said the dentist gave his own son the drug. After that, the boy began to remember he'd been molested. They said the drug could create false memories. They think the father planted the memories by suggestion."

"Could Star have given Deacon the junk?" Doc wondered aloud. "Could she have slipped it in his drinks?"

"No, it has to be injected. He should know if he's been injected. Does he have needle marks anywhere?"

"I don't know. Have the cops been snoopin' around?"

"Yeah, they wanna talk to you." She said. He heard the distress in her words. "Edward, you don't think they suspect you of anything, do you?"

"No, course not, but Deacon's my friend. If they've been doin' their homework, they've probably found the change in our partnership agreement. They might see that as motive."

"They wouldn't really, would they?"

"Deacon did with a little prompting from his so-called girlfriend. Katherine, I love you, but I wish you'd have never brought her into our lives."

"I've thought a lot about that. I'm not even sure how it happened. I just looked up one day, and there she was smiling and talking to me, like we'd always been friends. I thought she was perfect for Deacon."

"Deacon's comin', I've gotta go. I'll ask him about the needle marks, love you."

"Where you goin' now, what'll you do?"

"Don't know exactly, into town and see what's happenin'. Maybe it'd be best if we go to the police, and tell 'em what we know. I'm not sure. I'll call as soon as we decide."

"Edward, be careful," she whimpered, "I need you."

"Don't worry, hon, Deacon and I'll take care of each other." He said assuredly as he drowned in doubt. "Nothin's gonna happen. This will be over soon."

Deacon draped himself over Widowmaker like a sloppily added accessory.

Doc faced him, "Deacon, do you have any tracks?" He blurted out.

Startled, Deacon catapulted off his machine like a cowboy thrown from a horse, and landed with both feet flat on the ground. "Doc, what the hell...tracks?"

"You know, needle marks."

"Where do you come up with this shit? You know I don't do drugs. The booze is bad enough."

"Remember the drug that I told you about, Sodium Amytal? The lab found it in your system. Kat just told me it has the potential to alter memories. It has to be injected. Have you had any injections?"

"No, look," Deacon slid out of his jacket, held out both arms, and twisted them to show his smooth unmarked skin.

"Where else do junkies shoot up? Remember that guy we threw out of the Club for usin'? He used to shoot up between his fingers."

Deacon held out both hands, and spread his unmarked fingers. Doc scratched his head. "See, Doc, I told you, no marks. The lab must have made a mistake. 'Sides, don't you think I'd know if someone was givin' me shots? There would have been some soreness. Come on, let's get movin'."

Deacon walked to a nearby trash barrel, and spit out his gum. He pivoted on the ball of his right foot, and started back. He grimaced when his left foot met the pavement.

Doc watched intently as Deacon limped back to his bike. "Deac, where'd you say you hurt yourself? How'd you get that limp?"

A look of understanding flashed in Deacon's eyes. "I said, I didn't know. My toes on my left foot have been aching." He limped to the curb and plopped down.

Gingerly he pulled off his boot and sock. A noxious blast of sweat-permeated leather caused Doc to screw up his nose and draw back. He disregarded the smell, knelt, and took Deacon's foot in his hand. Between the big and second toe he found an inflamed area and several tiny marks. "Look at that," Doc pointed, "son-of-a-bitch, needle marks! Deac, there's only person who could have done this to you."

He dropped Deacon's bare foot, and wordlessly returned to his bike and the telephone.

"Now, who you callin'?" Deacon asked as he pulled on his sock.

"Thought I'd check in at the shop and see what they've heard. I don't know what else to do. I'm at the end of my fucking rope."

A familiar southern drawl answered after one ring. "Dawg," Doc asked rhetorically.

"Yeah Boss, where ar ya, you awraight?" Dawg asked in his clipped syllable chop.

"I'm okay—is anything happenin' there? Have the cops been around?"

"Nope, no law. Well, one a th guys thainks thar's a plain wrapper wif a pig down the block, but who fuckin' knows? Thar's weerd shit goin' on roun' here. Deac wif ya?"

"Yeah, why?"

"Got a message fer 'im. Some Mexcan broad calt here bout arr or so 'go. She saed ta tell 'im ta come down to the *Eads Bridge*. She saed don' be late. Saed he woon't wanna miss the Rev an Missus. Saed twas gonna be a great show. Saed be thar at five-turty, tanite, shaarp. Slut pissed me off. Fuckin' bitch saed I oughta fuckin' laarn ta tauk. So I says, 'look who's fuckin' taukin', ya stupid cunt.' Doc, what th hail's goin…?" The line was dead before Dawg finished the question.

Fear thrashed through Doc's chest and down both legs. "Deacon, saddle up."

Star heard the truck's profound rumble several minutes before the headlights came into view. She stepped onto the shoulder of the highway and stuck her right hand high in the air. She pulled her carefully designed body up, straight and tall, and smiled broadly. She knew she looked fantastic in tight jeans and leather jacket.

The airbrakes hissed loudly as the massive Peterbilt rolled to a stop. Dirty-white chicken feathers protruded from every cage in the tall stacks that populated the long trailer. The condemned birds cackled and squawked loudly. The pressure from the abrupt stop compressed them even more tightly together.

"Thanks buddy," she said with a sensuous smile as she climbed into the cab.

The middle-aged truck driver grinned. "My pleasure, babe, where ya headed?" Four lonely teeth protruded from his upper lip. "Name's William," he stuck a rough, callused hand across the broad console. "Bill, really."

"I'm Bridget, Bridge, really." She laughed mockingly.

The trucker laughed innocently. Star made sure her leather jacket hung open. He had a clear view down her black lace tank top. She crossed her arms at her elbows, pulled her shoulders in, and cast her eyes down. *Perfect cleavage, perfect breasts,* she thought conceitedly.

He seemed to hold his breath for a moment. There was a conspicuous stirring in his greasy jeans. *My gift,* she reminded herself.

He shifted the truck into second gear. "Where ya headed?" He asked for the second time.

"To the city," She said seductively, "Central West End, Kingshighway and Maryland, you goin' anywhere near there?"

"I'm goin' sort a near there. Hell, I got time," he said generously. "I'm ahead a schedule, and my log's hot. That means I've been on the road too many hours," he explained. "If a smoky checks me, I'm busted. I can drop you anywhere you want, so long as I can get my rig in and out."

"I appreciate it, and I'm happy to help cool off those logs of yours." Star leaned toward him, gazed into his eyes, and smiled. "I'm sure you'll be able to get your big rig in and out."

He followed her directions to the letter.

"Stop just up here. This is my building." Star was pleased with the look of surprise on his face as they pulled up to the corner of the luxury apartment building. She knew this facial expression well. He suddenly realized, he was dreaming. She was way out of his league. "How 'bout I give you my number. You never know?" She said coyly.

He answered without missing a beat. "Oh yeah, sure, you bet." He mined a crumpled piece of paper and a pen from the cluttered console.

Star scratched out the first set of seven random numbers that came into her mind. "Here ya go, Bill, thanks for the lift. She intentionally grazed his thigh with her right hand, twisted, and slid out of the cab.

The uniformed doorman pulled the glass door open and bowed stiffly, a prescribed bend at the waist. "Welcome home, Miss Luna. It is very nice to see you."

"Thank you, Fredrick. It is always good to be home. I will be going out in about an hour. Please have my Benz brought 'round." She commanded.

"I wish people wouldn't drive so fast on our narrow road." Grace commented to her husband. "I'm always seein' some poor dead pet. People are reckless." They sat side-by-side on their front porch reveling in the warmth from God's burning-yellow eye as it increased the speed of its descent to the horizon.

From more than two miles away, the dark car came into view as it rapidly approached. The vehicle disappeared twice as it lunged into dips in the two-lane county road. Translucent waves of heat radiated from the saturated asphalt and quickly dissipated in the cool air. The speeding car created barely visible ripples as it sliced neatly through the thermal inversion. "Probably somebody lost," she added, intently following its progress.

"In a big hurry, most likely goin' in the wrong direction," John contributed. He held his wife's hand tightly.

One-hundred meters from their driveway, the navy blue car abruptly slowed and wheeled hard into the gravel. Skidding tires threw pebbles across the lawn.

Startled, the Joneses jumped to their feet.

Heavily tinted windows hid the occupant. Simultaneously, with the cessation of the vehicle's forward motion, the driver's door swung open and a tall, brown-haired woman sprang out.

"What the…" the Reverend began.

She did not let him finish. "You know who I am, don't you old man." She laughed. "I can tell by the look on your face. It's lovely to see you both again after all these years, or should I say it's lovely for you to see me. I don't remember the last time. Don't bother inviting me in. We're not going to be here long enough to sit and visit."

"What do you want?" John's voice trembled. "What are you doin' here?"

"Who is she?" Grace asked. Without waiting for an answer, she demanded, "Why don't you just leave?"

"It's her, I told you. She's the other one, look at her." He whispered. "See the resemblance."

"Yes, Grace, sweet Grace, don't you recognize me?" She chuckled. "Don't you think even after all of my *expensive surgery* that I look like your beloved, David?"

John dropped his wife's hand. With determined steps, he started across the porch.

The woman, still standing by the car, pulled a dull black object from her purse.

John Jones froze as if hypnotized. She pointed the handgun at his face. "That's far enough for the moment, Rev," she said threateningly.

"What do you want with us?" Grace asked in a shrill voice.

"Oh, you'll find out soon enough. I have a real surprise for you two. Before we go, there's somethin' I want. You get it for me, Rev," she commanded. "I believe it's locked in your desk, a big yellow envelope. You know the one."

The color drained from his face. "I don't know what you're talking about." He said weakly.

"Your face says you do. You're a horrible liar. Be quick, and I won't hurt Grace. Bring me the envelope, unopened."

The Reverend returned in a very few minutes. Grace read the blue hand printed words: ***PERSONAL AND CONFIDENTIAL, OPEN ONLY IN THE CASE OF MY DEATH***. What is it," she whispered.

The other woman laughed a deep, guttural laugh. "Isn't that always the way. The bastards never tell us helpless females anything. This, doll, is some of our history. Something I want back."

Recently weakened adhesive easily released the flap. She extracted four items: two crisp, never-seen-the-light-of-day birth certificates; a tattered, faded black and white photograph, two halves married by tape; and a large brass medallion. In the photo, a tall, handsome young man leaned against an old Harley-Davidson. "My history, finally, I get back some of my history." She said with an awkward, melancholy voice. She held the birth certificates, compared the words, and shook her head. She held the photograph closer and studied the motorcycle, and then rubbed the medallion between her thumb and forefinger. She sighed a burdened sigh.

Her demeanor shifted, "Walk together slowly," Star demanded. "Get in my beautiful car. It's a symbol, you know, my ticket to a better life. A life I made for myself without you or your influence. I bet, when you sent my mother and me away with your little fucking money, you thought you had seen the last of me. After all these years, I've come to show you what you did to me. I'm here to exact my justice.

"Now, Rev, me and the Mrs. are going to ride in the back. I know you see as well as anyone. You'll be our chauffeur, now, you old bastard, get in the fucking car." She adroitly placed her stiletto in the small of his back and kicked him toward the open car door. The point of her heel ripped through his shirt and dug into tender flesh. She made a rapid pirouette, and recovered with the grace of a ballerina.

"Play nice, get in the car. We are goin' on the ride of our lives."

Star relaxed in the back seat and exuberantly pressed the barrel of the forty-caliber Glock against the Reverend's neck.

The late afternoon, early November sun hung low in the sky. The dramatic cityscape of downtown St. Louis cast overlapping shadows. The *Gateway Arch*, in its labyrinth of tiny, symmetrical machined patterns on stainless steel, trapped diminishing yellowish-orange rays of sunlight as they danced their final ballet of the day. The landmark cast its rapidly stretching, elliptical shadow upon the muddy surface of the Mississippi.

People streamed on and off the national park grounds like army ants. The last tour of the day exited the subterranean museum en-mass. On the waterfront, people queued up to board *The President* casino. A few hundred yards further downstream, families surrounded outdoor tables aboard a floating *McDonald's* restaurant.

Upstream from the Arch, an ancient decaying bridge cast an equipment-cluttered shadow across the broad expanse of water. Brownish-green moss clung to aging stone legs, which arched up from the river's surface supporting what were once multiple levels of traffic. Star admired the bridge. *Exactly like Deacon's dream,* she thought pleased with her own cleverness. Great lengths of rusting barges, compacted end-to-end and laden with coal, advanced north against the strong current.

On the west bank of the river just inside barricades, which blocked the entrance to the bridge, two lone motorcycles leaned on kickstands and cast ever-changing shadows on crumbling pavement. Headless helmets hung from handless bars. Rapidly cooling V-Twin engines popped and crackled. No people were visible on the bridge.

Reverend John Jones intentionally drove at a snails' pace; the woman was agitated. Occasionally, she buried the matte-black steel barrel of the semi-automatic pistol in the back of his neck.

Impatient, she uttered a curse and a threat. "Speed up you old son-of-a-bitch or else. This ain't a fuckin' funeral, but it can be." His perspiration soaked the leather-clad steering wheel.

It had all been a dream for too long. A family's history recorded in chalk and photographs on the walls of a closed-off room of a rented apartment in Los Angeles. As the time of fruition became imminent, as judgment day drew near, it was surreal, incomprehensible.   Star   glanced   over, unsympathetically, at the older woman. Grace Jones sat totally still, her face covered with her right hand, occasionally issuing a muted sob.

John studied the road ahead. He prayed for a police car. At every intersection, he strained to extend his vision. Silently, he asked God for forgiveness for all his shortcomings, and the strength to protect his wife and son.

Star studied his movements intently. "You can't fool me, you old bastard. I know what you're thinkin'. You can forget it. You won't see any cops. Even if you do, you're just gonna play it cool. I can do what I have to do with or without you and your old lady. I prefer with because it'll be a lot more fun, but try somethin' stupid, and I'll put a nice hole in Grace's lovely head. Then I'll give you one to match. So keep your shit together, and maybe I'll let you both live.

"Young lady, why are you so bitter?" John asked sincerely. "What has the world done to hurt you so much? Why do you have to punish others just to find relief? Perhaps I can help you if you let me."

"Bullshit! Bull—fucking—shit! You can't fucking help me now. You had your chance twenty-nine fucking years ago. Do you think paying my mother to leave was helping? You and I both know you did it for your own benefit, to protect your precious reputation. My bitch mother knew about my father and Grace. She knew all about their *special friendship*. You should have wanted to help me without a gun to your head. Although, I guess you're used to this. From what I hear, your precious fucking James David held a gun to your head for the first eighteen years of his miserable, fucking life.

"By the way, what did you discover, old man, during all your hours of following your baby boy in that stupid van? Did you learn that his name—his nickname, is Deacon? It's a joke. Don't you see, a cruel joke and you're the butt. He stands for everything you're against. Look at you, you miserable bastard, you still love him. You still want to protect him. You make me sick."

Hidden in the shadow of a construction dumpster, a short distance from the cooling motorcycles, Deacon Jones leaned toward Doc Williams and whispered. "What do you think will happen?"

"Deacon, you know the answer as well as I do." Doc replied in low tones. "How many times have we heard about a woman with a strong accent? Star is half-Mexican. You and I both know she's the one. She's on her way here, right now, and for whatever reason, she's bringing your parents. Your heart can't keep denying what your mind knows to be true."

"Maybe not, but—what about our connection, it's so strong? She walks into a room, and I feel a sort of electrical charge. Sometimes it's a rush of happiness, or a sweep of sadness; later I find out Star's happy or sad about something. We have the same tastes, the same desires, the same needs... She was made for me. Even Kat knew it the first time they met.

"Tell me, Doc, how can something that feels so good, be bad." Deacon shook his head. "How can someone so perfect, be responsible for all this?"

"You're in denial; I get it. I understand how you feel. Let me tell you a story that I've never told anyone.

"In high school, before I got Kat to notice me, I dated another girl, Gloria. She'd had a hard life, and I knew it. My parents told me not to see her, but I couldn't stay away. There was a rumor that she hung out with potheads and smoked dope. I didn't believe it. I asked her about it anyway, and she told me it wasn't true.

"One day in the locker room, I heard a guy, one of the *heads*, bragging about what a great screw she was. I laid into the jerk and ended up suspended for three days. I asked her about it. She denied it and refused to speak to me for a week. I thought I had lost her. One morning she came to my locker, sweet as ever, like nothing had happened.

"She drove an old red Chevy convertible. One night after school, I was on my way home, much later than normal. I saw her car with the top down parked near the end of a deserted street. I was afraid she was broke down or worse. I'm sure you can guess the end of the story. She was givin' her pusher a blowjob in the back seat in payment for a nickel bag of grass.

"Here's the real kicker. While we were datin', she occasionally let me cop a feel, but she'd never do me. She said she was a virgin, which made me want her more. Anyway, when I caught her givin' the long hair a BJ, I screamed her name. She didn't even flinch, just kept bobbin' up and down. Seconds later, she lifted her head, looked me right in the eye, and smiled.

"I'll never forget that moment for as long as I live, her smilin', and the guy's cum running out both sides of her mouth." Doc shook his head sadly. "God, I loved her."

In the half-light, Deacon saw tears on Doc's cheeks. "Jeezus, Doc, I'm sorry."

"Fortunately, I met Kat, and she taught me about real love. Although, you know, we had some of the same problems. Her dad was a big shot at the University; mine was the janitor. Her parents didn't approve of us. To them, I was from the wrong side of the tracks. Kat and I loved each other so we stuck it out. In the end, it all worked. I've never regretted marrying Kat, not for a moment.

"The sick thing is that I'm still occasionally haunted by the image of my girlfriend. I can close my eyes and see cum on her face. A couple of years ago, someone told me she'd died with AIDS. When I heard that, I cried. To this day, I really don't understand my feelings for her.

"This feels like the end for you, Deac; I know it does. It's how I felt that night with Gloria, but it's not the end. Someday you'll find the right person. When you do, it'll be better than you could ever imagine. Trust me."

"I was so sure Star was the one. It's hard to think she isn't. Would you call what you felt for Gloria a connection?"

"I don't know…" Doc suddenly stopped talking and crouched down. A car was slowly turning onto the bridge. "Let's get out of sight." He whispered urgently.

The dusty blue Mercedes rolled to a stop. An empty beer bottle exploded under a tire. Startled by the sound, Doc and Deacon jerked back. From atop a passing tug, a foghorn wailed. The men held their breath; the engine stopped.

The end of a busy day sonata filled the air, a cacophony of sounds from the interstate highway, the city on the west, and the river on the east.

Deacon cautiously drew a switchblade from a leather sheath sewn inside his boot. He squeezed the brass button. With a decisive click, a razor-sharp blade snapped out of a walnut handle and locked open.

Doc, with a sound like the tearing of cloth, opened the Velcro flap of the knife case on his belt. With his thumb, he deftly flipped out the finely honed burnished blade.

Shoulder-to-shoulder, they crouched, still as death, and low to the ground. Buttocks rested on boot heels.

Deacon checked his pocket watch. Five minutes remained until 5:30. He shifted his gaze from the car to the motorcycles. *They must be able to see our bikes,* he thought. *Why are they waiting?*

TWENTY

A MINUTE, which seemed like an hour, passed. Deacon flinched, in part from anxiety, the rest due to the lack of feeling in his legs. He wavered and lost his balance. Doc grasped his arm and steadied him.

Without moving Deacon whispered impatiently. "What are we—are they waiting for?"

"Don't know, five-thirty, maybe. We have to let her make the first move."

"I can't stand this." Deacon tried to move. Doc's grip on his arm redoubled.

Distant church bells began to chime. *Funeral bells,* Deacon thought. He tensed, a powerful adrenaline rush flowed through him, and his muscles tightened. It's time. The muffled, reverberating sound of the last ring died away. The driver's door opened.

Doc's squeeze telegraphed his anxiety. *We must hold our place.*

The driver of the car stepped out. Deacon gasped and let out a nearly inaudible sound, "My father."

The Reverend remained on the opposite side of the car. His profile, what they could see of his head and upper torso, visibly trembled like dry branches rattling in a fall wind. He stood between the door and its opening. His head hung miserably, forward, and to the right. His shoulders stooped. He nodded as though in agreement with an unseen someone.

He made a visual sweep of the bridge pausing at the dumpster then continuing past Doc and Deacon. They held their places, frozen.

The final threads of the setting sun illuminated the Reverend's face. When his visual search reached the motorcycles, he stopped and stared hard, his lips moved.

Deacon stiffened, straining to hear. The distance was too great, and the ambient noise of the city and the river too loud. He heard nothing.

Doc whispered. "I don't think he saw us, just the bikes."

The Reverend, his stance unnaturally rigid, began to sway in non-concentric circles as though his equilibrium was ebbing away.

Deacon blinked repeatedly. The adrenaline in his system began to dissipate. He fought to maintain consciousness. A voice screamed inside his head. *Is my other personality trying to take over?* He resisted; the bridge spun around him.

The Reverend cowered. The rear driver's-side door opened. Long dark-brown hair came into view, a woman. She exited abruptly and kept her back to Doc and Deacon.

Behind the brunette, Deacon's mother came stumbling into view. She landed on her hands and knees at the rear of the car. Mrs. Jones covered her face as though to protect herself from an impending blow. Nothing happened. She lowered her hands to her lap and sat among the debris wearing the countenance of a beaten prisoner. Slowly, methodically, she struggled to her feet and shuffled to her husband's side. Together they backed away from the car, three equal steps, and then froze, arms linked together.

An intense obsession, a barrage of anger, disappointment, and rage enveloped Deacon like a chemical injected directly into his cerebellum. He sensed something about to happen; his heart pounded. A cavalcade of excitement, nervousness, anxiety, and a strange sense of fulfillment plunged through him.

He whispered. "It's not her. That's not Star."

Doc answered in hushed tones. "Don't move. I'm not so sure."

The brunette took one step toward her captives. She spread her long legs in a haughty stance. The muscles in her calves formed strong lines, sculpted by high-heels. She tilted her head back and began to speak. Her words swelled to an urgent shout. *"Soy Estrella."* She exclaimed in perfect Spanish. *"Mi mama me llamo así, por ser la Estrellita de su vida. Hoy, soy la Reina de sus vidas. Voy a decidir sus destinos."*

Deacon heard her clearly. *She can't be Star,* he thought, trying to convince himself. *She never learned her mother's native language.*

With hardly a hesitation, she began again, louder, her voice somehow changed. Gone were the melodic cant, and distinctly cut syllables characteristic of Spanish. In their stead was the pragmatic, measured-delivery of English. A paralyzing chill swept over Deacon. He recognized this voice.

"James David, Deacon, JD, or whoever the fuck you think you are, we can't see you, but I know you can hear me. Unfortunately, you didn't choose to follow your heritage. You should have learned the language of your people. If you had, you would have understood what I just said. Since you did not, I'll translate…"

"I am Star. My mother named me so because I was the little star of her life." With each word, the rapidity of her delivery increased. She slipped away on a tangent, and added a personal commentary. "Estrella and Bridget are here too, but they can't come out." She resumed the translation. "This is my party. Today, I am the queen of your lives. I will decide your destinies." Her mounting diatribe reached a crescendo, ending with a sweeping flourish of bronze arms, long red nails, and a deadly weapon.

Star paused, "Today is a special day for us. I have planned it for a very long time." She raised her voice a few octaves. "Deacon, are you getting all of this? I said it's a special day; we're going to celebrate our heritage, your heritage. Your friend, Doc, moved up my timetable a little. Tomorrow was to be our day, the Day of the Dead, *el Día de los Muertos*. It's okay, today will work. The Aztecs called this date the Day of the Innocents, *el Día de los Inocentes*. The cool part is our ancestors believed that life is a dream from which we are awakened by death. Several people are going to be rudely awakened before this night's over. Too bad you don't have the guts to come forward and face me." She said cruelly. "Don't you have enough feeling for these poor people, whom you call parents, to defend them?"

Deacon leaped to his feet. "What do you want? Why are you doing this?" He was oblivious to the shooting pain in his stiff muscles.

"Well, well, a brave act at last. Welcome to the party, doll. Please don't make any sudden movements. This lovely pistol of yours has such a hair-trigger. I wouldn't want to hurt anyone, at least not until I'm ready. You must have so many questions." She pivoted a quarter-turn, and glared at James David. "You've been asleep your whole fucking life." She swung the pistol back and forth between Deacon and the Joneses like as though she could not decide upon her target. "That, you stupid bastard, is your fucking problem."

"Now, my dear, ridiculous marionette, come here. Let's have a family reunion."

Deacon inched toward the car.

"That's it, just a little closer," she said beckoning him with the pistol. "Where's our beloved Doc?"

Concealed in the small of his back, the handle of Deacon's open knife protruded slightly above his belt. The razor-sharp blade sliced through his shirt and into his flesh; he ignored the pain. He reached his mother and took her in his arms. Affectionately, he touched his father's neck and whispered, "I'm sorry."

"Now, isn't that just too sweet? You didn't even know where in the fuck they were for ten goddamn years, and suddenly you're fucking sorry."

James David turned to face Star. He looked hard at the caricature of the woman he thought he knew. Nowhere could he find any semblance of Estrella. Even her eyes were different. They were a hatred-filled brown.

"What do you want with us, with me?" He asked angrily. "I thought you loved me?"

"So fucking many questions. I do love you in my own way. I want to tell you a story; it'll be fun. It'd be a shame for me to have gone to all this trouble and you not understand. It's about regret. I want you all to regret your lives. Don't worry, in a minute I'm going to tell you how the festivities will play out. Then, with a little input from the good Reverend, we'll explain why. Before we get started, I want Doc's ass out here where I can see him."

"Doc isn't here." Deacon tried to sound convincing. "He's gone to get the police."

"I doubt that. We're not that far from downtown. He could have crawled there by now. No, I think not, but I'll play your little game. Let him stay in hiding. Be warned, let me hear one movement, one anything, no matter whether it's him or not, and momma Grace dies. No matter what, if anything happens, my fault, your fault, it doesn't matter, the old bitch dies. I'm an expert shot, and as you know, this Glock has a hair-trigger."

"Let's start with how this story ends. I'm going to kill the old bastard, the bitch, and your best friend with this pistol, your pistol. The same one you used to kill a defenseless hooker not many hours ago. Then I'm going to shoot you in the knee. I'm not going to kill you. I'll merely break a few bones so the cops can easily pick you up. I'll do it at close range at the perfect angle. It'll appear as though, you, being the clumsy son-of-a-bitch that you are, accidentally shot yourself in the process of the senseless slaughter of your friend and family. Then, I'll give you your pistol back—a pity, because by then, you'll be completely out of bullets.

"You, of course, will tell the police all about me. Since I don't exist, at least not so anyone would know," she smiled an arrogant smile, "they'll easily convict you. You'll spend the rest of your life dreaming of me and your demons while you wait for *el señor* electric chair."

"Make me suffer if that is what it has to be, but not my parents and Doc. Leave them out of this. Did you really frame me for those horrible murders? Did you make it seem as though I raped those women? How did you? How could you?"

"Wasn't everything a work of art? I even had *you* believing you did it, thanks to a few injections of Sodium Amytal. I put this place, this bridge, in your dreams; I made you fear it. The rapes, now that was sheer genius," she bragged. "I captured your sperm in my diaphragm, and injected it into *your* victims."

"Why Cynthia Thomas, she was a lesbian."

"I'm no fucking lesbian, if that's what you're thinking. I'm a lady of joy, a prostitute, a call girl, a whore. My body is my, very profitable, stock and trade. Sex with her, and with you, was just business. Today is my big payday. Sweet, innocent Cynthia, it was so sad. She was just like you. She thought Bridget was the love of her life, too bad, right? Her sexual preference and her initials made her an easy mark. I wanted everything to be perfect. She was a small sacrifice for the betterment of humankind, don't you agree? Besides, Bridget did have fun although the bracelet was over the top, a complete waste of money, extravagant cunt."

"You're a monster," James David screamed. "All those people died so you could hurt me."

"I'll take that as a compliment although not completely accurate. Garvin Brown was the exception, stupid pimp. He followed me from California. The fucker knew my history. I had to eliminate him. His brother was my mother's and my pimp." She continued in an emotionless monotone. "They were both dead weight. I got rid of them when I was almost nineteen, the night I gave myself a coming out party, and moved to Beverly Hills."

"I had originally intended that you would kill only women. I thought the serial killer thing would fit you nicely. Everything worked out after all. Cutting Garvin in half was a stroke of genius. I even convinced you that you did it. You've been the perfect puppet."

"Let the others go," James David pleaded again. "If you want me, take me. Settle your score, whatever that is, with me alone. Please, don't hurt my parents."

"Very noble, but the Joneses aren't as innocent as you think." She snarled at the couple, "Are you my dears?"

"I don't know what you're talking about, young lady," the Reverend answered indignantly. "Perhaps you think you know more about us than you actually do."

"Perhaps, my ass," she said harshly. "We'll just see, won't we, your holiness? Why don't you tell James David the truth? Cut the bullshit and tell him what you've been hiding since the day he was born. Tell him before you make me so fucking mad that I shoot your wife. You know the story as well as I do."

His face reddened and minutes passed. He cleared his throat. "Son, many years ago when this woman was born, we knew her mother. Your mother and I agreed that they needed help. Her mother was an unfortunate soul, a Mexican, with few opportunities. We gave her a little financial support so they might move to California…"

"Liar, liar, liar," Star cried. "Bullshit, bullshit, fucking bullshit!" With violently trembling hands, she waved the gun wildly. "Tell the goddamn truth!" Star angrily spread her legs, gripped the Glock with both hands, and assumed a shooter's stance. "You don't want to fuck with me, Rev'. One of my john's was a cop. He gave me protection and shooting lessens, and I fucked him. We both learned a lot. I can't believe this. You're fuckin' wearing me out. I'll finish the fucking story myself.

"You wanted me and my mother out of your lives. So you paid her off. You bought her just like all the other tricks. Only you fucked up. You didn't count on me. Your deal was with my mother, not me. Now, you old sack of shit, tell him why. The truth this time, my patience is wearing thin, and you aren't prepared to see me angry."

"All right, please, just calm down. James David, I'm so sorry to tell you this, your Uncle David was this girl's father."

"Oh, my, God!" James buried his face in his palms, and then turned to Star. "You mean to tell me, I fell in love with—I've had a relationship with, my cousin? You knew all along. You miserable... we committed incest, and you knew?"

"Oh, doll, that ain't the half of it. Go on, Rev, tell our boy who *his* real father is," she ordered. "Don't fuck with me. Tell him, tell him now."

"Son, forgive me. I always wanted to be your father. David, my little brother, was your father. He was killed a month before you were born. Your mother and I thought it would be in your best interest if we raised you as our own. Please, understand. We never wanted you to know. We didn't want to hurt you."

"Jesus Christ!" James David collapsed to his knees. He looked up in disbelief at the tired figure who he thought was his father. "Mother, you had an affair with your husband's brother," he began to sob, "then decided to hide the truth from your bastard son."

Star laughed. It began as a soft, guttural chuckle, which became increasingly louder until tears ran down both cheeks. "Goodness, James David, you are so fucking *naïve*, even I can't believe it. A minute ago, I was your cousin; now, I'm your half sister. You still don't get it, do you? Do I have to hit you over the head with the truth? Tell him Grace, the suspense is killing me."

"James David, sweetheart, how can I say this. I love you; I'm so sorry, but I'm not your birthmother." Mrs. Jones wavered and leaned against her husband. "I loved David, your father, in a very special way, but we never had a physical relationship. David was your biological father, and this woman's mother was your natural mother."

"Everyone sure is sorry all of a sudden. So, what do you think, bro? Wasn't sex with me fantastic?"

"My, dear, God, you're my sister." James David dropped his face to the tarmac and dry heaved.

"Yeah, doll, I'm your sister, and I loved playing you. Shit, it was easy. You, were so easy. Fuckin' you, fuckin' with your mind was like pickin' low hanging fruit. I didn't even have to reach. You practically leaped into my hands."

"But why... why do you hate all of us?"

"First, understand this. We aren't just brother and sister. We're fraternal twins, *gemelas*, dizygotic twins. We share the same rare blood, and probably more than fifty percent of the same DNA. That's why you feel connected to me, why we sense each other. I've become an expert at getting inside your head. Those voices you hear, they're all me," she said proudly. "Fuckin' cool, huh. It was all extremely useful when I was manipulating you."

"This is too incredible to be true," he shouted. "We don't have the same birthday. Yours is in May."

"I thought you were supposed to be a genius?" Her question dripped with sarcasm. "Do you think that my birthday is the only thing I didn't lie about? As for why, it's simple, they chose you. The Jones family chose you, and turned their backs on me. They decided to raise you as their son, and in the same instant, condemned me to a life of prostitution. You had it made. You took the fucking opportunity and shit all over it. You could have done anything, gone anywhere. You had the perfect life. The dream was within your reach.

"Do you understand me? You threw it all away. I'm willing to kill for what you wasted." The veins in her face swelled. Her skin became a patchwork of red blotches. Invisible plastic surgery incisions became hard white lines; manmade beauty gave way to grotesque reality. "You are a selfish, stupid son-of-a-bitch, and today I'm going to make you pay. I'll take away everything good in your life, and replace it all with absolute regret."

James David felt her anger swell; her pain was stifling. He heard her voices inside his head, the two others, not Star, crying and pleading. He winced. In her face, he recognized the same struggle that he felt.

"It's the bitches," she said matter-of-factly. "They want out. I have forbidden them to come out, and they're pissed. I forbade them both because of all the trouble they've caused lately.

"It started with Estrella. After we first fucked you, on that last night in Sturgis, she felt sorry for you. She wanted to tell you the truth. She thought we could come clean, and everything would be great. I shut her down, and locked her in that very day. Then Bridget tried to pull the same shit. After we killed Cindy, the stupid lesbo wouldn't quit cryin'. She was in love with Cindy. She wanted to go back to LA. I put a stop to that, too. I closed her off from the world. What you hear inside your head are the two woeful whores, begging to get out." She stopped. Her eyes became lifeless spheres; her consciousness seemed gone.

No one made a sound or dared move. Deacon eyed the gun and weighed the opportunity. Star's eyes rolled; she began to shout. *"No quiero ser una prostituta; ni quiero ser la hija de una puta."* Her lips curled back in a snarl and revealed perfect white teeth. She repeated her declaration in English. "I don't want to be a prostitute. I don't want to be the daughter of a whore." Dulled-brown retinas became empty, emotionless orbs.

Deacon looked into eyes he had thought were blue, and realized he knew her not at all. "Even your eyes—your eyes are different."

"I went to a lot of trouble for that deceptive little detail. Fucking theatrical contacts dry the shit outta my eyes. It was especially hard with you always looking over my shoulder like a lovesick puppy. Look closely, doll. These are my *real* eyes," she laughed, "*the windows, to my soul.*"

Something in her visage changed. Deacon felt a shift in her demeanor. He was sure she had willed the change. He experienced the strength of her gravitational pull. Her black essence revealed itself, fueled by jealousy, remorse and a suffocating need for revenge.

Star caught his look; her eyes flashed. Deacon experienced the ponderous weight of her shroud of madness. Reality crawled. He heard her ethereal words delivered in slow motion.

"Would you like to see," she calmly asked, "the ultimate demonstration of our connection? Take your jacket off," she ordered. She pointed to the tattoo on his left bicep. Wrapped tightly around the cross, the venomous snake's terrifying eyes glowed red. "Remember when you got that tattoo, the night of our twenty-first birthday?"

Deacon answered weakly, "I remember."

"That was the night when I first experienced our true connection. I suffered with the sting of the needle; I stepped into your mind. I smelled your boozy friends. I saw through your eyes. I heard your voice describe the ink." She paused, turned, and began to lift her blouse. "I want to show you what I experienced. You must witness our conjoined fate." She fully exposed the bare skin of her back.

Deacon staggered backward. The image sprang from her flesh like an exploding bomb. Etched on her bronze skin, in the small of her back, was a tattoo. The cross and snake were smaller, the detail and proportion were perfect. It was Deacon's tattoo.

She snickered, "Doll, I've been dyin' to show you this. You have no idea."

"What have I done?" The words were not Deacon's. They came from the Reverend.

"That's right, you son-of-a-bitch," Star screamed turning her wrath on the Reverend, "you did this. You did all of this!" She brandished the pistol in an arc. The barrel rapidly passed each of the men, and stopped at Grace's heart. "And now you'll pay."

When the gun barrel centered on Grace, the Reverend grabbed her arm. With one unplanned motion, he shoved her behind him, and stepped into the blast. Deacon watched in horror as the forty-caliber hollow-point ripped into his father's chest, mushroomed, and smashed through his heart. His mother jerked violently. The mangled lead exited the Reverend's back, and with waning force penetrated her side. The Reverend dropped straight down like an accordion. His eyes locked wide open. All semblance of life was gone before his body hit the ground. Mrs. Jones let out a strangled cry, and succumbed to the weight of her dead husband.

Doc vaulted from his hiding place, knife drawn, and ran toward Star. He shrieked hysterically, "You bitch…"

Star diverted her attention from the Reverend. She turned the pistol on her brother, and squeezed the trigger. Her aim was higher than she had planned. The lead tore into his left thigh, and nicked the femur. Deacon half-fell, half-thrust himself upon her, drew the switchblade from his belt, and with a single strike imbedded the blade.

She saw him lunge, and jerked back to avoid the gleaming blade. She screeched in pain as it penetrated her abdomen. Deacon slammed against her. The Glock exploded in her hand; fire flashed from the barrel. He grabbed her hair. They bounced apart and rolled in opposite directions. Deacon's wounded leg hit the pavement hard; it stung like another bullet. He frantically attempted to cover the open wound, and found her brown wig wound tightly around his fingers.

Doc stumbled backward. Blood gushed from his shoulder. Star sat up. She was only six feet away from Deacon. With both hands, she grasped the knife handle, and pulled the dripping, crimson blade from punctured flesh. She rolled onto her hands and knees, lifted herself with great effort, and limped away.

Deacon crawled rapidly after her dragging his bleeding leg. She fired two wild shots. Bullets exploded against broken pavement showering Deacon with debris. Hopping upright on one leg, Deacon bounded forward. She reached the railing in the same moment he caught her. They slammed into the oxidized steel of the deserted bridge. Star hit first, waist high, and tumbled backward over the barrier. Deacon reached for her. She caught his hand and looked up into confused eyes.

Deacon saw himself in her face like looking in a mirror. With all his strength, he gripped her hand. "My life was difficult," he labored to speak, "but with Doc and Kat's help, I made something good of it. Yours was difficult, too, I know, but you made it worse. Together we could have had something, something normal. We could have been brother and sister, a family. Instead, you turned our lives into something horrible. You made us both despicable, incestuous monsters."

She opened her mouth, "I—I," were the only sounds. Remorse flickered in her eyes. Her grip relaxed; Estrella's fingers began to slip from Deacon's hold.

The gun slipped away. It turned end-over-end as it fell. A moment later, Estrella opened her hand and followed. Deacon watched in despair. She disappeared into the muddy water. The impact rippled the surface in rapidly expanding concentric circles. There were no other movements on the surface, no bubbles, and no sign of life.

Deacon dropped to one knee, slumped to the pavement, and looked back at his mother. Grace clasped her side. Her face was pale and her breathing heavy. Doc staggered to his feet. He pressed tightly against the blood flow from the bullet wound in his shoulder.

Deacon looked again at the surface of the Mississippi. A sharp, unexpected pain sliced through his body. He cried out and clasped his uninjured right side.

At last, James David, *Deacon,* Jones remembered all of the things he had never known, and he understood them all. It was all important. He had needed to know; he had needed to understand. He realized, even though she was his twin, his missing half, she was different. His sister was not like Deacon at all. She was an anomaly with a burdened, black essence, a *Dark Star*. He had been right since the beginning.

Unquestionably, she was his cure.

[7]But we have this treasure in earthen vessels, to show that the transcendent power belongs to God and not to us. [8]We are afflicted in every way, but not crushed; perplexed, but not driven to despair; [9]persecuted, but not forsaken; struck down, but not destroyed;

II Corinthians 4:7-9

9000273R1